From *Heart Mates*

A half step closer, him or her, she wasn't sure who. Their auras kissed.

Pure male heat rolled over her skin, edged with a virile, wild magic. Shivers ran with abandon over her flesh as a tremor hit her low in the belly.

If she leaned in a fraction of an inch, she'd touch him, skin-to-skin...she swallowed hard. As much power as she felt rolling off him, touching would close an electrical circuit, and she'd be the one fried. "Look, I'm trying to find my Aunt Linda."

His gaze dropped to her mouth. "She owns the bookstore."

"Yes." Under that silvery gaze, her lips felt too full, throbbing. The word was hard to form. She licked her lips.

His pupils dilated until his eyes were pure black, riveted to her mouth. "Your aunt has a photograph of you." He slid a finger under her chin.

All her breath expelled from her lungs. Without oxygen, she let him tilt her face to one side, then the other. The throbbing in her lips intensified.

The matching throbbing in her groin was almost painful.

His lids lowered, lazy with promise. "Your nose is longer than I expected."

Just what a woman wanted to hear. "Thanks?"

"Your nose is unique, like your scent. Exotic. Deeply enticing. I want to kiss you."

He was right on top of her, sending frissons of energy through her. Staring up into his eyes, half-shuttered by passion-heavy lids, she managed a rasped, "Um, that's not a good idea."

"I misspoke. I don't want to kiss you." He took her face in both big, hot hands.

"I need to."

"I loved the book!" ~DebA, Night Owl Reviews on *Heart Mates* **TOP PICK**

RT Reviews TOP PICK "A must-read!" ~ RT Reviews on *Passion Bites*

"What a **brilliant, action packed, paranormal adventure and romance this proved to be**!" ~Splashes Into Books on *Mind Mates*

Heart Mates

To survive, they'll have to find the missing pieces—starting with their own.

Pull of the Moon book 2

Sophia Blue wishes the cute little doggie she's found in her aunt's abandoned magic shop could talk. Maybe he'd tell her if the old woman has wandered off on a walkabout, or if there's foul magic afoot. Odd how the scruffy little fur ball seems to understand Sophia's every word.

Just a few years ago, she might have cast a spell to translate the dog's ear-piercing yaps. But her magic is out of her reach, locked away in penance for mistakenly helping an evil wizard.

Noah Blackwood was the last person to see Sophia's aunt before she hit him with a spell gone sideways. By night he's two-hundred pounds of authority, a respected local pack leader. By day? He's twelve pounds of poof dog. A tasty morsel for the five anti-alpha wolves gunning for him.

The instant the sun goes down and Sophia's eyes meet Noah's, fire ignites between them in an incendiary kiss. But when the evil wizard reappears intent on murder, Sophia must break through killing layers of pain to find her magic. And Noah must reclaim all that he is—even defy the law—to claim the woman his heart knows is his mate.

Warning: Contains a sassy ex-witch princess who hasn't picked up a wand in four years, and a rare alpha wolf who proves attitude knows no boundaries. A little drooling, a lot of panting, and a few nips in all the right places. Flea collar not included.

Look for these titles by Mary Hughes

Now Available:

Romantic Adventure

Edie and the CEO—Crimson Romance

Falling ~~on~~ for the Billionaire

Cin Wikkid: April Fools For Love

Hot Chips and Sand

Bad Boy Billionaire's Lady: Lovless Brothers

Playing With Fire: The Battle of the Bands

Biting Love/The Ancients

Bite My Fire—Entangled

Biting Nixie—Entangled

The Bite of Silence—Entangled

Biting Me Softly—Entangled

Biting Oz—Entangled

Beauty Bites—Entangled

Downbeat—Entangled

Assassins Bite—Entangled

Passion Bites—Entangled

Biting Love Nibbles

Night's Caress—Entangled

Pull of the Moon Series
Prophecy Mates
Heart Mates
Hunt Mates
Mind Mates

Standalone
Black Diamond Jinn

Coming Soon:

The Classic Billionaire's Newshound (Lovless Brothers)
The Genius Billionaire's Hacker (Lovless Brothers)
Night's Kiss (The Ancients)
Night's Bliss (The Ancients)
Soul Mates (Pull of the Moon)

Heart Mates

Pull of the Moon

Mary Hughes

Heart Mates

Digital ISBN: 978-1-940958-15-6
Print ISBN: 978-1-940958-16-3
Samhain Edition Edited by Christa Soule
Cover by Scott Carpenter

First electronic publication: April 2015
First print publication: April 2015
Second electronic publication: May 2017
Second print publication: May 2017

DEDICATION

To Gregg, for keeping me in tea and cheese curds during those long nights doing promotion. Best batch ever, honey.

To Christa Soule, who's brilliant not just in flashes but all the damned time. How do you do it?

My thanks to awesome author and pet expert Renee Wildes for vetting (heh) King's grooming. All mistakes are my own.

Added for the second edition—thanks to the Blurb Wizard for the great blurb and Scott Carpenter for the amazing cover. It must be a burden to have to carry that much talent around, lol.

Chapter One

Noah Blackwood opened the door to the Uncommon Night Owl Bookstore, knowing full well he was walking into trouble.

He'd only been alpha a few days, but he already had a sense for when members of his pack were in trouble—and when they were *causing* trouble. Sure enough, as he glided soundlessly across the threshold of the bookshop, his foot struck broken glass. He scanned the store with a narrowed gaze.

Seventeen-year-old Marlowe stood to his left, beside a front display case. His dirty fingers were wrapped tightly around something, caught in the act of stealing it.

Marlowe was a bully in training and a young man with too much time on his hands.

By bloody tooth and claw, Noah would give the pup something better to do.

As he closed the door and strode toward Marlowe, Noah realized the pack youth was frozen in place, fingers squeezing the thing as if he *couldn't* let go.

And that the thing was a foot-long psychedelic capped tower that looked uncomfortably like an erect penis.

Noah scowled. He wasn't sure what was more unnatural, that frozen boy or the flower-power dildo.

A rattle of beads from the back of the store caught his attention.

"*Mr*. Blackwood." The store's proprietor—Linda Blue, who styled herself as some sort of seer—swept apart a back curtain of beads and trundled out. "You need to keep better control of your people. You're better than the old alpha Scauth, of course—"

"Alpha? You know about shifters?" Noah stared at the small, round woman. The magical communities were secretive and small. A mundane human, even a seer, shouldn't know about the pack. "How?"

"That's beside the point...oh my." As she neared, her hand fluttered in front of her ample bosom.

Magic flared in his sight, nearly blinding him. She'd cast a spell.

Damn it, she was a *witch*.

Noah's palm pressed automatically to his chest, shielding his wolf medallion. Well, that explained how she knew he was pack. Witches were trouble. Big trouble. The sooner Noah got Marlowe out from under her feet, the better.

"This won't happen again, ma'am." He half-growled it, his inner wolf close to the surface.

"And how do I know that, Mr. Blackwood?" She looked down her long nose at him, a difficult feat considering Noah was almost a foot taller.

Angry Marlowe had put him in this situation, Noah wanted nothing more than to take the boy and leave. But witches took careful handling. He controlled himself and said mildly, "Let me talk with the boy. You'll see."

She waved a hand, and Marlowe staggered as if released. Noah's hackles rose. A witch who could freeze a wolf was no mere dabbler.

Marlowe dared to snarl at him. The idiot.

Noah seized the pup by the scruff of the neck—and Marlowe swung at him with the pink rod.

Noah saw red. The rod was a doodad in a magical store full of doodads that did who-knew-what—and the pup was swinging it like a bat? He wasn't an idiot, he was an imbecile. Snatching the rod from Marlowe's hand, Noah hoisted the pup until his legs batted air.

Snarls changed abruptly to thin whines.

Letting the pup meditate midair on his errors, Noah set the rod gently on the display case. Barking dogs, he didn't know how close he'd skated to disaster. Noah gave the pup a good scold, letting his roiling anger and alarm bleed into his tone. When he set him down, he rapped his nose for good measure.

The boy slouched, as if his tail were tucked between his legs.

Noah turned to the witch. "I'm sorry for the boy's behavior, Ms. Blue. Naturally, I'll pay for any damages."

"Well..." She rocked on her toes and Noah could see her mind working. He waited for the worst, but her plump cheeks turned rosy. "If it can make us friends...apology accepted."

"Thank you." Friends? With a witch? He'd rather pal around with a rabid badger. "I'm glad to have this settled."

He grabbed Marlowe by the shoulders and marched the pup toward the door. The witch hustled past them to open it.

She misjudged the distance and plowed into them both. Noah twisted to catch her from falling.

She blinked up into his eyes, beaming. "Oh, thank you!"

Her girlish batting disoriented him just long enough for Marlowe to twist and duck away.

The pup, laughing, ran to grab the dildo then dashed toward the back of the store. His running fist pumped the tower in the air like a bizarre personal barbell.

"My vibrating skyscraper mushroom!" the witch cried.

"Mushroom?" Marlowe, as if *trying* to aggravate the damned witch, turned and crowed. "It's a psycho dildo 'shroom!"

The witch flitted after the pup, spinning her fingers like a thousand itsy bitsy spiders, her jewelry clacking like an antique train. "One for the money, two for the show."

Noah launched himself after her. Twist his tail, she was casting a spell. She looked sweet but if she had real power, well, he'd seen the destruction of mages' battles. "Don't—"

"Three to get ready and four—"

"No!" Dread kicked Noah to leap for the boy.

"—to go!"

He cut eyes back. Air warped toward him, wavering like a hot day. Before it hit, Noah tackled the boy, taking him to the floor. The impact took the rod from his hands, flying in an arc through the beaded curtain of the back doorway.

Noah raised his head.

The warped air rippled past them, sailing into a free-standing Snow White oval mirror near the doorway.

The spell rebounded off the mirror. No, the mirror didn't just bounce it. It augmented it.

Noah shoved to his hands and knees as a glittering tsunami of magic whooshed out of the mirror, heading off to his left. Damn it, this was why he hated magic. Unpredictable, uncontrollable. The spell shot into a glass curio cabinet full of pictures, hit one, and ricocheted—

Straight into his face.

It punched him like a fist. He spun on his knees and fell onto his back, magic shivering into his skin like a thousand tiny barbs. The spell spiraled down into him, condensing in the middle of his chest...and then nothing.

While Noah lay there panting, Marlowe leaped to his feet and disappeared through the beads.

Barking dogs. The pup had probably scooped up that damned mushroom on the way.

Noah wrestled to his elbows. His nose hurt like he'd taken a real fist. The witch packed quite a wallop for looking like a sweet Mrs. Santa.

Weaving fingers fluttered suddenly in his face.

Acid splashed through him. "Lady, don't—"

"Reveal." She stared down at him in plate-eyed horror, her face draining of all color.

"*What* in blazes is going on?" His words were more growl than voice. Normally, he had excellent control of his wolf. But this, on top of being forced into the alpha fight and the challenges to his new leadership, would make even the calmest wolf howl. He shoved himself to his feet. "What did you hit me with?"

The witch's fingers covered her mouth. "You felt that? Oh my. Oh dear. This is not good. This is very not good."

"If you don't tell me what—"

"Nothing. Everything." The plump woman flitted to the mirror. She traced its dark wood frame with fluttering fingers, her eyes surprisingly intent.

"Lady, I don't know what you're talking about. But that was some serious magic."

She whirled, skirts flying. "How do you know that?"

"Same way I know you're a witch." He tapped his nose.

"That's impossible. No one can sense a witch."

He shrugged. "I can. I'm pack alpha." The truth, in so far as it went.

She whirled back to the mirror, studying it so intensely Noah was surprised it didn't blush. She was muttering to herself. "Impossible. Magic is paradox. Witches *sense* the paradox but shifters *are* the paradox. A shifter sensing magic would be like...like a color sensing itself."

Typical witch. No real answer. "Just tell me what you hit me with, Ms. Blue."

The witch's cheeks pinked. "Call me Linda."

He tapped his dwindling reserves of patience. "Nice to meet you, Linda. I'm Noah—stop that!"

She wagged fingers at him, muttering.

Noah stepped sharply back, too late. The spell hit him with a brief glitter. "Damn it, I hate sparkles."

"You *saw* that?" Her eyes widened like hobbit doors. She spun, trotted to the curio cabinet, opened it, picked one of the pictures, and carried it back to him. "It hit Sophia's photo before it struck you. Do you know her?"

Sophia. The name rang like the purest bell in his mind.

Then she pushed the picture into his nose, and the woman's face hit him harder than the spell.

Smooth, elegant, so beautiful he wanted to howl. *Sophia*. Glossy bronze curls, elegant nose, and eyes that punched him in the gut. Big, intelligent eyes, yet something in her gaze hinted that if a man got her someplace private, they'd do some amazing things—

Noah backed away. He'd *never* heated up that fast. Damn it, what had the witch done to him? He tried to speak, but nothing came out. He swallowed and tried again. Still nothing.

Desperate to hang onto his control, he closed his eyes and used his three-two-one descent to his quiet place, one of the few things he'd kept from his childhood. After dipping a toe in the cool, calm waters of rationality, he opened his eyes again on the witch. "No. Never met her."

She tapped the frame against her lip. "Interesting."

"Linda, enough. *What hit me?*"

"The tiniest of hexes." She bustled to put the picture back then trundled to an armoire to lift a folded white sheet from the shelves. "A simple bur."

He shook his head. "That didn't hit like a bur."

"Yes, well, it took a few detours first." She closed the cupboard, trotted to the mirror and threw the sheet over it. The cloth slithered into place like silk. She twitched a few places to cover the mirror completely just as a bell tinkled from the front of the store. The sound of the door opening was followed by a beam of dawn sunlight lancing across the floor. "There, that's taken care of. I—oh dear."

She spun and stared at the front door.

"What's the matter...*yip*?" Suddenly dizzy, he pressed a hand to his head. Or tried to. A paw wavered in front of his face.

"We're closed." Linda's tone was strained.

Noah shook his head to clear it. He felt so strange. He finally managed to focus on the front door where an older woman stood, hands over her mouth, staring at *him*.

The woman stuttered, "The door was open and I... D-did that man just turn into an animal—?"

Noah froze. Had he shifted without meaning to? That hadn't happened since he was in diapers. He reached for his human...and nothing happened. What was going on?

"No, no. That's an illusion." Linda bustled to the woman and turned her away. "All mirrors and such. Come back tomorrow." She hustled the woman out, closed the door, and collapsed back against the jamb, hand against her forehead.

"Mr. Blackwood. Noah." Heaving a breath, she straightened and trotted toward the back of the store. "You stay here. I have to go check out a few things."

"Yip?" He couldn't quite believe what he was hearing.

"I'll be back as soon as I can." Then, in a flurry of hairpins and a rattle of beaded curtain, she was gone.

"Yip yip...? Yip!" He ground his teeth. Witches. Couldn't trust the lot of them. Always secretive, and not in the necessary, protecting-the-pack way. He started after her, using the long-legged lope that was his wolf's stride...and upended, landing on his back, little furry legs batting above him.

That was when he found out he was a fifteen-inch dog.

Chapter Two

Sophia Blue stared at the broken bookstore door. Her brother had spoken with Aunt Linda this morning, but since then, they'd heard nothing. Now it was nearly sunset, and Sophia was officially worried. Heart thudding, she cracked the door open.

She peered into the store's shadows. Shivered. She'd never felt so naked without her magic.

"Aunt Linda?" Her voice echoed in an empty way.

No bustling medicine ball of an auntie swooped down on her. No lecture on finding a husband. No bosom-suffocating hug.

Just darkness. Emptiness.

"Aunt Linda, where are you?" Sophia's hand rose to clasp her pearl necklace, hard little knots under her fingers. Nothing looked out of place in the arcane bookshop, but with the jumble of shelves and showcases, every available inch crammed with crystals, herbs, candles, and books, it was hard to tell.

She stepped into the store. When glass crunched under her feet she jumped so hard she nearly fell. Her gaze plunged to the floor.

Broken shards glittered warningly in the dying June sunlight—more than would fit the fist-sized hole in the door's crosshatched pane.

Her spine iced. She released her necklace to jab a hand into the pocket of her banker-chic suit coat for her pepper spray. Her fingers landed on smooth metal. It reassured her.

Anybody but Aunt Linda, and she'd have called the cops. But involving mundanes in magical business was a bad idea. Besides, the Blue family still hadn't gotten over being treated like marshmallows by the courts of the 1600s.

"Auntie, where are you?" Clutching her pepper spray, Sophia eased farther into the store, gaze searching. The old-fashioned register seemed undisturbed. Ditto the dust on the heavy bookshelves.

Her neck prickled. She turned.

The showcase next to the door was smashed, a confusion of dream catchers, incense boxes, and heaped costume jewelry inside. The hairs on her nape rose. "Break my broomstick..." She clenched her eyes at the curse. She'd been without power for several years now. But old habits were hard to break.

A faint rattle from the back of the store snapped her eyes open. "Who's there?" Her voice shook. "Auntie?"

No answer.

But she'd recognized that rattle, the beads curtaining the back doorway. If not Aunt Linda, then who? Mr. Kibbles, Auntie's cat familiar? *A burglar?* Fingers so tight around the pepper spray they nearly dented the can, Sophia forged deeper into the store. Past the bookshelves. Past the reading area with its chairs and sofa and big

Aladdin carpet, once a sun-drenched haven for her girlhood summers spent reading.

Now just shards of glass and empty echoes.

Swinging beads caught her eye, strands which curtained the private kitchen exit of the old-fashioned storefront. *Someone had just stepped through that doorway.*

A burglar? A murderer? A *demon*?

She swallowed dry air. "Auntie? Mr. Kibbles?"

No answer, not even a meow.

She released the spray to find her cell phone. Not to call the mundane police or even the Witches' Council, whose Enforcers only came out for big things like demigod infestations. But she was alone, hundreds of miles from home with a car that had broken down on the way here and barely limped into town, and she needed to alert *someone* she was walking into trouble.

She texted her brother, *Auntie's door broken,* hit send, and looked up.

A shaft of red sunlight beamed through the store, stabbing a back display case like a laser.

A portent.

Every hair on her body stood straight. She wanted to check the kitchen, but no witch ignored portents. Not even ex-witches. Veins throbbing with cold, she edged toward the showcase.

The red shaft spotlighted two wands, placed in an X.

Both had been hers.

Sophia swallowed hard. *Her* wands, the subject of a portent? Why? They weren't special. Her learner's wand was typical for a young witch, pink and sparkly. Heart pounding, she put away her phone to pick up the wand, intending to return it to its box, covered in peeling boy band stickers.

The moment she touched the wand, she smiled. Even baby spells danced, wonderfully magical, with the pretty pink stick. Someday another young witch would find learning magic fun with it. She settled it into its box and put the box on the bottom shelf.

Then she picked up the smooth, seductive length of the second wand. Carbon fiber, light, strong, and precise, here was a serious amplifier of magic. The handle still fit her palm like a living part of her. She'd had it with her constantly.

Until the day she sealed off her magic, four years and another lifetime ago.

Her smile died. She shoved the wand into the first empty space she saw.

Stars and moon...*damn* it, what were these wands doing here anyway? She'd given them to Aunt Linda on consignment. Not special, but the learner's stick was in top condition and the carbon fiber wand was professional, handmade, and priced to move. It was suspicious she'd never managed to sell them.

Then again, Auntie was rather haphazard about her stock.

Sophia sighed and rolled her shoulders, trying to roll out some of her tension. Where was Aunt Linda? Was this simply another of her famous walkabouts, as when she'd wandered off in search of Bigfoot to complete her Magical Creatures of the World autograph set?

Plausible...except for that broken glass. And the portent. And the moving beads...

Sophia resolutely headed for the kitchen doorway. She put a hand on the beads to part them.

A furred streak shot through the doorway—straight at her.

Demon! Sophia jumped back. She landed braced, heart thudding in her ears, fumbling for her pepper spray. Nothing immediately attacked.

"*Yip yip yip.*" The cry, bouncing off floor and glass cabinets, was as piercing as a jet engine.

A Siren? Death by sex wasn't so bad, but she'd rather avoid the soul-stealing part. Her hand landed on the spray.

Cold and wet touched her shin. *Zombie…?* She gasped and lost her grip on the can. Her gaze darted down, dread coiling inside her.

A dog sniffed her legs.

She blinked. Nope, still a dog down there, nosing her ankles. Or a doglet, rather, a terrier no bigger than a football. Heaving a deep breath to slow her thudding heart, she bent to ruffle his or her head. "Hello there, sweetie."

Its little tail started wagging, like a ceiling fan set on whap.

"Auntie finally got a pet, huh? How's Mr. Kibbles taking it? Not well, I bet. What were you doing in the kitchen?"

She headed through the beads into a room redolent of warm memories, sugar cookies baking, and Auntie's comforting-if-oxygen-depriving hugs. The kitchen was fairly tidy. No sign of a burglar or an auntie.

But a big fat yellow tabby sulked on top of the refrigerator. Mr. Kibbles wasn't the stereotypical black, but Auntie wasn't a typical witch.

The little poof dog trotted in behind her, yipping as if he or she was offering suggestions.

Mr. Kibbles hissed.

The dog, instead of jumping or barking at the cat, sat regally on its haunches and gave the cat the Look. Powerful magic, wielded unknowingly by mundanes, the Look was the sword-sharp "if you do this the world will end" eye-communiqué given by spouses the world over.

It was not given by rat dogs to fat orange cats.

Sophia laughed, ruffling the dog's bangs. "I'm seeing things, doggie. Worried about Aunt Linda, I guess."

The dog transferred its attention to her. He—or she—barked three times, with grave authority, like a bank president admonishing someone who'd tried to cash a bad check.

"What don't you like, me calling you doggie?"

It nodded.

She blinked in surprise. The dog couldn't understand her, could it?

Nope. Unless it was a shifter or familiar—but dogs never were. Too artless. Dogs—the ultimate WYSIWIG, What-You-See-Is-What-You-Get, complete with slobber and jumping on the couch. This dog couldn't be a subtle shifter or wise familiar. She shook off the idea. "What should I call you? Curly?"

The dog shivered then gave a single, sharp yap.

"No, huh? Mitzy? Sweetie?"

That got an actual growl.

Sophia laughed again, surprised she could with glass on the floor and Auntie missing. But for some reason this little ball of fur made her happier. "If Auntie were here you'd get Oogywoogiesnookums. The fat one up on the fridge was Umpylumkins until I talked her down to Mr. Kibbles."

The dog sneezed, stood, and turned his-or-her back on her—hmm, from behind that was definitely a *he*.

"Impressive package for a little guy. How about Prince?"

The dog cocked his head over his shoulder at her. Yipped doubtfully.

"Close, huh? What about King?"

The dog turned toward her, his bark enthusiastic.

"King it is." She laughed again. "King of the Poof Dogs."

The dog snipped a yip, turned his back, and stuck his snout in the air.

She stopped laughing. Was she just imagining that eerie intelligence?

Well, yes. Unless Arcane Animal Husbandry 101 had been completely overturned in the last four years.

The orange lump on top of the fridge, on the other hand... "Mr. Kibbles, do you know where Auntie went? There's a can of tuna in it for you."

In answer, he leaped from refrigerator to countertop to floor and padded out the back of the kitchen. Familiars could take human form, but Sophia had never seen Mr. Kibbles as anything but a cat. She followed him to the hallway.

He sat by Aunt Linda's slippers, washing his face.

Auntie's *slippers*, instead of her shoes. Sophia's spine ran cold.

Behind her, King yipped. She glanced at him. His little brow was furrowed, and she almost heard his, "What's wrong?"

He couldn't understand, but it was comforting to pretend he could. She bent to pat his head. "It's nothing, sweetie. Aunt Linda's walking shoes are usually here." It meant Auntie had left under her own steam. But if she was okay, why wasn't that glass swept up? The door repaired? Why wasn't she answering her cell phone? "She's gone outside."

He barked at the word "outside".

"Oh dear." Where was Linda, that she'd left this poor doggie without his walkies? "I'm so sorry, King. I have to find Auntie first. I'll take you for a walk later."

As a stopgap, she laid papers on the kitchen floor.

Then Sophia returned to the store proper, thinking maybe Aunt Linda left a note by the register, or tacked to the community bulletin board.

The register was on a counter near the front of the store. She found the pad of paper her aunt kept to figure tax—the register was that old.

The pad's top sheet was blank. Sophia was trying to see if she could make anything of the dents by turning the pad this way and that in the dying sunlight when a bell clanged *right behind her*. She leaped out of her skin, her nerves flaring like live wires. The pad dropped from her hand and hit the floor with a thud.

"Yip?" King, who'd followed her into the store proper, gave a small, concerned bark.

"It's okay." She put a hand to her breastbone, where her heart was trying to dent it from the inside. "It's just the landline."

Auntie's store phone was a wall-mounted monstrosity with separate cones for ear and mouthpiece. Sophia picked up the bell-shaped earpiece and leaned in to speak into the trumpet mouthpiece. "Uncommon Night Owl. How may I—"

"What the hell," a bear-like voice growled, "did you do to Noah?"

Noah.

All her fear evaporated in a rush of heat. The name sang along her spine like strong magic. Her belly did a little shimmy.

She barely managed a professional, "Who is this?"

"Who's *this*? You aren't Miz Blue."

"I'm *a* Miz Blue." Summers cashiering here kept her from chewing the rudeness out of Mr. Growl. "I repeat, who are you? And who's Noah?" Her tummy shimmied again and the heat in her blood flushed goose bumps along her arms.

Mr. Growl started swearing.

"Hey. I'm not even sure those are all real words. No answers until you give me some."

"I'm Mason Blackwood," he bit out. "Noah's cousin. He's the leader of our...group."

"Group, hmm?" Mentally, she substituted the word "pack". Shifters couldn't recognize witches, but witches could identify shifters. Aunt Linda had mentioned that the local wolf clan recently had a change of alpha. The Scauth pack was renamed Blackwood for the new alpha Noah Blackwood...

Her whole body shimmered.

She nearly dropped the phone. Stars and planets...damn it all. That was *lust* running delightedly up and down her body.

Witches and wolves and lust—extremely, totally *forbidden*. Lightning coming down from the sky, gods hitting the smite key forbidden.

"Where's Noah?" Mason growled in her ear.

"I don't know..." She dribbled off as she barely recognized her own throaty purr. Putting a hand to her pearls, she thought cool bankerly thoughts, about compound interest and mortgages and the clink of the coin machine sorting dimes and quarters into slick paper sleeves, pounding hard cylinders into tight sheaths...good heavens, where had *that* come from? "Why would you think your cousin was here?"

"Miz Linda Blue had a problem there in the wee hours of the morning with a boy in our group."

The wee hours, when the store alarm had gone off.

Mason went on, "She called Noah in to handle it."

"That's not right. Auntie handles her own problems."

"Not for our group," Mason growled. "We police our own."

And didn't that just have the pawprint of secretive shifter all over it? "If it happened so long ago, why are you first calling now?"

"I'm not. I've been trying since dawn. Noah went, but he never came back."

"Well, I'm sorry. I haven't seen him." About to hang up, she paused. Noah was at the store after the alarm went off. He was possibly the last person to see Aunt Linda. "I need to talk with him, too. Tell you what. There's an outside chance he's upstairs. I'll go check, and then we can talk again."

"Blackwood Small Engine Repair, Third and Pine." Mason hung up.

Sophia stared at the ear piece. Typical shifter, a male of few words—and most of those growled. She'd meant "talk" over the phone. She hung up with a shrug. Denizens of the magical communities did prefer face-to-face over technology. Well, most of them did.

Heading for the steps, she considered what she might find upstairs. Not her aunt. Even if Linda had been working in the sales bins, she would have known the instant Sophia was in the store. Auntie might not have heard her if she was taking a nap in her room in the back, but leaving her store open without someone to mind the registers? Not likely.

Sophia mounted the steps.

Even less likely that Noah—*shiver*—was in her aunt's guest room, sleeping. Probably nobody was up there. But in case a burglar or the person who'd broken the door and display glass hid upstairs, she scooped out her cell phone and readied her thumb over her brother's speed dial. Just to be safe.

King hopped up the stairs after her, yipping a double bark that rose at the end, like a question. Like he was saying, "What's going on?"

A talking dog. She was either completely nuts, or had a great premise for a new reality show.

But it made her want to answer the question. Oh, what was the harm? If a burglar hid upstairs, he already knew she was here. And talking to a dog wasn't insane, only thinking he actually answered was.

"I just don't like the picture I'm getting, King. The store alarm went off last night. Or rather, early this morning. Well, my brother Gabriel had rigged it to notify him, and he called her right away. My aunt answered, but she sounded stressed. She babbled about being in a spot of trouble, said that she'd call him back—but she never did. Now, she's not only gone, this Noah"—*shiver*—"has disappeared too. I don't like it at all." Reaching the top of the stairs, she automatically started sketching a simple locater spell for her aunt.

Pain. Pins and needles jabbed both hands. With a gasp, she clamped her hands to her sides. The pain died down.

King gave a concerned yip.

"I'm fine." But her heart was thudding and her forehead was prickling with sweat.

She searched Auntie's two bedrooms and a bath, methodically, checking closets and under the bed. Nothing out of place.

The store half, in the front...well, Auntie had learned shopkeeping in the sixties, complete with round rose-colored spectacles, peach wine, and her best friend Mary Jane. Sophia was never so happy as when the shag carpet had come up...and off the walls.

The dog followed her on her search, as quiet and alert as a bodyguard. Not big enough to guard a mouse, but she was glad for his company. This was supposed to be a quick visit to make sure Auntie was okay, not all bloody sunlight and portents.

No burglar, but no Noah either. Time for Mason's.

She clomped downstairs but before she could leave, Mr. Kibbles meowed at her. Loudly. She'd promised him tuna, and a familiar's metabolism meant he'd get cranky if he didn't get fed—and when Mr. Kibbles got cranky, Auntie's heirloom linen got shredded. Sophia poured out the last of the cat food into his pointedly empty dish and plopped a can of tuna on top.

While the cat familiar nom-nommed with a room-rumbling purr, she put down fresh water for both animals then hunted for dog kibble. No bag, not even an empty doggie dish.

"Have you been eating cat food, sweetie?"

King's little face screwed up and his tongue pushed out repeatedly.

So buy some, after talking to Mason.

Sophia headed for the front door, adding *sweep up* to her mental list as she crunched gingerly through the broken glass. Her hand was on the doorknob when a sense of *wrongness* made her look up.

Beyond her car, across the street. She stopped breathing.

A hooded man lurked in the shadows, intently watching her.

Chapter Three

Sophia swallowed fear as cold as crushed ice. She tried to see the figure's face—but the hood shadowed it.

The head raised. A glimpse of man-chin... He turned and disappeared.

She clutched her pearl necklace. Her whole body felt cold.

King yipped. *Are you okay?*

She inhaled deeply, pushed the air out, and shoved aside her shock with it. "I will be." She was saying it to herself, not answering the dog. Really. "I've got to find Aunt Linda. According to Mason, Noah was probably the last person to see her. He might be able to tell me what happened or where she went—if I can find him." The streetlight outside flared on. Sunset was only minutes away and complete darkness would fall soon after. She put her hand resolutely on the doorknob. "So, next stop, Mason's garage."

King yipped eagerly and trotted toward the door as if he'd come too.

"Oh no, sweetie." Turning, she bent and pushed him back gently before he stepped on the broken glass. His body was surprisingly sturdy for such a little guy. Maybe the weight of that swinging package. "No walkies now. Use the paper."

"*Yiiiip.*" He scowled at her. It was equal parts scary and adorable.

She felt herself weakening, but Aunt Linda might not have time for her to wait. She pushed the dog away more firmly. "King, *no*. You can't come."

He howled his dismay—like a soprano wolf.

She snapped straight in equal dismay. *King is just a dog*. Jerking the door open, she skipped through before he could tag along and quickly closed the door after her.

His aggrieved barking followed her out.

* * *

Noah stood at the edge of the broken glass and barked after the stunning but annoying woman Sophia. How dare she leave him?

He winced at the embarrassing soprano yips that came out of his muzzle.

Dropping to disgusted haunches he snuffled a breath out. He sucked air in through his nostrils to calm himself, then tried yet again to shift, either human or wolf. He'd been trying all day. It was as effective as it had been the first three hundred and fifty times, which was not at all.

He'd have thought that, after a whole day as the poofball, he'd have at least gotten used to it. But no. He still went ass over teakettle when he'd tried to catch the woman.

She had the most amazing eyes. Star-shot blue, like the moon sparkling on a Grecian sea. Strong nose, pure skin, kissable lips—

His tail bone vibrated. His hindquarters popped up at the buzz, the startled reaction of his inner...well, not wolf in this form, but his inner canine. His human mind knew it was his cell phone, probably his lieutenant Mason calling again, slightly fewer times than Noah'd tried to shift.

Normally, Noah could shift whenever he wanted. Day or night, and any time of the month, though the full moon made it easier. His grandpa had explained that it was because they were magical werewolves. Clothes shifted in with them when their wolf came out, including whatever mechanicals they were carrying.

Which meant right now the phone was a giant internal joy buzzer. Noah could've spent a few minutes nudging it out, but why? It wasn't like he had hands or a voice to answer the call.

He trotted around to shake the buzz off, nearly planting his face on the floor because of his stubby little legs. Nearly two hundred pounds of human, and two hundred pounds of wolf, Noah was finding fifteen pounds of terrier unbelievably hard to work with.

Cursed by a witch. Bad enough. But *he* had to be cursed by a witch with a lousy aim and a wicked sense of humor.

Then the beautiful Sophia had shown up. His tongue lolled out and he panted at the memory. Amazing eyes and lips as sweet as ripe cherries...he shook himself.

The *witch's niece* had shown up. *Never* trust a witch.

Although, just because Sophia's aunt was a witch didn't mean Sophia was one. He didn't know about witch breeding like he knew about shifters, but he knew enough to guess the gene for doing magic wasn't dominant, unlike the gene for being magic.

Sophia certainly had been chatty. He wondered if she would have been as chatty with the man Noah as she had been with the dog King. Probably not. The thought rather wounded him.

The last of the sun disappeared.

Mist fogged his brain. Needles stabbed his legs. He stumbled and fell sprawling to the floor.

He came to...human.

And naked.

* * *

Sophia considered taking her car to Mason's, but it had barely gotten her here, and she didn't want to push her luck. Matinsfield wasn't that big, a rubber band of a town stretched along Main, so it was no big deal to walk.

Her power walk—her natural pace, not running from scary hooded guys at all—propelled her along the street. Streetlights stuttered on, jarring her already tender nerves. Dark, empty storefronts didn't help. It saddened her that there were so many. Aunt Linda had said the town wasn't doing so well, but she'd never dreamed it was this bad.

A few places were open. Her step lightened passing the new FreshFresh submarine sandwich shop. Only three thousand people, but Matinsfield had three of the chain sub stores, a retail peculiarity that seemed to work despite itself.

Like a witch attracted to an alpha...?

Nope. I'm not going there. "Keep your ass unsmited, Sophia."

Turning north on Pine, Blackwood Small Engine Repair was the last building before the town ran out. She'd expected a rickety shack and cracked blacktop so was surprised by a sweeping skirt of neat red pavers around a large cinder block building. Despite the local economy, the store was obviously doing well.

She'd also expected lawn mowers and snow blowers, and while there were some of those, the biggest window was filled with motorcycles.

Leaning her palms against the glass, she stared in awe at cruisers, sportsters, and off-road bikes, all lovingly displayed.

Inside, cool air caressed her cheeks. She ran a finger along buttery leather jackets and sleek carbon fiber bikes, everything she could want for her riding pleasure, including some bitchin' helmets.

But she was here for Mason. She walked through the store, searching for him. A quick survey showed her the store was empty, but a single door across from the main entrance flashed with light.

*   *   *

"Damn my aching paws." Noah raised his head and shook it, reassured when hair flopped around his skull instead of doggie ears. "About time the witch's hex wore off."

His wolf prodded him to leap up and run after the gorgeous Sophia...run to *Mason's*, that was. He resisted his beast with a willpower born of lifelong practice. He'd gotten to be alpha at the impossibly tender age of twenty-nine through brains, speed, brains, strength—and brains. Checking his surroundings with eye and ear and most importantly nose, he sensed no immediate danger. Well, if you didn't count the fat cat in the kitchen.

If it was possible to be fatally annoying, Mr. Snippy Kibbles had a lock.

Noah climbed to his bare feet. He flexed his fingers then stretched all his muscles, his body cramped from wearing the small dog all day. And though he usually shifted forms smoothly and easily, that transformation had *hurt*.

He checked rapidly that all parts of him were present and in working order, including his package, the one Sophia had called impressive...that made him preen...damn it, he was a deadly wolf and deadly wolves did *not* preen.

His clothes lay in a heap next to him. He cautiously prodded them. Usually anything he wore on his human body stayed on, and shifting back naked made him uneasy. But the clothes seemed normal.

Must've been the hex. Dressing, he pulled his cell phone from the jeans' pocket. His lieutenant had called only a dozen times, not the five hundred it seemed. No message. Mason was as cautious as Noah.

Noah rapidly considered his options. *Go to Sophia...* He clamped his eyes shut. No. Debrief with Mason. *Then go to Sophia...* Fine. She was the witch's niece, and he owed the witch money for damages to her store.

It had absolutely nothing to do with Sophia's pure, kissable mouth, the sexy sway of her hips... "Bite me." His eyes flew open, and he jabbed Mason's speed dial.

He was in the process of giving Mason a flash update when his lieutenant interrupted with news that a gorgeous woman had just come into the garage.

Sophia had arrived. Noah clipped a goodbye, rushed out the door, shifted to wolf, and bounded off into the night.

* * *

Sophia pushed open the door into a garage.

Oil and metal stung her nose. Darkness surrounded her, broken only by a bright light filtering from her left through a couple sets of tall shelves. A *kerchunk* of tools came from where the light was. To her right were outer doors, garage and people.

She moved forward. The tall shelves broke the floor into six bays, three on each side. Straight ahead, leaning nonchalantly on its stand like a gal's wet dream, was the sweetest-looking motorcycle she'd ever seen.

She floated nearer. *Ducati* graced the gas tank. A hole marred the frame. Engine parts littered a worktable that, swept together, might fit the hole.

It was a measure of Sophia's love for her aunt that she moved away from that motorcycle. And the fact that maybe *Noah* was here. Her heart beat faster at the thought.

She followed the clangs to the last bay.

Working under the shop light was a tall, heavily muscled man wearing jeans, grease, and not much else. He applied a wrench to a big cruiser, his back to her. She was still half the floor away when he spun.

Power-filled eyes startled her. Chocolate irises, ringed in unusual, rich copper, said here was a strong magical being. A beta at least. No wedding ring.

He wasn't single because of his looks. Those eyes were made for low bedroom light. His shaggy brown hair was streaked with gold. Combined with the heavy muscle on his big frame, his chiseled lips, and his square jaw, he was one appealing wolf.

"Who are you?" He growled it.

Okay, that wasn't so appealing. *Shifters.* The animal within always snarled through. "I'm Sophia Blue—Linda's my aunt. We spoke on the phone. You're Mason, I take it?"

His stance relaxed, and he set aside the wrench, grabbed a couple of wipes from a pop-up container, and cleaned his hands. "You're here about Noah?"

"Yes." Sophia kept her own body relaxed and her gaze steady and slightly averted. No sense antagonizing the wolf in Mason. *Thank you, Arcane Animal Husbandry 102.* "My aunt is missing, and Noah was probably the last person to see her. I thought we could try to find him."

"I know where Noah is, now." Mason's growl was back. "So do you."

"Me? I don't know where he is. How could I?" Yet even as Sophia spoke, a snarl of awareness seized her.

Mason said, "He phoned just a minute ago. Said you named him Kin—"

"—someone to help," a bass voice thrummed from the dark depths of the garage.

Sophia spun. That masculine voice, vibrating with power, plucked a long string of throbbing need deep inside her.

A tall, broad-shouldered figure emerged from the blackness, gliding into the sharp white light with a smooth prowl that was all muscular grace, extraordinary strength, and endurance.

Her entire belly turned inside out at the sight of the man.

Powerful frame. A fall of black hair over a high, regal brow. A face that was all dangerous planes. Eyes that gleamed with intelligence. He was total alpha—dominant, deadly, and sexy as hell.

Her own eyes widened, her jaw dropped, and her heart knocked "Some Enchanted Evening" against her ribs—before her hormones exploded. Not really, but the man gave her a full-body rush.

He stopped a few feet from her, standing with breathtaking stillness.

Werewolves were usually ruled by their aggression, so the man's cool composure was even more striking.

Definitely a were, though. His honed jaw was textured with the rough, black morning-after-sex stubble all male wolf shifters seemed to have.

Her body splashed with a hot *me want* of desire.

Then their eyes met.

Power shows in the eyes. This man had power, and to spare. Irises of pure silver stunned her even as his pupils opened to her like velvety black pools. She fell in and happily drowned.

"Noah, finally." Mason's voice came from behind her. "I found Marlowe, but he'd already gotten rid of the..." He cleared his throat. "The thing. I read the kid the riot act, made him do some work around here, and sent him home."

"Good." Noah's answer was for Mason but his gaze was still locked on her. He took a step nearer, his eyes flashing. "You're Linda's niece."

"Yes." Nervously, she fingered her pearls. Sucking in a breath to steady herself, she got a lungful of hot male and nearly imploded when her body zinged like every cell was shouting *alleluia*.

Shifter, she scolded herself. Worse, he was pack alpha, bound to be mated. An ex-witch slavering after a mated alpha?

Smiting was happening for sure.

He glided another step closer, his muscles sliding easily under his skin and clothes. Raising his hand, he caught her fumbling fingers and stilled them.

The warm pads of his fingers, pressed against her skin, were stunningly sensual. Her belly stirred with hot response, her breasts tightened in excitement, and her lips fell open because she was having trouble breathing. Her brain had turned to mush, though, because she started wondering how bad a little smiting might be.

He lifted her hand from her pearls and brought it to his nose. Finally those remarkable eyes closed as he inhaled. A tiny, appreciative smile curved his lips, as if he were enjoying the bouquet of a fine wine.

"You smell amazing." His voice rippled with a low, sensual growl.

A groan bubbled up in her throat.

When his lids lifted, his gaze had gentled. The wolf within was very strong, but the man controlled it utterly.

Her groan emerged as a whispered whimper.

A half step closer, him or her, she wasn't sure who. Their auras kissed.

Pure male heat rolled over her skin, edged with a virile, wild magic. Shivers ran with abandon over her flesh as a tremor hit her low in the belly.

If she leaned in a fraction of an inch, she'd touch him, skin-to-skin...she swallowed hard. As much power as she felt rolling off him, touching would close an electrical circuit, and she'd be the one fried. "Look, I'm trying to find my Aunt Linda."

His gaze dropped to her mouth as she spoke. "She owns the bookstore."

"Yes." Under that silvery gaze, her lips felt too full, throbbing. The word was hard to form. She licked her lips.

His pupils dilated until his eyes were pure black, riveted to her mouth. "You're the gor—the woman in the picture."

What had he been about to say? Gorilla? Gourmand? *Gorgeous?* "What picture?"

"Your aunt has a photograph of you." He released her hand to slide a finger under her chin.

All her breath expelled from her lungs. Without oxygen, she let him tilt her face to one side, then the other. The throbbing in her lips intensified.

The matching throbbing in her groin was almost painful.

His lids lowered, lazy with promise. "Your nose is longer than I expected."

Just what a woman wanted to hear. "Thanks?"

"It's a good nose. Honest. Elegant. I like it."

Instantly the throbbing was back, but she pushed it away, mirrored it by stepping back. "An honest, elegant snout is still a snout."

He followed her. "Your nose is unique, like your scent. Exotic. Deeply enticing. I want to kiss you."

He was right on top of her, sending frissons of energy through her. Staring up into his eyes, half-shuttered by passion-heavy lids, she managed a rasped, "Um, that's not a good idea."

"I misspoke. I don't want to kiss you." He took her face in both big, hot hands.

"I need to."

Chapter Four

I need to kiss you, too, Sophia thought, dazed. *Wolf, witch, forbidden.* Yet she needed to fuse her lips to Noah's with an urgency that bordered on insanity.

She dug for the last of her self-preservation and parted her lips to say something, anything, to avoid smiting.

Which only made it easier for his mouth to claim hers.

He pressed his open mouth to her parted lips, his tongue slipping into the gap like hot silk. He teased at the sensitive flesh of her lips until, with a groan, she opened wider.

At the invitation, his tongue speared into her mouth like a blazing flame.

Desire curled deep in her pelvis. He tasted male. Exciting. A man, but his wolf was strong in him, his kiss full of dark and wild magic. She groaned again. His matching groan was more a growl.

Heart thundering in her ears, she lifted on her toes for more.

His kiss slanted and deepened, the wild taking of the wolf—but also the mastery of the man. A man who knew how to give a woman what she wanted. What she needed.

She opened wide to his plunging tongue. In response, his fingers threaded through her hair, pulling her closer. Their bodies melded like two hot candles.

Mason cleared his throat.

She groaned at the interruption.

Noah lifted his head with a soft sigh.

Without the liquid caress of Noah's hot, expert mouth, the moment was broken. Sophia's sanity returned. *What have I done?* Witch and shifter...no, not, *never*. She gathered enough tattered willpower to step out of his arms.

"I'm sorry..." Her voice was breathy. Damn, she'd revved up fast in the wolf's embrace. She tried again. "I'm sorry that happened."

"Why?" He stepped back too with crossed arms, his biceps and pecs bulging. "I'm not."

At the sight of all that male strength, she swallowed her tongue, totally forgetting why she should be sorry. Oh yeah, shifter/witch taboo—but he wouldn't know she was a witch. And even if he did, he wouldn't care. Most shifters pretended the Witches' Council didn't exist.

"Hey," Mason said. "I didn't want you two to stop. I just wanted to let you know that if you're going to get *friendly*—" Mason's grin was so big Sophia wanted to punch him, "—I'm heading out now. There's a couch in the office. Lock up when you're done." He lumbered off.

"Stars," she said. "What was that all about?"

"He's encouraging me to find a wife." Noah grimaced.

Noah wasn't mated. *Yes*. No. None of her business.

But poor Noah. He had his own Aunt Linda, nagging for the pitter-patter of little paws.

He thrust his hands in his pockets, incidentally framing all that was glorious. With the confident way he stood there, bigger and badder than anything, it was hard to feel *too* sorry.

He nodded after Mason. "I should go, too."

"Wait. Before you do...I came here because I wanted to talk with you."

"Why?"

"Why? Um, well, the reason I wanted to talk with you is..." What had she wanted to ask? Are you dating? What's your phone number? *What size condom do you wear?* She rubbed her eyes. "My aunt Linda." She dropped her hand and met his silver gaze. "I think you were the last person to see her at the bookstore. Do you know where she went?"

"I'm sorry, no. She left before I did, but she didn't share her plans with me."

Disappointment gnawed Sophia's gut. "Can you at least tell me if she was okay?"

"Yes." His response was immediate and reassuring. "Don't worry about your aunt. She was fine. A little flustered, but fine."

Sophia smiled inside. He'd seen her worry and hadn't hesitated to comfort her. He must be a very good alpha.

"I'm relieved to hear it. What about that boy my aunt called you in for? Was he still in the store at that point?"

"Marlowe? He's my responsibility. But I can assure you he will be punished and your aunt reimbursed. In fact, if you want to get repairs going, I'll personally vouch for the funds."

"Thank you." All that muscle, and responsible too. Some little she-wolf was going to be very lucky someday. "But that's not what I meant. I'd like to talk with him. Do you know where he lives?"

Noah's gaze shuttered. "The boy knows nothing." The reply had "back off" stamped all over it.

As if that would stop her. She gave a mental shrug. She'd simply have to get Marlowe's address another way. "Okay. Well, I'd better get back to the bookstore. If you think of anything, come see me, okay? The sign will be Closed, but I'll be there."

"You and me. Alone." His molten gaze ran over her, chasing a shiver from her head to her toes and back again. His gleaming eyes lingered on her mouth so long her lips swelled and started throbbing and she had to work not to lick them. Finally he said, "Let me get this straight. You want me, a stranger, to come into the bookstore, where we'll be alone, together—after what just happened between us?"

"Uh...yes?" Although, put like that, reinforced by his hot all-over gaze, it sounded like an invitation to ravish her.

He shook his head, more disbelief than a no. "You're temptation on a stick. I'm not quite that masochistic."

"Me?" Holding out her arms, she looked down at herself, at her banker chic of navy-blue pants suit, pumps, and pearls. "Have you been chewing Viagra? I'm no cover model."

"I've never cared for *eau de airbrush*. Believe me, your real beauty is far more seductive."

Her gaze snapped up as his eyes fired white-hot on her, a beastly hunger that was pure *wolf*.

That look promised instant ravaging. Hot, hard, animal sex.

She swallowed, long and hard, all the way to where she was wet. She wasn't completely certain she'd stop him.

He took a single step toward her. Her heart thundered in her ears as his gaze blazed so hot it threatened to consume her.

Then he clenched his eyes shut. His hands fisted, and he inhaled so deep his nostrils flared. A second breath.

Then he relaxed, his eyes opened, and the man was fully in control. "Good luck finding your aunt. I'll see you out."

Sophia's heart hammered for a new reason now. Wow. An alpha with that much fire, harnessed by that strong a self-control? It almost made her long for ears and a tail.

He gestured toward the door.

Turning, she saw only a dark blob, and hesitated. She'd stared at the bright shop light too long.

He put a hand on her spine to steer her out.

His big, hot hand seared her back. Her lungs seized up.

Urging her into motion, he said, "Look, I understand you're worried about Linda. I do have resources that might help. I'll give you a call later."

"Thanks." Sophia tried not to jump on that. Noah Blackwood was far too tempting. Never mind not encouraging *him*. She didn't want to encourage herself. "A call...a *phone* call...would be perfect."

* * *

Outside, Noah disappeared into the night. Sophia shivered on the sidewalk, wishing just a bit that he'd stayed with her.

Right. And if he'd stayed, would he have let me track down the boy Marlowe? No, it was better for both her search and her libido that Noah had gone.

She considered using her phone for an Internet address search. But wolves were secretive. Without the boy's last name, she wasn't sure of netting him. Fortunately the town's premier news source, the Misses Jamies, was on her return route to the bookstore.

She struck off south.

Matinsfield had changed since she'd been here last, a new Green W drugstore on the corner and a SuperDuperPriceCutter past the ballpark, but the sisters still lived in their brownstone in the center of town.

If there was any truth to the zombie rumor, they always would.

Which reminded Sophia of the creepy hooded man. Every shadow seemed to stir as she dashed from streetlamp to streetlamp, trying not to look victimish. By the time she hit the Jamies' front walk, her heart pounded and her breath rasped.

So relief flooded her when Miss Almira, tall and thin with long front teeth and shoe-polish black hair, threw open the door.

"You're finally here. Have you gotten the Uncommon's door fixed?" Almira latched onto Sophia's arm and dragged her inside like a snake taking a frog.

Sophia's relief evaporated. "I was going to call—"

"Gladys Louise will do that." Almira raised her voice. "Gladys Louise! Get Frank Fixit on the line."

Heavyset Miss Gladys Louise, short wavy blonde hair going gray, eyes small and bright, bustled in with a tray of cookies and lemonade. Almira and Gladys Louise were a set of fifties' sitcom spinsters in twinsets and pleated skirts whose noses twitched at the slightest hint of gossip.

"Sophia! Sit, dear, sit," Miss Gladys Louise piped. She always piped. "Wonderful that you came. Now Noah doesn't have to handle this problem all on his own."

Noah. Sophia's lips vibrated in memory. She pressed her fingers to them to still them—and found them soft and swollen from the wolf's kiss. Her cheeks filled with heat.

Almira gave her a narrow-eyed, arched-eyebrow stare.

Sophia grinned and pointed. "Oh look. Is that lemonade? I'm awfully thirsty."

Almira relented with a little *hmph*. "Gladys Louise?"

"Make sure she tries the chocolate chip cookies, Almira." Gladys Louise set the tray on the table and poured. "I whipped them up fresh. I'll go call Mr. Fixit now." She bustled out.

Sophia picked up a tall sweating glass, her throat suddenly parched. Her broken-down car had made the trip long and dusty. Nothing to do with alpha-buzzing lips at all.

She took a big gulp.

And promptly sucked her uvula into her nose. Gladys Louise had flavored the drink with a dash of lemon zest—and a quart of brandy.

Coughing, Sophia set the glass down. She managed, "Do you know where Aunt Linda is?"

"No, we only knew she'd disappeared when Mason called us, trying to find Noah." As Almira spoke she filled a small plate with cookies and set it in front of Sophia. "Did you ask him?"

"Noah? Yes, I just talked with him. But he hasn't seen her since the boy broke into her store—a local named Marlowe. I thought he might have more information. Do you know where I can find him?"

"Marlowe? He lives with his older brother, east, past the gas station." Almira's mouth pinched as she pointed. "You don't want to go there, though."

"Why not?"

“Sophia?” Gladys Louise stuck her head out the kitchen door, an old-fashioned handset complete with curly black cord at her ear. “Is tomorrow good? Eight a.m. is Mr. Fixit’s first opening.”

Sophia grimaced. “Could he come tonight? I’d pay extra.” Auntie didn’t believe in indoor locks, and while her wards were good at shrieking alarm, they didn’t actually stop anyone. Sophia couldn’t sleep in an unsecured house, not with that hooded guy lurking.

Mr. Kibbles wasn’t much of a watch cat.

“I’ll try, dear.” Gladys Louise disappeared back into the kitchen.

Sophia set down her glass and picked up a cookie. Her fingers sank in. “Why shouldn’t I visit Marlowe?” She tried a bite. Sugar and flour melted in her mouth.

“You know I’d never gossip or say an unkind word about anyone.” Almira nibbled her own cookie.

“Of course not.” Unless it was followed by an *I’m kidding* or a *bless his soul.* Then unkind was somehow okay.

She stuffed a second cookie in her mouth to stop herself from saying that.

“Marlowe is the exception. He has wandering fingers. Cash, jewelry—women. His brother, Killer, is even worse.”

Sophia swallowed hard. “Ah.”

Almira *tsked.* “You’re going anyway, aren’t you? You Blues always were stubborn women.”

“We prefer focused.” That made Sophia smile. She brushed her hands on her slacks and rose. “Thanks, Miss Almira. I appreciate your help. I’d better get back to the bookstore and batten down as best I can.”

“Good news.” Gladys Louise bustled out of the kitchen. “Mr. Fixit fit you in—a personal favor to me.” She blushed.

"Thanks." Sophia blinked. From that deep red blush on Miss Gladys Louise's face, the favor was very *personal.* "I don't need to know the details, but I owe you."

"Do get home as quickly as possible." Almira walked Sophia to the door. "Things aren't what they used to be in Matinsfield."

"Dangerous," Gladys Louise agreed. "Especially with that hooded man lurking about."

Sophia spun on the stoop, heart suddenly pounding. "W-who?"

Almira raised a critical brow. "You sound like an owl."

"Shush," Gladys Louise said. "We call him X."

Sophia swallowed a lump of ice. For the Misses not to know something was unheard of.

"Otherwise we'd have said 'George' is lurking about, or 'Heathcliff' is lurking about, or—"

"Right. My mistake. I'll be off now." Sophia stuffed her heart back in her chest and headed to the bookstore.

* * *

Mr. Fixit was already at the Uncommon Night Owl, replacing the glass. Gladys Louise must've made one helluva promise. Sophia said, "I don't suppose you could update the lock too?" The door still had the old-fashioned rod-style key it had come with in the 1800s.

"I'll order 'er up tomorrow." He finished the inside glazing. "Don't touch this or bump the door for a few days. I'll send your aunt the bill."

"Actually, you can send it to Noah Blackwood." She flipped on the lights. The sign was set to Closed and she'd lock the door after Mr. Fixit left. Hopefully there wouldn't be too many disappointed customers. Aunt Linda often kept irregular hours.

"I like Blackwood—he pays promptly." Mr. Fixit clicked the door shut behind him.

Through the window, Sophia watched him go. Her gaze drifted to the dark shadows across the street. She was alone in the store, and though the door was fixed now, a boy breaking in the first time had shown how easily it could be done. Her heart thumped faster.

Brrring.

She jumped. Nearly zapped the wall phone with a short-out spell but managed to stifle herself in time. *That call might be Auntie.* She ran to answer.

Grabbing the old-fashioned ear trumpet, she panted, "Hello?"

"Doing marathons now?" Gabriel's deep voice held a hint of amusement.

"Hello to you too, brother dear." She tried to control her breath. A witch, scared of a little dark? She'd never hear the end of it. She managed to wheeze, "I was out searching for Aunt Linda. I just got back."

"You need to work on your stamina."

"Sure, as soon as you work on your manners. Are you calling for a reason?"

"I was worried. You texted that the door was broken—and then nothing. I tried your cell, but you didn't answer. It's been almost an hour. Why were you so late getting there in the first place?"

She checked her phone. Two missed calls. She took it off vibrate. "I had car trouble."

"I thought I fixed that."

"Yes, but..." Normally, technology mixed with magic like lemonade and potato chips. Theory had it that a witch's magical aura—or neural fields or whatever—fritzed the technology.

Sophia's technology was fine, with a little help.

Gabriel was a wizard prince—but more, he was a Choice Buy Techie Titan. He dealt with bit-challenged mundane users all day, so it was easy for him to make recalcitrant technology sit up and rumba, even for witches. Something to do with aligning rare earth elements in the logic-gated components. Sophia tried to listen but her eyes glazed over.

"You couldn't have done anything about this. It was a mundane failure. A carbegumerator injector thingy."

"Gotta love injector thingies. Update me."

She told him about the boy-wolf Marlowe tripping Auntie's store alarm, and Auntie calling in the pack alpha to handle it, without mentioning Noah by name. "Now Auntie's gone, but nobody knows where."

"Cap'n Crunch me. That's not good."

"I have a lead on the boy. I'll try him tomorrow. Oh, and Auntie got a dog."

"What kind?"

"A little poofy one."

"Now I'm scared. Those fuckers are like stealth sharks. No ankles are safe. About Aunt Linda." Gabriel paused, and Sophia knew she wouldn't like what was coming next. "If you would do a simple reveal spell—"

"Not happening."

Gabriel blew out a sigh. "Okay. I'm not going to backseat drive. But anytime you want to talk about it, I'm here."

"Thanks." When it counted, Gabriel was the best brother in the universe. "So anyway, I'll be talking to

Marlowe tomorrow. Oh, and Noah said he'd call if he got more information. I mean phone, not call *here*—"

"Noah? Who's Noah?" Gabriel's tone was brightly inquisitive.

"Nobody. Nothing. Gotta go." She hung up. *Whew. Dodged that bullet.* She turned away from the phone.

A man's shadowed face loomed in the door's crosshatch.

Her heart skipped. "Who...?" Her voice cracked, her mouth suddenly dry. She tried to swallow, but it was hard. "Who's there?"

"Me. Sophia, open up."

Noah. Any trouble she'd had swallowing disappeared in a sudden influx of saliva. She ran to open the door to him.

He stood there, filling the doorway, as still as the night. More, night's apex predator, dark and deep and born of enormous strength.

It both scared and excited her. She swallowed again.

Against the doorjamb's height tapes, she saw he was actually several inches above six feet. Miles of shoulders, acres of chest, light-years long legs, dark flannel shirt and jeans worn white—framed by the doorway, the man looked like a hard-hewn Paul Bunyan.

She fell back a step, fanning her face. In the race between fear and excitement, excitement took the lead by a nose, then by a big long lick. If she got any hotter she was going to fling the door wide to jump his bones. Not a good ending for the new window panes. "Um...c'mon in? Watch your feet. There's broken glass."

The garage's half light had softened his details. Now as he surged into the store, his hard features cut like the prow of an icebreaker. Carved, determined jaw. No-nonsense mouth. Silver eyes so narrow they sliced. Sophia automatically backed up a few more steps.

He stopped and stood, fists on hips. Dominating her aunt's store, he wasn't just regular-guy handsome. He was breath-sucking, eye-watering, gut-punching, great gods above can-I-have-him-please stunning.

And *taboo*, damn it.

One black brow rose. "What's that rattling?"

Demon...? She glanced down. She was futzing with her pearls. She deliberately released them and lowered her arm. "Nothing. Close the door, please. Softly—that glass is new."

He shut the door with a gentleness that, given his alpha power, made him even sexier.

Her stomach flipped happily, and things below began to purr.

What is it about this man that, every time I see him, I suddenly think about nothing but sex?

"So why'd you come?" She winced. *Come.* Talk about sex on the brain. "I thought you were going to call."

"I knew the lock was broken. I wanted to make sure you were okay." He glided toward her.

The surging force of all that was Big, Dark, and Yowsa pushed her to flee. She spun and trotted toward the sanctuary of the reading nook. "I'm fine. As you can see. I can take care of myself."

"I'm sure you can. But I think I can help." Two long-legged strides brought him beside her.

Her own gait hitched.

His muscular legs worked easily, his hips rolling like well-oiled pistons. An intense desire seared her to fuse herself to those powerful thighs.

She clenched both pearls and teeth. What was wrong with her? She was a staid banker, not a wolf with an estrogen problem.

But maybe that was part of the issue. She was surrounded all day by civilized banker-men in suits and ties, and Noah was a breath of fresh air compared to them. Wild, howling at the moon, biting the nape of her neck and making her his...

Yikes. No wonder the Witches' Council forbade witch/shifter sex. It had nothing to do with their fear of insane werewitch *duals* born with innate power *and* the ability to wield it.

It was because when a witch met the right sexy shifter, she lost her damned mind.

This *intense* attraction...now she understood why, to make absolutely certain witches and weres never got naughty parts within unclothed miles of each other, the Council had made the penalty as harsh as possible.

Death.

"Um, why don't you take a seat on the couch?" She waved vaguely at the cozy seating, scattered couches, chairs, and throw pillows. "I have to...um, I have to..." Spinning around for an excuse to get miles away from insanely attractive male wolves and death penalties, her gaze lit on the door. Closed—but not locked. "I have to make sure customers don't wander in."

It was only as she clicked the lock home that she realized she'd trotted back to the door and locked it with all the subtleness of a dog sniffing butt.

A low growl thrummed through the store. Slowly, she turned.

Noah stared at her, silver eyes blazing. Her gaze locked helplessly with his...until he moved to adjust his jeans.

Then her eyes dropped to the biggest Jiffy Pop she'd ever seen. Too late she remembered what he'd said at Mason's.

He was thinking what they could do, locked together alone in a closed store.

The worst part was, she was wondering too.

Chapter Five

She'd locked the door.

Noah had hustled Sophia out of the Blackwood garage because their kiss had his wolf howling so loud he couldn't think of anything except getting her naked under him. The way she reacted to him, giving so honestly of herself, took his breath away. Never before had he tasted a woman so lively, so bright—so *right*.

Which was so wrong. Alphas screwed other shifters, and strong shifters at that. They rarely screwed fragile humans, and they especially didn't screw witches' nieces.

It confused him, and a confused alpha was a dead alpha, so he'd hustled her out and run the other way as fast as he could.

Leaving her unprotected. His spirit rebelled against that.

Needing to protect her, he'd latched onto his promise to talk with her. He'd come here, rehearsing what he'd tell her. She'd asked for his help, and he had information, but he didn't know her phone number to call, so he'd come in person.

Then she'd locked the door, and the heat roaring through him blew away all his lies.

He really just wanted—*needed*—to see her again.

And now they were alone inside a locked store. Stealing a kiss in front of Mason was nearly his undoing. If the firestorm of lust now pouring through him was any indication, the next hour or so would destroy him.

But what sweet, sweet destruction.

She must've caught something of what he was thinking because she blushed a very pretty pink, the same shade as her lips. Then she glanced down at his crotch and flushed a luscious crimson, the same shade as her lips after he'd kissed them so very thoroughly.

Slow down, boy. She's human, not shifter. "I thought if we rehashed what happened last night, we might be able to pinpoint something to find your aunt. Why don't we sit?" He started for a chair then saw a sofa and headed for it instead. They could sit side by side on the sofa. Easier for talking. They'd sit together and he'd slide his hands under her staid jacket, under her top, up the creamy skin of her belly to her bra, lifting the cups to reveal her breasts, nipples ripe for his suckling until she writhed beneath him, screaming *"Take me..."* Clenching his fingers, he coached himself to start with talk. Sliding his hands under her suit coat, lifting her top and discovering if her nipples were that pretty pink or luscious crimson could come later.

"All right. Just a minute."

Her voice was husky. He liked that a lot. He got to the sofa and turned.

She was shrugging off her suit coat jacket, revealing soft naked shoulders and a long creamy neck.

His groin wrenched tight, and his tongue fell out of his stupid mouth.

Human. Not so fast. He shoved his tongue back in and thought deflating thoughts.

Then, carrying the jacket, she started toward him with a sexy sway.

His eyes locked onto her rolling hips and bouncing breasts. His tongue fell back out, his cock ballooned against his fly, and he started panting like an idiot. It was shockingly hard to control himself.

Shifters were preternaturally sexed, sure. But he'd never *lusted* like this, so hot, so fast.

Fortunately she didn't see, her gaze on her objective, the old-fashioned coat tree at the edge of the big carpet. He had time to reroll his tongue and give himself a mental cold shower while she hung up her jacket.

He'd barely managed to pull himself back from the edge when she finished with the coat, lifted her gaze, and started toward him.

She hadn't seen, but she must've picked up on something because, with all the soft, overstuffed furniture, she perched primly on the only wooden chair in the whole area. Her knees were pressed together and her lips were almost as tight.

He'd love to loosen them—with his tongue. He wasn't sure if he meant her lips or her knees. The thought started his groin pulsing, and before he embarrassed himself, he sat, casually crossing his legs.

"So what happened last night?" she asked.

Talk, damn it. "It started with Marlowe. The kid is trouble because of his older brother, who's even bigger trouble." Killer was inner cadre for the old, corrupt alpha.

Because of Killer, Marlowe was a bully in training. "Marlowe broke into your aunt's store while she was here."

Sophia's hand fluttered to touch between her breasts. "He hurt my aunt?"

"No..." Noah's gaze followed the hand helplessly to her bosom. His tongue wanted to be that hand. *Sliding under her top, testing the weight of her breast, suckling her until she was writhing...* He clenched his eyes, hoping it would help.

Even without sight, simply from the curl of her scent dusting the air, his body hardened.

If I didn't know better, I'd say she's my mate.

His eyes shot open in shock at the thought. He knew better. Shifters of any caliber rarely mated non-shifters. Alphas, never, because how could a non-shifter lead the pack in a hunt?

His body didn't want to be rational. It wanted to strip her of that staid pantsuit, throw her onto the couch, and pound into her until she screamed with a full-body release.

His brow broke out in a thin sweat. He had to get himself under control *now*.

She eyed the couch beside him, the one where he'd been imagining her naked and arching and moaning her pleasure.

He clenched his jaw, reined in his wolf, and moved to sit on a different couch. "No, your aunt was okay. Otherwise I would've punished the kid immediately. But he did steal her vibrating 'mushroom'." A dildo if Noah'd ever seen one.

From the pink blush rising up Sophia's delectable cheeks—he barely stopped himself from licking them—she'd seen the thing too.

"Anyway, Linda called me in." He gave her the rest of the story, except for the hex. It had already worn off and hadn't done any real damage.

Sophia listened to him without interrupting, a sexy furrow of concentration on her brow.

To stop himself from licking *that*, he said, "How did you know Linda was missing?"

"Auntie's a bit...Bohemian. My brother set up an alarm on the store. He'd put a nannycam on her if she'd let him." One corner of her mouth tipped up.

He wanted to lick that corner so badly he nearly howled.

"We're a touch overprotective, but since our parents' deaths, Gabriel and I only have Aunt Linda."

That kicked Noah's head out of his pants. "I'm sorry. Why isn't your brother here, taking care of things?" His words were roughened by a growl. Men who left their women alone in times of need should be neutered with a meat cleaver.

She eyed him nervously.

His expression must've reflected his thoughts, unusual for him. He cut the growl. He'd never hurt her—he'd never hurt any woman—but she didn't know that.

She smiled ruefully and relaxed. "Gabriel's working out of state. My place is only four hours from Matinsfield, so I volunteered to drive up."

"That was good of you." Her caring made her even hotter to him.

"Say." She tapped her lip. "Do you think maybe Auntie went to confront Marlowe? Get her, um, 'mushroom' back?"

There was that blush again, just as lickable as before. "It's possible." He shrugged.

Sophia's eyes dropped to his shoulders and widened.

Well, well. She was impressed by his body? His wolf pranced proudly inside, and maybe his man did a little, too. "She mentioned needing to check out a few things. Do research."

"Do you know why?"

He shrugged again, just to watch her eyes widen and enjoy her enjoying him. Linda probably wanted a good hex to throw on the kid since the original had backfired.

"Well, maybe the boy knows." Sophia stood. "Let's go."

He stood too. "What?"

"Let's talk to this Marlowe and find out if Auntie visited him."

Her sweet, soft flesh anywhere near that hoodlum? Noah's veins fired. "Absolutely not. That pup is trouble with a capital T. His older brother is trouble with a capital A-to-Z."

She bit her lip, her pearly white teeth denting the lush red pillow, making him want to lick *that*. He briefly clenched his eyes. Even on the back of his lids he could see nothing but her. With a despairing sigh, he opened his eyes.

"I was going to wait until tomorrow, but really, the trail is getting colder with every minute's delay." She grabbed her suit coat from its hook and dug in a pocket. "I'd hoped you'd come with me, but I guess I'll have to make do with my pepper spray."

She headed for the door.

He intercepted her in three strides and lay a restraining hand gently on her arm.

Her bare arm.

His fingers pressed to the smoothest, silkiest flesh in the world. His body went instantly rigid. Her soft little gasp didn't help. He swallowed his lust, a long, hot sword of it. "Sophia, please. I don't want you anywhere near those brothers."

"To be honest, I don't want to go either."

"Good. Then let's go back to the couch—"

"But I have to, don't you see?" Her gaze searched his for understanding. "It's not like Aunt Linda to go off without telling me or my brother. If you're right, Marlowe may have been the last person to see her." She slid from his fingers and started again for the door.

He needed to stop her. He rationalized it in his head—Marlowe was pack, Noah was alpha, and it was his duty to protect humans from the worst of his pack.

But really, he simply wanted to protect Sophia, with a need that burned white-hot inside him.

No immediate ideas how, though, with her determined to leave, not without tying her up...his body hardened again, so *wrong*, but entirely too enticing an idea. He shook himself. He was an animal, but he hadn't lost all humanity. Surely he could keep her from walking out that door in a way that was urbane, gentle, and didn't give away anything about the state of pack affairs?

His wolf took it out of his hands. He grabbed her and spun her into his embrace. His arms wrapped around the softest curves in the world. Her eyes, gazing up at him, were big and blue, her lips the sweetest pink.

So he had to. He really did.

He kissed her.

Her lips parted on a gasp of surprise. He fell into her sweet mouth. Her breath was warm and minty, her lips plush, velvety. His whole body rose to the feel of her, the scent of her, the taste of her. He thought it couldn't get any better.

Then she sighed and nestled in, wrapping her arms around his neck and stretching herself along his torso until every inch of them touched.

His whole body went haywire. The press of her, taut in some places, soft in others, exploded pleasure along his skin.

And still it wasn't enough. He wanted to kiss her, to cuddle her, *to be moving inside her*—everything, all at once. His need rose so swiftly, so fiercely, that his control temporarily evaporated. Mouth devouring hers, he lifted her and carried her to the couch.

His human intervened, trrying to slow things down, to settle her on the couch and sit beside her so that they could slowly explore each other.

His wolf spread her flat on her back, exposing everything to him in a perfect position to plunder.

She whimpered. *Too fast.* He reined hard on his ragged control. He was wolf, but she wasn't. She needed a gentle touch, a sweet seduction. He leaned in and floated his palms along her bare arms.

Her hands found his shoulders, her fingers dug in, and she pulled him on top of her with a desire as fierce as his own.

The tattered reins of his self-control snapped. He stretched out over her, his body completely covering hers—and fused his lips with hers.

She moaned into his mouth and her fingers slid up his neck to curl into his hair. His wolf urged *more, harder*. His kiss roughened, his tongue plunging deep inside her glorious heat.

And she...she opened to him. Accepted him, wolf and all. Her lips parted to give him greater access, and her thighs spread to nestle his hips.

His wolf howled, reveling in it, in her. At her splendid welcome, his cock sprang full, the bright need shocking him. He cupped her head with both hands and took what she offered, returning it in full, his tongue plunging hard and deep.

She began to ripple up into him. His groan ruffled with the beast's sexual growl, he rolled his hips against her in return. It dragged his pumped zipper along her pants seam. She gasped into his mouth, soft breath billowing. He rubbed himself into her again, this time deliberately long and slow. Her eyes widened and locked on his. She began to pant.

He searched her gaze and read surprise there—but not surprise at the speed. Surprise at so much pleasure.

Still, she was only human. He said the words. "Do you want me to stop?"

"Well," she panted. "This *is* pretty fast."

His wolf growled. He throttled it. "But do you want me to stop?"

A beat. "No."

He gave her a fierce smile and rewarded her with a hard stroke of his hips. She moaned and her knees fell completely apart, her legs limp with pleasure. He wanted to slide his hands up her ribs, caress her breasts, tease the tips to tight snaps, but his wolf had other ideas.

He leaned one forearm beside her head, used his freed hand to open her prim slacks, and with a snick of button and zip, he slid his fingers into her panties.

He stroked naked skin.

She jerked at his touch, gasping. Then she moaned, low and long. He'd never heard a sweeter sound. His fingers delighted in her slick warmth, over and over. She was sweet and warm and womanly and he was in heaven.

Her hands wrapped around his triceps, fingers digging in. Urging him to do more, harder, faster. His heart pounded in quickening desire. Her hips tilted, yearning toward his stroking hand. His cock strained against his zipper in response.

He slid a finger inside her and was rewarded with a louder groan. He shifted his hand to cup her sex while pressing his finger firmly inside her. With his palm, he started pumping.

She whimpered. Whispered, "More."

"I know." He kissed her, deep, wild. She arched into him. He drove his tongue into her mouth. She sucked at it.

Desire splashed hot in his belly. His cock was straining so hard it was about to burst.

Bite her. He was nearly overcome with the sudden need to take her like a wolf, to throw her up on her knees and fasten himself to her and plow her with rough strokes, to mate like an animal and howl.

He broke the kiss, appalled at himself. How could such a rough act appeal to him? *He was a beast*. She whimpered, as if underlining the fact.

Then she pumped her hips against his hand and licked his chin, urging him to do exactly as he pleased. *She wanted him, beast and all.*

Her simple acceptance undid him. It brought sudden clarity; the rough act didn't appeal—he wanted to take her in the traditional way, in front of the pack to proclaim her as *his mate.*

By his fangs and claws. How was this possible? Confused, he dropped his head into the crook of her neck.

Her scent, heady and ripe, filled his nostrils. His wolf opened his mouth...and he barely managed to turn his bite into a gentle nip. Her tender flesh was like silk, dusted with the scent of jasmine and woman. She tasted of fresh fields lightly kissed with dew.

Didn't matter how, where or why. Only who. His blood boiled up and over into a low growl. He thrust a second finger into her and stroked.

She arched into him, breasts pressing against his chest, hips into his belly. Staid navy slacks and a thin blouse didn't stop him from feeling every feminine curve stamped into his skin like hot irons.

Panting into the crook of her neck, he tried to get himself under control. She undulated and rubbed against him in wild abandon. "I'm almost there...please, Noah."

His cock was ready to rupture. He could barely keep his fingers steadily stroking her. She was so wet and hot he could just imagine grabbing her hips and plunging deep into her sweet naked body, sinking into her wet welcome—

She stiffened and cried out. Her muscles contracted around his fingers, so hard it shot pulses down his arm, straight to his erection. He came in his pants like a green pup, and it was wonderful, the best. Sound evaporated as the world around him exploded with bright lights, all the colors of the rainbow and more, so bright his eyes hurt.

He pulsed an infinity of perfect pleasure, locked in her arms.

Sound zoned back in, his rasping breath and heart thundering in his ears...and soft, even breaths.

He blinked. The bright lights resolved into the Uncommon Bookstore. He and Sophia lay on the old reading sofa.

Sophia had fallen asleep, a tiny smile on her face. He gazed at her in wonder.

From first meet to orgasm in less than a day. Even for shifters that was incredibly fast.

Yet it felt right. Almost as if...

His mate?

No. Couldn't be. Not a human.

His heart slowed as his body cooled. The wet in his jeans cooled past the point of discomfort. Still, he didn't move, needing the contact with Sophia—until it occurred to him that she might be uncomfortable too.

He slid off and went in search of a blanket. After that disastrous hexing last night, the aunt had gotten a sheet out of an armoire to cover the mirror. He found it, opened its doors, dug up a light woven blanket, and returned to drape it over Sophia.

She sighed and snuggled in. His heart swelled.

He shushed it. Human. Not his mate.

Still, he pulled a chair near to her and watched over her as she slept.

* * *

The wizard known as X picked up the hem of his silk robe to stalk past the disgusting wolfman into the dirty trailer. X's familiar hopped off his shoulder, refusing to enter the filthy place. His familiar, X thought, had the right idea.

When X saw what was waiting for him, he stopped in his tracks.

A ragged, stick-thin female cowered in the corner of the trailer. Scowling, X took out his tool, a foot-long rod that was the color of air-bubbled blood. The tool warmed in his hand. He circled it at the cringing female to activate its analytic properties; it would tell him how much magic the skeletal wreck actually had.

At the readings, he snarled. "Can it be? Have you actually found a wolf scrawnier, sicker, and poorer than the rest?"

"She's not pack," the wolfman whined. "Since the new fuckin' alpha came, this is the only fuckin' wolf we could get."

X sneered at the pathetic creature. At *Killer*. What a burlesque of a name for a stupid, dirty animal. "That's your excuse? A new alpha?"

"He's watching us too closely. Doesn't let any females go out alone. Sends fuckin' Mason along or goes himself."

"So? One of him, *five* of you." X's eyes rolled in contempt. "Deal with him."

The wolfman swallowed hard. "Blackwood's different. Master, we got him to fight the old alpha before he was ready, like you said. But he *won*. He's so fucking strong... You have to give us more. Give us something to help crush the fucker for good."

"You want *more*?" X's seething fury exploded. "When you offer barely adequate tribute as it is?"

Killer flinched.

X reined in his righteous anger. For now, he still needed the beast. “Do I not already provide you with drugs to make you more powerful, amulets to help lure whatever female you want, make her do whatever you want?”

The wolfman hung his head. “Yes, master. But this new alpha is just too much—”

“Stop complaining.” Idiot anti-alphas. Big men when beating up on bitches and pups, but let a real challenge face them and they were whiny girly dogs.

“Yes, master.”

“Have you at least uncovered information on Blackwood?” X turned from the pathetic loser to put one hand on the female’s forehead and ready the tool in the other.

“Yes, master.” The wolfman practically whimpered.

“Then I will be generous. Find me a weapon and I will ensorcell it. What have you discovered about Blackwood?” The young alpha was a mystery. Nobody seemed to know where he came from or who his parents were.

Which made him a prime candidate for the wolf X sought.

“He comes from Mason’s old pack out west. But get this, master. Blackwood wasn’t born there.”

“That’s all you have?” X glared at the pathetic Killer.

“Mason’s old lady is dead, master, and no one knows who Blackwood’s bitch mother was.”

“*Imbecile*. Answer me this. *Is he the one we seek?*” Spittle flew onto X’s chin. He wiped it away with an automatic fastidious flick. “Never mind. It’s obvious you couldn’t find a pimple on the end of your dick. I’ll know the answer soon enough.”

He turned to the bitch, slapped his hand against her forehead, and triggered the talisman.

Magic sucked out of her, flowing into him. She deflated like a ball. He pressed harder, following her as she slowly collapsed to the floor. She didn't move, other than her gradual shriveling, didn't even whimper.

Drugged to her gills. At least the wolfman had done one thing right.

When she'd collapsed into a pile of useless biology, X removed his hand. Stood, stronger and younger and flush with magic.

He turned to Killer.

The wolfman's face was white. X almost used the talisman on the pathetic excuse for a were. But no, Killer had his uses.

All the power-hungry anti-alphas across the country were useful. X manipulated them, playing on their lust and greed and fear to make them do his bidding. With the right incentives, the anti-alphas weakened their own packs and made them vulnerable. They lined up their own females for X's draining.

And most importantly, they prodded key young dogs into premature alpha fights.

The fact that Blackwood had actually won made him all the more interesting.

All the anti-alphas were useful, but this pack held a special place in X's heart. Matinsfield would be the site of a long-overdue revenge. He smiled to himself.

"Will this switchblade do, master?"

X's visions of revenge cleared to the sight of Killer, offering a palm-sized handle.

"Let's see." X took the case. With the flick of his thumb, a wicked blade erupted straight out of the top, slender as a needle and sharp as hell. It was a weapon of surprise, of deception. X was astonished Killer was smart enough to own something this clever, this deadly. Even the troublesome Blackwood wouldn't see it until it was far too late. "Yes, this will do nicely." He stabbed the tip of the knife into his finger.

The wolfman flinched.

X's blood boiled out, sizzling onto the metal like water on a hot oiled fry pan. Gradually the bubbling subsided, the blood sinking into the blade as if it was being absorbed.

"You must whet the blade's appetite before it can be used." X retracted the blade and handed the knife back to Killer. "Let it taste the blood of its prey, as both man and beast."

"You mean stick fuckin' Blackwood?"

"You have no poetry." X snapped his robes around him and stalked toward the trailer's exit. "Stab him *twice*. Man, then wolf. When it is blooded, return it to me and I will finish the poisoning. And Killer?" X turned in the doorway, eyes narrowed, until the wolf trembled appropriately. "Next time, make sure the bitch is healthy." He swept up his golden robe and stalked out.

Chapter Six

Sophia woke as the world brightened with predawn, a smile on her face. She felt wonderful, better than she had for years.

She opened her eyes and felt even better.

A luscious man, pure art in black hair and silver eyes and broad shoulders, watched over her. Protectiveness gleamed in that intelligent gaze, along with the masculine satisfaction of a man who'd given her the best orgasm of her life.

Happiness burst inside her like a radiant dawn. It had been months since she'd had any kind of orgasm, much less one as perfect as that. And she'd not just won the orgasm lottery, but he'd stuck around and was gazing at her with such tenderness? Keeper.

"Hi." She felt a little shy. It'd also been months since a guy had seen her first thing in the morning.

"Sleep well?" His deep voice, roughened with a little morning growl, made him even sexier.

"Wonderfully. I must have been more tired than I realized. Well, with the drive and worrying about my aunt—*my aunt.*" She sat up abruptly. A blanket fell to her waist. He'd covered her. That was incredibly sweet.

But her aunt was missing and she'd lost minutes...hours...how long? She tossed aside the blanket. "I can't believe I fell asleep. Why didn't you wake me? What time is it?"

He raised one black brow. "Which do you want answered first?"

"Time."

He pointed at the window, where impending sunrise brightened the glass. His expression turned puzzled, then alarmed. He leaped to his feet.

"Noah? What's wrong—?"

"Stay there." He fled toward the kitchen.

She rose and started after him but was slowed by her open pants sliding down her hips. "Noah?"

He'd already disappeared through the rattling curtain of beads. If he was looking for the bathroom, he was going to be disappointed. Those were in the store.

As the beads settled, she struggled toward the kitchen, wrestling her clothes straight. "Noah, what's going on?" It occurred to her that maybe he'd suddenly regretted what they'd done.

Maybe he'd sneaked out the back.

She poked through the beaded curtain into the kitchen. "Noah, if you're still here, say something."

Silence. The room was empty except for a floor covered by pristine newspaper.

An orgasm, a sweet smile, and a thoughtful blanket, but then he'd run away? Happiness shriveled as regret thickened her throat and lynched her muscles of strength.

Shoulders slumping, she wandered back into the store. Finding herself at the sofa, she collapsed.

A yip raised her head.

"King." Her mood immediately brightened. At least *someone* loved...um, needed her.

He jumped onto the couch beside her. She picked him up, and when he licked her face enthusiastically, she giggled.

A banker, an assistant VP, *giggling*. But the poofball made her feel light as a girl. "Noah's gone, King. You just missed him." So did she. No, she didn't miss *him*. She missed the backup he could have provided when she tracked down Marlowe. "Too bad I can't have you as my protector."

The dog yipped and wiggled, the universal language for "down". When Sophia set him on the floor he scampered to the front door. Well, skittered actually, toenails clacking like he was trying to stride but his little legs were too short. What a strange combination of cute and assertive.

He stood before the door and yipped a couple times, wagging his tail expectantly. She realized he stood on bare, clean floor.

Noah had swept up the glass.

All that walking sex appeal, *plus* tidy? Where did she sign up?

King yipped. She got to her feet. "You want walkies?"

He *grred* a definite "no".

"Something to do with outside, though?"

The *grr* transformed to a happy little yip.

She smiled. There she was, imagining he was talking again. "This is about Noah?" At another yip she said, "You think Noah ran out on me too, huh?"

King growled. He stalked on stiff little legs toward her until he stopped directly in front of her and nailed her straight in the eye. That stern look said, *If you think Noah ever runs out on his responsibilities, you don't know him at all.*

Sophia was momentarily shocked. Then she laughed. More likely his stare meant, *Let me out before I burst a faucet.*

"Okay. I'll try to find your leash." But despite searching, she could find neither leash nor collar.

Tapping her pearls, Sophia stood there. What to do? Let him out and hope he didn't run away? Or slip out to buy a leash and risk his anointing Auntie's porous hardwood floors and mint-condition Persian carpeting? Although if the papers in the kitchen hadn't been used, maybe there already was a surprise waiting for her somewhere else.

King started pawing the front door. Maybe she could improvise a collar? Something the size of her wrist...? Fingers tapping at her necklace, her gaze lit on a glittering display of costume necklaces and bracelets dangling on metal trees near the register.

She got an idea.

Aunt Linda had a fondness for antique jewelry. The rhinestone and paste on display, whether sparkling pink and robin's-egg blue or emerald green and ruby red, were all mint condition.

Sophia picked out a sapphire bracelet as King trotted up with an annoyed *whuff*. "Hold out your neck."

He cautiously extended his head.

Kneeling, she fastened the sapphire strand around his furry neck. The bracelet was too loose.

She took it off and selected a smaller one, which happened to be a bright pink.

King growled.

"Quiet. You get a collar or you don't go out."

King bared teeth and started yapping loud and fast, as if he was reading her the riot act. He even stomped once as if for emphasis, his package bobbling in a way that reminded her forcefully he was not in any way an "it".

"*Okay.*" She put the pink bracelet back. "Happy now?"

King gave a final snarl and shut his mouth.

"This doesn't mean I think you can understand me." She sorted through the rest of the bracelets. "Wereterrier? Please. Shifters don't come in any domesticated breed but cat, and cats don't count. Even house cats aren't truly domesticated." She picked out an emerald bracelet with a hook on one end and a chain on the other. Not as sturdy as the blue or pink with their solid clasps, but it had the advantage of being sizable. "Although one might argue all ferrets are weres. Does this one meet with Your Highness's approval?"

King gave a disgruntled yip, but he sat still while she put it on. It seemed secure so she tied some thick string onto it as a makeshift leash. Retrieving her jacket from the coat rack, she and the dog headed outside.

First morning light dusted the sidewalk and glittered off dew, golden light that made the whole day seem fresh and ripe with possibility.

Sophia nearly shared her thoughts with King, realized how foolish it was, and clamped her lips.

Oh, heck. If talking to King made her feel good, what was wrong with that? In fact, maybe "talking to King" was really only working through her problems out loud. That wasn't crazy.

Although the thinking-he-answered part probably was.

But who was around to notice? She smiled again. "So, King. Where do you think Noah went? Should we try to find him?" Given everything she'd heard about Marlowe, it would be nice to have the big strong alpha by her side.

With a yip, King whirled and trotted in the other direction. Her gut jolted. Had he understood and caught Noah's trail?

He trotted toward a tree.

She laughed. Right, the dog could "understand" her. "Okay, hurry up and do your business. I'd like to get this confrontation with Marlowe over with."

King whirled again and almost upended himself, like he was expecting a bigger counterweight than his little stub of a tail. He recovered immediately, braced his hind end, and barked at her like he meant it.

"Fine." She raised a hand. "Do your business and I'll take you back inside before I go."

"Yip *yip*." King glared.

That was a "no way" if she'd ever heard one. "Well, I'm going to Marlowe's, and I'm going now. Are you coming or not?"

He gave a disgruntled "yes" of a yip.

She hid a smile. "Then let's go."

She thought she'd just knock and ask a few polite questions. But when she got to the address a block past the sidewalk's end, she was confronted by a yard-circling hedge as friendly as bailed wire. Remembering Miss Almira's warnings, fear splashed into her stomach.

She crunched with King up the driveway through the weed-choked lot. A hand-painted sign with red drips read, *Go away or get shot.*

Subtle.

The sign was corny, and she wanted to laugh off her fear, but as she mounted the stoop to the rusty trailer with the dirty windows, King gave a worried little yip. Maybe wondering if she was going through with this. Heart pounding in her ears, she was asking herself the same thing.

Deep breath. She knocked on the door.

It swung open. Five-ten of punk-assed teen werewolf stared groggily at her.

"Marlowe?" She kept her stance and gaze neutral, not aggressive, but not victimish either.

His eyes sharpened on her. "Who's asking?" He stepped out onto the stoop, crowding her back.

Not just a punk-assed were, but a bully.

Sophia opened her mouth to give him a verbal slap, but before she could, King leaped between her and Marlowe, the brave little thing.

The dog yapped sternly. She could practically hear him say, *Knock it off, kid.*

"Damn dog." Marlowe kicked King before she could stop him.

Or kicked *at* King. The dog leaped nimbly to one side and the boy's foot swished air. The whole time, King kept yapping, not angry so much as telling the kid to shape up pronto or else.

Marlowe swore, tried another couple kicks, and missed. With an irritated spit to the side, he turned his attention to Sophia.

Oh, the look that kid gave her, from head to toe and definitely in between. Her palm itched to slap him. But questions first. "I'd like to talk with you. May I come in?"

King threw her a look that clearly said he thought she was nuts. She shrugged. She couldn't disagree.

Marlowe sneered up his attitude. "Sure. Yum, yum."

"Ew. I'm probably nearly a decade older than you."

"Ain't you heard of cougars?"

"Ain't you heard, cougar beats wolf?" A giveaway that she knew about werewolves, but she was tired of the boy. She shouldered past him into the trailer, King following silently. She thought it telling that the dog refused to sniff around.

Trash cluttered the place. Not clutter like her aunt's store. There was clutter from an active mind, clutter from folks too tired to clean, clutter from kids, and clutter from illness.

Then there was the miasma of filth-in filth-out, like a snake's nest of sloughed skin. Her own skin crawled.

The trailer was mottled like a snake's skin too, with amber light. The sun, struggling through the grimy windows, hit sills lined with beer bottles, splotching everywhere—except one corner.

A single red bottle lit that corner like weeping blood. *A sign.*

Death had happened here.

Horror scorched Sophia's veins. She automatically reached for her magic, to cleanse the place with fire.

Pain met her instead of her power, her skull exploding in a headache. She released her will, vowing to find out what had happened and make whoever was responsible pay.

Marlowe pushed inside past her then turned with a grin. "Welcome to your worst nightmare." It was a rehearsed line.

"Grow up." She straightened to her full height and looked him in the eye. "I have questions about your theft. Why the bookstore?"

"Me? Theft?" Marlowe overdid the innocence. "Maybe old lady Blue needs better protection."

King sat on disgusted haunches. She didn't even bother contradicting the kid. "Who told you to steal from her?"

"Kille—hey. No trick questions. *I* didn't steal anything."

She held both hands up. "One more. Did my aunt come here to retrieve her property?"

"Please. We don't allow scrawny old hens like her with us prime bachelors."

And again, ew. That and King's yip of warning were her cues to exit. "Thanks. I'll be going."

"I don't think you will." Marlowe's eyes flicked to a spot behind her. His slow, lurid smile made the hairs on her nape rise.

"My brother's right," came a growl from the doorway. "You ain't fucking' going nowhere."

She turned, relaxed, easy, but inside her nerves were screaming. "You must be Killer."

"In the fuckin' flesh." Filling the doorway was an f-bomb of a werewolf on toothpick legs. "Speaking of fuckin' flesh..." He grabbed his crotch and bumped his hips.

She ground fists into her eyes, trying to scrub out her retinas. Killer was Marlowe but heavier, hairier, and not as subtle. Now she knew where the kid had learned his suave way with the ladies.

The wolfman sauntered toward her. Her heart jumped to her throat and started hammering. She breathed through it, trying to be ready for fight or flight.

Pain unexpectedly seared her side. Biting back a yelp, she slapped her hand against the pain.

A hard length met her palm—the carbon fiber wand. It had appeared automatically in her blazer pocket, primed with battle magic. Materializing on her need, acting as if it was still hers.

Her past rose up inside her like an avenging angel. She could instantly downgrade this ass with a whip of the wand.

She reached into her blazer...and her brain and body suddenly muddled into an incoherent mash of terror.

Shame, sealing her magic away, dying...

While she reeled, King leaped between her and Killer, barking angrily at the he-wolf.

The wolfman snapped teeth at the dog. "Looks like I'm having me a snack first."

Fear for King blazed through her muddle. For the little dog's sake, she grabbed the wand and focused.

A lightning bolt of pain ripped through that hand, up into her skull, and down into her heart before ripping out the other hand.

She shrieked and let go of both the wand and her will. She'd thought maybe...but not just shame kept her from using her magic. Her heart thudded in devastation.

Some seals were not made to be broken.

"That's the shriek you'll make when I'm fuckin' you." Killer took another threatening step toward her.

King darted in to nip a warning at Killer's ankles then leaped back as if to protect her.

"Oh noes." Killer pointed a sarcastically trembling finger. "The nasty doggie's guarding you. I'm sooo scared."

King stood quivering at the ready. Poor brave dear. She couldn't let him get hurt for her. Without her magic, she had to resist the mundane way. Lifting her breastbone, she said in her coldest voice, "Move aside. I'm leaving."

"Not before you and me have some fun, girlie." Killer stepped in and grabbed her arm, fingers biting.

King leaped, tearing the string leash from her hand. As Killer grabbed her, the dog ran through wolfman legs, trailing string, slaloming a figure-eight, winding the string around Killer's ankles.

She yanked out of Killer's grip. The he-wolf, thrown off-balance, tried to step wider to steady himself.

King leaped back. The line snapped tight.

With a roar of anger, Killer toppled, slowly, like a tree. She could have yelled *timber!*

She hopped back as he crashed in front of her.

"Hey!" Marlowe grabbed for her.

She automatically hammered an elbow back into him. Luck made the point land right in the bully-boy's gut.

Shoving past the flailing wolfman, Sophia unhooked King's bracelet and freed the dog of the string. "Let's go!" She dumped the bracelet into her blazer pocket as she ran for the door.

Marlowe shouted. Sophia spun to defend herself—as the kid stepped on a pile of frozen dinner cartons, skidded on their coated surfaces, and smashed into a wall.

King nosed her toward the door. *Great minds, thinking alike.* She ran.

Roars and shouts came from the trailer as she blundered down the gravel drive. She hit asphalt and put on speed. Her lungs sawed and her heart pounded as she pushed her muscles to the limit. King churned his little legs alongside. Civilization and the start of the sidewalk on East Second seemed miles away.

A full-throated howl from the trailer drove needles into her spine. She shot a glance over her shoulder.

A gray wolf leaped from the bramble hedge, landing braced on four paws. Killer. His shaggy head twisted from side to side, searching for her. He'd be after her the moment he caught sight or scent of her.

She tried to run faster, but her legs trembled, her breath rasped painfully, and her heart thudded like it would explode.

A second howl turned her insides liquid and made her stumble. Marlowe. *Got to keep going*. She pushed on.

Her feet thudded onto gas station pavement. Pain shot through her side as she made the final leap for the station's door. *Salvation*.

It was locked.

She grabbed her shooting side and staggered to the neighboring FreshFresh. Also locked, its Closed sign taunting her. King yapped angrily and nudged her ankles to go on.

Whimpering, she started for the next building west, an accountant's converted brownstone. She stumbled up two steps, swung into the doorway and knocked desperately.

No one answered.

She fought panic's rising burn. Would she have to run all the way to the bookstore?

Killer's howl changed. Sophia spun. He'd caught her trail and ran toward her with a wolf's ground-eating stride. Advanced Creatures 401 taught her they could go almost forty miles an hour.

Killer leaves the trailer two blocks away going forty miles an hour. Sophia starts at the same time and must cover a block limping and huffing badly, going three mph if she's fricking lucky.

She'd never make it to safety in time.

King growled, low in his throat. Coldly angry, the growl was almost scarier than Killer's howl.

But a growl wouldn't defend them. Fumbling for her pepper spray, she edged out of the doorway and trembled her way down the steps. Groping for the spray the whole time.

Instead of the pepper spray, her stupid hand kept landing on the stupid wand. Pain jolted her each time. Her eyes blurred with tears of frustration.

The wolf was almost on top of them. King, on the sidewalk, wasn't doing anything but growling. They were out of options. Using magic would hurt her or worse, but she had no choice.

She whipped out the wand.

Her head exploded in pain. Her hands ached like they were cramped around live wires. Her heart froze in her chest. She gasped for breath.

The wolf leaped for her.

Chapter Seven

The wolf arced toward Sophia. Her bowels froze. A slavering mouth filled her view, inches from her nose, a mouth full of sharp teeth—and the mouth suddenly emitted a piccolo howl of pain.

Sophia's eyes dropped to Killer's body, where King, who'd launched himself into the air at exactly the right time, had latched on to soft wolf belly with tiny jaws of steel.

The wolf curled and fell back to the sidewalk, King still attached. Killer, dropping onto his side, bicycled his legs to push the small dog off.

King hung on despite the scrabbling horny untrimmed wolf toenails. But his dear little nose scrunched, his eyes clenched tight, and spatters of fresh blood marred his fluffy fur.

Sophia's fingers finally unclenched around the wand, and as her pain ebbed and she started breathing again, she thrust the stick into her pocket—where her hand finally landed on her pepper spray. Heart beating hard, she yanked the can out, flipped back the hinged cover, thumbed the button, and leaned in close to the wolf.

She released the stream directly into his face.

Killer yowled, pure pain. He started morphing from wolf to human, several bone-cracking moments.

Marlowe's wolf bounded into sight. He saw Killer and screeched to a halt, eyes wide. With a howl, he came running.

Sophia snatched King and tried to flee. The dog was still attached to Killer and she had to tug.

King's teeth tore off a few layers of Killer-hide.

The instant King came free, she ran. The dog was a furious fuzzy tornado yapping his displeasure. Blood decorated his muzzle, not all of it his.

Her protector. She hugged his sweet sturdy little body to her. His head ended up pressed between her breasts. His yipping stopped abruptly, along with any movement. And then his tail began wagging and he wiggled happily in her arms.

Her last sight of Killer was as a man kneeling on the sidewalk, clawing at his streaming eyes, Marlowe trying to help and getting swatted.

She ran all the way to Aunt Linda's, clutching King to her chest. Her hand trembled as she unlocked the bookstore door. She darted in and nearly slammed the door behind her. She was out of breath—not just panting, but the kind of wheezing rasp from scoured-off layers of lung.

King, despite bleeding from numerous scratches and abrasions, licked her face like he was trying to reassure *her*. The sweetie. The imbecile. Why had he attacked Killer like that? Man-Killer was gross, but wolf-Killer was big, fast, and deadly.

When she could breathe without danger of puking, she set King down and locked the door. Although, even gross, human-Killer would have hands. The lock wouldn't keep him out.

Her palms broke out in a cold sweat. Sticking them under her arms, she peeped through the window. Without magic, she was a sitting duck.

A profound longing surged through her—she wished Noah were here. With his strong presence, she wouldn't worry about Killer as a wolf or a man.

King gave a pained yip.

"What's wrong, sweetie?" She immediately dropped her own worries to kneel beside the dog. "Are you hurt?" She parted his blood-smeared fur, looking for wounds. The fur was too thick for her to see anything.

She had to get him to a professional. But the only vet was miles away, and she wasn't sure her car would make it.

Her eye landed on a flyer, tacked to Auntie's "Local Businesses" bulletin board. *Matinsfield Happy Tails Pet Store* blazed across the top, and just below *New Grooming Salon NOW OPEN!*

She nodded. Maybe not a full-fledged omen but surely a good sign, literally. "King, I'm taking you to the doggie salon."

"Yip, yip." King barked rapidly, as if he was trying to talk her out of it.

She silenced him by scooping him up and hugging him to her bosom. He again stilled, then wiggled happily.

Too spooked to stop and hunt up more leash string, she hugged the dog firmly in one arm as she let herself out and locked up. Hurrying across Main, her eyes were open for pissed-off wolves.

Her cell phone rang, startling her so badly she nearly threw up her heart.

The ringtone was her cousin Daniel's. Should've calmed her, but instead her dread increased, the same as getting a call at three a.m. Lungs pumping, she pulled out the phone.

It pulsed red.

Magic-enhanced to signal a 911 emergency. She nearly cracked her cheekbone answering. "Daniel? What's wrong?"

"The first knell has struck." He intoned the words, the solemn wizard prince. Since Daniel was a playboy, this strange, serious tone rattled her even more. Then he said, "*You* have been chosen to carry the burden."

"Me?" The words hit her with an almost physical blow. "What burden? Wait. Are you talking about that crazy poem?"

Last October Daniel had discovered the Avignon Quatrain, fabled lost prophecy of the great wizard Jean-Dion d'Avignon. Supposedly a sort of treasure map, they hadn't been able to decipher it.

"*HEART beats for a wolf and a Blue.*" He recited it like a chant..

"But it's been nearly a year," Sophia sputtered. "We decided the prophecy is a fake."

"*You* decided it's a fake," Daniel said in his normal baritone. "Mostly because it named you first."

"It doesn't name *me*." Why did everyone insist Blue meant her? She was hyperventilating. King yipped and licked her chin. "Total coincidence my last name is a color. And anyway, prophecies are all image and metaphor. Clear only in retrospect."

"It's a little more specific than you make out." He recited the full Quatrain.

HEART beats for a wolf and a Blue
MIND is focused by Light
SOUL belongs to those who are True
The KEY unlocks the Night.

"So there's a wolf too." *Noah was a wolf.* Her body shimmered. She ignored it. "Big whoop."

King gave a short yowl. She was squeezing him so tightly she was in danger of cracking his ribs. She let up immediately.

"Cousin Arianna had a vision. She says Heart, Mind, and Soul are pieces of the Key. She's adamant that you're the Blue to find the heart piece, and she *is* the seer in the family. So I have to ask you...fall in love with any wolves lately?"

"That's taboo." Even and especially wolves with silver eyes and clever hands attached to all that was tall, dark, and *umm-hmm*. "Maybe Aunt Linda met someone. She's a Blue. Or Arianna. Can't be me. I just got my life on track. I'm not messing it up with love."

"I see." His dry tone said he did see, too much. "Well, that's a problem. Because if it's not you, who is the Blue I need to warn?"

"*Warn*?" She screeched to a halt so fast she almost smoked her heels. "Warn about what?"

"Red script appeared beside the first line of the Quatrain. A warning."

"Daniel," she growled. "Stop teasing me."

"If you're not the Blue in the prophecy," he countered, "why should you care?"

Sophia wished for a smite button of her own. "Because it's a warning. Everyone needs to heed a warning." She waited.

His silence was a pregnant reply.

"*Arg*. All right, because it might—*might*, mind you—be about me."

"Good enough." His tone was smug, the bastard. "It says, 'Beware the Hungry Ghost.'"

"Hungry Ghost? I don't like the sound of that." Shivers started coursing down her body. She catapulted into a walk, fast, trying to shake them off. "What does it mean?"

"Not sure. In Buddhism the Hungry Ghost has the appetite of a mountain but the throat of a needle's eye. A person who tries to fill emotional needs with physical possessions."

"Why don't you just say greedy?"

He sighed. "Being a banker has really dulled your sense of the poetic. Can't you just picture it, a huge growling empty stomach trying to suck empires through a drinking straw of a throat?"

"You're a playboy, Daniel. You see nothing wrong with a big appetite."

"I *was* a playboy." He paused. "Look, just do me a favor, okay? Keep your eyes open for the Heart."

"Whatever it looks like."

"Sophia..." His tone was a warning.

"Yes, all right."

"It's important. I think you're right on top of it. If the wrong person gets their hands on that Key, the world as we know it will end."

"Thank you, Mr. Apocalypse."

"No joke, Sophia. The red script has ramped up the danger. Your competition is devouringly evil."

"*All right*." She hung up, shuddering.

King wiggled in her arms. The poor, brave dear. Hungry Ghosts and prophecies would have to wait until she knew how badly he was injured.

Chapter Eight

The sign on the pet store door was turned to Closed. Sophia's chest shot with disappointment.

A plastic clock hung below the sign, red hour hand distinctly pointing at nine. She took a quick peek at her phone for the time. Seven.

She rolled her eyes at herself. Right. What was the world coming to when stores weren't open at dawn?

Okay, if not here, the vet. Still hugging the dog to her breast, she thumbed up a search on her phone in case Matinsfield had gotten a new emergency clinic for animals since she was here last. But no, the closest vet was ten miles out of town, and the closest animal emergency clinic at least twelve. Could her car limp ten miles?

King yipped. He was shivering. Could he last ten miles?

A light snapped on inside the pet store. Hope surging in her breast, she peered in. Movement inside set her heart pumping. She tried the door.

It was open. She eased inside and set King on the floor. "Hello?"

Light spilled from a small glassed-in area to her left, about the size of a vet's examination room.

"Yip!" King barked the same sharp warning he'd used for Killer.

She stepped back just as a man glided from the darkness.

He was all sculpted cheekbones, brilliant black eyes, black hair, and sexy mouth begging for a nibble... Her breath caught. If she hadn't met Noah, she'd have been drooling. As it was she felt uncomfortably hot.

King's yip turned distinctly cross.

"One moment." The gorgeous man tossed a shopkeeper's logoed apron over his head.

Instantly the tug of attraction was gone. As if, by donning the apron, he'd put on an asexual envelope. He became, not a man, but a dog groomer in ordinary jeans and open-collared Oxford shirt, a means to taking care of King.

Almost magically.

Sophia frowned at the man. Still the same chiseled face, twinkling eyes, and thick lustrous hair. He didn't appear magical, but the only way she could be sure was to look at him with her third eye. The witch's eye wasn't magic, so she could still do it, but it was uncomfortable. She'd only used it a couple times in the four years she'd been mundane.

"Welcome to Do Doggie 'Do." The man's voice was deep and sure. "How can I help you?"

She decided the eye wasn't worth the bother. "I thought this was the Matinsfield Happy Tails pet store."

"It is. Currently merging with the Do Doggie 'Do chain of in-store pet grooming boutiques. I'm here to get the franchise off the ground." He pointed at King. "Cute little puppy. Serious *aw* factor."

King growled.

She said, "King isn't a puppy. He's a brave warrior. In fact, he injured himself defending me from a much bigger, um, dog. But his fur is matted and I can't tell how badly he's hurt. I was hoping you could see if he needs medical care."

The groomer's lips curved in an almost-smile. "Normally we tell owners to take injured pets directly to a veterinarian. But I'll wash him down, and we'll see what we shall see. Feel free to browse while you're waiting." He reached for King.

The dog's growl turned distinctly chilling. Braced on four paws, his fur rose, and his lips pulled back to expose his fangs.

Tiny cute fangs, but trickling through Sophia's *aw* was a sense of apprehension. Did King sense bad things about the man? She cleared her throat. "I'd better come with him."

"Certainly." The groomer's smile changed, as if secretly pleased. "This way, then."

He led them to the glassed-in grooming booth. Just outside it, King balked. Sophia cajoled him and scolded him and finally picked him up and carried him. He stopped fighting at that. He really seemed to like it when she hugged him to her breasts. The sweetie.

The grooming table was metal topped with grooved vinyl. Clamped to one corner was a tall pole, a short crossarm at the top making a half-T. A leash hung from the arm. It swung uncomfortably like a hangman's noose.

The groomer unhooked the loop from the table's arm. "Let's just get your little man secured."

King growled at the leash and tried to squirm out of Sophia's arms. He wouldn't let the man put the loop over his head. She finally had to threaten the dog with leaving him at the store while she searched for Aunt Linda to get him to cooperate.

Yes, he probably couldn't understand her. But it worked.

The groomer dropped the loop over King's head and tightened it, two fingers between the leash and fur for space. "We'll leave it a little loose for him," the man said. Then he led Sophia, carrying the dog, into an attached room smelling of shampoo where he clipped the leash to a wall hook beside a sink. "Set him in here." While the groomer washed and rinsed the dog, he adopted a sugary voice. "Who's a good puppy? Is Kingy-wingy a good boy?"

A low thrum threaded the air, King growling again.

The man laughed. "Good news. Just scrapes under the blood. I can treat them."

She let out a relieved breath. "That'd be great."

He unclipped the loop from the wall and indicated Sophia should take King back into the grooming booth, where she set the dog on the table. After anchoring the loop to the half-T, the groomer used a foot pedal to raise the table's height. Then he turned to a selection of bottles on the nearby counter top and picked up an amber one. "Tell you what. I'll throw in a trim and style for the little fella, no charge."

King's low growl developed a distinct knife-edge.

Sophia tapped his nose. "King, be nice. He's helping you."

Casting a doleful eye at her, the dog quieted.

Her mind wandered as the man applied antiseptic. Why had Noah left in such a hurry this morning? Where had he gone, what was he doing? Was he thinking about her as much as she was thinking about him?

Mooning over a man she'd just met. She shook her head at herself. She was here to find Aunt Linda.

Okay, she'd talked to Noah, Mason, the Misses Jamies, and Marlowe. She didn't know who else to talk to. Maybe she should just give in and use her Witch's Sight to survey the scene of the crime. Although Noah had given her a pretty thorough rundown on what had happened, there were traces she could pick up with the witch's eye that he wouldn't have seen.

The groomer finished treating King's scrapes and turned the dog around on the table. "My my, this little man has quite a big package."

King shot him a look that would've frozen fire.

The groomer simply smiled as he toweled, blow-dried, and brushed out. Then he thumbed on the clipper, releasing a burnt dust scent.

King's low growl promised serious mayhem.

The groomer laughed. "Just a trim, little man. No big deal."

With a grumpy yip, King turned forward.

The man pursed his lips as he worked. He had gorgeous lips, very kissable.

The groomer shot Sophia a look out of the corner of his eye. Somehow she forgot about lips.

As the clipper buzzed and growled, her mind turned back to Noah. He hadn't wanted her to interview Marlowe, concerned about his brother Killer. It occurred to her that anybody who concerned Noah Blackwood had to be pretty damned dangerous. Was Killer behind the wall of the trailer weeping blood?

She shook herself. Not thinking about Noah anymore.

Or any less.

She sighed.

"All done. What do you think?"

Sophia looked up. The groomer had given King an adorable, fluffy trim, complete with a pink froufrou of a bow clipped between his perky ears. She smiled. "Cute."

"What do you think, puppy?" The groomer picked up a mirror and held it before King's face.

Odd that the man would show the dog his image, like a hairstylist to a client. But no odder than her thinking King answered her.

In the mirror, the small dog's bright eyes fastened on the frilly pink bow—and went very, very narrow.

Dead silence.

Suddenly King went ballistic, snarling and snapping, the loop lead whipping.

The man danced back, barely keeping body parts out of teeth-stapling range. Sophia alternately shouted and soothed, but the dog refused to calm down.

King's paroxysms loosened the table noose. He slipped free, jumped off the table, slid past their frantic outstretched hands, and ran directly to a file cabinet. With a hump and twist, he used the cabinet handle to pry off the bow.

Sophia's jaw dropped. The dog was amazingly facile about it, as if he'd planned the whole series of maneuvers. Cool once he was loose. No wasted motion.

Just like a certain alpha.

Damn it, she had Noah on the brain, a fever, and the only cure was more Noah. Or cowbell, she wasn't sure.

She rested her forehead in her palm and sighed.

* * *

As they left the pet store, King strode ahead of Sophia, a gait which should have been impossible with his short little legs, but he managed it. He also managed to keep perfect tension on his new black leather leash while completely ignoring her. Yes, he was a dog and couldn't talk. She knew from his stride and the way his nose pointed in the air that he was ignoring her in offended dignity.

"I don't see why you didn't like the bow. It was cute."

King stomped on, the extra swing to his male parts a clear, *I do* not *do cute*. She smiled.

As they walked, her smile faded. Where to go next? The bookstore was the obvious answer, but for Killer. The wolfman hadn't followed her to the store, and there was no reason to think he'd know she was staying there—except for the fact that Matinsfield was a small town. It wouldn't take much digging to find her.

But she still needed to locate her aunt, so she headed back to the Uncommon Night Owl to do her duty. Besides, that was where her suitcase was, and she was smelling a little ripe.

Inside the store was cool and dark, but her gut was churning. Worried about Killer, but also uneasy about using the Sight. Frankly, she'd rather pet a porcupine. She shut the door. Locked it. Removed King's leash. Fed the animals. Put fresh water down. Answered all her emails and updated her social statuses in three places before she knocked the phone between her eyes.

Avoid much? She shut her eyes and reached mentally for the etheric.

Witch's Sight rode a magical gray line. While mundanes could do Sight, it took a whisper of power. So when she opened her third eye, because of the way she'd sealed off her magic, her head tingled unpleasantly. She gritted her teeth and pushed through it. It'd only get worse.

With her third eye focused, she lifted her physical lids and scanned the store.

A red ring pulsed where the mushroom had been, Aunt Linda's version of a theft-reporting device. Too bad Auntie hadn't put a locater spell on the thing—or on herself.

The doorway was tinged bright yellow-red. Someone had gotten a surprise bordering on shock here, enough for the emotion to bleed onto the etheric. The thief? Or Auntie?

Sophia's head started throbbing. The eye was taking its toll. She didn't have all day. She started walking the store.

Midway in, another splotch of gold-red surprise floated just above the floor. Jagged skid marks leading to the splotch lit the air, evidence of a cast spell. Frowning, she stopped.

Magic potential couldn't be seen, which was why even a witch couldn't reliably tell another witch on sight. But actual magic was visible, whether it was injected into a thing like an amulet, pulsed within a living being like a shifter, or cast raw by a witch as a spell.

A thrown spell left traces of its path.

This skid was from a spell—and it was fairly fresh. Probably Aunt Linda, but strange, because as a single-element witch, she didn't often throw spells because of the fast power drain. Auntie preferred potions and amulets which drew over time.

But if not Aunt Linda, that left the mysterious hooded man, and Sophia didn't like that idea at all.

She tried to glean more information from the skid, peering more intently at it. The intense concentration gave her a bigger headache, like squinting too long.

But she was able to tell by the jagged nature of the skid that the spell was a hex.

Her hands started aching, bone-deep. She followed the skid. It led her to a glass case of pictures. She bent and peered inside. Scratch that. It had hit *her* picture.

Her heart started misfiring. She knocked a fist into it. It hiccupped and caught. Even the trickle of magic she drew for her third eye was catching up with her. Time was running out. She moved faster.

The skid made a V out of the case. She trotted the length of the trace to a cloth-draped piece of furniture—from the shape, a freestanding full-length oval mirror.

She reached for the cloth to uncover it.

An etheric eye as big as a house zoomed in on her. *One searches for Noah.*

Her heart stuttered. A second eye, behind the first, lanced into her. *One hunts him.*

She fell to her knees, dizzy, gasping, hands clutched to her chest. Her whole body felt weak and fluttery.

Her last impression before she lost consciousness was King, yapping frantically and licking her face.

Chapter Nine

She was Sleeping Beauty, her prince kissing her awake. Sweet and coaxing, male lips smooth, enticing...*hot and wild...*

Sophia's brain came online. That wild taste didn't belong to a fairy-tale prince. It was *Noah*.

She was on the floor, on her back. His strongly muscled body was hard and heavy beside hers. It felt like heaven. She sighed in pleasure. This was what it would feel like, waking up to him every morning.

Well, except for the being on the floor bit.

Unless he liked things kinky. At the thought, she wriggled happily.

"Sophia," he murmured against her mouth. "I was worried. Are you all right?" He started to lift his head from hers.

"I'm fine." She captured his head with one hand, stopping him, her fingers threading his silky hair. "Keep kissing me and I'll be better than fine."

His head remained stubbornly raised. "You collapsed...I mean, you were sprawled against the floor as if you'd collapsed. Are you sure you're okay?"

Explaining about her third eye and the hex was a sexual non-starter. And she wanted him with a shocking need. Maybe waking to his kiss had shortcut around her inhibitions, or maybe, having already experienced one Noah-induced orgasm, she wasn't so worried about Council prohibitions. She said, "I overdid it. It may have looked like I collapsed, but all I needed was some serious sleep. Got it, and I'm okay now...unless you stop kissing me. Then I will *not* be okay and *you* will have serious problems."

He chuffed a laugh and bent to press his lips sweetly to hers.

Sweetly, from the alpha. What was she, his little maiden aunt? Pulling his mouth hard onto hers, she wrapped her other arm around his ribcage and tried to lever him on top of her.

Something in Noah's big body changed at that. Heated red-hot. It reminded her that this wasn't a mere dream prince kissing her, but a wilder royalty, more dangerous and elemental.

He eased himself on top of her. As he did, his hand slid behind her neck to clasp her nape. She'd felt a dozen men do that, but with Noah it was different. As if, instead of fingers, hot teeth closed on her neck, to hold her firmly in place for pounding sex.

Lust gushed through her at the thought.

"Sophia, your scent..." He groaned and drove his tongue deep into her mouth.

She moaned and opened to him, both lips and legs. Gravity did the work, bringing his hot torso nestling between her spread thighs, warming, then scorching her sensitive flesh.

He'd feel even better skin-to-skin.

She slid a hand between them to fumble with her slacks. His fingers came to help. Strong yet nimble, they made quick work of her fastenings. When he lifted off her to ease her pants and panties down the curve of her hips, she groaned with the loss of his weight.

Almost immediately he returned to nip down her jaw. His body pressed against the naked flesh of her exposed belly, only his flannel shirt between. She wriggled happily as he nipped to her throat.

Pinned by his weight, his teeth sharp along the tender flesh of her neck, she could almost feel the predator's bite. But the wolf was tempered by the man as his sharp nips alternated with warm kisses and licks. The combination along with the heat of his breath on her neck sent shivers riding along her flesh from crown to toes.

Her heart thudded faster. She lifted her chin to give him better access. At the same time she hunted for his waistband. His jeans button came open with a hard push-tug. She cranked on his zipper, lost patience, and dived in, expecting boxers or briefs.

Shocked, she felt satiny warm flesh instead—his cock, peeking up to greet her.

He shifted his hips so that she could shoehorn her palm past his waistband into his pants. She glided along the length of his hard, growing erection. It was thick and sleek and she yearned to feel it inside her.

As she rubbed, his breathing got ragged. His mouth pressed to the crook of her neck and sucked gently. His hand was busy flipping open blouse buttons. *A multi-tasking male, ooh.*

But while his touch on her naked nipples would be nice, she was burning up elsewhere. She abandoned his pants to grab his fingers and tried to redirect his hand to where she wanted it, between her legs.

His growl revved darker. “Not yet. I want you totally naked.”

She thrilled. Shivered. “You too.”

He lifted his head and stared into her eyes. His were a silver so bright they burned. “Oh, yes.”

His mouth seized hers. She gasped, her jaw falling pliant and yielding to him. He plundered her to the limits. And when she was insane with want—he stopped.

“Damn it, Blackwood—”

“Naked, remember?” Straddling her hips, he rose to his knees over her and made short work of her blouse and bra. She half-lifted to strip them off. He grabbed them from her and tossed them to the side.

And then he was suckling her breast. She sank back to the floor as her nipple surged up to meet him. He suckled it then started plucking the other until she arched with a moan. Until her urgency drove her to thrash against the floor. “Naked,” she gasped.

“Yes.” He completely stripped off her pants and panties, then fell on her breasts again, suckling. Desire flaming through her, she rolled her hips into him.

“*Naked,*” she shouted, then panted, “You.”

That ripped a dark growl from him. He surged to his knees above her and without unbuttoning, stripped off his flannel shirt with a rise of chest and biceps, a long stretch of muscle along his ribcage and a flaring of his lats. The man was all lean, luscious muscle. She petted everything she could reach, delighting in silky skin and a light dusting of hair that tickled.

His jeans were already unbuttoned, the top of his erection straining in the gap. He tore his zipper open, rolled one hip onto the floor then rolled onto his back, peeling the pants off as he went. He came up on his knees, the pants in one hand.

His erection strained eagerly for her.

She nearly lost it at that. The monster cock jutted proudly from his body. *What will that feel like inside me...?*

Tossing the pants, he came to lay beside her, his body flush with hers, and leaned over her to kiss her. As his tongue mated with hers, he slid his other hand between her legs.

She was already so wet his fingers sank deep. They both moaned.

He stroked her sex, gently at first and then with increasing insistence. Her hips began to jerk in excitement. A mini-explosion rocked her. He kept stroking and she built higher and higher. Dizzyingly high.

Achingly close to the peak.

Winched to the point of no return, she grabbed his hips and tried to lever him to where he'd do the most good. He chuckled and moved to accommodate her, kneeling between her parted thighs. He lowered himself slowly until his erection bobbed against her mound, on the cusp of making everything perfect.

The wall phone jangled.

She groaned and tried to ignore it. Grabbing his head in both hands, she brought their lips together and kissed him as if she could deafen them both with her enthusiasm.

The ringing stopped.

She sighed and reached between them to circle his cock, lovely and thick in her hand. She stroked, feeling it grow even fatter. He'd feel like heaven sinking in—

Brring.

"Damn it." She clunked her head on the floor in disgust.

"Who is it?" Noah's growl was just as frustrated.

"I don't know. Could be a supplier—or a customer."

"Or a telemarketer. Don't answer it." He slid a tongue along the sensitive tendon of her neck.

"Not a telemarketer." Auntie's phone was spelled to reach down the line and zap any telemarketer with a twenty-four-hour truth spell. They'd learned to stop calling long ago. She raised her head again. "It might be important."

"Might not." He followed that long glide of tongue with a little gentle sucking. "And you're close..." He slid a hand onto her clit.

She arched into his hand, the crown of her head clunking the floor again. *Yes, please.*

As if it agreed, the phone stopped ringing.

"They'll call back." She pumped her hips against his clever fingers. "Right?"

"Certainly. In the meantime..." He reversed himself, threw his leg over her head, pushed her thighs apart, curled strong arms around each and dropped his head between her legs.

She'd barely comprehended their reversed position when the hottest mouth in the universe assaulted her sex.

"*Aaahrgh!*" Her legs tightened in response. Her thighs wrapped around shoulders so broad they could have been redwoods. His breath scorched her. She moaned.

His tongue was rough and insistent, lapping her over and over, long sweeps paying special sweet homage to her clit. She arched against him with a strangled sound, bowing so hard she'd have pushed a normal man off. She barely moved the alpha.

She grabbed his thick erection just out of self-preservation. She didn't stroke it so much as grip it rhythmically, her rudder in the storm.

"Harder." His growl rumbled against her belly. When she clenched him tighter, he slid a finger into her and tongued her clit. She whimpered. He sucked. She trembled so violently her bones rattled. He used his superior weight to hold her steady while he sucked and thrust again and again.

Her mouth was hot and swollen. Needing to suck too, she pulled his cock to her and swirled her tongue over the head.

"*Yes.*" He thrust a second finger into her. It slid in like she was drenched.

She bucked against him, on the precipice of the biggest orgasm she'd ever had, rolling toward her like an avalanche.

Coming. She opened her mouth over him and sucked him down.

He shouted and climaxed. The heat and force of him overwhelmed her, triggering her own orgasm.

She burst, pleasure swamping her in huge, hard waves.

Brring.

Her heart, pounding in her ears, drowned out most of the phone's jangling. His mouth worked her rhythmically through the orgasm, his fingers driving into her sex, wringing even bigger contractions from her.

Somewhere along the way he pulled out of her mouth and turned his hips to the side. His fingers gentled, easing out her last bits of pleasure.

Wow. That orgasm had totaled her. Even now, her body rang with the aftershocks.

As the contractions ebbed, peace settled in their place.

Brring.

"Damn it." Peace broke. "That's the third callback. I have to answer."

"I know." He rolled onto his feet and held out his hand.

She took it, her eyes flicking to his cock, hanging satisfied, though still heavy and thick. As she came to her feet, her naked breasts swayed with unusual weight. Swollen. She went to the phone. Even her hips worked differently, languid, extra-fluid. Her inner parts were swollen too and walking brushed everything in all sorts of exciting, distracting ways.

She was wrung out, totally satisfied...and yet shockingly, she wanted to do it again. Only this time face-to-face, with tab A in its proper slot.

It took all her willpower to reach that phone. "Uncommon Night Owl, how may I help you?" Her voice was husky.

"Sophia!" Aunt Linda sounded quite chipper. "I'm absolutely fine. Just ran into a tiny spot of trouble with Noah's hex. Looking for a cure. Be back soon. Ta-ta!" *Click.*

That shocked Sophia out of her languor. "What? Wait!"

Only a dial tone answered her.

"Damn it, *damn* it." She jammed the earpiece onto its hook, wishing for a regular handset and a satisfying slam. Well, at least now she knew the hex's victim. Poor Noah.

"What's wrong?" Noah growled *right behind her.*

She spun with a squeak. Should've put King's belled collar on *him.* "Nothing." Everything. "That was Aunt Linda. She's fine, which is good. She's looking for a cure to—" In the nick of time she realized he might not know he'd been hit with a spell.

"To my hex?"

"Yes." She glared her frustration at him. "Why didn't you tell me?"

"I thought the problem was solved, so I omitted it."

"Omitted... You mean you lied. You lied to me?" Why him, why now?

She'd trusted the wrong man at the wrong time and promised herself she'd never make that mistake again.

Only she *had* made that mistake, and worse... Her gaze slid down the rapid rise and fall of Noah's heavy chest. Below, he was coming to attention again. And damn her, that thick, jutting erection made her want to climb on and yell yee-hah so badly she burned with it.

Yeah, worse, she wanted to make that mistake yet again.

A witch rubbing naughty parts with a wolf was bad enough. Having intercourse—*making love*—with a man who'd just lied to her?

He was actually growing bigger under her gaze. She could see his cock throb. Looked painful. She should at least help him out with that.

No, I shouldn't. Not her problem. He was an alpha wolf. He'd have no problem finding some little she-wolf to raise her tail.

Sudden pain stabbed Sophia's gut and propelled her into motion. "Doesn't matter." Grabbing her clothes as she went, she headed for the stairs. Aunt Linda was okay. Sophia could put inappropriate wolf/witch attractions behind her.

She could go home.

And why didn't that make her happier?

Trotting upstairs, she turned resolutely for the bedrooms. Despite knowing the penalties, she'd been two seconds from humping Noah like a bunny. Willpower alone wouldn't cut it. This was one of those decisions she had to make by changing the environment.

Time to get away from temptation. Get out of there ASAP. She'd have to find a place for King but... Speaking of, where was King? She slowed, puzzling at it.

Noah leaped up the stairs after her. "Sophia, wait."

Panic flared. She scrambled for the bedroom and managed to make it inside just in time to shut the door in his face. His strong face with that sexy stubble, those broad shoulders, those capable hands...she nearly popped the door open again. Clunked her skull against the door as if it would drive her insane stupidity from her head.

"Sophia, are you okay?"

"I'm fine," she called back. "Go away."

Clothes. Clothes would keep her from doing the unthinkable and jumping his bones. Or, even if it didn't stop her, it'd delay her. Hopefully. She wasn't discounting the possibility of strip-shredding like the Hulk. She fumbled on her bra, wishing she could be like the groomer and don asexuality with an apron. At least then she wouldn't clench her teeth simply from her swollen nipples and sex brushing *air*.

"Sophia, let me in."

Without a lock he could walk in any time, but maybe he didn't know that. "I'm getting dressed." She shrugged on her blouse and left it unbuttoned while she slid on panties and pants, dancing over to the bed while she zipped and buttoned to haul her suitcase out from under. Her haste stirred Auntie's crystal dream-catcher, hanging in the window.

"I won't stop you. But we need to talk."

Click.

The door opened behind her. She spun, hastily buttoning.

Noah glided in, big and silent—and still *naked.*

She pointed. "C-cover that."

He carried his clothes. His answer was to slowly press his crumpled jeans over his groin with one strong hand. Tendons stood stark in his forearm, emphasizing his strength.

Sophia groaned. Urges flooded her, the insane need to shove him to the floor, climb on and play Chutes and Ladders on his naked chest. Which bulged most intriguingly as he took a deep breath then slowly let it out.

A pendant emerged briefly, unseen before because it nestled between his impressive pectorals. Or because she'd been fixated on his thick, vein-throbbing...arms. *Yeah, right.*

The small lacquered piece was a sleek black animal shaped like a wolf.

"You're leaving." He breathed again, and in the lift of those heavy muscles, she forgot the wolf, forgot everything, forgot even her name in the desire flushing through her, surging to her extremities and pooling heavily in her lips and groin. She couldn't relieve the renewed ache between her legs, but she did lick her lips.

His eyes dropped to her mouth and he groaned. "Why do you have to be so beautiful?"

Me? What about you? She shook with longing, so hard it scared her. She tried to put words between them. "You said my nose was too long."

"You remember the strangest things. Sophia, please don't leave. I need your help finding Linda."

"I'm afraid Linda doesn't want to be found. Could you get dressed?"

"With you watching? No."

"Well then, could you at least stop breathing?"

He smiled. "That's my line."

She smiled back; she couldn't help it. The ultrabad alpha was compelling enough. Leavened with a touch of humor, he was irresistible. "What if I turn around?" She suited action to words. Though the image of him, naked, *breathing*, was burned on her retinas forever.

"Sophia, please. I need you here." His voice was underlined by the sound of denim riding up long muscular legs.

Imagining him in jeans and nothing else, she clenched her hands against a flood of desire. "Why do you need to find Auntie so badly?"

"I can't tell you the full details." His tone rumbled with a low growl.

More secrets. She hated secrets. She wished King were here, the uncomplicated little doggie with his happy little yip... He was oddly quiet. Oddly *missing*.

Her mouth fell open, events rearranging themselves in her brain.

King, missing at night. The unused papers. Noah, missing during the day. King, howling like a miniature wolf. Seeming to understand her.

It gave her weird ideas.

No, no, no. There were weird ideas and then there was getting a new white coat that tied charmingly in the back—by the arms. Did King have clunky glasses and bad hair, and Noah a cape and a curl, and she was too dense to see they were one and the same?

Never seeing King and Noah at the same time. Both males assigning themselves as her impromptu bodyguards.

Her fingers tangled in her pearls. No more secrets. Not ever again. "Noah, tell me the truth." A fair amount of time had elapsed since he started dressing so she dared turn. "Are you the dog..."

He was pulling on his shirt, muscles sliding under his skin as he worked, as gorgeous donning it as he was taking it off. His jeans were still open, baring lots of bronzed skin along with a trail of black hair she wanted to follow with her tongue.

All the breath left her lungs. She managed a whispered, "...King?"

He finished pulling flannel over abs, tucked and zipped. Her gaze, finally released, rose to his. He'd been looking at her the whole time, and there was a pleading depth to his silver eyes. "Sophia, please let me explain. Yes, I'm King. Your aunt hexed me."

"You fur-faced liar." Anger tore through her haze. "My aunt would never throw a hex on a good person."

"Not on purpose. She was aiming for that little thief Marlowe."

"Oh." Sophia's anger deflated. *That* sounded like Auntie. Her aim wasn't the best—honestly, she couldn't hit a Hummer with a handful of magnets. "How do you know she hexed you? Only witches can feel magic."

"She told me." Flags of color darkened the skin over his cheekbones. Then she saw the question hit him. "How do you know *that*? Are you a witch?"

She grabbed her pearls. "I don't do magic." The truth, as far as it went.

Some tension seemed to go out of his big body. "I was wondering. Your aunt is."

"I know."

"The reason I didn't tell you about King...*couldn't* tell you...well, do you know about shifters?"

"Yes."

"I'm a wolf. Pack alpha, actually." He slid a look out of the corner of his eye, as if he was checking her reaction. To see if she was impressed?

She was, and not simply from the fact that he was alpha. But because he was brave and loyal and coping really well despite the curveball her aunt had thrown him...and it didn't hurt that he had a body like a stallion. "So?"

"So if my pack knew I'm stuck as the dog during the day, it'd be the end of me."

"What?" She blinked at him. "Why?"

"Remember Killer? I outweigh him as a wolf, but I'm sure he'd love to challenge a fifteen pound doggie."

"You can't shift at all?"

"Not during the day."

"That's some hex." Sophia shook her head. "And at night?"

"Then everything's okay. After sunset, it's like the hex is gone. I can shift, man or wolf. But if a challenge comes during the day...I *must* get this hex off me."

"You will. Aunt Linda is searching for a reversal. She'll be back soon."

"You don't understand." He shook his head. "*Soon* isn't good enough. Killer's not the worst of the lot. I can't chance any of them learning about my disadvantage."

"There are more like Killer?" She goggled.

"The old alpha's cadre. Five anti-alphas, each more tricky and treacherous than the last. Every second I'm under this hex is another second closer to, not *if* they find out—but when." He spread his hands in a gesture of appeal. "Please help me contact Linda."

He had such strong, capable hands. They'd feel marvelous spread over her skin, urging her to ride faster...damn. Lust was eating her brains.

"Noah." She used his name to signal she knew this was serious. "I hurt for you, but I simply have no idea where Auntie is." She shook her head. "She'll be back when she's ready."

His jaw clenched visibly, as if she'd hit him. "But—"

"I'm sorry. There's nothing I can do." And if she stayed one more moment she'd lick that clenched jaw then rip his shirt from his body and lick all his muscles until they clenched too under her tongue.

"Sophia, please—"

"I have to go." She grabbed her case and spun past him toward the door.

A shaft of moonlight sheared through the crystal dream-catcher. A rainbow of colors dotted the walls—and a blue beam speared her in the eye.

A wolf and a Blue.

The prophecy. The Key. Her cousin Daniel. *Have you fallen in love...?*

Perhaps *she* was the Hungry Ghost, needing Noah with a desire that would kill them both.

And if not the Ghost, there was always the Witch's Council's headsman.

Get away. Urgency propelled her. She raced out the door and fled downstairs.

Strong dread drove her out the front door and onto the sidewalk. The *empty* sidewalk—and emptier street. She stopped, bewildered.

Her car was missing.

Chapter Ten

A stone rattled across the street, as if it had been kicked into the concrete gutter.

Sophia's head jerked up.

A man sauntered off the curb toward her, his hood darkening his features. "Hello, Sophia."

Even without seeing his face, *she knew that voice.*

Shock numbed her. Her guts shredded, her brain threw *run, run, run,* and acid poured into her veins as her heart started pumping overtime, but she stood frozen.

Last time she'd seen him, four years ago, he'd worn a pale gold robe and a snooty attitude. Now he had on jeans, leather shoes, and a hoodie, but the snooty attitude was the same. She managed a breath.

"Rodolphe." She was proud of how normal she sounded. "Don't suppose you know anything about my missing car?"

"Yes, actually. I'm afraid I have to keep you in this backwater burg a little longer. The fun's just starting."

As he approached, she could see he looked younger than he had four years ago, and flush with power. She swallowed hard, not liking that. What was he doing here, and why now? "Are you an ass, or do you just play one on TV? The fun's just starting, huh? What does that mean?"

"My dear little witch." He smirked. "Always so many questions."

My dear little witch. That scraped along her nerves like a wire brush. He'd always called her that. She'd thought it was an endearment. *Gullible twit that she was*. "Maybe not enough questions."

His face split in his white, even smile. She'd thought it attractive once. Now she saw the gloating, the smug.

The door shut behind her. Noah had padded out. Hopefully he hadn't heard Rodolphe calling her a witch.

Noah's strength and heat at her back thawed her. "I could care less about your clumsy threats. Where's my car?"

Rodolphe's gaze never left hers. To a man, Noah was the bigger danger, but not to a witch. Then again, Rodolphe didn't know she was no longer any threat to him, either.

"Your rattle-trap is around the corner. I accidentally 'broke' it. In the battle between powerful magic and technology, well, you know which side invariably wins."

She managed a toothy grin in reply. "Except for the last time we met."

His smile disappeared. "Last time was an aberration." He lashed out with, "Too bad your aunt left. I had a little surprise for her."

She clenched fists. "Bastard."

"Enough." Noah took a single step and was somehow in front of her. His stance was deadly, the wolf who protected his own. "Leave."

While she was impressed, acid for the alpha flooded her stomach. Rodolphe was a wizard. Noah's challenge was sure to be met with magic, and a shifter couldn't hope to compete.

Rodolphe straightened as if surprised. "You dare to tell me what to do?" He reached in his pocket.

Noah took one threatening step forward.

Rodolphe flinched; then he scowled. "You won't be so bold after I deflate you like a balloon."

As his hand rose from his pocket, something pink in it, Noah leaped and pinned the wizard's arms in a bear-hug. Rodolphe struggled but didn't move the powerful alpha one jot.

"Drop it." Noah's voice was all growl. "*Now.*" He goosed the word with a squeeze to the wizard that nearly cracked ribs.

"All right, all right!" Rodolphe's voice squeaked like a little girl. The pink thing fell back in his pocket.

"Sophia. Get the leash."

She hesitated leaving Noah with the other witch, but against all odds, it seemed the shifter had actually won this round. She darted inside, grabbed the new leather leash, and returned it to Noah.

Noah bound Rodolphe's hands behind him, then gave him a little push. "Now go away."

Rodolphe stumbled before catching his balance. He covered it with an irritated shrug. "I have business elsewhere anyway. I'll be seeing you soon, dear Sophia." He gave her a mocking wink and stalked off. A stumble or two spoiled his stalk.

Noah's glare followed Rodolphe until he disappeared. "Bite me. Who was that?"

Sophia sighed. "Trouble. Let's go inside. I have to call a tow truck. I can explain to you while I'm waiting." Then she'd have to call the Witches' Council and explain more thoroughly to their Enforcer.

"Mason can fix your car." Noah followed her through the door, growl still in his voice. "Sophia, who was that?"

The wolf's presence was a strange mix of comforting and dangerous. "The long story takes a while. The short story? That was the biggest ass you'll ever meet—should've been liposuctioned years ago."

"Given. But what's his name?" Almost as an afterthought Noah added the words she'd hoped he hadn't heard. "And what did he mean when he called you a witch?"

Her step faltered, heart stuttering. She didn't know why, but she got the clear picture that he didn't care for witches. Well, most shifters didn't. And it was just as well if it killed the attraction between them. But it still made her sad. "Could you phone Mason for me?" She couldn't look at him.

"Sophia—"

"Please?"

"Fine." He stalked off.

She fled to the reading area and collapsed into one of her aunt's chairs to try to pull herself together. Clasping her elbows, she gathered the tatters of her self-control. She'd thought Rodolphe was out of her life for good.

Why now? With her magic she'd have been more than a match for him. But without it she was in danger.

Worse, Noah was in danger, too.

He'd painted a big target on his back by not only challenging the witch, but beating him. Rodolphe didn't take defeat well. Next time he wouldn't stand within leaping distance of the wolf. Stars and moon, how could she stop Rodolphe then, how could she fight him without magic? Pepper spray and stern looks wouldn't stop a wizard.

She could run. Hide. Throw up. None of that would help Noah. She grasped her pearls so tight she nearly crushed them.

"Sophia, what's wrong?"

She opened her eyes to see Noah was off the phone, his silver gaze concerned. Bigger than big, stronger than strong.

But even an alpha couldn't hope to defeat a wizard in the long run. Noah had to get out now, while he could. Protect his pack, maybe by getting them to take a vacation. South, like Illinois, or Texas, or Rio de Janeiro. She'd heard Brazil was nice.

"Who is that man?"

She'd love to go with him, but once he heard the full story, he'd never want to see her again. She hitched a breath.

He sat next to her. "Tell me."

"Damn it." She briefly clenched hot eyes. "Why do you have to be so persistent?"

"It's a gift." He gently gathered her hands from her pearls. "Let's start slow. Who was that wizard?"

She blinked at him. A tear trickled down her cheek. "How do you know Rodolphe's a wizard?"

Noah touched his nose. "Your aunt smells different. The hooded creep had the same scent, only nastier." Before she could ask another question he gently thumbed the tear from her skin. "You don't. You smell like running free through a meadow on a spring day."

His deep tones gave the words a poetry. Sophia blushed. "That's sweet." But her gaze cut away. He wouldn't say such sweet things once she told him the rest.

He took both her hands. "Sophia, please. I need to know if he's a danger to my pack."

"You do." Her chest iced. She needed to come clean, but to see the warmth in his eyes wither and die... The ice melted into unshed tears. This would take fortification. "Well, I told you the long story was long, right? How about I tell it over some tea."

She didn't give him a choice, popping to her feet and leading the way to the beaded curtain.

In the kitchen, she silently busied herself filling the teakettle.

He leaned, arms folded, against the wall.

When the kettle was on the stove over a high flame she took a deep breath. "I was born a witch." She glanced at him to see how he took it.

He flinched. "A *witch?*"

That hurt, but worse was coming. "Proud of it, at one time." She paused getting the box of tea, shame pricking her nose and eyes. "I was strong, with ability across multiple elements. An, um..." She cleared her throat. "A witch princess."

"You're a *what?*" He stiffened like she'd sprouted a rash.

"Hereditary witch princess." She winced. "Although I prefer gene-recruited. But yeah. Long silk robes, power wand, sparkly tiara, the whole deal. Noah, please. I'm not a witch anymore, and this is difficult enough. Sit?"

Silver eyes narrowed like she was going to turn him into a toad, he nonetheless nodded and took a chair at the kitchen table.

She got down mugs, pressed leaves into two diffuser balls, and settled them in the mugs with dual *clinks*. She stood a moment, her hands on the mugs, gathering her courage. “Once upon a time, I embraced everything being a witch meant. Like the kid who wants to grow up to be president or prime minister, everything I did was fueled by determination to reach the top—High Minister of the Witches’ Council.”

“The Council. Sweet running prey.”

“You know about the Council?”

“Stories.” He shuddered.

“At least it’s not a crime syndicate, right?” She tried to laugh and failed. The kettle whistled. She brought the mugs to the table then went back to turn off the stove, retrieve the kettle, and bring it back to the table, its whistle dying slowly. Her hand shook pouring steaming water over the tea diffusers. “I studied hard and practiced every talent I had and by the time I reached university I was the best damned freshman witch you ever saw. But even among mages, you can’t get to the top on talent and hard work alone. You need connections.”

“You’re a damned royal witch. What more connection do you need?”

The anger in his tone rippled unhappily up her spine. Her shoulders drew in as she returned the kettle to the stove. She couldn’t look at him when she returned to the table. Grabbing the ends of the diffusers, she tried to dunk them both at once. She fumbled it, sloshing tea onto the table.

With a small *tch* he took the mugs away from her, firmly but not unkindly. As he rose to get the dishcloth to wipe up, she sat with clasped hands. Without his burning silver gaze it was easier to say what needed to be said.

“My connections would have been my parents. But they died in an airplane. A midair explosion.”

"Oh, Sophia." He returned to her, tossed the cloth, and took her clasped hands. "I'm so sorry."

Her fingers relaxed under his. "I had my brother to help me through it. And Aunt Linda."

"How old were you?"

"I was eighteen. My brother was twenty. The crash spurred Gabriel's need to make tech work with magic."

"You don't have to tell me the rest." Noah gave her fingers a squeeze then released her hands to retrieve a jar of honey. He dosed her mug with a couple generous dollops of gold.

"I really do. I don't want to, but I need to." She met his gaze.

He searched her eyes. Compassion touched his face. "Then let's talk somewhere you'll be more comfortable." He lifted both mugs and took them into the store, where he sat on a couch.

Following, she sat beside him. He handed her her mug, barely cool enough to hold, but the heat—and the sympathy in his eyes—strengthened her to go on. "I enrolled in the Council's page program, hoping for a recommendation. At first I was a general gofer, fetching coffee and mail. I moved up to data entry on the Persons of Magic census, not popular but high-profile."

She paused to sip, fingers wrapped around the hot mug. "I caught the eye of a very powerful water wizard named Rodolphe."

A low growl emanated from Noah's chest.

"On the surface, he was everything I wanted to be. Successful. A sharp dresser. A sharp mind, or at least he had answers for everything. A sharp smile. Everything about him was sharp, which should have been a big red warning. But I was nineteen years old and thought I knew every-damned-thing." She blinked. A thread of wet heat ran down her cheek. "I knew just enough to hurt myself."

Noah put an arm around her shoulders in silent support.

Something deep inside her eased at that. "The Council's upper house is hereditary, but mages in the lower house rely on training, raw power, and connections. They work hard to get where they are, the best of the best. I was excited to come to Representative Rodolphe's notice." She shook her head. Such an idealistic idiot.

"You were nineteen and had no one to tell you better."

"You're being kind. Gabriel didn't blunder like that. You wouldn't have either."

"I've made my own mistakes." His flat, pained tone told her he had his own bitter history.

"I'm sorry." She set a hand on his, to comfort him, but the simple touch eased her knotted shoulders too.

Their eyes connected briefly. The bright silver of his was more than she could bear. Her hand flew to her pearls and she looked away.

A beat. Then he prompted, "Rodolphe?"

"He said he'd known my parents. 'My dear little witch,' he said. 'They'd want me to shepherd your career.' That sold me. I was thrilled when he made me his assistant. But while he pretended to reinforce my training, he subtly skewed it. At first it was simply, 'We work hard, so we make the hard decisions.' I was all about hard work, so I lapped that up. Then he shifted to 'People need us to make the hard decisions.' Then, 'People *expect* us to make the hard decisions. It's our duty.'" She grabbed her pearls harder. "And then, 'We make the decisions. It's our *right*.'"

"Sophia, you were young."

"Not so young by then." She fisted her pearls so tight she bruised bones. "I haven't even told Gabriel the full story. I was twenty-two, under Rodolphe's influence for three years, when he came to me with a 'special project'. 'Terrorists,' he said, 'are planning a heinous attack on the mundane capital.'"

"Damn my paws."

"Yes." She laughed with no humor. "Blindly idealistic, I didn't ask questions, or at least, not the right ones. I didn't ask what kind of attack or where his information came from or even ask for proof. All I said was, 'Yes sir. What can I do?'"

He set aside his mug and hers and enfolded her in his arms. Trembling, she went on.

"Rodolphe said the terrorists were storing cash and account information in a mundane safe. 'We can cut off their funding, stop the attack before it ever gets started, if we rob that safe.'

"At that point I did show a little brains. 'What about the mundane police?' I said. 'Can't we tell them and let them handle it?'

"He said, 'No, my dear little witch.' He always called me that, my dear little witch. I thought it meant that he cared about me—I thought it was sweet. I never noticed he only used it when he didn't want me asking questions."

Noah growled, "I'll kill him."

She pulled from his arms, her eyes flying to his. He'd defend her, even now? "Thank you, but you may change your mind after you hear the rest. I remember that day so clearly. Rodolphe took my face in his hands. It was so *sweet*, and I thought he was going to...that he was...well. When I was most vulnerable, he hit me with 'Sophia.

People expect us to make the hard decisions. We *need* to do this.'

"And because I trusted him, because I believed in magic and my heritage, I said meekly, 'All right.'"

Noah pulled her back into his arms. His warmth ate the shivers away.

Eventually she squeezed out a tear and straightened away from him, wiping a thumb under her eyes. "There's not much left. Rodolphe said, 'My dear little witch, you have the most important job of all. I am giving you your first mission. You must break into the terrorists' bank and capture those funds.'

"A mission. It sounded so special. I was scared and proud. I thought he'd given me this mission because he respected my power, my training—my excellence." She twisted her hands in her lap. "Of course, it was really because the safe had complex electronics, and my brother Gabriel had spelled my wand against tech misfires. Rodolphe knew that—I'd boasted of it, gullible little twit that I was. So I used my technology-proof magic to get into the bank, open the safe, and retrieve sixty thousand dollars in cash and account information for another two hundred thousand. A quarter of a million dollars. I gave it to Rodolphe and thought I was a hero." She twisted her fingers so hard they were white, but she didn't feel the pain, overpowered by the sword's edge of memory.

Noah took her hands and gently untwisted her fingers. So gentle.

She gazed into his face, willing him to look at her, to really *see* her. To know the worst.

His silver eyes held no condemnation, only deep sympathy.

Hers were brimming and her throat thick as she said, "The money wasn't for a terrorist attack. It was fundraising for a little girl's kidney transplant. I'd stolen the money that was supposed to save a child's life."

"God." The silver mirrored.

"You can't hate me worse than I hate myself." Her only comfort.

"I don't hate you."

She swallowed hard. And again. Only after a third dry swallow could she go on. "When I found out, I was horrified. I flew to Rodolphe's office for an explanation—dope that I was, I was sure he had one, sure that it was all a horrible mistake—but he'd gone. It took me a while to realize that he'd fled. That he'd lied to me and had known what the money was for all along.

"I told the Council's Enforcers everything. They set a tracer spell on him, pinged him in the next city over. Ready to come back. The jerk honestly thought I'd take the fall for him.

"The moment the tracer hit him, he threw up a blinding spell and ran, hopping onto an ocean ship before the Enforcers could catch him. They continued to try magical means to locate him, but he'd been on the enforcement committee. He knew their methods and countered every one.

"The possibility of catching him became slimmer and slimmer. So before it was too late for the child, I leaked the information to the mundane police."

Noah sat straighter. "You told the cops about magic?"

"No, of course not." She dashed the back of her hand against her wet cheeks. "Only that Rodolphe had raided the girl's fund and fled. It was enough. The mundanes tracked him to Europe and recovered the money. A combination of fingerprints, passport tracking, and database searches saved that child."

"Thank goodness." Noah released her and sat straight. "I understand why you hid this from me. But as a witch, I'm begging you. Remove the hex. Help me to defend yo...my pack." His eyes blazed with fierce protectiveness and practicality, better than condemnation, but perhaps that would come later.

"Noah, I want to, but..." She raised her gaze to him. He shimmered in her view. "I told you the whole sorry story so you'd understand exactly why I *can't* help. I hurt that poor girl when I meant to help and...I couldn't go through that again. So I...I..." She couldn't say the words. Settled for, "I'm no longer a witch."

"That's not possible. Magic is born in."

"How did you know that?"

"Reason," he said quickly. "My shifting ability was born in, so I figured yours was too. Isn't it?"

"It was. But when the horror of what I'd done crashed down on me, I took...steps." She looked away. "My powers and my heritage, the things that had once made me so proud, now stood for stupidity. Gullibility. Guilt. I was shocked how deeply and unthinkingly I'd embraced Rodolphe's message, how blindly I'd followed him, just because he was 'one of us'." She paused. "I sometimes wonder...would I have made the short, fatal step to assuming that superior ability meant a superior right?"

"No. Sophia, you care too much. You empathize."

"You have no proof."

"Oh, but I do. It's all in how a person treats small animals. You honored and respected King. You're nothing like Rodolphe, and you never will be."

Her eyes found his, reading the deep surety in his face. Her heart made a lump in her throat. She swallowed, managed a hoarse, "Thanks." A simple word for profound gratitude. Even though she'd admitted the worst, he still defended her. He was a natural protector to the end.

She backhanded her wet, swollen eyes. "I didn't want to risk it. So I locked away my magic. A Head-Hands-Heart ritual." She glossed over what she'd had to do to seal the locks.

"Noah, I smell mundane because I am."

Chapter Eleven

Noah reeled. First because Sophia was a witch, the thing he hated and feared most. But then because somehow her magic—magic that was born into her—was gone, and she wasn't a witch anymore.

Yet of all the shit going down, the most important takeaway was that, unless he found some way to reverse his hex, he couldn't protect her from Rodolphe.

And his pack, although somehow that had become an afterthought to her safety.

She stood to take out her phone. "I'd better get this over with."

"I already called Mason."

"Not Mason. The Witches' Council. They'll send an Enforcer to deal with Rodolphe."

"You can't." He put a hand on her wrist, stopping her. If an Enforcer came, Sophia would leave. How could he protect her from Rodolphe if she left? "What if the Enforcer finds out I'm hexed? It'll just muddle things worse."

"No, they won't blame that on you. If anything, he'll go after Aunt Linda."

"Won't there be a penalty for that?"

"Well...yes." She nibbled the lush pillow of her lower lip in thought. Noah wanted to be her teeth. "If Auntie had hexed a mundane, the Council would slap her with a thousand-dollar fine and sixty days in lock up. For hexing a were, that'll go up to five thousand and six months. But the hexing was unintentional. A good arcane lawyer can probably argue it down to just the fine."

"And if she can't?"

"Doesn't matter. Stopping Rodolphe trumps a fine and jail time. Beside, Auntie's been in jail before, protesting during the sixties." She took out her phone.

"But why muddy the waters at all?" he said desperately. "You studied magic, right? Maybe you can find an amulet or premixed spell to lift my hex before the Enforcer even gets here."

She gave him a penetrating stare. "How do you know about premixed spells?"

He opened his mouth, shut it again. He wanted—no more, he *needed* to be honest with her. But explaining would involve secrets he'd kept for decades. He gave up one precious truth. "My mother worked for a wizard when I was a pup. I learned it there."

Strangely, revealing that to her felt...right.

"Oh." Her stare eased and she put away the phone, easing the knot between his shoulders. "I can try." She stared at him, tapping her chin. "I need to know what kind of hex she put on you. Since I can't *reveal* it..." She waved vaguely, but he'd already known "reveal" was a spell. "You'll have to tell me what happened. Better yet, *show* me."

She strode to the middle of the store. "Show me everything. Where you stood, where Aunt Linda stood.

What gestures she made. What she said." As Sophia became absorbed in the problem, her confidence and expertise shone through. Admiration rose in him. She must have been one hell of a witch.

He came to his feet and followed her, soundlessly from habit. Her movement had stirred the air, filling it with her delicate scent. Nearing her, he instinctively reached out, a man's desire to touch and a wolf's need to possess. He pulled back at the last instant. "Everything?"

She jumped at his voice. "How did you get there?" Almost immediately she shook her head. "Wolf, yeah. Never mind. Yes, as clearly as you can recall."

He showed her, including Linda's little weaving gestures.

"That's really good." She stared again, her gaze as penetrating as a truth awl. "Almost a perfect bur hex. If you had magic, you could have really cast that."

His face heated. "Good memory?" Her gaze sharpened even more. He smiled innocently.

Her gaze dived to his mouth. She must have liked what she saw because her irises dilated, her nostrils flaring slightly. Her lips parted. She licked them, her sweet pink tongue caressing glossy lips. His wolf approved.

And somehow he was kissing her again.

He crushed her to him, her small body soft and warm, her mouth tasting as bright and crisp as crushed mint leaves, her scent flowering like jasmine...so female. So...his.

His?

He pulled away and saw his hands entwined in her hair, the glossy dark ribbons around his fingers. His wolf had done that.

She opened her remarkable eyes. Stars stirred in their depths, and his mouth throbbed to take her again... "You've got to stop doing that." Her voice was husky, like honeyed whiskey.

You started it with your lip licking warred with *I can't stop* and *I want to kiss you forever.* None of those were acceptable responses, so he forced himself to untwine and step back. "Did that tell you anything?" His face heated. "About the spell, I mean."

She cleared her throat. "Yes and no. What you did was a bur hex—but a simple bur only makes you break out in hives or lose your hair, not mess with your intrinsic shifter magic." She bit her lip, teeth so white against the plump, rosy skin.

He took an unguarded step toward her, needing to put his mouth on her, but stopped himself in time.

Still, she caught him staring and must've seen his hunger because she blushed. "Something just occurred to me. I was looking for Auntie with my third eye...well, you don't need the details. But did the spell hit objects? Bounce?"

So he had to explain about the mirror and the picture. As he spoke she pursed her luscious lips in thought and it was all he could do not to take them up on their ripe invitation.

When he finished, she nodded. "The mirror or picture must have changed the hex. Let's check out the picture first." She walked toward the cabinet in the back of the store.

He watched her move, savoring her efficient grace. "You were really good, weren't you? Princess aside, you worked at your magic."

She stopped at the pictures, her back still to him, but her rolled spine said she was embarrassed. “Yes.”

“Why? You wouldn’t need it for politics.”

She glanced at him, her cheek flushed a rosy pink. Damn, every time he saw that, he wanted to lick her rosy skin...*everywhere* she was rosy.

She cleared her throat and took out a daguerreotype. “After I retired from the Council, I was going to go into research. This picture?”

“No. The photograph of you.” He glided to her side. “My lieutenant Mason’s into research too.”

“Your beta?” She put back the daguerreotype. Lifted out her own photo and frowned at it.

Noah snorted. “Beta implies second. Mason could lead the pack as well as me, maybe better. He doesn’t want to. But he’s definitely not second class.”

“I didn’t mean any slur by it.” She coughed. “I know wild wolf packs are more like a family. That the fighting and hierarchy are a wolves-in-captivity thing.”

He considered her. She really was remarkable, both a good brain and a good heart. “Wild is wild and civilization is civilization. Even a city as small as Matinsfield qualifies as a wolves-in-captivity thing.”

“I’m sorry.” She paused, and he could see her curiosity warring with her innate sensitivity and tact. “You don’t have to answer this, but you mentioned more wolves like Killer. Is it worse than that? Do you have a lot of fighting to quash, as alpha?”

“Being new makes it worse. The pack is still testing me. Sure, it’s mostly at the instigation of the old alpha’s lieutenants, but once tempers flare I have to stop it, and it doesn’t matter who started it...” Damn, he was babbling. What about her made him yap like an excited pup?

She reached to give his hand a brief squeeze—the kind that made his hand happy and his cock jealous. She said, "The hex must make it doubly hard."

Oh yes, that was what. Her obvious interest in him. The true interest a friend would show.

Or a mate.

He clamped down on that. Him and a witch? Never, not ever.

But he *wanted* her. He met her starry eyes, fringed with those long lashes, her gaze filled with sympathy. He wanted to dive in and drown... He shifted to watch her talk, her glossy pink lips shaping words that made him swell with the desire to kiss her again. Kisses wouldn't hurt, would they? Maybe a little meaningless hot sex...?

His whole body flushed, fever rising, pulse racing. Meaningless? Sex would never be meaningless with Sophia.

She stepped back, her eyes wide and her fingers rolling her pearls. She'd set down the frame. "There's nothing special about the picture. Let's check the mirror." She hurried past him, headed for the draped oval. Her face was ruddy.

He clenched his teeth. Idiot. Every stupid lustful thought must have shown clearly on his face.

Bigger idiot. Sophia was checking out, alone, the mirror that had warped a simple hex into something dangerous.

He rushed after her.

Only to be stopped by a loud *hiss*. Noah's hackles sprang high.

A big orange lump sat in front of the mirror, emerald eyes narrowed at them both.

The cat hadn't been there a moment before. Noah would have smelled him. Bloody claws, he would have felt all that attitude miles away.

Sophia bent to pat the cat, then straightened and raised a hand to remove the sheet from the mirror.

The cat jumped to its feet and hissed again.

She paused, hand still out. "What's wrong, Mr. Kibbles?"

"You talk to cats?" Noah worked hard to keep the growl out of his voice and was mostly successful.

"Talk to them, and pay attention to them, if they're as smart as Mr. Kibbles." She lowered her hand and focused on the cat, who again sat primly beneath the mirror and started washing his foreleg. "I shouldn't touch the mirror? I need to look at it, though. It's important."

Noah glided to her side. "I wouldn't trust the word of a cat." When Mr. Kibbles paused washing to narrow his eyes, Noah added, "Not just you. I wouldn't trust any cat."

"He's not a cat," Sophia said.

Noah grimaced. "Looks like a cat. Smells like a cat. Snippy like a cat." As King, he'd had words with Mr. Fat Kibbles.

"Mr. Kibbles is Auntie's familiar."

"How's that different from cat?"

"Familiars are carriers of arcane knowledge. When they warn, you listen."

Noah crossed his arms. "Yeah, well, if he's so smart, why is he still a cat?"

"He doesn't have to be. They're born as their animal, but later they can become human, or any intermediary form between."

He stared open-mouthed at her. "You're not saying he's a *shifter*?" He was vaguely offended. He had nothing in common with a snippy *cat*.

"Not exactly. Familiars can only change shape after name-bonding."

"Name-bonding?" Ice chilled Noah's blood. "What's that?"

"When the witch gives the familiar its true name. It shows that the witch understands the honor of being in partnership with such a wise being."

"I see." Something about that disturbed him deeply. "What if name-bonding doesn't happen?"

"Well, the familiar is locked in animal form until named. If the witch comes into her full power without naming the familiar...? It's only happened a handful of times." She paused, looking unhappy.

Cold fingers of dread kneaded his stomach. "What?"

"The familiar's brain tries to expand to adult size. But locked in its smaller animal cranium...well." She cleared her throat. "Within a few days the familiar goes insane, then dies."

The dread dug into his chest and exploded into horror. If that happened to his beloved—

Noah straightened suddenly, hurling away his half-formed idea before it could become whole. He was a *wolf*. Wolves didn't have familiars.

"What's wrong?" Sophia's star-shot eyes filled with concern.

"Nothing." Immediate distraction was in order. "Do you have a familiar? Let me guess, it's a cat. Where is he?"

Her mouth curled crookedly. "*She* stomped off in a huff when I gave up magic. I think she's sulking somewhere in the Bahamas."

"If you're bonded, how can she leave?"

"Bonding doesn't mean slave. Kat is independently wealthy—she made some shrewd investments early on. They're *wise*, Noah. When a familiar takes the time to communicate, it pays to listen." Sophia eyed the mirror then the fat orange fur ball. "But in this case, Mr. Kibbles, we need to know how the mirror affected Auntie's hex. It's for the sake of Noah's pack." She reached for the sheet.

A dark shiver of foreboding rolled over Noah, an earthquake of premonition.

He'd only felt it once before—the day magic had destroyed his life.

Instinct grabbed him. He stepped in to seize Sophia's wrist, stopping her from uncovering the mirror.

Their bodies met.

Her eyes flew up, darkening. She pressed her lips together, drawing his gaze. She had the prettiest pink lips.

While he was distracted, the sheet slithered from the mirror.

Light struck it, a bright flare. Power hit him at the same time with an almost physical impact. Sophia flinched.

"Damn it." He grabbed her in both arms and spun, as if he could shield her from a magical attack. The mirror glowed faintly in his periphery. "First, your aunt hexing me, now this." This was what he got for being attracted to a witch. He released her to snag the sheet and toss it back over the mirror. "Damn witches."

She drew herself straight. "Did you want me to help you or not? Because you're sure not acting like it."

He stilled immediately. Closed his eyes. Breathed deep. "I'm sorry. That wizard my mother worked for...something happened because of the magic. Something bad." He opened his eyes. "I want your help, Sophia. I need it. *But*."

His gaze cut to the mirror and he scowled. "I don't want you near that thing."

"That's not logical."

He turned his scowl on her. "I don't care about being logical. I care about you being safe. I don't want you near the mirror, and I especially don't want you anywhere near that Rodolphe, with him so obviously hungry for revenge."

"*Hungry?*" She clasped her pearls and frowned. Then her eyes flew to his, her pupils constricted to pinpricks.

* * *

Sophia stared at Noah. He was right. Rodolphe didn't just want revenge, he was hungry for it. *Hungry,* like the Hungry Ghost.

Her chest hollowed out. Stars and moon, if Rodolphe was the Hungry Ghost, not only she and Noah were in danger from him. If the Ghost found the pieces of the Key, the world as they knew it would end.

This was no time to worry about saving her aunt some money and inconvenience. She had to call the Council.

She pulled out her phone and began thumbing through her contacts.

"Sophia, don't." Noah looked more desperate than a five-thousand-dollar fine and six months in lock up would merit.

She'd have to worry about that later. "Rodolphe is more dangerous than I knew. We need serious help. We need a Council Enforcer."

"Even with your aunt facing a fine and jail time?"

"She brought it on herself."

"Marlowe brought it on. My pack member, my responsibility."

"I'm sorry. You may get fined too. But lives are at stake. More." She found the entry and pushed connect call.

"But Sophia..." Anguish showed in his silver eyes. "What if a mundane witnessed the hexing?"

Sophia frowned at him, the phone ringing in her hand. "What do you mean?"

"A lady walked in at dawn. *At dawn,* Sophia."

The implications hit her just as the call connected. "Council general office. How may I direct your call?"

Sophia's head reeled. A woman—a customer—had come in at dawn, *just as the hex would have taken effect.* Had she seen Noah transform? Sophia palmed her forehead. Well of course she had. There was that extreme surprise that had bled onto the etheric. And if the woman was shocked by a transformation, that meant she wasn't a witch.

A mundane. Auntie, unintentionally or not, had revealed real magic to a mundane.

"Hello? Is anyone there?"

Any witch or wizard who, by action or inaction, doth betray the existence of true magic, shall suffer capital punishment.

The Council was not known to be lenient on that. They'd hang anybody and everybody. Literally. Because if mundanes found out about magic, it would cease to exist.

Magic was about *possibilities*. Like poor Schroedinger's cat, sitting inside that box, both alive and not—until some chump opened the box and looked inside. The act of looking collapsed the magical possibilities into one mundane reality.

Nutshell version—magic only worked if the box stayed shut.

It was why all three magical types were so secretive about it. Shifters were beings of magic. They couldn't manipulate it, but they'd cease shifting if it disappeared. Familiars were conduits of magical wisdom but couldn't manipulate it either. They'd be locked as their animals if magic ceased to be.

Only witches could "touch" magic. They had an inborn ability to feel magic and shape it without opening the box. Nobody knew why. A gene, an environmental factor, neural fields, witches as elevated beings, take your pick.

Sophia thought witches were just crazy enough to believe in all possibilities.

"Hello? Who's there, please?"

Aunt Linda, while not known for having her head firmly on her shoulders, still had a head. Sophia couldn't say that if the Council got wind of this.

"Sorry." Sophia clapped the phone to her ear. "Sorry, I misdialed. Tech misfire, you know how it is." She quickly ended the call.

Okay, her aunt was safe, at least for now. But Sophia knew that meant it was her against Rodolphe—alone.

No, Noah would try to help. But the next time, the wizard wouldn't be caught off-guard. Which meant Noah was in danger, unless she could protect him. Her breath froze.

Of all the terrors facing her, Auntie's danger, Rodolphe's return, the possibility of Rodolphe being the Hungry Ghost, Noah being in danger beat them all.

How could she protect Noah? More, how could she protect him without magic?

* * *

The morning Sophia's aunt went missing, a dozen hours before Sophia entered Linda's bookstore, a raven spread his wings and caught an updraft, soaring into the dazzling first-morning light.

This was the day.

Three nights ago, Raven's master had finally revealed himself. After two and a half decades waiting, Raven rejoiced at the surge of magic of his witch. He'd flown two straight days, chafing each night as he was forced to rest. But he knew he wasn't far now. Today was the day.

Today, he'd find his master.

Today, the young wizard would bestow Raven with his true name, the name he should have had decades ago—if not for the dark time.

Four-year-old Raven was hunting when he was captured. Hooded. Taken somewhere cold and dank. Something horrible was done to him that perverted his bond and loyalty to his master.

Released and returned home, Raven wanted to scream, heartsick at what had happened. But he was locked in his animal form. He'd tried to caw the problem, but his master, also four, was too young to understand.

A week later the dark witches came. A cyclone of magic rose up between Raven and his master. Raven clawed to get to the boy. But the need was more than loyalty, a dark urgency that made Raven scrabble. Dangerous, tainted... He'd have resisted, but he felt the boy's fear through the furious fighting. He flew toward his master with everything he had, everything he was.

Hard magic pushed him away. Royal magic. Even using all the secrets he knew, it wasn't enough to combat that mature power.

And then bitter magic came to Raven's aid. By then he was panicked enough that he didn't question the odd taste, just used it to beat through the hard magic.

The royal magic blasted him out of the air. There was only darkness.

Raven came awake on the roof of the house. His master was gone. Raven took wing, searching, but not even a taste of his master's magic remained.

Nulled? Or *dead*?

No, if his master were dead, Raven would be as well.

So he waited. Magic kept him from aging as a natural raven would. He tried to use the time productively, growing in strength and wisdom, but until his master named him, he'd be a bird, without hands.

It was hard to read a book or do an Internet search lacking a simple opposable thumb.

And then, in his twenty-ninth year, *finally*, he felt the wizard's power flare. Raven took off instantly.

There was a strange aftertaste to the flare, a physical, almost beastly violence. But the magic was strong, the strength of a prince. Almost...stronger. How strange. Nothing was stronger than a full-blooded wizard prince.

Now, today, Raven would finally have hands. Finally, he'd have a name. The optimism ate through the dark chill on his neck.

As the sun cleared the horizon, his master's power—cut.

Raven fluttered midair. He cawed and flew in a circle, trying to sense the power, to find that huge well that had drawn him across the continent...but nothing.

This was impossible. A parent might mask a child's magical signature, but once the magic was tapped, the mask burned clear. The freed magic was like a direct line from mage to familiar. Not even death cut it off so entirely, so abruptly.

It was as if his master was no longer a wizard.

The raven's head cocked. No longer a wizard...or perhaps no longer human.

Chapter Twelve

"What are you doing?" Noah couldn't seem to help himself from following Sophia as she flitted around the store, gathering packets of this, snips of that.

"I don't know if Rodolphe will be back—he's a coward. But either he'll return or he'll send someone to do his dirty work, and you're vulnerable. The hex makes it worse. I can't solve Rodolphe, but I *can* try preparing a potion to neutralize the hex."

"Good. That's good. But it's just a hex, right? Can't you use something, I don't know, prepackaged?"

She stopped to stare at him. "You picked up quite a bit at your mother's employer. Yes, most hexes clear up with a generic unhex. Auntie sells 'em in bulk, ten for ten bucks." Her gaze flashed to the side. "Oh, *there's* her fennel." She grabbed a handful of seeds, counted five into her other palm and dumped the rest of them back.

"But...?" he prompted.

"Hmm?" Her star-shot blue eyes focused slowly on him. "Oh. But Auntie never did her spells by the book. She'll have added her own twists. I'm using a simple unhex as the base, but I need to, well, spice it up at bit."

She muttered to herself as she worked. He caught "triangulation" and "original spell interacting with secondary boosters" as she studied picture and covered mirror from different angles. Then she was off searching again.

While she put together the potion, Noah tapped fingers on a glass-topped case and worried. What if Rodolphe came back before she freed him from the hex? How could he protect her? Worse, what happened *after* she freed him? Would the urge to kiss her and stroke her pretty...everything...disappear?

Or, potentially worse, would he find out this insanely strong attraction was real?

He wasn't used to feeling unsettled and didn't like it. "I'm going outside."

"Fresh air?" She was nose deep in some spellbook. The elegant sweep of her nose distracted him for a moment.

"Sure." Really it was to walk the perimeter, to make sure Rodolphe or Killer or someone even worse wasn't out there, ready to pounce.

And maybe get a little privacy for a phone call. To talk this out.

He must be *really* unsettled if he was thinking of that.

Outside, he prowled around the bookstore three times, seeing and scenting nothing. The fourth time he pulled out his phone to call the one person who might understand his problem. Mason's cousin Zoe.

Noah and Mason's mothers were sisters. Zoe was Mason's cousin on his father's side. Zoe was the reason Mason had curtailed his wandering a few years ago to join the then-Scauth pack. Zoe's mother was sick. To make ends meet, Zoe had gotten a job in Milwaukee, but the money she sent wasn't getting to her ailing mother, thanks to Scauth and his bullies. Mason stopped that, but when he saw Zoe and her mother weren't the only wolves suffering, he'd called in Noah.

Zoe, unknown to everyone but her alpha, was now Zoe Light and mated to a wizard.

"Noah? What is it?" Zoe answered out of breath, as if she'd been running or doing gymnastics or making lov...

He clamped mental blinders on. "I have a problem."

"Scauth's lapdogs harassing you? You just have to say the word, and Daniel and I will be there."

"Not yet. Your boyfriend's why I'm calling."

"Boyfriend?" She snorted. "Boy implies little. If only you knew how far off that is." Springs creaked, like bodies shifting in a bed.

Noah squeezed his eyes briefly in pain. "Look, your—whatever—is a wizard, right? I'm calling about a witch."

That shut Zoe up.

"She isn't able to do magic, and another wizard threatened her. Is she vulnerable?"

Zoe conversed with her non-boy-toy in a low tone. Then she came back on the line. "Hell yeah, she's vulnerable. Who is this ex-witch, Noah? How did you meet?"

"It's not important." His jaw clenched against a growl. *Sophia was vulnerable*. He'd have to stick close to her to defend her. And if dawn came and they still hadn't removed the hex...well, as the bite-sized doglet, it wouldn't be as easy, but what he didn't have in size he'd have to make up for in heart.

"Noah, it might be the most important thing there is. I need to know. What, Daniel?" In the background, a deep voice murmured something about *taboo* and *prophecy*.

Taboo reminded Noah that the Witches' Council had some insane prohibition against witch-shifter sex. He shrugged. Most wolves ignored the Council as much as possible. But he wondered about the prophecy.

Zoe came back on the line. “Are you attracted to her?”

“Of course not.” Not counting his inexplicable need to touch her, kiss her, *fuck her*, every time she was near. Or every time he smelled her, or every time he thought of her, or even heard her name...bloody claws and fangs. *Attracted* didn’t even begin to describe how he felt about her.

“Then why are you asking?”

He said the first thing that sprang to mind. “Duty. My duty, to the pack. I have to get rid of a damned hex to keep the pack safe. The ex-witch can help me.” That was why. No other reason.

“You’re lying,” Zoe said dryly.

He knew that. “Maybe.”

Who wouldn’t be attracted to Sophia, with her beautiful eyes and fine face and soft body made for his hands...and her *loyalty*. Yes, he admired her traveling hundreds of miles to come to the rescue of her befuddled aunt. It wasn’t all about body parts. He admired Sophia’s caring for the dog King, trying to protect him before she knew his secret. Chafed at it, but admired it.

“Noah, listen. Sex with a witch is a problem.”

“I know the stories, power-mad duals, yada-yada. I think the vaunted Council simply can’t stand a bit of fur in the blood. Besides, she’s an *ex*-witch.”

“The Council won’t care about nuances. What now, Daniel?” The phone muffled and he could barely hear her say, “Prophecy’s her problem, not his.” She came back on the line. “Noah, please. The Council is deadly serious about inter-magical sex. Why do you think Daniel and I move every few weeks? Get out of there now, before anything happens between you two. It's best for you both."

"She's in danger. I can't leave. I'll just say no to sex." So she smelled wonderful and looked like his wettest dream. Didn't mean he had to act on his desires. He could keep her safe without bedding her, couldn't he?

Couldn't he?

Sure he could.

Zoe sighed. "Okay." The sigh meant it wasn't okay, but she wasn't going to scold him about it anymore. In the background was more deep murmuring. "Daniel says if you want, we can try to help with the hex you need removed. We can be there in a couple days. Less if we fly." Her voice tightened. "Planes are iffy with wizards, but Daniel has some tech from his cousin that betters our odds."

"I'd love your help, but I don't want you to have to drive all the way here. And I especially don't want you risking your life."

Again Zoe covered the phone and in the background he heard Zoe and Daniel talk. He was arguing about a prophecy, and she about a witch and wolf who needed to work things out on their own.

Noah's mind was chewing on protecting Sophia. He just had to set his goal, protect her without jumping her. He was nothing if not good at setting a goal and going for it, straight on and full steam ahead.

Steamy, full breasts...

He growled at himself.

"What the hell was that?" Zoe said. "Noah, are you in danger?"

In danger? "No." Yes. More than he'd admit. Keep Sophia safe *without* bedding her? Welcome to hell, and oh yeah, here's a boulder for you to push up the "down" escalator. "Look, while she's in town I'm just going to bodyguard her." *Body*guard. Now there was a word that conjured up all sorts of images, naked, steamy images...

Damn it, he was so fucked.

* * *

Sophia's eyes were on the potion she was making. But her ears were on Noah. He'd slammed back into the bookstore and immediately swung into pacing. For a heretofore silent beast, he was making all sorts of noises. Snorts of disgust. Huffs of displeasure.

Guttural grunts that made her think of sweaty bodies and tangled sheets.

She glanced at him, prowling the curios for the third or fourth time. When he moved, it was like his wolf, all muscle and limber strength. Oh, to have that power caught between her thighs.

She discreetly smacked herself on the forehead. Job to do here, with dawn creeping ever nearer. Unhex Noah then figure out how to fight the Hungry Ghost without magic...she started hyperventilating. No, no, she wasn't certain Rodolphe was the Ghost. No reason to panic. She refocused on Auntie's red leather spell book. Her purple scrawl in the margins helped Sophia think like Linda. *Cloves for forked spells,* she read. *Two to break, three to heal.* She found a bottle and poured out a handful to count three.

"Is it done yet?" Noah snarled right in her ear.

Her whole body jerked. The cloves flew into the air like a mini-explosion. Clattered to the work countertop.

She spun. He filled the space before her, to the point that she had to brace herself on the counter. "It'll be done when it's done."

"I can't protect anybody with this hex. Make it done faster."

"Yes, sir." Her sarcastic salute lost something when her voice and hand trembled. One thing she could say about him, the wolf had presence.

She picked up the cloves and he went back to his long-limbed stalking, poking and growling among the artifacts. Either he was getting anxious about the approaching sunrise or the modified bur was really starting to dig under his skin, or...well, this was how her boyfriends acted when they needed to get laid.

But that was the one thing a big ol' alpha wolf didn't have trouble with, wasn't it?

She dropped three cloves into the beaker and put the rest back into their bottle.

Unless he felt forced to stick with her until she freed him of the hex. Stuck, he couldn't find relief. That would explain his searing hot kisses and her amazing orgasms. All that rampant sexuality with only one convenient outlet—her.

Her jaw tightened so hard she crunched teeth. He'd kissed her because she was the nearest set of lips? And she'd stupidly responded, and the rest had followed. Maybe not, but she hadn't gotten laid recently either, and irritation spiraled up inside her like a drill. She snapped, "Will you stop that growling?"

He spun, going glass-lake still, absolutely focused on her. She swallowed hard, caught between feeling special and feeling like prey. Just as her knees were about to give, he stalked closer. "Is it ready now?"

Burn my comets. "Let me check." She turned back to the beaker on the counter, stirring the liquid until it shimmered a soft pink. "Yeah, as ready as it's going to be. As long as the hex wasn't too skewed by the mirror, this should work."

"Don't forget the picture," he rasped, moving aggressively into her space.

She whirled and pressed back. Her hips hit glass counter. She swallowed again. "The picture isn't magic."

"No? Then why do I need to do this every time I'm near you?" He grabbed her and kissed her.

She gasped. The amount of tongue on impact...and teeth...stars and comets, it was hot. She grabbed his hair in return. Maybe this searing heat between them was just convenience on his part, just restlessness on her part—but it felt like more, a *lot* more, full of deep, heartfelt need.

She kissed him back, thrusting her tongue so hard she practically torqued it down his throat.

He grabbed her hips and lifted her onto the counter, shoving Auntie's big spellbook to the floor. It hit with a thump that shook.

She twisted to reach down for it.

His mouth landed on her neck, on the sweet spot under her ear. Suddenly she could care less about paper and print over the meeting of hot flesh.

She arched into him. He stripped her of her suit coat, tossed it onto the counter and returned to tasting that sweet spot. His palms glided up her flanks, found her breasts, cupped and squeezed. She seized his broad shoulders, solid anchors in the storm of need.

"I don't know," she gasped. "Why?"

"Why what?" His breath billowed against the delicate skin of her neck.

Tantalizing nips and kisses along her sensitive neck made her fears slip out. “Why *do* you need to kiss me? Because I’m convenient? Handy?”

He lifted his head, silver eyes wide. “*Handy*?” He snarled it. “Is this handy?” One hand flattened on her breastbone and pressed her back.

Her shoulders hit glass, her head hit air.

“Is this *handy*?” His mouth found her nipple, wet the cloth, and suckled her through bra and blouse.

She arched with a gasp. Oh yeah, he was a shifter all right, going straight from attraction to action.

“No. This is not *handy*. This is need so deep it slices my guts into ribbons.” He bit her nipple, lightly, but the zing of desire shot sweet urgency into her flesh.

She raised her head, neck muscles protesting. His crown filled her sight, black locks begging for her touch. She feathered her fingers over pure silk.

He suckled through cloth, plucking the other nipple erect. She moaned. Desire heated her veins, her muscles, made her soft and yielding. Her neck gave out and her head fell back and she just enjoyed.

He unbuttoned her blouse, still suckling—lithe, strong and dexterous on top of it. Lifting her bra he applied that hot dexterity directly to her puckered nipple with his steamy mouth and rasping fingers.

She shot straight up. *Ye gods*. She writhed as his mouth tortured her, tongue and teeth and rough caressing fingers. She nearly shrieked when he settled down to some really good sucking.

And she wanted *more*. She speared fingers through his thick hair, speaking her need through them. Pulling him closer. Pressing him downward.

He chuckled. “I’ll get there soon enough.”

She slit her eyes and found her hands pushing him toward her belly, toward where his mouth could really do some good.

Temporary insanity? Too many balance sheets and not enough bedsheets? Or because no other man could bring her to a fever pitch, satisfy her like he could?

He started moving down, kissing the sensitive flesh on the underside of her breast. She sighed and released her head to hang. His tongue tickled the fine hairs on her solar plexus. Her breath hissed out. Potions and hexes and even worry about Auntie temporarily disappeared, licked away by the fire of that tongue.

Down, down he went, her belly boiling with anticipation. A pop of button and zip, and her trousers were undone. *Now we're getting somewhere*. She petted whatever part of him she could reach, urging him to do more, faster, harder. He winched material down her hips. She lifted, wanting him where she throbbed most.

Cool air hit her heated flesh. She moaned.

He took a deep, appreciative breath. "Sophia, love. Open your thighs."

Her slacks ringed her knees. His panted breaths heating her sex, she winched her legs as far apart as the open waistband would let her and squirmed, raising her hips to meet his mouth...

Crack. Liquid splashed her stomach.

He yanked her off the counter, bundling her in one arm, his head swiveling as if he expected an attack.

Nobody was there.

His face was wet. Sophia traced a finger through the sheen on his cheek. Charred pink, slightly viscous. She had to resist the urge to tongue the same path over his strong cheekbone.

He set her carefully on her feet and used the tail of his shirt to wipe more charred pink off her belly. It smeared gray. "What happened?"

"The potion." She turned to the countertop where nothing was left of the beaker but broken glass and blackened potion. She groaned. "We triggered the unhex potion."

"How?"

She pulled up her pants. Not only the beaker was broken—the mood was too. "Strong emotion can do that."

He poked the glass shards. "Did it work?"

"I don't know. It's expended."

"The hex is gone?" He started to smile. "I don't feel any different. Are you sure it worked?"

She hesitated. "I'm sure it activated. We need to wait for dawn to see if it worked."

"And if I don't turn into King, it worked?" He nodded. "All right. Just in case, we should find a plan B."

She sighed and finished dressing. "Right. I'll do more research."

Noah's eyes followed her fingers, the silver of his irises almost molten. He cleared his throat. "I'd better stay out of your way. I'll just poke around for something to protect us while you read."

"Sounds good."

She hit the books while Noah prowled the store. She squirmed a bit as she read—the burst beaker hadn't entirely broken the mood. But as she worked she cooled down and became absorbed in a blue grimoire. Absentmindedly, she lifted the book and took it to sit on a couch in the reading section. He eventually found a book, slid into a nearby chair, and started reading too.

It was nice. Companionable. As the minutes turned into hours, she relaxed, feeling almost like being at home.

She'd found a reference to a possible eliminator potion when Noah made a strange whuffing noise, as if he'd been punched in the gut. She jerked from the book. "What's wrong...?"

The sun speared through the front window. Noah wasn't there.

The doglet, quivering with anger, stood in his place.

"Stars and moon. I'm so sorry, King. Or should I say, Noah." Failure ripped her gut.

He yipped. Three times, like, *It's okay*.

"It's not. I tried but...Noah, I need to look at the mirror."

Yip, yip, yip. *No, no, no*.

"I have to." Stomach churning, she rose, set the blue grimoire on the couch, and strode to the mirror. Noah yipped at her heels the whole way.

Resolutely, she grabbed the sheet and yanked. It slithered to the floor.

The glass revealed was old, yellowed, and so ripply it could've been from a funhouse. Cavorting around the darkling glass were carved cherubs.

And snarling demons.

Every hair on her body stood straight up. She jumped back. King/Noah yipped in concern. Mr. Kibbles, who'd just come in, flashed under the linen cupboard and hissed.

"Yes, yes, you warned me." Any serenity she'd found reading with Noah was gone. She leaned against a nearby display case and let the shakes work their way through. She didn't like this out-of-control, endangered feeling. "I'll be okay. Maybe something hot first. Coffee or tea." She managed to pick up the sheet and throw it back over the mirror before starting for the kitchen.

Noah cut her off, bumping against her ankles. Turning her toward the upstairs.

She tried again. He herded her as efficiently as a sheepdog.

"What do you want?" She blinked at him, then the stairs. "There's nothing upstairs but sales items and bedrooms...oh." That was why she felt so trembly. Except for passing out for a few hours, she'd been up for twenty-four harrowing hours straight. "You're right. I'll be more efficient with a nap. The daytime wards will let me know if Rodolphe comes back. I'll research those demons when I'm fresh."

She slogged upstairs, set the alarm for ten a.m. and slept right through it.

She woke, groggy, when the sun was low in the sky. She stumbled into the shower before remembering Rodolphe then washed fast. But hot water and a good scrub made her feel better. She'd donned her suit pants and was about to shrug a plain white blouse over her bra.

Thoughts of a silver-eyed male stopped her.

No, she didn't want to tempt more wolf/witch forbidden action. But wowing him a little couldn't hurt, could it? The suit had a skirt. She changed into it and a pair of thigh-high hose. Then she dug through her luggage for her executive heels and The Camisole.

From her pre-banker days, the camisole was a spaghetti-strap tank with a built-in bra. Great for kicking around college bars, out of step with her current mature image, but she'd kept it because she felt sexy as hell in it.

And yeah, not to tempt taboos, but she hoped Noah might like it.

Besides, under the suit coat it would look staid enough. She wiggled into the spandex top and glanced at herself in the dresser mirror.

She looked smokin' hot.

Her cheeks heated. She quickly threw on her jacket and reached for her executive-row tall pumps, four inches of stiletto death.

She slid her feet in, took another look in the mirror and saw legs a mile long. Long enough to wrap around all that was tall, dark, and bangsome.

Face hot, she went downstairs.

Noah-as-King lay at the bottom, stretched out in front of the stairs, his eyes shut. He looked dead.

Her heart goosed. "Noah?"

His lids sprang open. He yipped, *What's wrong?*

A soldier, sleeping when he got the opportunity, but still protecting her. Her pulse slowed. "Nothing. Look, I thought of a Plan B. I'm calling my brother for help."

Noah's tail wagged.

She speed-dialed Gabriel. He greeted her with, "Found Auntie yet?"

"She phoned. Said she's okay."

"Did she say why she isn't home?"

"She hexed someone accidentally. Well, it started out as a hex. The spell rebounded a few times, altering it. A picture and a mirror. Actually, that's why I called. To bounce some ideas off you."

"Heh," Gabriel said. "Bounce, mirror."

Sophia paused. Her world was all out of whack and her brother was making puns. A profound sense of normalcy comforted her. "You have a weird sense of humor."

"Adorable, not weird. That's my secret ploy to weed through the many females who throw themselves at me. The woman who loves my humor will be my true love."

"You mean the one who loves you *in spite* of your humor."

"That works too."

"Look, about the mirror." Sophia told him about the carvings.

Gabriel said, "Shoot me a picture."

She removed the sheet, careful not to touch the glass or the frame, aimed her phone, and clicked. She wasn't actively using magic, but she still had the potential locked inside her, and some artifacts could respond to that. "I'm worried how the demons might've affected the spell."

"So Auntie wasn't practicing safe hex?"

"Twirl my broomstick. I hope bad puns aren't infectious."

"*Pfft,*" he said. "They're hereditary."

"You're probably right," she mourned. "But sex-linked, like male-pattern baldness."

"Good one."

Noah trotted closer, maybe trying to see what she was doing.

"Don't touch." She waved him back. Bad touch for her was potentially explosive touch for an innately magical being—like a hexed werewolf.

"Who are you talking to?" Gabriel said.

"Someone in the store. Here's the picture." She sent it to him.

There was some keyboard tapping and humming. Suddenly the humming stopped. "We've got trouble. The resolution on your jpeg was for suckage but I have an interpolating program that—"

"You hear that sizzle? That's my brain frying."

"Hah. You want my help or not?"

"The price may be too high."

He laughed. "Okay, I'll give it to you straight. I tweaked the image to show magical detail. For which you owe me, Biggeth Timeth."

"No way. You made me drive up here. I don't owe you diddly squat."

"Who taught you cussword math? It's diddly *over* squat, where squat is really shit. Means small and stinky, worthless—"

"Do you have a point?"

"Those demons mean the mirror was a *malifier*."

Sophia's heart plunged out her feet. Then she shook her head. "I don't believe it. Auntie wouldn't have kept something pure evil in the store."

"I said *was*. Auntie added cherubs. She made it an *assistere* instead."

"A helping mirror? That's good. Right?"

"Well..."

"That doesn't sound reassuring."

"The hex struck the mirror, then your picture, right? You're tied in."

"Yes, that's why I feel this overwhelming need to be with..." She trailed off as the implications hit. Gabriel thought she was helping Noah, not because she wanted to, but because she'd been spelled to.

The attraction was all the hex.

"Need to be with who?" Her brother's voice was brightly inquisitive. "Spill."

Spill about kissing...and more...with a wolf? Immediate distraction was in order. "So is the mirror helpful, or not?"

He chuckled. "Avoiding the topic. Oh, it's got to be good. Okay, the cherubs are helpful, but like pepper in a stew, the demons will still have an effect. There's a fifty-fifty chance you'll hurt the hexee rather than help him."

"No." She gasped the word through a suddenly tight throat. "I might hurt Noah?"

The dog growled. No words but the meaning was clear. *You'd never hurt me.*

"Noah?" Gabriel's brightly inquisitive tone cut through. *Nosy brother alert.* "The hex hit Noah? Or is he the one you feel this overwhelming need to be with—?"

"Oops, *bzzt*. Sorry, can't hear you *bzzt crackle crackle*. The techmeld must be wearing off." She hit end.

Good gods. A fifty percent chance she might hurt Noah? Even one percent was too high. She slid the phone into her coat pocket, darkness seeping into her bones. Noah was certain she'd never harm him, but what did a doggie werewolf know, even one whose mother worked for a wizard?

Was it helpful that, just as she visited Marlowe's trailer, Killer happened home to take a chomp out of King's hide? Was it helpful that evil-blast-from-*her*-past Rodolphe was here?

No, it was not helpful. Even Noah's lusting after a witch in the first place was Not Helpful with a capital NH.

Just like that poor transplant patient four years ago. Sophia meant to help, but instead she was putting on the hurt. *It was happening again.*

As if to underline her dismal thoughts, a rock sailed through one of the front windows—and all hell broke loose.

Chapter Thirteen

Shattered glass pocked against the floor in front of the window in a tinkling shower. Then a crowbar thrust through, clearing the pane of glass, sending shower after shower cascading musically to the floor.

Amid the tinkle of glass, Noah's drill-sergeant yip got Sophia's attention. He nosed her behind a couch. She clutched the back of it and stared at the destruction of her aunt's window.

A howl from the front sidewalk froze her breath in her chest.

The little dog that was Noah leaped in front of Sophia's couch, legs braced. His tiny growl was pure menace.

A snarling wolf jumped through the window and landed with an audible whump on the floor. He was a big, barrel-chested gray with scraggly fur. A second, dark gray wolf leaped in behind him.

The barrel-chested wolf howled its challenge.

Just as the last of the sun set.

In front of Sophia's eyes, Noah's little legs wobbled. He fell.

She cried out and skirted around the couch to help him.

Black smoke roiled up from the dog's form, obscuring it, billowing larger. She reared back. The smoke cleared.

In the dog's place, Noah leaped to his feet—naked. He shook his head as if to clear it, black hair shuddering.

From the front of the store, the barrel-chested wolf launched into a run, thundering toward them.

Noah snapped to attention, his silver-sharp eyes stabbing at the wolves as he gently used a barred arm to urge Sophia behind the couch. She went, thinking he'd join her. But he only stood there, tall and proud and naked.

The wolf had almost reached him. In the front of the store, the other wolf began shifting to human, joints popping, bones snapping, lumps sliding under his skin.

The barrel-chested gray, fury in its yellow eyes, leaped.

With a roar, Noah charged to meet it, his arm crooked before him like a raised shield.

The wolf ripped a chainsaw snarl and to her horror, chomped onto Noah's raised forearm.

Noah whirled, grabbed a carousel of jewelry from a nearby counter, and smashed it upside wolf skull. The gray yelped and let go.

Noah's arm was red and raw like chewed meat. Sophia, eyes brimming with tears, glanced around her, desperate for something to bandage that arm. *The linen cupboard.* She rose to a crouch, prepared to dash the length of the store.

Beyond them, the other wolf's limbs elongated, his spine unrolling. He stood with a crick of neck.

It was Killer. He pulled a knife from one pocket and charged with a roar.

No time for first aid. *Get in the fight.* She dug in her pockets for a weapon.

Noah, face set like a locomotive's grill, raised the dented stand. His arm weeping blood, he ran to meet Killer's charge.

They met in a clash. Noah swiped the stand into Killer's arm. The blade flew. It clattered to the floor, spinning to rest a few feet from Sophia.

She crept out from behind the couch and reached for it. It was a slender switchblade.

Killer dove for the knife, nearly plowing into her, and came up with the knife in his hand. Their eyes met. She flinched. Killer raised the knife to cut her.

Noah seized Killer's wrist from behind and jerked. Killer spun up to a crouch. They grappled for the knife.

Behind them, the big barrel-chested wolf stumbled to its feet.

Pepper spray. Sophia jabbed a frantic hand into her coat pocket.

The stupid wand that wasn't hers kept getting in the way.

Killer switched his knife to his free hand and slashed the blade across Noah's face. Noah flashed an arm up, deflecting the knife and stopping it from taking his eye. But it cut to the bone.

Blood sheeted down his cheek, dripping from his chin.

"First fuckin' blood." Killer grinned viciously.

"No!" Sophia finally found the small can. She leaped to her feet and dashed in with the spray.

Lightning-fast, Noah punched Killer, bang in the Adam's apple. Killer fell back, hacking. Noah smashed the stand into Killer's skull, so hard the stand burst into a pile of metal rods.

But behind him, the barrel-chested wolf braced on four paws, quivering, and leaped onto Noah's back.

Sophia pivoted to let loose a stream of pepper spray directly into the wolf's beady yellow eyes.

It howled and fell to the floor, scrabbling.

"Sophia!" Noah spun and shoved her aside.

The wolf blindly chomped where her hand had been. Wolf teeth punched Noah's arm and grimly hung on. Noah let out a soft groan.

Sophia screamed and beat wolf skull with her fists. The wolf let go. Bone and tendon were visible in Noah's arm before the red holes filled with blood. Her stomach swapped with her throat, but she kept pounding the wolf.

Killer stumbled to his feet and lurched toward the front of the store. As he passed Sophia he shouted, "Attila, here!"

The gray wolf cringed from under Sophia's beating hands. He staggered toward the voice.

The blinded wolf took refuge behind Killer, who slashed the knife side to side in a clear "back off".

Screw that. Sophia raised her pepper spray, aimed for Killer's face.

"You fuckin' win!" Killer raised a hand in surrender, his other on the wolf's ruff, backing slowly away.

Behind her, Noah released a low groan. Sophia glanced over her shoulder. He leaned heavily against a counter, bleeding from numerous cuts and bites. Red rivulets forming on the glass scared her.

The fight was over. Noah needed her. Needed bandages.

"Don't move." She mimicked shooting Killer with the pepper spray before pocketing it and sprinting to the armoire. She threw open the cupboard and grabbed a sheet to tear.

"Hey, Sophia Blue," Killer rasped from the front door.

Clutching the sheet, she turned.

He held up something long and psychedelic as the wolf limped out the door behind him. Aunt Linda's not-a-vibrator. "Your old mentor says hi." He lobbed the mushroom at her.

She flinched.

Noah's hand shot up. He grabbed the mushroom out of the air.

Whole, uninjured skin filled her vision.

Noah lobbed the thing back at Killer. The wolfman caught it automatically. In a double-take, he looked at it in his hand, looked again, and swore.

Noah started for him.

Killer scooted.

Noah pursued him, slashes and bites gone but still distinctly naked.

She dropped the sheet and ran toward him. "*Noah.* Wait."

He stopped. Turned and strode to meet her and swept her into his arms. "Are you all right?"

"I should ask you that." She ran her hands over his skin, hardly believing there wasn't even a scratch. Healed through shifting? She'd only been turned an instant. Incredible that he could shift—twice—in that short time. In her relief she wrapped arms around his neck and blurted, "It was me. They were after me."

"No, Sophia. Those are two of the assholes I was telling you about. Their hard-on is definitely for me. This is the last straw. When this hex is gone I'm taking them out permanently."

"You're not listening." She pulled back to look into his eyes. Make him understand. "They had no way of knowing you were here. They came to hurt *me*. Didn't you hear

Killer? Rodolphe sent them. He sent those two wolves to attack, and you were injured—badly—because you were forced to defend me."

He frowned as he searched her eyes. "I wasn't forced to do anything."

"You don't know Rodolphe. He's sly. He hurt a little girl through me." Her fear bubbled like acid. "He hurt you, because of me." Because of the hex, and it would only get worse. She would not, *could* not let it.

Key to magic be damned. "I have to go." She pushed out of his strong arms and ran upstairs.

* * *

Noah watched Sophia's slim backside disappear up the stairs. She was leaving *again*.

Noah's wolf howled out against it. *Stop her.*

But how, besides tying her up? Which wasn't appealing in the least—until he added *naked on a bed*. Then, the idea was alarmingly interesting. Though, if she wasn't into it too, it was likely to earn him a nail-clipper neutering.

He followed her upstairs. This time, he knocked. "Sophia, wait. What about my hex?"

"That's the point." Her voice, coming through the door, was thready. When she burst out a moment later her nose and eyes were red. She trundled a suitcase behind her.

His heart leaped into his throat. "Where are you going?" He couldn't help a lonely pup whine. "I need your help."

She retracted the handle, lifted the case by a side handle and clomped awkwardly down the stairs. "It's pretty obvious I'm *not* helping."

He followed. “Please wait. Think. Even if you can’t do anything about the hex, you’re safer here, with me—”

“That’s the problem. I’m safer with you, but *you* aren’t safe with *me*.” She flashed him a look he couldn’t decipher as she set the case down, took a couple tries to extend the handle, got it clicked into place, and started for the door. Her legs wobbled.

He was distracted for a bare fraction of an instant by her legs, long and shapely in hose and needles for heels.

In that instant she made it to the middle of the store.

He hustled after her. “You can’t leave. Please.” He was begging. He never begged. But she’d been upstairs most of the day with him stuck as the small dog, only his toothpick claws and fangs for defense, and then she’d come downstairs in that skirt and heels that made her legs miles long, and it was just damned good luck he’d stopped drooling and become a man in the nick of time to fight the two wolves. If he hadn’t, she’d have been injured or worse. The gashes and holes he’d suffered could have been in *her* creamy skin. Adrenaline pumped through him at the thought, so hot and furious that he shook with the force of it.

Fuck this. If it kept her from injury, he’d beg like a toddler. “*Please.* I need your help with the hex, and...and you need to get the window repaired, and...and you can’t leave.” He didn’t understand how, but his gut told him that, even after so short a time, she’d come to mean the world to him.

“I have to.” She trundled her suitcase behind her across the wooden slats of the floor. Each clack-clack-clack drove a nail of despair into his heart.

She opened the door, shoved her case through, and stepped outside.

She really was leaving him.

It skewered him, hurting more than the fight, hitting him like a fist to the gut. Like multiple fists, to the jaw, the gut, the knees. He crumpled, caught himself on a display case, and managed to croak, “Wait!”

She didn’t. He grabbed up his pants and hopped into them as he ran after her, catching up just as she stopped and stared at the empty street. “Right. My car is at Mason’s.”

She started off with a determined stride, shortened and made wobbly because of that skirt and those high, high heels. He could only be grateful, and not just because they made her behind as perky as a poodle.

He leaped in to grab the case’s handle, pretending to help but really snagging it to stop her from getting away. She wanted to go, to leave him, and his heart was breaking.

“Auntie will help you,” she was saying. “Or Mason, or...or... *anybody* but me.”

“I don’t *understand*.” His shattering heart made it a plaintive cry. “Why are you leaving me?”

She stopped, thank goodness she stopped, her hands dropping to her sides as if her limbs were leaden too. She shook her head. “You don’t understand. Well, why would you? It’s not like you’re a witch.”

He winced. “You could try explaining.”

She blew a frustrated breath. “I’m hexed too.”

“What? How? When?” He dropped the case to enfold her in his arms, to pet her hair, to reassure himself that she was uninjured, at least for now. “What do I do? How can I help?”

She laughed from deep within his embrace. “Not like that.” Her tone was a little embarrassed and a lot muffled. “The mirror’s demons malified the hex. Since it hit my picture, it sucked me into hurting you. Can you let up a little? I can't breathe."

"You'd never hurt me." He held her at arms' length. "I don't believe it."

"Doesn't matter." She tugged against him and he released her reluctantly. "I'd never be able to live with myself if I did." She bit her lip.

He honored her for that. Witches had power. They didn't always have consciences to go along. Sophia obviously did.

He honored her, but he had to make her see she needn't worry about him. "Sophia, look at me." He stepped back and flexed his muscles for her. He hadn't had a chance to put on more than his jeans, and he enjoyed the way her eyes darkened and followed each ripple. "I'm an alpha wolf. You *can't* hurt me."

"I wouldn't mean to, but I most certainly could." Her back snapped ramrod straight, and her words were snipped. That was the witch princess talking.

He smiled. "All right, maybe you could, but even if you're powerful enough, I maintain you'd never hurt me. You're *good*. That means more than any carved demons."

She sighed and met his gaze. Hers was infinitely sad. "There's no way to know for sure."

The way her eyes glimmered with tears, she meant more than the hex. Somehow, she meant *them*. Unless he could straighten her out, immediately, she was going to leave him and never return.

The challenge went straight to his alpha bones. "You need proof?" He snapped his fingers. "Your aunt's spell book. I bet something in there would reveal the hex's nature on you."

She was already shaking her head. “Without a witch to do the spell—”

“Or a potion.”

“Didn’t work before. Something complex like this...” She shrugged.

He wanted to howl. Then he thought of something better.

“You’re just *giving up?*” That would challenge the witch princess. “Not even going to try putting our heads together?”

“Well...”

Got her. Before she could throw another rebuttal his way he picked up her suitcase with one hand and urged her toward the store with the other. “Let’s talk this over inside.” His palm covered the small of her back. He had to work to keep his hand from sliding down to cup her perky, sleek bottom.

“Well, I suppose we can try. But put some clothes on.”

“Yes! Of course. No problem.” He bundled her through the door. Caught her running her eyes over him and made a muscle with one raised, crooked arm, bulking the biceps, flexing it for added measure. “Of course as a shifter, I’m quite comfortable in the nude.” He glanced at her.

She’d sat and averted her gaze, her cheek that luscious pink.

Gotcha. While she wasn’t looking, he dashed off with her suitcase and hid it behind the register display case.

Dressing, he then called Mr. Fixit, who promised, with the enticement of double time, to be right over.

Noah found the big red spell book behind a counter on the floor—remembered the hot kiss that had sent it there—squashed his need for her, and brought the book to the couch.

While Mr. Fixit repaired the window, Noah and Sophia sat side by side, turning the book's pages together. He relaxed as they pored over the illuminated vellum. It was comfortable, nice. Like old mated wolves.

He squashed that thought too.

"I'm all done," Mr. Fixit called.

Noah rose to pay the man. He returned to the couch to see Sophia staring down at the book with a definite frown.

He glanced at the open page as he sat beside her. The title, done in careful calligraphy, was Mortal Reveal, subtitled *A Mundane Reveal for Altered Spells*. "What's that?" He read the text out loud. "'To see the nature of a spell that's been magnified, altered, or both, gather final target, any intermediates, and all magnifiers.' I wonder what that means?"

"Final target is you, the magnifier is the mirror. Intermediate...that's my picture. Me."

"The mirror, you, and me. Okay." He went on reading. "'The target must engage in the most powerful form of creative physical magic that mortals have available, in conjunction with any intermediates and magnifiers.'" He turned to her for clarification.

"Creative physical mortal magic..." She stared at him, blushing furiously. "It's talking about *sex*."

He could only gape at her. "Sex with the mirror?"

"Sex, *in front* of the mirror—between *you and me*."

Hot desire shocked him, like water splashed on a sizzling griddle. He swallowed, hard. Him with a witch? Should've repelled him. Should have sent him howling from the room.

But sex with *Sophia*... He wanted it so badly he had to clench his hands to keep from reaching for her. He grew claws into his palms, the pain giving him the barest edge of control to hold his place.

It had to be her choice too.

* * *

Sophia stared into Noah's eyes, silver as a mirror. She needed to leave, but those eyes, that face, that brave heart, they all tethered her, made it physically painful to walk away.

She'd felt it on the sidewalk. Like a huge rubber band joined them, stretching tighter with every step apart.

So she'd come back to the bookstore. She'd *wanted* to find proof it was safe for her to stay.

But this particular proof? Her belly flipped at the thought of sex with him. It was wildly, wickedly tempting. Her body clamored for this excuse to have him.

Unless he felt coerced into it. It wouldn't be right if he didn't come to her freely, of his own will.

She could ask him, but she didn't want to be seared by an immediate, mortifying no. So she searched his face for a clue as to how he felt. The damned wolf could be damned controlled when he wanted to be. Nope. Not a hint.

Until she saw a faint flush riding his high cheekbones. Clenched fingers in his lap. The barest shifting of his weight toward her, instantly checked. His silver eyes burned mirror-bright.

He wanted her too.

She rejoiced. Then she despaired. What if the hex was fueling this? What if it was a bad hex, but they'd find out it was bad only *after* sex cemented their connection—because what she was feeling, what was in his eyes, tolled like a bell of forever.

"So let me get this straight," he said. "You and me...and *sex*." His body tightened on the last word.

Hers did too. Need coiled deep between her thighs, the kind of tightly wound desire that could quickly spring into something large and ravenous. "*Yes.*" She cleared her throat. "Yes."

His nostrils flared. He leaped to his feet so fast, she wondered what he smelled coming off her. It did give her some much-needed space.

Then, to her shock, he smiled like a naughty boy. "I'm willing if you are."

She groaned. Good thing he didn't know the alluring power of that knowing-yet-boyish, eager-yet-patient, and definitely masculine smile. Her body flushed hot, prickling with anticipation. "It's probably the hex. I can't believe I'm considering it."

Need and fear, spinning like a tornado of conflict, pushed her to her feet. She peeled out of her jacket, staring at the mirror, still uncovered from taking the picture of it. Sex with Noah, magic meeting magic.

Four years of being mundane—including mundane, conservative sex. She hadn't missed any part of her magical side. Until now.

Until him.

Dangerous, because she felt like she knew him when she didn't. Dangerous because they were going too fast.

Most dangerous because she wanted it so badly.

"Talk to me, Sophia."

Big hands wrapped around her arms. Her blazer dropped from her hand onto the edge of the carpet.

Noah turned her to face him.

Her camisole meant they were skin-to-skin. Not bankerly professional, but at that moment she appreciated the comfort of touch.

"Tell me what you need from me. Or talk to me, and we'll work it out."

He wanted her too, but he wouldn't push. The deadly beast was also a gentleman.

She pressed palms to his chest. Something chunky lay under his shirt in the valley of his pecs. She put off the decision a moment longer by poking it. "What's this? I got a glimpse before. It looked like a wolf."

"Yes." He drew a leather thong from inside his shirt. Hanging from it was a black enameled wolf. "My mother gave it to me when I was a boy. I wear it in her memory."

"That's sweet." She brushed a finger over smooth cool metal and felt just the whisper of power. "You're a caring man, aren't you?"

One corner of his lips rose as he threaded the thong back into his shirt. "Don't tell. It'll ruin my big bad alpha reputation."

She smiled back, her heart warming. "Okay. Then I won't mention that this, you touching me, is both sexy and nice."

"Nice?"

"Reassuring. Comforting."

"Ah. Well, as long as you don't mention it, I'll keep doing it." He folded her into his arms, her face pillowed on his taut pecs, her nose in the middle of all that smelled good. He kissed her hair, then rested his chin on her head. "I won't tell anyone it's good for me too."

She nestled in with a happy sigh.

Several seconds passed. Then he said, "Would it work?"

"Sex before the mirror?" She sighed again, but not out of happiness this time. "Yes. A tantric reveal would certainly tell us the truth. But..." She fell silent.

"There's always a but, isn't there?" He grinned down at her, unseen but felt in the change of the shape of his chin against the top of her head. "I'm ready. Hit me with it."

"I'm worried the hex is rushing us into a bad decision. Not just a bad decision, but an irreparable one. There's a reason the Witches' Council forbids a witch to have sex with a werewolf."

"Ah." The grin disappeared.

She opened her mouth to protest that the results were unpredictable and mostly bad, ranging from spontaneous human combustion during intercourse to monstrous, power-hungry offspring.

Something—maybe her inexplicable feelings, maybe trying to let him down gently, maybe simply tired of justifying herself—stopped her. She only said, "I have to admit it feels right."

He gave a soft sigh, as if he'd waited a lifetime for her to say those words. "Then why don't we try it? Sophia, between the two of us, what can't we handle? What can't we work out?"

"That's the problem. We don't know."

"You're right. We don't know." Noah turned her and held her at arms' length. "And we won't know until we try." He released her and strode to the mirror, unbuttoning his shirt as he went.

So decisive. It must make him one hell of an alpha.

He stood before the mirror, facing it. She realized he'd stopped exactly where he could see her face—because she could see his. That wasn't the alpha staring back.

That was the man, gazing hungrily at her.

"You're so beautiful." His eyes met hers, his blazing silver. "I knew that when your aunt showed me your picture, but meeting you, being with you...you're beautiful clear through. When I saw you leaving me—it hurt, Sophia. I don't know what I'd do without you."

She blinked. "Are you okay? Your mouth is open but alien words are coming out."

He laughed. "Better than okay. My mouth is open and the truth is coming out, and it's set me free. The words were burning my brain. But I couldn't say them. Me, attracted to a witch? Heresy, insanity!"

It was insane; it was the sweetest of music. She felt torn in two. "I think that hex has mutated on you, and not for the better."

He twisted toward her, throwing the flare of his lats into relief, and held out a beckoning hand. "We can do it. We can do anything."

At the words, she felt a surge of optimism. Maybe the two of them, together, *could* accomplish miracles. She went to him and positioned them with the mirror at her back and him in front of her.

"Okay, first I'm going to see what kind of power we can generate." Last time she'd used Witch's Sight, she'd passed out. But this time she'd only take a glimpse.

Placing her fingertips on his chest, she took a deep breath, closed her physical eyes, opened her third eye, and looked at him.

His eyes, seen on the etheric, burned a silver so hot that flames of desire licked her from toes to crown.

She gasped and staggered, third eye slamming shut, her physical eyes flying open.

Before she could fall, he seized her, wolf fast, and pulled her tight. His molten silver gaze blazed directly into hers, melting her from the inside.

His body was scorching, pressed intimately against hers. Her heart slammed into overdrive. Her blood lit with fire.

His hand slid down her hip, perhaps to steady her, but when she wriggled against him, he grabbed her bottom and squeezed. She moaned and rose the few millimeters to tiptoes. Her hips collided with his. He winched them together and she could feel his cock unfurling in intense interest.

He speared fingers into her hair and kissed her.

She opened to him. His tongue thrust inside, filling her with a wild, animal hunger. His deep growl underscored his possession of her mouth, his tongue diving and lashing until thrills shivered down her throat into her breasts.

Both his hands were on her backside now, caressing, cupping, massaging. Her hips shifted up and back, like a cat in heat.

In response, he tunneled one hand under the waistband of her skirt.

Directly onto her skin.

She sucked in a shocked breath. As if he expected it, was waiting for it, was *courting* it, he speared both hands under the loosened waistband. Diving down into her panties, his palms slid directly onto her buttocks.

He groaned. “Damn, you’re creamy smooth. Can’t wait to taste you there.”

She parted her lips to respond. He thrust his tongue down her throat again. She moaned. His mouth opened aggressively, his jaw working as he tongued her even deeper.

Her fears disappeared in the fire of his claiming. She threaded her arms around his neck and kissed him back. Her heart pounded and her breath rasped, with excitement but also the waistband, with both her and him in it, was too tight. "I...I can't breathe."

He immediately withdrew one hand. "Sorry."

She was too, momentarily bereft of the heat of that big hand.

Then she felt a tug and the pop of a button and the waistband gave. She could breathe again—until his mouth reclaimed her with fierce heat. She was panting and breathless in an instant.

Skimming one hard palm over her backside, he maneuvered the other into the low neckline of her camisole. Her breastbone raised in response, as if her breasts were begging for his touch. He delved deeper and cupped one, his hand fitting it perfectly. She sighed and relaxed into that warm, perfect hand.

Then he gently tweaked her nipple. She squeaked.

He captured her squeak in the dark cave of his mouth. His tongue began to thrust in hot wild rhythm. His lips were fierce and his shifter's stubble rasped her skin. He kissed her, pinched her, kneaded her, *overwhelmed* her.

Her blood sang with need and her skin was on fire. Her breasts swelled and throbbed, nipples tight as nuts. Her pelvis churned with tense, growing need.

In counterpoint, her muscles melted with desire and her sex softened in anticipation, warm and damp and silky against her panties.

The opposing forces clashed and crossed, building bigger and bigger, waves of hunger that made her so hot and needy she shuddered with it.

He stopped. Spun her.

She confronted their reflection in the mirror.

His arm wrapped around her ribs, tendons and muscles tight with claiming her. Her eyes were huge, her pupils dilated so wide that her eyes were almost black. Her lips were red and swollen, and so were his.

Hesitantly, she whispered, "Is it the hex doing this?"

"No. It's *us* doing this." Holding her firmly with one arm, he drove the other under her neckline to cup her breast. In the mirror, the mound that was his hand began to squeeze gently, like a breathing animal.

"What are you—*ohh.*" He'd slotted her nipple through two fingers and pinched. She arched violently.

"Sex. You and me. In front of the mirror." He slid his other hand into her skirt, his fingers tunneling under her panties to make his arm an esker running from her waistband to her mound. Bending, he put his mouth by her ear. "*Now.*" He slid one finger along her slit.

Thrust *into* her.

She whimpered. One big finger inside her, his thumb on her clitoris, he squeezed, gently, rhythmically, in time with the tugging on her breast. She was caught between his hands, hot-wired nodes zapping electricity through her. Her hips began to rock and a moan bubbled through her parted lips.

"You smell amazing." He buried his lips into her neck, kissing the delicate skin. "A rosebud opening."

Her trembling expanded into delicious shudders.

"Sweet. Heady. Lickable." His warm, rough tongue lapped her neck, her collarbone.

She started purring like a cat, a tiny portion of her mind wondering insanely if he was turning her into a shifter. "But if the hex is trying to distract us... *Oh.*" She gasped as his probing finger hit her sweet spot. Lightning need streaked through her. "It *must* be the hex."

"Why?" He slipped a second finger into her, stretching her with warm wonder. He began rocking against her, their hips pressing together deliciously.

"*This*. It's so fast. Magically fast." She let her head fall back against his chest, raising her chin to give him better access to the skin of her throat. Her brain squealed it was a sign of submission to an alpha wolf, but she only wanted his hot, talented mouth on more of her skin. He responded by tracing the tendon with his tongue.

"And 'this' is...?" He ground his hips into her buttocks. His erection pressed huge.

She shuddered, delighting in his hot slick licks down her throat. *This* was hot, potent wildness. Abandoning planning, thinking, throwing out anything but fiery, reckless *feeling*.

"I want you," she whispered.

He revved a growl that came from the pit of his belly. "I've never heard words so beautiful."

"But so hot...so fast..."

He nipped her neck with an alpha's powerful growl. "It's *not* the hex. This is you and me, Sophia. *Us*. Look, see what I'm doing to you. Acknowledge it, acknowledge *us*."

He drove his fingers deep inside her.

She gasped, her eyes popping open, and looked.

Every muscle in his body stood out as he held her fused to him. His hands worked her hard, almost brutally.

His gaze, his whole focus, was concentrated on *her*. On giving her as much pleasure as he could. And not her as the intermediary in the hex. But her, Sophia. That blazing focus told her the shocking truth.

He meant it. It wasn't the hex doing this to him. He wanted her.

And she... Her skirt hung loosely from her hips. Her legs were spread wide, and the rougher he worked her the farther they spread. She wanted him so badly she was flushed and visibly trembling. Her back was arched, her breasts thrust forward, and she was grinding into his hand. Grinding her butt into his hips, feeling his erection grow.

It stunned her how powerful her desire was. His desire. *Their* desire. He was right. It wasn't just him doing her, or her doing him. They were doing it together.

Grabbing the hem of her camisole, she dragged it up her ribs past his arm, tugged the cloth over her head, and threw it away.

He sucked in a breath.

She seized his hand and slapped it back on her bare breast, feeling the nut of her nipple rasp his palm. In the mirror, his eyes were glowing so brightly they practically burned.

She wanted them on *fire*.

Her skirt was already unbuttoned, and her writhing had worked the zipper halfway down. She opened it all the way, almost botching it because she was trembling so hard. The skirt slid down her thighs to crumple around her ankles, leaving her clad in nothing but panties, thigh-high stockings, four-inch heels, and him.

His hand was as gorgeous squeezing under her bikinis as it was on her breast. It felt even better. His thick cock, pressing urgently against her panties from behind, would feel even better yet, skin-to-skin.

It might have been the hex's fault to start. But this was happening, it was happening now, and it wasn't the hex's fault any more. She wanted it.

No, she wanted *him*. And if she were honest with herself, she'd wanted Noah Blackwood from the moment she figured out he was loyal, brave, and sexy as hell.

Chapter Fourteen

She snagged the inch-wide elastic of her bikini panties in either hand and pulled down. Without bending, she only managed ten or so inches, but it was enough to uncover Noah's hand and a whole lot of her private skin.

He let out a low, rough howl. Dropped to his knees. Grabbed her hips in both hands, tilted her back, and pressed a kiss to her sex.

His mouth was searing hot. She screamed. He lapped at her roughly, beating her with his tongue until she whimpered her need. Until she grabbed the frame of the mirror to keep from being shoved into it headfirst. It tingled under her hands, but her whole body flushed with a more powerful fever.

He must've sensed she'd found purchase because he lapped harder, thumbs spreading her for his onslaught.

Urgency flamed along her slit, exploding into her pelvis, settling hot and heavy and throbbing.

In the mirror her face was flushed, her bare breasts heaving. His fingers dented her hips, his skin dark against hers. She saw flashes of his chin, moving savagely against her.

She felt nothing but bliss. Sharp pleasure built, higher and higher the faster he worked her. He ground and ravaged with his mouth until she ached for him to fill her. Until she was needy, hollow, *in anguish,* and she'd implode unless he fucked her right now.

"Noah...*take me.*"

He stood and lost his pants in one fluid motion. Seizing her hips in his big hands, he tilted her up.

She was too short. But instead of crouching to fit, he wrapped one arm under her breasts, one around her hips, and lifted her off the ground.

Her pumps fell off her feet and hit the floor with a clatter. She dangled from his arms, naked but for her thigh-high stockings and the panties banding her knees. His lips moved to her nape, his breath hot enough to scorch. The edge of his teeth took hold. And just nudging her sex...

Her eyebrows rose. Heavens, he was big. Instinctively she grabbed the mirror frame—just as he drove himself in.

Her aching channel shouted with joyous fulfillment.

Her eyes flew open. In the mirror, they were wild. Her mouth dropped open too, red and wet in reflection.

He thrust. Her whole pussy clenched with a thrill of response. She gasped. Urgency sang from her sex, branching up into her body. He thrust again, harder. Every cell opened inside her to bright sensation. She clenched the wood frame. He set up a steady, strong rhythm, holding her firmly with arms and hands and teeth, and she closed her eyes and gave herself over to the growing waves of tightening sensation.

Her ears filled with the thwack of his muscular belly hitting her smooth buttocks, almost drowning out her panting. Her heart raced in her chest, thudding so hard she could feel it. Her skin prickled as moisture rose. Her ears rang as her pussy cried out in pleasure and wept for joy. He thrust deep and ground down. Her body's eager response to him released a tsunami of wet along her thighs.

She slit open her eyes to see steam clouding the mirror, her breath, misting and clearing in rapid succession.

"Sophia...my heart...you're incredible." He began circling his hips with each deep thrust.

She whimpered her pleasure, her pelvis full and heavy and hot. He was the incredible one, smooth and slick, filling her to bursting...and then he drove himself in to the hilt. Her pussy clenched hard. "I'm...I'm..."

He adjusted her in his arms to slide two hot fingers onto her clitoris.

Orgasm swelled on her horizon. Ballooned huge, filling her whole sight.

He pounded into her twice as hard, her swollen clit bouncing against his fingers until she screamed. His thrusts deepened, slowing, each scouring her to the core of her being. One. Winding so tight with pleasure it was pain. Two. Pushing to the very pinnacle of rapturous agony.

"Sophia." He groaned and crushed her to him, so tightly that they fused. "Now, love."

Love. It triggered a powerful release. She came hard, so hard her eyes clenched against the brilliance of it. A keening cry forced its way from her throat. Wave after wave of contraction and release plowed through her. He buried himself inside her and came with a shout. They shuddered together, her contractions seeming to lengthen and reinforce his, his tugging cock adding to hers, going on and on.

The waves rippled out into joined pleasure that was wildly, deliciously sweet.

As climax eased, he set her gently into her shoes. Her eyes opened. In the mirror, her face looked sated, tired, and satisfied.

Behind her, the sweep of Noah's black lashes rose in the mirror. She prepared herself for the burning silver of his piercing stare.

His eyes were softly glowing. Sated, like hers. Satisfied.

And gold.

* * *

"Noah? Come help Mommy with the cookies."

The small boy ran into the kitchen, his second-favorite room. Four-year-old Noah's favorite place was the book room, where his mommy had her big loom and the hard man had the soft reading chair, smelling of leather and paper, warmth and love. The boy adored crawling into the hard man's lap for a bedtime story. His favorite stories were about princes and princesses who wielded wands and skin-prickles, or what the man called magic. "How can I help, Mommy?"

His mother held out a cookie. "Taste this."

He loved helping but especially with this. He took the cookie and tasted it thoroughly. Seriously. He wanted to do a good job for her. "It's good. Even though it's oatmeal."

Her smile was the sun coming up for him.

The hard man swept into the kitchen. The man always swept, his purposeful stride unfurling his long star-and-moon robe. Noah's mommy had made the cloth on her loom. She worked for the hard man, and she and Noah lived with him.

She held out a cookie to the hard man. The man smiled and Noah's mommy smiled back. It was a different smile than she gave Noah, smaller, more adult. Promising things other than hugs and cookies. Noah didn't like that smile because it meant his mother and the hard man were going upstairs where Noah was not allowed.

Noah thought about pouting, but his mother's smile turned to him. She handed him another cookie, this one chocolate chip.

He tasted it with the same seriousness, but his mouth couldn't lie. He smiled back. "This is great!"

His mother wasn't listening. Her nostrils flared. "Simon."

A bad feeling rolled over Noah, bitter like weeds.

The hard man's head came up. "I hear. They're coming from the front. Take the boy. Go out the back."

Wrapping Noah in one arm, she clutched the hard man's robe with her free hand. "Simon. You come too."

"I must hold them off. Take the boy, Hayley. Quickly." The hard man pushed Noah's mother toward the door, gently, but Noah still growled. The man paid no attention to Noah, his gaze locked on Noah's mother. "Go. For the boy's sake."

She blinked shiny eyes. Noah was angry with the man for making her cry. She gathered Noah and urged him outside.

They ran down the garden path leading to the big woods. Suddenly Noah realized someone was missing. "Raven! Mommy, we have to go back for Raven."

"Not now, honey." She tried to tug him along, but he dug in his heels. Raven was more than his pet, he was his friend.

Suddenly a cyclone of star-spangled wind whipped around the corner of the house—headed straight for them.

Magic. Noah could feel the skin-prickles from here. His mother stopped tugging on him, knelt, and pulled him into her arms. Her heart was drumming and she trembled against him.

The hard man popped between them and the magic cyclone, his star-and-moon cloak snapping in the wind.

He raised a hand. Noah saw a greeting.

The wind died, revealing three black-robed men. Noah's skin buzzed, bad, *wrong*, like nasty wasps. His hackles rose. The hard man had shoved his mommy away and was now meeting bad men.

Caw, caw. A blue-black bird flew around the corner of the house.

"Raven," Noah cried, and tried to rush for him. His mother's arms tightened and he couldn't get to his friend.

Following the raven was a fourth robed man, but his silks were pale, and an ivory fur collar curled around his neck. He stood back, arms crossed, watching.

The hard man pointed his wand at the black-robed men. Noah only cared about his friend. "Raven!" Noah struggled loose from his mother's arms and ran toward him.

Below Raven, the hard man's face paled. "No!" One palm shot out toward Noah, the other at the bird.

A wall of wind slammed into Noah. He pushed against it, churning his legs as hard as he could, but he couldn't get any closer to his pet. He called, "Raven, come."

The ivory-collared man pointed at Raven and started chanting. Raven began to win through.

The hard man turned white. His palm still flat toward Noah, he spun up his wand.

Pointed straight at Raven.

The bird shot into the sky like a missile. He got smaller and smaller, a bird, a blotch, a dot, gone.

A single black feather floated to the ground. Noah, face wet, struggled toward it.

The hard man aimed his wand at the feather. It exploded. Noah shrieked.

Noah's mother wrapped arms around him, picked him up, and ran.

Over her shoulder, Noah saw the black-robed men bookend the hard man and shoot horrifying magic at him. The hard man, after a final glance toward Noah and his mother, jerked as if he'd been hit in the back.

He fell. He did not get up. Noah felt the hard man's sparkles disappear, and for a moment was frightened.

No. The hard man had destroyed Raven, Noah's friend. He'd pushed Noah and his mommy away to meet the nasty robed men.

Noah was not, could not be sorry for the man.

The ivory-robed man motioned toward Noah and his mother. Bad feelings bit Noah's tummy. His mother crashed with him through the outer thickets, still too far from the deep woods to hide.

The black-robed man ran after them, wand pointing ominously.

"Mommy!" Noah grabbed his mother's shoulder to get her attention. "The bad man."

She slashed a glance back. Then she whispered the word Noah was never to say, so viciously that winter stormed in his chest.

She set him down to throw her daggers. As his wand spewed fire toward them, the blades *thunked* into the man. The stream of magic cut off, but not soon enough.

The leading tongues of magic snapped like a whip into Noah's mother. She cried out and fell to one knee. Her hand slapped her ribs.

Blood dripped between her fingers.

"Mommy. Your wolf!" His wolf healed his own owies.

She shifted. Bright red streaked her fur. It scared him.

But when she nudged him with her muzzle, pushing him toward her shoulders, he mounted as she'd taught him. He didn't know what else to do. The hard man was gone. Raven was gone. He dug his fingers into his mother's fur and held tight.

She ran. She ran so fast the wind slapped his face. If Raven had been flying with them, it would have been fun. But now...

He didn't understand. Why had the hard man made Raven go away? Why had he pushed Noah and his mother away?

Noah clutched his mommy, sad and angry and scared. No, being scared was for babies. Angry.

Noah's mother ran off and on for days. The bright red on her fur never dried. More leaked out. It smelled funny; it felt *wrong*. It buzzed like the black-robed men had.

Days and nights blurred passed. Eventually, Noah's mother stopped outside a tiny shack in the forest.

She turned human. But her skin was gray like a wolf, and her breath came in gasps. The gash on her flank was fiery red.

Noah was frightened. Why hadn't turning wolf taken care of her owie? He reached to touch his mother's wound.

She took him by the shoulders, stopping him. "Noah, listen to me. You must never again use the skin-prickles, do you understand? No magic from now on. Can you do that for me, honey?"

She was so serious, so gray. Even the gold of her eyes had gone dull. He would have agreed to anything she asked, but especially this. Skin-prickles reminded him of the hard man. Noah used a big word he'd heard but never understood before now. The hard man had *betrayed* them.

He never wanted to think about the hard man again.

"Yes, Mommy."

"Good." She seemed relieved. "Now wipe the magic away, as Simon...wipe the magic away as you've been taught."

Noah closed his eyes and *didn't* think of the hard man. He pictured the squeegee his mommy used to wipe down the showers and scraped the skin-prickles off himself. They trickled down his body into a pool at his feet. He was about to shake them from his toes when his mommy spoke again.

"Good. Here." His mother drew a thong over her head. It was attached to a medallion the size of his palm. Her black wolf. She'd let him play with it before, but she'd never taken it off.

She kissed the wolf and whispered a single word. *Hide.*

She looped the thong over Noah's neck. The wolf fell onto his tummy.

As if the wolf called the skin-prickles, they rose like a rope of water. They spun through the medallion into his belly button as if sucked in. He watched the tail of magic disappear. "Mommy, why are you giving me your wolf?"

Her eyes glistened. "It is—was—your father's. He gave it to me because he loved me, and I'm giving it to you because I love you. You're a big boy now, Noah. A brave boy. The wolf will help you remember that I love you."

Two days later she was dead.

Chapter Fifteen

Noah opened his eyes, dazed from the most spectacular climax he'd ever had, and was immediately riveted by the sight of Sophia's eyes in the mirror. Magic eyes, irises like a warm sea sparkling with moonlight. Paradise at night.

Paradise. He closed his lids and savored the scent of her, the feel. What they had done was the most amazing...*she* was the most amazing...well. He admitted to himself he'd wanted to do this since the moment he'd first seen her. He opened his eyes again to look his fill. Caught sight of his own eyes in the mirror.

Gold.

His irises were gold, the color of...bloody claws and paws. He spun away, yanked his pants one-handed to his hip, and started to hunt for his clothes.

"What's wrong?" Sophia said.

He glanced at her. She looked confused, beautiful, hurt. He nearly ran back to her, to hug her and kiss her and make the confused and hurt go away.

But damn it, he'd *mated* with her. He'd mated a *witch*.

He wanted to howl, wanted to run away from the reality of it. Mating was the most intimate thing a wolf could do, like inviting another soul under his skin.

A witch. Like the hard man who'd betrayed his mother and him. Like the evil warlocks who'd come that day.

His head throbbed. He'd sworn to never trust mages again. And now he was mated to one?

He stared at her, echoes of memory made flesh. He wanted to escape, but he couldn't. He couldn't leave her unprotected—nor could he leave her looking so hurt.

Veiling his gold irises with half-shut lids, he returned to her and wrapped arms around her. He only relaxed after he cupped her head against his heart. Without his hand to hold his still-open pants, they started sliding down his hips.

She snuggled in, a warm, soft bundle, and none of that seemed to matter.

He sighed. What did he do now? She felt so absolutely right in his arms. He didn't know if his brain or the mating was telling him that. It no longer seemed to matter.

Fucking marvelous. His body had settled right in, accepting her as his mate, even glorying in it.

His brain and emotions were *way* far behind. This was a disaster. For years he'd tried to believe he was a full-blooded shifter, even though he'd suspected his mother's relationship with the wizard was something closer than employer and employee. So, all right, sex with a witch could happen. Even having children was possible. But mating? Never. Happened.

Right?

Except his mother's eyes had been gold, too.

But the wizard's eyes were silver. Even if Noah's mother had mated, it was one-sided. How else could the wizard have abandoned them? If they'd truly been family, Noah would've felt remorse amputating his connection with magic afterward.

"Your eyes changed color," Sophia said from the depths of his embrace. "What does that mean?"

He throttled a groan. She'd seen. The only bright side was that she didn't seem to know what it meant.

He thought about lying for all of a second. *No.* Even if this was the most unnatural mating on the planet, she was his. He couldn't lie to her.

He could, however, equivocate. "It's complicated."

Was it ever. He was riding a roller coaster between extreme joy and scared shitless.

He could just imagine how she'd react if he told her. *You are now a wolf's mate.* Disgust would be the least of it. Witches were even more prickly about purebloods than shifters, just look at the hereditary council. "Hereditary" had the stamp of bloodline all over it. He was sure every last royal witch and wizard would be horrified—right before they cut off his balls, or whatever penalty they had for this particular taboo.

"It's always complicated," she said dryly. "Look, I know we started out to prove the nature of the hex, but what happened...I mean, I want you to know I don't sleep with every guy I meet. Not that we did any sleeping...well."

He felt her blush more than saw it, a heating between his pecs, and smiled. It was so sweet, so cute... Bite his wolfie ass, his emotions were lining up with his body. He groaned.

Only his mind remained the holdout, detached, doubtful. Sane. This could *not* be happening.

Therefore he had to find a way to make it unhappen.

His body froze at the thought. His emotions ran like knives through him. His heart thumped painfully.

She said, "But I think we have to do it again."

"Again?" Where'd that eager little yip in his voice come from? He'd been the dog King too long. "Why?"

"I think it worked—I think the hex was revealed—but, um, I didn't have my eyes open to see it. Not my physical eyes and not my third eye."

"But we climaxed together." And how special was that? "Proof positive everything is good. So you can stay."

"Good sex proves... Where did you get that idea?" She leaned back in his arms to look into his eyes.

He didn't want her to see the gold, didn't want to remind her he was evading her earlier question. He tucked her face back into his chest.

Then her words seeped through. "*Good* sex?" That wasn't just good sex, it was exceptional. The best sex of his life.

The most fabulous orgasm he'd ever had wasn't the shared paradise he'd thought? Was this like his mother, a one-sided mating bond? Worse, was this all his pitiful ego, needing Sophia to be as overwhelmed as he was?

"The sex was amazing," she said. "But it doesn't prove alignment. Even evil can indulge in pleasure."

Of all that, he only heard the sex was amazing. *Yeah*.

"Noah, are you listening?"

"Of course." Mostly. "If you can't tell the hex's alignment by the climax, how can you tell?"

"By looking into the mirror at the *moment* of climax. A positive alignment reinforces. It makes everything glow. Negative dims the reflection. I don't suppose you were looking?"

"No." He'd been *feeling*. "We really have to do it again?" He couldn't help the hopeful little catch in his voice. "It's the only way?"

"It's the only non-magical way. But not the only way." She wrestled out of his hold. "There's a reveal spell. It's pretty simple." She started hunting for her clothes, finding her little white top first and pulling it on.

For an instant, he thought she'd figured out his secret. That she wanted *him* to do the reveal.

Then she picked up her skirt and pulled a serious-looking black wand from its pocket. She fingered the stick. "It keeps coming back."

"*You?* You're going to do magic? After you locked it away?" He was appalled. "No. Not for me."

"It's not like you can stop me." She scrambled into the skirt then looked at him and blushed hard. "Aren't you going to dress?"

He stood straighter. Even after they'd satisfied the itch, she liked what she saw. *Yeah.*

"Please?" She looked away.

For her, he pulled up his pants, zipped, and belted. He left the shirt unbuttoned. "Sophia, I remember when Killer chased us from his trailer, you tried to use that wand. You were in obvious pain. I don't want you doing anything that distressing. If we can find out the hex is good simply by having sex again—"

"No!" She put a hand on her cheek as if to cool it. "Sorry, but I've reconsidered. Last time, I couldn't keep my eyes open. Nothing makes me think this time would be any different. Can you promise you'd keep your eyes open?"

He gave her a grudging, "No. But would it hurt to try?"

"Something is driving us together." She glanced at the mirror and her cheeks turned downright ruddy.

"Something incredibly strong, which makes it very, very dangerous."

His gold eyes in the mirror were as bright as coins. Strong? She had no idea.

"Reinforcing it with sex is too risky, especially when a simple reveal would tell us. Then if the hex is beneficial, great. But if it's not, I'd get out of your life, pronto."

Get out of his life? "Too late," he muttered.

"What?"

"Nothing. Can you promise me there's no price?"

"Yes." Her hands clenched, and she couldn't quite hide the agony flashing across her face.

He scowled. "Don't lie. Not to me."

She sighed. "No, I can't promise."

"Then no, you can't do it."

She opened her mouth as if to argue then simply shook her head sadly and turned toward the door. "Then I have to go."

Anguish shot through him, sharp, breath-stealing, as if she'd ripped out his heart. "You can't go." His tone revealed more of his pain than he meant. "You can't go...without your car."

He'd said it automatically, to cover. But the more he thought about it, the more he liked it. A walk to the garage would buy him time. "Mason might have it ready. Let's go check."

"Well...I suppose." She reached for her coat, still on the carpet from when she'd dropped it, and picked it up.

He intervened, nabbing the wand from her with one hand and the coat with the other. Surreptitiously, he dropped the treacherous stick into one pocket. He snagged her elbow, spun her away, and steered her toward the door—nonchalantly tossing her jacket onto the coat tree as they passed.

"But I'll need my coat—"

"It's too warm. You want to sweat? When we get your car, you can come back for it and your suitcase. If the car's ready." He steered her outside.

"I suppose." She locked up then started west on the sidewalk.

He followed. She swung along in her skirt and heels. His eyes felt glued to the swing of her hips. He kept remembering that under that skirt was a pair of thigh-highs, lacy panties and nothing else.

Distracted. That was bad. If they were attacked, he'd be no protection for her. He caught up. As they walked, his hand sought hers. She took his without seeming to realize she was doing it.

They walked hand in hand. Also bad if they were attacked, but he couldn't seem to stop touching her.

He opened his mouth to say something, anything, and couldn't think of a safe topic—sex, hex, mating? So she was the first to break the silence.

"You know, you don't look forty years old."

"I'm not." He finally focused to stare at her in consternation. "I'm twenty-nine."

"So young?" She stared back at him, incredulous. "Wasn't it suicidal to challenge?"

"Well...yes." Shifters lived long lives and didn't come into their full strength until their forties or fifties at the earliest. He'd only won because he'd matured early, and because he'd pulled on his mage heritage at the last minute.

"Why'd you do it?"

"Instinct?" He'd never put his reasons into words before. Now, for her, he tried. "Jobs are scarce here. Seems like half the pack moved away to find work. The ones left...well, stronger is supposed to help weaker, but the alpha, Scauth, and his inner circle were lazy. Living off the sweat of the iotas and omegas. The pups were starving, their mothers overworked. Mason tried, I tried... It was just *wrong*."

"Starving children?" Her spine stiffened with affront. "My aunt would never tolerate that."

"I doubt she knew. Pack takes care of pack." He slid an arm around her waist, his excuse to guide her around the corner, but his real reason to smell her better, to feel her heat, her vitality. Her compassion. "Linda might have known something and tried to help in a way we wolves would accept," he amended. "A couple years ago, before Mason asked me to come to Matinsfield, I got an anonymous message hinting that I'd find answers about my childhood here. I think now maybe that was your aunt."

Her gaze was on his mouth. "So you've been here a year with starving children and didn't fight until now?"

"Before, you thought I was nuts to fight at all, now you think I was nuts to wait even a day?" He wanted to take up the unspoken invitation in those beautiful eyes, those slightly parted, soft lips. "Slan Scauth got his position through backstabbing and trickery. I was trying to build up a power base first, so I'd have solid support for my leadership against his deceit—and his inner circle of bullies. But Scauth went through his midlife crisis in a rather spectacular way, and I couldn't wait." Nearly raping a teenager had been the last straw. "Now I have five ex-lieutenants who hate me, and only Mason to support me."

He snapped his snout shut. He hadn't meant to say that, hadn't meant to worry her. But she was so easy to talk to.

"Even more reason to get you unhexed as soon as possible." She fell silent, a frown on her face.

She was silent as they entered the shop, silent all the way to the garage, a silence that began to worry him.

Finally she said, "Look, I'll stay as long as what I'm doing helps. But if I do one thing that crosses the line, I'm leaving. And if Rodolphe attacks me again, you let me handle it, do you hear?"

In all that, he only heard she was staying. He was relieved—until Mason appeared from under Sophia's car, scowling.

"Damn, Noah, I'm glad you're here. I just had a visit from the Fucking Five. It's a disaster."

Mason rarely got upset. With his size, strength, and smarts, he could handle anything, so why stress?

Yet from his words and the way he kept pulling hand wipes and cleaning his hands—and the fact that he didn't seem to notice Noah's golden eyes—he was definitely perturbed.

"The anti-alphas? What did they say?"

"I don't think she—" Mason jerked his head at Sophia, "—should hear."

Definitely pack business. Noah turned to tell her to leave.

His wolf howled denial. Unnatural or not, she was his mate.

Noah shook his head. So much for wanting to keep the mating bond secret. "I understand. Now you understand. Whatever you have to say to me, you can say in front of

Sophia. I don't have any secrets from her. I *can't* have any secrets."

Mason blinked. His nose twitched. Frowning, he sniffed. His eyes met Noah's, and his eyebrows jumped into his hairline. "Oh shit. Oh shit, shit, shit. You two are ma—"

"*Made* up, yes. We've resolved our differences and are working together."

"What are you talking about?" Sophia touched her pearls. "What's wrong?"

Mason opened his mouth. "You two. You're—"

"Getting impatient." Noah glared at the blabbermouth. When Mason still hesitated, Noah used his alpha growl. "Beta, report. *Now*."

"Yes, sir." Mason didn't look happy, but after a deep breath, he started. "A group of pack 'representatives' came here an hour ago looking for you—the usual crew of five." He grimaced. "They said the majority of the pack was behind them."

"On what?"

"What else? Your leadership. They're full of crap. The majority of the pack is *not* behind them, but the females are so used to being pushed around and abused by the males—" Mason's wolf rasped into his voice, "—instead of being protected and supported like they should've been, well, they probably just gave in."

"Even though they're safe now?" Sophia said.

"It's only been a few days," Noah said. "They have to unlearn years of fear."

Mason said, "Those assholes have been constantly grumbling since we packed Scauth up and carted him off. I've been here longer. I should've seen this coming."

Premonition ruffled Noah's fur. "Bottom line it."

Mason cut a glance at Sophia. "They've issued a full Alpha Challenge."

"The fuck they have!"

"What's that?" Sophia practically vibrated with her need to know, her need to help. She wasn't going to wait quietly on the sidelines, apparently. No missish little mate, but one who could match him stride for stride... *Bloody claws, I did not just think that.*

With a reassuring squeeze to Mason's shoulder, Noah turned to her. "Nothing big. When the alpha isn't taking responsibility and control of the pack, it's a single twenty-four hours to prove he's up to the challenge of leadership on all counts."

"But usually it's only issued after plenty of time for him to try," Mason said. "The minimum before this was nine months, and that was only so short because Doghouse was obviously screwing the pooch...literally."

"Ew." Sophia grimaced. "So it's like impeaching an elected official? There's a vote?"

Noah shifted his eyes. "Kind of like."

"Not really like," Mason said. Noah would've stapled his second's mouth shut but Sophia was watching. Mason yapped on. "It's a full HUFF, starting with the hunt tonight."

"Right," Noah said. "That gives me a couple hours. Plenty of time to prepare. Now about Sophia's car—"

"What's a HUFF?" Sophia jumped in.

Persistent woman. Pride warred with consternation, but Noah's practicality won out. She'd keep asking until she had answers. He'd give her enough to satisfy her curiosity. "A ceremonial Challenge Hunt." He left it at that.

But naturally Mason was being Mr. Helpful. "It *starts* with the hunt. That's what the HU stands for. At moonrise, which is slightly before one a.m. tonight, the alpha and his mate lead the pack in a hunt to prove they can provide."

"The alpha and *his mate?*" Sophia said.

Stapling would not end at his lips, Noah decided. Balls would be involved.

Then her pretty brow wrinkled as if the thought of Noah having a mate other than her was painful, and he wanted to fold her in his arms and reassure her that only she was his, and he hers.

Mason must've wanted that stapler vasectomy because he was still talking. "The Hunt is followed by a Challenge Fight. That's where a challenger fights the alpha for his mate."

Noah shuddered. If anyone took Sophia from him...

"There's that mate thing again," Sophia said. "Is the pack there for that too?"

"All important events take place in front of the full pack," Mason said.

"Okay, if the hunt is at moonrise, and this all happens within twenty-four hours..." Sophia tapped a finger against her pearls. She obviously was considering the risks, formulating a plan. Damn, she was impressive. Maybe she'd even guessed the main problem. "When is the fight?"

She'd seen it. Noah gave in to the inevitable and told her. "When sunrise clears the tall meadow grass. Two hours after first daylight."

When he was fifteen pounds of fur. A full-grown wolf against his doglet. Losing was almost inevitable.

And the winner would take Noah's witch.

Chapter Sixteen

His witch.

Somewhere between Noah's eyes taking on the mating color and now, his mind had lined up with his body and emotions.

He'd come to think of her as his mate, and no temporary about it.

Damn it.

"Daytime?" Sophia said. "That's not good. All right, let's hear the rest. If HU is hunt and F is fight, is there a second F?"

Fucking-helpful Mason opened his mouth to reply. Screw the stapler. Pretending to stumble, Noah pivoted and kneed Mason in the gonads. "Oops."

Mason lifted from the floor with a yelp. He skittered back, hand protectively covering his privates, and gave Noah a bewildered look. Then his eyes cleared, and his sheepish expression let Noah know that the message was received—and that Mason wasn't permanently injured.

Noah spun back to see Sophia staring at him suspiciously. "I'd prefer to concentrate on the first hurdle. The Hunt."

“All right,” she said. “Problem. You’re not mated.”

“Sure he is,” still-fucking-helpful Mason said.

That did it. Next time Noah wouldn’t pull his kick. Testicles would meet tonsils.

But Mason’s words meant he’d already accepted Sophia as their alpha female.

Would that be so bad?

Noah gazed at her. She was bright, beautiful, spirited, and determined. Perfect for him.

He crushed the wistful thought. She was a *witch*. Like his father. Never trust witches.

Although, just because he hated his father didn’t mean he had to hate all witches, did he? Of course not. Hating all witches based on his father abandoning his mother and him would just be psychotic.

It was okay, what he felt for Sophia. Okay that his fingers ached with the need to touch her, that his mouth throbbed with the need to kiss her. Definitely not hate. Was the opposite of hate. Was lov...

Not hate. Right. Done deal. Glad that was settled.

Of course, the rest of the pack might not be so easily persuaded to accept her, especially after they found out she was a witch. Most wolves could care less about the Witches’ Council as long as it didn’t impact their day-to-day lives, but since this mating was a Council taboo, it might carry a big price tag, too big for the pack to accept. He was going to have to find out what the penalty was one of these days.

Mason continued, “The problem is, Noah’s mate has to hunt as a wolf.”

Okay, Mason had a point. Even if there was something in the magic shop to turn Sophia into a wolf, there was almost no chance they’d find it in that clutter before the

Hunt. If only he didn't have that deadline. Why did it have to be tonight?

It didn't. He hit his forehead, hard, nearly flattening it. "By my sire's bloody paws, why should I cave to this so-called representative group? If it's the usual five, I'll just go convince them they've made a mistake."

"You mean talk them down?" Sophia said.

"Well...yes?"

Mason snorted. "Wolves, talk?"

"So you'll fight them?" Sophia folded her arms. It plumped her cleavage in that little white top most enticingly. "Five against one? You already got hurt fighting just two. Noah, please don't."

He raised his eyes to meet her gaze. "A very wise woman once said to me, 'It's not like you can stop me'."

"Touché. All right, then can't you even the odds somehow?"

"Listen to her, Noah." Mason crossed his arms too, although Noah wasn't tempted to look at his cleavage. "If they'd fight fair, that'd be one thing. But I don't trust them not to gang up on you."

"Maybe I can help," Sophia said. "Who are the five?"

Noah bristled. "You're not getting anywhere near those—"

"Killer." Mason ticked up one finger. "Attila." A second finger. "Bonnie and Clyde." Two more fingers, and then his thumb, pointed down. "And Ivan. Noah, you'll have to take Ivan last, or you'll be exhausted before you even start."

"Not Marlowe?" Sophia asked.

"The pup is trouble," Noah said. "But he's not old enough to be a real threat. Ivan is. He'll definitely be last. And you won't be coming."

"Take Mason with you, then." Sophia looked grim.

Noah shook his head. “I can’t look weak.”

“Pretend he isn’t there to fight. Say it’s to discuss pack business and you need him as a secretary, or something.”

Mason started nodding. “Listen to Sophia, Noah. She’s smart.”

Noah glanced between them. Both his mate and his second were wearing their determined faces. If he didn’t give in, he wouldn’t put it past either of them to go around him to “help”. Or worse, they might collaborate. Mason could take care of himself, but Sophia and those five...? He briefly closed his eyes and shuddered. “Fine. If it’ll get you both off my back, I’ll take Mason.”

Mason relaxed. “Good.”

“But you.” Noah shook a stern index finger at his second. “Stay back. Only interfere if it’s an emergency. My status as dominant is already shaky.”

“No problem, except for Bonnie and Clyde. They’re almost never apart.”

“Bonnie?” Sophia said brightly. “I can take care of her.”

Noah whirled to face her. “You won’t go anywhere near that bitch.”

“What bitch can resist shopping?” She dazzled him with a grin. “I’m not going to fight, only distract. Don’t worry about me.”

Not worry about her? Not in this lifetime. He grabbed her arms. “You are not—”

“Noah, sweetheart. Goose-gander? You can’t stop me.”

His mouth remained hanging open. She’d called him *sweetheart*.

* * *

Sophia stared into Noah's wonderful golden eyes. He thought she didn't know. He was avoiding the whole issue of his eyes turning colors because he thought she didn't know what it meant.

He was mated. To her.

Which, she reminded herself, was *forbidden*, not just yanked-before-the-Witches'-Council-and-castrated forbidden, but death.

Strangely, she worried more about the impact on poor Noah's sex life. One-and-only mated wasn't bad for her; Blues were monogamous women. But Noah? Shifter mating was the ultimate of monogamous relationships. Exclusive and forever, meaning if Noah never had a child by her, he'd never have a child.

Mated. 4-evah.

She'd always thought shifters got the raw end of the sex deal. The idea of fate—or magic or the great Wolf in the Sky—picking your partner seemed weird enough. But then being stuck with that mate your whole life long? Arbitrary and capricious and definitely not fair.

But now that she was experiencing it, it didn't feel arbitrary or capricious. It felt inevitable and right.

Should have scared her. She wasn't scared at all.

*HEART beats for a wolf and a Blue...*and Avignon's predictions always came true. She shook the thought away.

Noah didn't seem too scared either. Maybe he suspected, as she did, that the whole thing was counterfeit. A consequence of the altered hex that would fall apart with the unhexing.

Although in the meantime, if she was the Blue of the prophecy, he was the wolf. Which meant if the Hungry Ghost was after her, he'd be after Noah.

Beware the Hungry Ghost. Big reason to break the hex ASAP and free Noah from the mating.

On the other hand, breaking the hex would leave him mateless for the Hunt. Unless he could find another mate in a scant two hours...

Something deep inside her snarled at that. Noah wasn't finding any mate but *her*.

Heat washed over her. Did she have an inner wolf somewhere? She probed the snarl like a sore tooth, gingerly, hoping it was her imagination.

The wolf snarled again. She didn't like getting poked.

Sophia's nape hairs raised. Clang her cauldron—she had an inner wolf. How the hell had that happened?

The hex? Or the sex? There certainly had been enough magic swirling around them. Or maybe Noah's wolf rubbed off on her when they'd been rubbing bodies...stars.

Her wolf snarled again. *Protect our mate. Beware the Ghost. Find the Heart.*

Well. Whether inner wolf or subconscious venting, it spoke truth. First things first. Help Noah survive the Challenge by putting it off until she could find a way to shift.

Time to go shopping.

"Sophia." Noah's deep voice broke into her thoughts. She realized he was staring closely at her, almost deep enough to read her mind. Sure enough, he said, "You are not going to Bonnie and Clyde's."

He couldn't stop her, but that stern look on his beautiful face meant he certainly was going to try.

She gave him a bright smile. "Would I do that?" She put a finger to Noah's lips to forestall any arguments. Apparently her flesh had been sensitized by their time in front of the mirror. Skin-on-skin contact poured barrels of lust through her veins. Him too, if his pained face was any indication.

Her whole body clenched with want, so intense she shuddered. But the shock also made his grip on her relax.

She recovered first. Popping from his hands, she spun for the garage's people door.

He started after her with his ground-eating stride.

"Don't worry," she flung over her shoulder. "I'm just going to my aunt's bookstore."

"Why?"

"Auntie has a barrel of basic calm charms. Overstock. Might help with a rampaging shifter or two. Say, if you want to get your convincing done before one a.m., hadn't you and Mason better get started?"

He slowed at that, albeit reluctantly. "You're not going to Bonnie's?"

"How can I? I don't know where she lives." She scooted through the door and outside. She hadn't lied. She had no idea where Bonnie and Clyde lived.

But the Misses Jamies would.

The bad thing about eternal busybodies was that they were always poking their noses into their neighbors' business.

The good thing was that meant they were always home.

Gladys Louise met Sophia at the door. The heavy-set sister wore a frilly red apron that matched her apple cheeks. "Come in, come in! Aren't your eyes bright and your hair nicely mussed."

Sophia's mouth dropped open. "I'm sorry?"

"Very stylish, that right-out-of-bed look." The twinkle in her eye made Sophia wince.

"Hello, Sophia." Almira, appearing behind Gladys Louise, waved Sophia in. "We've been expecting you."

That froze her, open-mouthed again. She managed, "You were?"

"Noah has trouble. You'd want to help, but you'd need more information. Oh, shut your mouth. You look like a fish." Almira steered Sophia to the couch. "Albeit a nicely mussed one."

Sophia shut her mouth and let herself be directed. Miss Almira Jamies could have made a mint as an air traffic controller. Cheeks broiling, not thinking about why she looked nicely mussed, Sophia collapsed onto a cushion.

A sweating pitcher of iced tea waited on the coffee table. Gladys Louise poured her a generous glass. "Oh. A man left something for you here." She handed Sophia the glass then reached into a pocket of her apron and pulled out the psychedelic rod.

"Your aunt's vibrator," Almira said when Sophia only stared.

"It's not a vibrator." Sophia took it. "It's a skyscraper mushroom."

"It doesn't vibrate?" Gladys Louise piped.

"Well it does, but..." Face flaming, Sophia sipped iced tea, sucking an ice cube into her mouth.

"It's nice, of course," Almira said. "Though mine is bigger."

Sophia choked on her ice cube.

Gladys Louise piped, "The double-ended ones are better."

Sophia swallowed the ice cube whole. She coughed while Almira helpfully pounded her on the back. "Gladys Louise uses it for sore muscles. What did you think?"

When her coughing subsided, Sophia said, "I came for Bonnie and Clyde's address. I can't go into details—"

"The Alpha Challenge?" Almira said.

So much for secrets. "Yes. Noah's going to get the anti-alphas to drop it. I need to distract Bonnie so he can talk to Clyde alone."

Gladys Louise nodded encouragingly. "And how had you thought to do that, dear?"

"Well...take her shopping?"

Almira snorted. "The only kind of shopping Bonnie does is the lifting kind."

"As in shop-lifting," Gladys Louise piped helpfully.

"Isn't that taking the Bonnie and Clyde names to the extreme?"

"They picked their own adult names," Almira said.

"Shopping's a nice idea dear," Gladys Louise said. "Except for the fact that Bonnie doesn't go shopping, of course." She cocked her head, her eyes bright beads, like a little bird. "Maybe you should add an item or two from your aunt's stock of magical persuaders. Just in case."

"You might get Bonnie to a bar." Almira nibbled a cookie. With her long front teeth, she looked like a tall mouse. "She likes to drink."

"Good idea," Gladys Louise said. "She even has her own mug at the corner tap."

"Which one?" Sophia asked. There were at least five corner bars in a six-block radius.

"The one next to her house, of course." Gladys Louise gave her the address.

"Thanks." Sophia took her aunt's mushroom and left.

She trotted down the sisters' hedge-lined front walk, intent on getting to the Uncommon Night Owl Bookstore to pick up a magical means of helping convince Bonnie to leave, in case straight begging didn't work.

A rustle brought her head up. Behind her. She turned.

The front walk was empty—except for a couple leaves fluttering on the hedges.

Neck prickling, she turned slowly back and continued on her way, turning from the sisters' path onto the city sidewalk, her ears open. Would've been easier with a wolf's preternatural hearing.

But even her human ears caught the click of toenails behind her.

She whirled to see a dog-like rump disappearing into the hedge. Not King—bigger. Black, with a suspiciously bushy tail.

Frowning, she turned again. Worked up a whistle and nonchalant saunter, she traipsed along in seeming oblivion for half a block.

She spun on her toe.

The animal trotting behind her froze, standing directly under a street lamp.

It was a wolf.

O-kaaay. The question was, shifter or natural? Cause if it was a *wolf* wolf, she was in serious trouble.

Come to think of it, if it was a shifter other than Noah or Mason, she was probably in trouble too. Well, unless it was Moon Moon, the Mr. Bean of werewolves.

Human or animal? She tried to see its eyes without staring. Creatures Studies taught her Canidae took a direct stare as a challenge.

The wolf's eyes looked like—eyes. Well, hocus her pocus. Who made up the idea that only shifter wolves had human eyes? What a load of crap. Round iris, round pupil, the only difference between human eyes and wolf eyes was that the opening revealed much less white.

The amused gleam in those black eyes, though? Definitely human, and an annoying human at that.

Sophia's fists landed on her hips. "Are you Mason? No, don't answer. It's bad enough you're out where anyone can see you. Follow me."

She stomped off. Damn it, Noah was supposed to take Mason with him. Instead he'd ordered Mason to protect her? She could protect herself. Mason was so getting a butt chewing, followed by Noah when she saw him next.

Ooh. Chewing Noah's butt, those hard rounded muscles... No. Righteous indignation here.

Arriving at the bookstore, she hesitated. The physical lock looked fine, but with Rodolphe in town... Sure, he was a coward, a danger to freshmen witches and helpless cars, but running from a real threat. But if he wasn't the Hungry Ghost, that only meant the Ghost was still out there.

Bracing herself, she took a quick peek with her witch's eye for signs of tampering, keeping half an ear on the wolf. Nothing alarming popped up. She'd have done a full reveal but migraine auras streaked like jagged lightning through her vision, warning her pain wasn't far away. She closed her third eye, unlocked and opened the door, strode in, and turned on the lights.

The wolf trotted in behind her. The moment she shut and locked the door, the wolf's edges blurred. Its form unfolded, morphing. Fur retracted, lean limbs lengthened and thickened with masculine muscle. All fours reared onto two, back unfurling and head rolling up while legs and arms and torso lengthened. Clothes blossomed to cover him just before he finished forming. In less time than it took to describe it, a man stood before her in jeans and a jacket.

It was the hot man from the pet store.

Without the apron he was very sexy indeed. He stood at his elegant ease, black hair curling carelessly around his fine ears, thumbs in his jeans pockets, hip cocked. His sharp eyes told her that, despite being a dog groomer, this man was not one to cross lightly.

"Did Noah send you?" she blurted.

"Hmm." The corner of his mouth curled. "If I say yes, I could be lying. If I say no, you'll run. I'll say 'yes'."

"Right. Stupid question." She normally wasn't stupid, but she'd had a rough couple of days, culminating in the shock of incredible sex, her mate having to fight, and now these brilliant, penetrating black eyes. "Okay. Who are you?"

"Someone to keep you out of trouble."

In the pet store it seemed perfectly appropriate not to know his name. Now it rankled. "Did Noah ask you to watch me? Are you in his pack?"

"I owe the Blackwood pack a favor," he said, answering nothing. "I happened to overhear him trying to get his second to follow you, to 'Keep her from getting herself killed', which I interpreted as keeping you out of trouble. Watching you in action, though...now I understand what he meant."

She flushed. "Noah's overprotective. What I'm doing isn't dangerous." Or at least it wouldn't be, after she combed Auntie's stash for a helper item. She stowed the mushroom under the register—oh, there was her suitcase—and started searching, one eye on the nameless man.

"Not dangerous?" The man's very fine lips quirked in her periphery. "Noah's usually a pretty good judge, both of people and situations."

"He's emotionally involved. It's clouded his judgment."

The man raised one black brow, arching high. He sniffed delicately, his fine nostrils flaring. "Ah, yes. I understand."

Like he hadn't smelled the sex before. Which reminded her, she'd have to stay downwind of Bonnie and Clyde. "Don't pretend not to have super-smell. I know you're a shifter."

The man shrugged. "I can shift." The twinkle in his eye hinted at implications with a capital Imp.

She snatched up a calm amulet from a nearby barrel. Not for the five anti-alphas—for her, so as not to smack Mr. I-Can-Shift to the moon. He was not only annoying, he'd obviously had a lot of practice at it.

"Whatever." She opened the cabinet nearest her, labeled *Last Chance Sale!! (unsorted)*, revealing shelves littered with magical paraphernalia: wands, scrolls, loose crystals, potions in jewel-toned glass vials, and amulets both simple and gemmed. No way to tell what any of them were, at least not in the mundane way.

So she opened her third eye to the possibilities. Immediately the competing chatter of the talismans crowded her. "Pick me, pick me!" they cried. "You need help. Pick me!"

Oh great. Leave it to Auntie to have obnoxiously helpful talismans. Sophia felt like Alice in *Alice's Adventures in Wonderland* where the cakes all cried, "Eat me". Or was that *Through the Looking Glass*? Then she remembered what a big bad alpha shifter and she had done *in* the looking glass...staying in Wonderland, then.

The talismans' voices were getting louder, shriller. Her head started to throb. To stave off a headache, she dropped the calm amulet, reached into the cabinet, and picked one.

Behind her, gorgeous no-name guy cleared his throat. "Good choice...if you're trying to kill her."

She cracked a physical eye. She held a foot-long copper rod with an ivory ceramic handle on one end and a small ball at the tip of the other. It looked like a toy wand. She turned it over to read the label. "Lightning rod. Used for ritual electrocutions."

Her eyes flew wide, all three of them. *Yikes*. What the hell was Auntie doing with a thing like that? She tossed it back.

"Although it *would* clear the field for Noah," Nameless Guy went on. "I think you can turn the level down."

"Like a magical stun gun?" She still left it in the cabinet. "How'd you know I was looking to clear the way for Noah?"

The corner of his mouth quirked. "The Jamies are a bit deaf. I could hear you through the front window."

"You were *eavesdropping*?"

"Please. I prefer aural fact-finding. What you don't know *can* hurt you."

"Look, I just want to get Bonnie out of her house without raising suspicions. Clyde would know something was wrong if I zapped her."

"How about this?" He reached into the cabinet near her head. Her hair crackled, and she shivered as he brought the thing out past her, like it was covered in electricity. Unless his personal aura was just that potent. He handed it to her.

A clear plastic case held a small multi-colored disk, about four inches in diameter. "It looks like a coaster."

"Ulysses S. Grant's coaster, to be precise. You want to get Bonnie to go out drinking, correct? This will make the urge an obsession. Slip it onto her person, and she'll immediately want to visit a bar."

"Won't she just pop a beer from the fridge?"

"No, that's not how it works," he said with such exaggerated patience that she wanted to beat him with a humility bat. “It heightens whatever she loves most about bars. Take a closer look.”

“Fine.” Opening her third eye she saw the coaster would indeed prompt the desire to visit a bar or tavern. And something more...she reached for it but couldn’t quite tell.

“C’mon, Sophia, you’re not marrying it. Take it and let’s go. Knowing Noah, he’ll start with Bonnie and Clyde, specifically so you won’t be exposed to Bonnie.”

“Crispy fried cobwebs. That’s just like him, isn’t it?” She shut her third eye and opened her temporal ones. Coaster in hand, she headed out the door, locking it after them. “I wish he wouldn’t. I don’t need protecting.” She started east, then stopped.

“Everybody needs protecting at some time or another. Including big bad alphas. What’s wrong? If you’re going to get there before Noah does, you’d better hurry.”

“I need to hide the coaster. I left my coat in the store.”

“Put it in your skirt pocket.”

“If it fits.” She slid the case into the skirt pocket, then stuck her hip out to look at it. “It bulges.”

“So she’ll think you’re happy to see her. Come on. Noah won’t take long to convince Mason to head there, and you frittered away half that jawing with the Jamies. You have maybe five minutes.”

“Right.” She started up again, setting a brisk pace for four-inch heels. “You’re coming along? This isn’t just a favor to the pack, is it? What’s in it for you?”

His lips quirked. “You’re a sharp little witch, aren’t you? I have a bike that’s a bit specialized. Mason’s the only one who can keep it in top condition.”

“That vintage motorcycle in pieces?” She cut a penetrating glance at him. Something about his lazy saunter and lowered lids made her think he wasn't telling her the whole story.

"No, the Ducati is Mason's. At least his name's on the title. Of course, emotionally, it's Noah's."

"Huh?"

"Please. It's obvious that bike is Noah's promise to both himself and Mason that he'll fix what's wrong here in Blackwood territory."

"If you roll your eyes any farther, they'll stick looking at the inside of your skull. Although then you'll see your favorite person, won't you? That bike doesn't look fixed to me."

"Noah's a damned good alpha but he isn't a mechanic. He needs help. He hasn't admitted that yet, though. We're here."

"Right." Sophia took a deep breath and started up the curving front walk to Bonnie and Clyde's home.

Chapter Seventeen

After Killer's, Bonnie and Clyde's house was a surprise, a neat bungalow with a white picket fence and a freshly clipped lawn. A curving walk, lined by petunias of all things, led to a home that sat primly in a nest of neatly trimmed shrubs.

The nameless man stopped and morphed into the black wolf, this time flowing from form to form so fluidly Sophia knew he'd been deliberately showing her the process last time. Or maybe he was showing off now.

As she clipped up the walk, no toenails clicked beside her, either. She glanced at the wolf. "If you won't tell me your name, I'll have to give you one. How about Major Annoyance? Snarky Sidekick?"

His head tilted to look at her. One corner of his wolfie mouth quirked up. Then he leaped into the bushes and hunkered down.

She mounted the stoop. The front screen door was closed, the inside door open. She leaned in to peer through the screen, straight into wafting plumes of rough smoke, an El Sleazo cigar. The interior was quiet, dark, and stinky. Stifling a cough, she rang the doorbell.

Light, quick steps approached.

Bonnie opened the door. She was a surprise too, wavy blonde hair, white flip-flops, pink calf-length skinny jeans, and a short pink top with "Baby Doll" in sparkly letters. A swath of smoothly muscled tummy peeked between the top and jeans.

A strong, sweet cloud of perfume enveloped her. Between that and the cigar smoke, Sophia stopped worrying about the smell of Noah on her.

"What do you want?" Bonnie said.

"It's what *I* can do for *you*." Sophia gave Bonnie her best trusty smile and wished really hard on her lucky broomstick that Bonnie would let her inside, at least long enough to plant the coaster. "I'm from the American Barkeeping Association. You've won a *free* pass to the neighborhood bar of your choice."

Clyde appeared behind Bonnie. With his wiry muscularity, threadbare jeans, and skintight, yellowed beater shirt, he was gangster werewolf to the hilt. "Who is it?" He puffed a cigar around the words like a locomotive.

"Dunno," Bonnie said. "Someone selling something."

"It's free!" Sophia put on her bestest, honestest grin—and stuck her toe in the door. Hopeful didn't equal stupid. "May I come in to tell you more?"

Bonnie shook her head. "We're expecting someone."

"No problem. I'll be quick." Not throwing her out was as good as an invitation, right? She surged forward, so Bonnie either had to step back or actively resist. She stepped back. *Yes*.

As Sophia came inside, she slid the coaster case out of her pocket, eyeing Bonnie for likely hiding places. The shifter woman's pink spandex camisole was so tight every ounce of fat was smooshed up into her boobs, making spectacular cleavage. Sophia really wanted one, especially now that she'd met Noah...*argh*. Focus. If she could tuck the coaster in Bonnie's cleavage—

"This way." Bonnie spun and, with a sway of hips, took off.

Sophia squeaked and leaped after her. Clyde fell into step behind.

The door opened onto a cozy living room, a conversation area to one side boasting a tartan sofa facing two chairs, a pine plank coffee table between. An end table held a cordless phone.

Sophia thumbed the case's plastic tab as she followed. Now the only hiding place presenting itself was Bonnie's painted-on jeans pockets. She'd almost certainly feel Sophia sliding the coaster in. Maybe cover by giving Bonnie's rump a buddy slap? She'd have to hope she didn't slug her.

Okay, go for it. Sophia flipped the coaster case open—or tried. The case was the bastard child of a clam and super glue. She wrenched on it.

Bonnie turned just as the case came open with a snap.

The coaster flew out like bread from a toaster on crack. Sophia snatched at it, bobbled it, and barely caught it.

The room spun around her. An intense desire to go bar crawling hit her and grabbed her by the lizard brain, degenerating into *Me like beer*. She stumbled a few steps.

"You okay?" Bonnie stood in front of one of the chairs, and Sophia had stumbled to stand before the couch. The she-wolf reached a sympathetic hand over the table to steady her.

Sophia slapped the coaster back into its case by instinct alone. The dizziness receded. "Yes, I'm fine."

Bonnie dropped her hand from Sophia's arm to point at the case. "What's that?"

"Nothing." Sophia jammed the half-open case under her armpit.

Click. Shut again. Stupid case.

Bonnie frowned. "But—"

"Let me tell you about your marvelous prize. Free drinks at the local tap of your choice! One night only." Sophia's grin felt pop-riveted on. She dropped onto the couch. Apparently the coaster worked on contact. Maybe she could just hand it to Bonnie like a prize token—assuming it would come out of the case. Although if Bonnie dropped it, the jig would be up. "Open bar as long as you stay. Free-free-free!"

"Free is good." Bonnie sat down in the chair. "There's a nice bar right on our corner."

Yes, I know. Sophia's smile broadened until she was grinning like a maniac. Bonnie had fallen neatly into her trap.

Bonnie's expression froze, and she slid back in her chair as if not quite certain of Sophia's sanity.

Sophia lost the rapacious grin fast. "Imagine that. A bar on your corner would be ideal. Let's go!" She sprang to her feet. Maybe she wouldn't need the magic coaster to get Bonnie out of here. Maybe the magic *word* "free" would be enough.

"You can't." Clyde put a hand on Bonnie's shoulder. "Marlowe said you-know-who is coming."

"Oh." Bonnie's face fell. "I'm sorry Miss...Miss Barkeeping Association person. I can't go right now. Later?"

"Sorry, the rules don't allow that. I'll just have to give this Marvelous Free Opportunity to someone else." Sophia shrugged, pretending not to care.

"Okay."

Sophia gritted her teeth. "Too bad you're missing this Wonderful Never-To-Be-Repeated Offer. Free-free-free."

"Too bad. But thanks for thinking of me."

Enamel cracked. "One Time Only. Last chance."

"I'm sorry, Miss...whatever." Bonnie rose and gestured toward the door. "You can see yourself out."

Sophia started for the door with great reluctance. Double-bubble her toil and trouble; she'd failed to get Bonnie out of the way, and now Noah'd have to battle two wolf shifters at once.

Sophia stopped. Unless she, as his mate, could fight Bonnie while he thrashed Clyde. She cut a glance at Bonnie. The wolfwoman stood with the grace of a dancer or a martial artist. Considering the amount of slender muscle in her arms and torso, Sophia probably couldn't actually *fight* her for any length of time.

But she could distract Bonnie from Noah by taking a long time getting brutally torn apart. Yay.

A wolf's yip came from outside. An instant later arguing voices, getting louder, sounded like men coming up the walk.

One voice was Noah's.

Clyde grinned viciously around his cigar. "You-know-who is here."

Sophia's heart kicked into overdrive. Dammit, she would *not* fail her mate. She was planting that coaster on Bonnie's barely covered self if she had to insert it like a tampon. Sophia tore the case open.

As Bonnie passed her on the way to the door, Sophia shoved the coaster deep between the wolfwoman's boobs.

"What the fuck?" Bonnie looked down at herself. Her hand reached into her bosom.

Sophia froze. All was lost. She managed a grab at Bonnie's shoulder. "Don't—"

"*Hic.*" Bonnie swayed slightly. Slowly, her hand dropped. She hiccupped again.

Then her frown spun up into a come-hither smile. "Oh, Clyde. Clyyy-dee honey."

"Not now, Bonnie." Clyde hovered near the door, craning for a look out the screen.

She sashayed to him with an ultra-sexy hip roll and caught him by the shoulders. She practically draped her body around his. "Clyde, babe. Forget you-know-who. Let's go around the corner—and do it on the bar again."

Again?

"Are you drunk?" Clyde asked suspiciously.

"Didn' have a drop." She burped. She rubbed her foot sensuously—against his butt. Wow, she was flexible. "C'mon, babe. You know you want to."

Sophia felt a sort of triumphant horror. Apparently when Bonnie got drunk, she got horny and exhibitiony.

Another warning yip came from Annoying Nameless Guy. Sophia had mere moments to peel Bonnie off Clyde and get her out of here. "Come on, Bonnie, I'll take you to the bar."

"Oh, I don't know." Bonnie giggled, cut short with a hiccup. "I think you're too short to do it on the bar with me."

Sophia was speechless long enough for a nasal male voice to cut through. "An alpha should have pussy, not *be* a pussy."

"Attila's fuckin' right." That was Killer, nearly at the door.

Attila gave a nasal laugh. "You're screwed without a mate, Blackwood."

Sophia's chest iced over. Killer, Clyde, and Attila? She remembered the last as a big, barrel-chested gray wolf. Three against Noah? Mason would *have* to help. And if she couldn't spring Bonnie loose, she'd have to fight too, although without her magic she'd have to rely on her pepper spray...which was in her coat pocket, hanging at the store, damn it. Maybe the nameless man would join in to even the score, but she wasn't hopeful. She plucked at Bonnie's arm. "We need to go."

"Clydee, please." Bonnie grabbed Clyde's head and thrust it into her bosom.

Okay, maybe he'd suffocate, and it'd be three against three.

"Whatever you say, I *am* alpha." Noah's voice rang with confidence. "It doesn't matter what you will or won't accept."

Sophia tried to get Bonnie's attention. "Is there a back way—?" Too late.

The door opened.

A dark man with long mustaches surged onto the doorsill. "Our 'alpha' challenges the Challenge."

"Figures." Clyde's voice was a bit muffled.

Bonnie cooed. "Ooh, Attila. I'm so glad you're here."

Attila was built similar to his namesake, short and broad-chested with small eyes and a scraggly beard.

Bonnie released Clyde to drag Attila inside and give him a big smooshie kiss. "Wanna do a threesome?"

Clyde growled. Sophia nodded. Good, something to distract him from beating up on Noah.

Mason slid inside next.

Bonnie's eyes widened. Well, he *was* a handsome specimen of a man, big and muscular with his shaggy gold-streaked walnut hair. One hand still latched onto Attila, she grabbed Mason's wrist. "Oooh, a foursome." She planted Mason's hand—on her breast.

Clyde's growl darkened. Bonnie grinned.

Behind Mason, Killer shoved in.

The last time Sophia had seen him, he'd knifed Noah. Foreboding rippled unpleasantly along her skin. Unnerved, she cracked open her third eye.

A blood aura surrounded Killer.

She swallowed bile, her hand flying to her pearls. Comets and stars. Those murders in the trailer...

Her head began to ache. But the blood aura didn't quite touch him. An accessory then, not the killer. She peered closer, head starting to throb. A gold flame writhed in the aura.

Her eyes snapped open. A wizard was involved.

Daniel's evil wizard, the Hungry Ghost? Had Rodolphe graduated from stealing life money to stealing *lives*? She shuddered.

Then Noah stepped inside.

His eyelids were lowered, masking the gold of his eyes. Sophia breathed easier, seeing him come in last—it meant he'd allowed no enemies at his back. She'd half-expected him to play the indestructible alpha with the S on his fur.

But then the door opened again and the whole group slid forward into the living room as if a force-field had moved them. Sophia sucked in a breath.

The nameless man filtered in, still a big black wolf, leaving it a mystery as to how he'd opened the door. Her breath came out in a puff of relief. At least he hadn't left them high and dry.

Although if it did come to a fight, she wouldn't put it past him to sit back and break out the popcorn.

Bonnie brightened like the sun. "A sixsome, all for me."

Clyde growled, low and angry, in response. Sophia mentally pumped air. At this rate Noah wouldn't have to fight any of them, since they'd all be too busy with Bonnie.

Then Bonnie released Mason and Attila and clamped both hands on *Noah*.

Mine. Sophia roared and flew past astonished males like a tornado.

Bonnie's mouth was millimeters from fastening onto Noah like a French-kissing lamprey when Sophia grabbed her by the camisole straps and yanked.

Bonnie was bigger, but Sophia was powered by sheer rage. Bonnie came away shrieking. Sophia threw the wolfwoman from Noah with all her strength. Bonnie stumbled, crashing into Mason and Attila. Attila grabbed for her, got a handful of bosom.

The coaster popped out. It hit the floor with a rattle that made Sophia wince.

"What the hell?" Clyde snatched up the coaster, glared at it, then switched his glare to—Noah. "Whadchew do t' her?" He swayed in place, his eyes narrowed and vicious on Noah. He swiped his cigar from his mouth and, gaze locked on Noah, snuffed it by smashing the lit end into his own chest. Beater shirt smoldering, he dropped the crumpled cigar to the floor with a growl. "I'sh kill you."

The coaster had done its work, but apparently Clyde was a mean drunk—and he'd take his frustrations out on Noah.

Sophia blurted, "No, *I* put the coaster—"

"Fuck you, Clyde." Noah shook his head at her in a frantic *No*—and planted a fist in Clyde's face. *Crack.*

Clyde reeled back—before dropping the coaster to leap on Noah.

They grappled, not even punching and kicking, but shoving and scuffling with mindless violence.

"Fight!" Attila dove for them. Mason lunged for Attila, grabbed him, and yanked him away. They overbalanced and fell onto the couch, rolling and scrabbling.

Bonnie clapped her hands. "Fight, fight!"

Nameless Guy sat on his haunches and lolled.

Then Killer circled around behind Noah, where his kidneys were all too vulnerable.

"Noah!" Heart pumping and veins flushed with adrenaline, Sophia called a warning even as she leaped into action. She dodged snarling shifters, cut in front of Killer, and shoved him away from Noah with all her strength.

As Killer stumbled back, he grabbed her arms. He levered himself against her and not only kept his feet but whirled her hard into the wall.

She bounced off and hit floor.

Good news was, she rolled into Killer's toothpick legs, tangled his feet, and tripped him.

Bad news was, he was wearing boots. Damn, that hurt.

He fell on top of her. She shoved him off then huffed, lying there, trying to get her breath back.

Beside her, Killer scrambled to his feet. Damned shifter speed.

Noah's kidneys were still vulnerable—and he'd whipped out that slender, wicked switchblade.

"Nameless Guy," Sophia shrieked, hauling herself to her elbows. "Go, go!"

The black wolf boiled up to human; his smirk didn't change in the least. He tapped Killer on the back. "Outside, Fur Boy."

Killer spun. "Fuckin' what...?" He blinked, and his face blanked. The knife dropped from his hand. "Okay."

Nameless Guy calmly escorted Killer outside. Sophia staggered to her feet, her mouth agape as she stared after them.

"Oh dear!" Bonnie fell to one knee like a lame duck—right in front of Noah.

Sophia tried to get between them but her heel twisted and she stumbled.

"I hurt myself." Bonnie batted her eyelashes at Noah.

The damn alpha reached a chivalrous hand to help.

Leaving him open to Clyde, who cracked a fist into his skull.

Noah's face went white. He fell back, hand slapping to his head. Blood trickled from under it.

Sophia kicked off her shoes, winched up her skirt, ran two steps, and sailed a kick into Clyde's nuts, so fueled with anger she probably dented his prostate.

With a sound like a leaky balloon, Clyde fell to his knees, curling like a pill bug.

Bonnie squeaked. Dropping to the floor, she wrapped arms around him. "Clyde, honey, speak to me! Are you all right?"

The shot of adrenaline that had fueled Sophia suddenly left her. Collapsing against the wall, she held her aching ribs and gasped. Telling herself with a short rest, she could get back in the fight.

Noah, despite the blood trickling down his forehead, looked steadier. His feet were planted, and his eyes surveying the room were sharp. And Mason was actually winning against Attila. She let herself hope.

Then the screen door slammed open.

The room went silent. All fighting stopped. Even Clyde whimpered more quietly.

A man filled the doorway, so big he had to bend to enter. Clad only in stained sweatpants, he was frighteningly lean, a skeleton banded with muscle. He had fists the size of sledgehammers, a small cliff of a jaw, and brows that were bony shelves over insane eyes.

In a tar-paper baritone, he rasped, "You're dead meat, Blackwood."

Sophia swallowed dry fear.

He climbed through the doorway...and straightened. As his torso unfolded, it revealed a skull tattoo emblazoned on his naked chest. Its fiery tongue curled around his navel. His nipples were its dead eyes.

Sophia's knees buckled. She braced against the wall to stop herself from slipping to the floor. She wanted to puke but controlled that too.

Her first coherent thought was worry for Noah.

Her mate had speed, agility, and brains, but there were too many of them—and they didn't fight fair.

No coming out of this uninjured, not even any guarantee of a win. She swallowed her gall. She'd have to try to tap her magic.

If she even could.

Chapter Eighteen

The wand appeared in Sophia's skirt pocket, hot with battle magic.

She didn't question how it had gotten there. Wands, once claimed, had strange properties. She simply slid her hand into her pocket and touched its smooth carbon fiber surface. The wand reminded her of all she'd renounced.

But it was also who she'd dreamed to be. Witch princess, Royal Senator. *Madam High Minister*.

Maybe if she'd waited after Rodolphe's betrayal she'd have reconsidered cutting off her magic. In some ways she'd still been that young, idealistic fool, simply embracing the opposite of Rodolphe in the same blind stupidity.

She'd never know, because cutting off her magic wasn't "like" cutting off a part of her—it *was* cutting off part of her.

The ceremony required a death sacrifice. Being a lawful witch, that death could only be hers.

Being a smart witch, she'd done it in pieces.

Over a period of three days, she suffered three potentially fatal wounds involving head, hands, and heart.

But with a little luck, a lot of magic, and a powerful ceremonial rite, she walled off those deaths along with her magic in three metaphysical funeral domes.

She'd lived. But unlocking even a portion of her magic by breaking a dome could potentially kill her. At the very least, it would hurt like she was dying.

Break all three, and it really would kill her.

It would have been safer to simply expel all her power into another witch. Share Power was a spell used fairly often, sharing bits of magical energy that time and rest would replenish. More rarely a complete Evacuate was used, not fatal, but it was permanent. She hadn't been brave enough to become irreversibly mundane.

Or maybe even then, she knew she'd need her magic one day.

"Ivan." Noah straightened to his full height.

Sophia scanned for allies even as she prepared herself to tap her magic. Mason was locked in combat with Attila, and Nameless Guy was as good as gone. If she didn't want Noah to face the monster alone, it was up to her.

Didn't matter if using magic killed her. For Noah.

A deep breath shunted her horror into a place where she'd deal with it later, a technique learned from her brother the combat wizard. She hadn't studied fighting outside of her intro class, but she'd practiced with Gabriel, something she was grateful for now.

She wrapped her fingers around the wand in her pocket, the stick smooth and warm and good in her hand. Pulling it out, the fittings flashed in her vision, gleaming silver and gold against the black. Silver like Noah's eyes before the change and rich gold like after.

"Sophia, no!" Either seeing the glitter of metal, or even now attuned to her as his mate, Noah spun toward her.

Ivan, seeing the opening, launched a massive fist at Noah's head.

She screamed.

Mason's head jerked around, his eyes huge and horrified. He pushed himself off Attila, shouting Noah's name, and barreled toward Ivan at ramming speed.

Noah swayed to one side at the noise; Ivan's sledgehammer fist barely missed his skull.

Instead, it met Mason's jaw. All the speed force of the beta's lunge rammed into all the power of the huge wolfman's fist. Bone crunched at sickening volume. Spinning once, Mason went down.

Ivan swung at Noah again.

Hand trembling, she opened her third eye to fracture the funeral dome for the first of her trapped magic. The head seal. In her third eye, the dome shimmered like hardened glass.

Noah had already swayed out reach of Ivan's attack—but then Clyde shoved Noah between the shoulders.

As Ivan's fist clipped Noah's skull, Sophia slammed into her head seal. A horrible stereo *crack* sounded in her ears, one Noah's, one hers.

Hers was amplified by pain slicing through her brain. She choked back a cry. Squinting through her physical eyes, she saw Noah had run Ivan's bell with a stunning return punch of his own, but Clyde had leaped on Noah's back. Bonnie clapped her hands and jumped up and down like a demented cheerleader, but if she decided to join the fight, or Ivan recovered, Noah was in trouble.

Sophia's own situation was better. Squinting her third eye through a pounding headache, she saw a hairline fracture branching through her dome's glass. She raised her wand again, readying herself for the magic that would pour out—and as the crack lengthened suddenly, her face sheared in half with acid pain, agony spilling out instead.

She screamed and clutched her head with both hands. Her wand slapped against her cheek.

"Sophia!" Noah shook off Clyde's bear hug and surged toward her.

Clyde managed to grab Noah's arm. The alpha's momentum threw him into an arc around Clyde—toward Attila.

With a vicious grin of triumph, the mustachioed wolfman raised hands to seize the alpha.

Noah simply went with it—with a lifted knee.

His patella slammed into Attila's gut. With a whoosh of expelled air, Attila's grin disappeared. He tried to suck in a breath, couldn't.

Instead of shaking off Clyde, Noah curled in on his grip like a yoyo, and punched Clyde's temple. The wolfman reeled back.

Stomach heaving, vision blurry, Sophia breathed through her pain and reached for her magic. But her head seal was cracked, not broken. Her magic was still locked away. Damn it. Wiping her eyes, she saw Mason out cold, only Noah left fighting Clyde. And when Ivan and Attila recovered...without her fighting magic, there was only one move.

Retreat.

"Noah," she croaked. "We have to go."

Noah glanced at her—as Ivan slammed a pile-driver fist to the top of his head.

A small sigh, all the more horrible for how soft it was, and Noah collapsed to his knees.

As the alpha knelt, swaying, on the floor, the monster wolfman wound up for a finishing blow.

"Help!" Sophia screamed it, even as she opened her third eye, took kamikaze aim, and plunged with all her might toward the hairline crack.

Nameless Guy shot through the door.

She hit psychic glass. The dome's crack widened slightly—and two skillets of pain smashed her skull. Nausea wrung her guts like a washcloth. She gasped and staggered. Only running into the wall kept her from falling to the floor.

Nameless Guy cut between Ivan and Noah and slapped Ivan so hard he left a hand print on the massive wolfman's gaunt cheek. "Hey," he shouted in Ivan's ear. "Here, doggie, doggie. Yeah, you."

Ivan lumbered into a turn, swinging sledge-fists at Nameless Guy. Nameless Guy danced lithely out of the way. Ivan kept swinging like a bull. Nameless Guy kept doing the lambada, keeping Ivan occupied.

Noah stumbled to his feet. Relieved, Sophia shut her eyes, panting, and tried to get herself under control. But she felt it when, instead of dealing with Clyde, Noah headed for her. She snapped her eyes open.

Clyde grabbed for Noah's arm. Without even looking, Noah punched him in the face and kept coming for Sophia. Clyde's nose spurted blood.

"Clydee!" Screeching like a banshee, Bonnie launched herself, clawing, at Noah. Noah barely blocked her. Attila, breathing again, seized Noah from behind, tethering him for Bonnie's scratching. Blood and weals striped Noah's cheeks.

Despite all the blood dripping from various shifter wounds, it was the sting of copper from *Noah's* blood that cut through Sophia's awareness and went straight to her lizard brain.

She shrieked. *Mine*. Screw pain, screw magic. She leaped for Bonnie, grabbed the wolfwoman by both arms and pulled her off her mate. The wand, still in Sophia's hand, blazed against Bonnie's flesh.

With a pained howl, the she-wolf twisted loose. The fiery wand line on her arm must've burned like hell but either her adrenaline was pumping or she ignored it to fist her hands together—and slam them into Sophia's head like launching a volleyball.

Sophia's world shook and went suddenly, inexplicably silent. Light flared too bright. She crushed her lids shut.

Her skull exploded with pain. Sound rushed back but fractured, like it was filtered through crystal shards. She slit her eyes open. Her cheek was smashed to the wall, where she'd landed after the punch. Her vision buzzed like she was holding a blender at high.

Through her blurred sight she saw Bonnie scratching more long weals on Noah, Attila still attached. Behind them, Clyde tore strips off his own shirt and wadded them up his nostrils.

Sophia gritted teeth against a wave of nausea, pushed away from the wall, and stumbled toward them.

Bonnie spun on her and planted a fist in her belly. Pain exploding in her gut, Sophia folded in two.

Clyde swung a punch at Noah. Noah dodged—into Attila's waiting fist. Noah collapsed to hands and knees.

For the first time, Noah stopped fighting back.

Attila, Bonnie, and Clyde ganged up on him, less like a pack of wolves bringing down a great stag and more like a trio of vicious thugs. They went at him, pounding on him, raining blows on his head, shoulders, gut.

He made a small, terrible noise. Blood ran from his nose, his mouth, his ears.

Sophia willed her head to stop spinning and her guts to stay out of her throat. She tried to straighten, managed a hunched stoop, and raised her wand in front of her, two-handed. It blurred in her double sight.

Bonnie started to shift. Clyde howled, human voice changing midway to a sound far more animal and eerie. Noah feebly blocked Attila's punches and wavered to his feet.

Sophia tried to open her third eye. For the first time her vision on the etheric was blurred.

Bonnie's wolf circled Noah, darting in and out to nip at his hamstrings. Clyde opened huge wolf jaws and chomped Noah's shin.

Bone splintered.

Noah gasped, the sound more agonized than if he'd howled in pain, and fell to one knee.

Despite not being able to see the crack in her head dome, Sophia launched her will, herself, at the glass where she thought the fracture was.

She hit hard glass, bounced off, and slid to the bottom of a dark mental well.

Her physical eyes weren't much better off, but she didn't need detail to see Attila grab Noah's arm and wrench up.

The shoulder dislocated with an awful pop. Noah made a sound somewhere between a grunt and a pained sigh.

Sophia whimpered. They weren't just going to disable him.

They were going to kill him.

She wiped her physical eyes, clearing her sight slightly. *Maybe that will work with my witch's eye.* Blood pounding in her ears, desperate for even a thread of power to fight with, she mentally wiped her third eye then opened it. *Yes. There's the crack.* She braced herself—and smashed everything she had into that glass dome.

Cricks branched out like impending doom, opening everywhere. And as they opened, bolts of bright light shot out, directly into her brain. The precursor of her power, but not the power itself. She clenched her eyelids and doubled over, gasping.

Not enough. Her magic, still trapped, wasn't going to save them. *Magic's not enough.*

Like Rodolphe and the girl. Mundane authorities had come to the rescue, then. But now...

Suddenly she knew what to do. She opened her eyes, hobbled to the end table, snatched up the handset, and dialed by feel alone.

"Nine-one-one. What is your emergency?" The dispatcher was Sophia's summer swim instructor.

Sophia grunted through her pain, "*Help*. They're killing Noah."

"Sophia? What are you...no, never mind. Where?"

"Bonnie and Clyde's. Hurry!"

Keys clicked. "Our emergency units are on the other side of town. Five minutes. Can you hold on?"

Do we have five minutes?

She spun around, her stomach nearly evacuating. She ignored it to take count. Nameless Guy—gone. Mason—unconscious. Noah—bleeding and broken, his left arm hanging useless, against two wolves and a human.

Worse, the human was Attila—and armed. The mustachioed he-wolf scooped up Killer's switchblade, brandishing it with a bloody smile.

Five minutes? We probably don't even have five seconds.

That was when Noah's gaze lanced from the kicking, biting man and wolves, and his golden eyes met Sophia's.

Despite all his pain, he focused on her. Mouthed, "Get out of here."

Then he shifted too.

Under the mass of anti-alphas, she couldn't tell much about him, but Noah's wolf was dark and he was *big*.

So when Clyde hit Noah's wolf, Noah only staggered. But then Bonnie hit him mid-stagger and took him to his knees.

Attila leaped onto his back, stabbing him with the blade. "Second blood!"

Bonnie and Clyde piled onto Noah too, trying to bring him down, biting hackles and back and belly.

Sophia threw down the phone. *They're trying to kill my mate.*

Fury rose in her, so vast and pure it had no name. It shoved aside pain, nausea, and even sanity. She lifted her wand and pointed it at the wolves. Years of training lifted with it, flooding her in an instant. She pressed her thumb against the wand's metal inlays.

Silver and gold inlays, like Noah's changing eyes. A lucky resonance, serendipity, but magic worked that way sometimes. She knew intuitively what to do the moment she touched those inlays.

"I sing silver. I sing gold." In her hand, the wand began to hum, the metaphysical resonance becoming physical. "I sing to protect him that is silver and gold. Let my song burst forth." The vibrations reached a fevered pitch, higher and higher and higher yet, until the glass of the first seal *shattered.*

Shock waves blew forth. She trapped them with her song, spinning them into her wand, where they translated into potential energy.

Magic potential that she formed into reality with a snarled, "*Blast.*"

A bolt shot from the tip of the wand. The air before it compressed, then expanded in a concussion wave that threw the wolves and human flying, like toy jacks. Bang-bang-bang, they smashed into the wall, cracking plaster.

For an instant, it felt so damned good. Magic hadn't been a part of her life, it *was* her life. Joy welled up and burst inside her.

She'd forgotten what else she'd walled off with that first dome.

Brutal pain hit her head, a tsunami of death exploding into a thousand sharp razors that sliced her brain to confetti. She screamed. Silently. Like a nightmare, nothing came out of the rictus of her mouth. Tears streamed down her cheeks. She gasped and fell to her knees, her guts quaking until her death spewed from her depths.

"Sophia, oh, no." Shaking hands gathered her head to a hard wall of chest that pumped like bellows. A cheek pressed the crown of her head, confining the pain. A heart beat fast and furious under her ear.

The caressing hands, the thudding heart, caught her attention. Like being in a womb, they soothed her. Absorbed some of the pain, drew it out.

"Sophia." The voice resonated deep. "Love, please be all right."

Love. At the word she felt a click, and the worst of the pain, that jagged shard of death magic just...disappeared.

From the doorway, a slow clapping started. Sophia cracked a physical eye.

Nameless Guy, in human form, lounged against the jamb. "Very nice."

Noah released her to stalk over to Nameless Guy—and punched his jaw so fast she only saw his head jerk. Noah snarled, "Why didn't you get Sophia to safety?"

Nameless Guy only smiled.

And then, to Sophia's utter shock, Noah whirled his fury on *her*. "What the fuck did you think you were doing? *Why didn't you leave*?"

"You..." She rose to her feet, but the death magic, though no longer killing her, had mauled her insides like dough hooks. She staggered, managed to rasp out, "You were hurt. Dying!"

"I don't care! Those anti-alphas were primed for blood. They'd have turned on you next. Next time I say get out, you get out, hear?" He swept her off her feet. Carrying her, he stalked past Nameless Guy.

She was impressed by his concern and furious at his caveman way of showing it. "You can't order me around."

He stopped on the sidewalk and gently set her on her feet, only to grab her shoulders and whirl her to face him. Nose-to-nose, he growled at her, "Let's get one thing straight, Miss Hereditary Witch Princess. I can, and I will. For as long as the hex binds us together, *you* are my mate. *I'm* alpha. That means when it comes to pack safety, *your* safety, *you* listen to *me*."

Now was a fine time to finally acknowledge their mating. She met his fury with cold anger. "Then I guess it's even more important that we get that hex canceled out."

His pupils constricted abruptly, as if a killing pain had hit him. He didn't move any other way, could have been a statue.

"Fine." He released her.

Took two steps away.

Spun back and grabbed her by both arms. "No. You will listen to me, Sophia. I will not be in that position again, you in danger and me scared shitless that you're going get hurt or do something stupidly brave and die...I will *not* go through that again, do you hear?"

She seized his face. "I was scared too! You were bleeding and they were ganging up on you—"

"I'm not important. If anything happened to you—"

"The fuck you're not important. I'll show you how important you are." She grabbed his head and kissed him.

A shocked instant. Then he wrapped her in powerful arms and kissed her back, his mouth desperate on hers. He kissed her so fiercely her very bones melted.

"Sophia," he groaned. "Don't ever leave me. I couldn't stand it. You're my *life*, sweetheart."

He said it in the heat of the moment, and he probably hadn't meant it literally. But magic didn't care about that. When Noah, his arms wrapped in a warm cocoon around her, said the word *life,* she felt a second distinct click.

Her pain from breaking the death seal just...disappeared.

Opening her third eye, she gingerly poked her insides. The other two funeral domes were intact. But the first, the one she'd shattered, was gone. Nothing remained, no cracked rim, no razor-sharp debris.

Somehow, he'd swept death away. All with one unintentional word.

She gazed up at him in wonder. "What are you?"

His cheeks flagged with color. "Sophia...I haven't told you everything."

Whooping sirens interrupted him as the emergency crew arrived.

An ambulance and a squad car squealed to the curb. The patrol officer popping from the car was young, human, and inclined to arrest everyone on sight. Since Killer and Ivan were already gone, Nameless Guy had melted away, Mason was still unconscious, and Sophia had obvious defensive wounds, the officer slapped cuffs on the shifters remaining–including Noah, who made things worse when he refused to open his eyes fully for the booking camera.

Sophia tried to explain that the other guys started it and pressed the officer to release Noah, but the more she argued the more defensive the young human got. When it became obvious she was only making things worse, she shut up.

Except for refusing to open his eyes, Noah went quietly, a testimony to his self-control. The other wolves weren't anywhere near as disciplined. The town would be paying for a lot of bandages and disinfectant tonight.

After running back inside for her shoes, Sophia followed along to the jail. She could have used magic to get Noah released but wasn't completely sure how much she had freed–or if, after four years, she could wield it skillfully enough to modify behavior. Better to try to get him out the mundane way. She did manage to remember her swim instructor's name and used it ruthlessly to get Noah a separate cell from the other wolves.

"I called the hospital." Noah stalked around his cell, the only cell in the basement, basically a cot and uncovered toilet in a concrete and steel-bar box. "Mason's fine, and coming to collect you. When he gets here, go home and get some sleep."

"After everything that's happened?" She watched him pace, aware that she'd gotten used to his glass-lake stillness. It took a lot to rumple his emotions. “If you can’t sleep, what makes you think I can?”

He thumbed the bridge of his nose and sighed. “I’m being a thoughtless dick.” He used two fingers to wave her closer. “Turn.”

“What?” She turned, keeping eye contact over her shoulder. “Why?”

“This.” He dug fingers into the knotted muscles of her shoulders.

It wrung a groan from her. “That’s so good. I didn’t know how much I was hurting until now.”

“Shh. Relax.” He continued kneading out the knots until she was limp against the bars. He massaged down the sides of her spine. She rested her head against the bars in bliss. He continued to work her back muscles down to her waistband. A tug and zip and the skirt went slack against her hips.

“Wha…?”

“Shh,” he said again. “I’m just loosening anything that constricts blood flow.”

“Oh.” She closed her eyes and relaxed again against the bars, giving herself over to his soothing massage.

So it was a complete shock when a breeze played over her nipples.

Her eyes flew open. “Hey!” She glanced down. She was naked but for her panties, thigh high stockings and pumps, her clothes heaped around her ankles. She must have been worse off than she’d thought, because she hadn’t noticed anything but his magic fingers. Hopefully her magical aura would confuse the security camera, because otherwise someone was getting quite a show.

He blew again on her nipples. She turned. He’d wedged his face between the bars. His tongue mimed licking her.

Her nipples furled just from the sight. Desire curled into her pelvis.

It had been a long, frustrating, frightening night. Daringly she grabbed two bars, high, and leaned one breast into his open mouth.

He latched onto her nipple and suckled. Lust sprang hot and heavy between her legs. He reached through the bars and cupped her breasts as he continued to suckle. The globes swelled with aching need. He hefted them gently, pressing her need higher.

Moaning, she arched into the bars. She lifted one leg, bending it to rub her tender inner thigh against cool metal. His nostrils flared and he sucked harder. She lifted her thigh higher, turning her knee out until her lace-covered mound rubbed against the bar.

"I'd like to rub against something else." She gazed hungrily at him.

With a growl he stood and got rid of his clothes with a quick zip, a few plucked buttons, and a couple shrugs.

Then he stood there, naked and gorgeous, his muscles rippling in all sorts of interesting ways just from breathing.

Her foot dropped to the floor. She leaned into the bars and moaned.

Slotting his arms through the bars, he grabbed her hips and pulled her into him.

Her sensitized flesh pressed equally against cool bars and hot male. She scrubbed herself up and down, purring her pleasure. Her skin slid easily along the metal but burred with the friction of his hair-rumpled flesh.

He clamped her hips to the bars, pinning them with one hand while he ran the other up her body to twine fingers in her hair. He pressed her head gently forward.

Their mouths met in a kiss, all the hotter for the fact that they couldn't mesh completely because of the bars. When he sucked her tongue to hold her in place, frissons of deep need shuddered along her entire body. She thought about disappearing the bars then got a better idea.

Breaking the kiss, she wiggled out of his hold. His eyes flared a bright gold. He wrapped hands around the bars and stared hungrily at her. She stood just out of his reach and smiled naughtily.

"Come here." The wolf was in his voice.

"In a minute."

His powerful body was framed and highlighted by hard steel. She looked her fill. His cock, already jutting toward her, rose eagerly at that.

So she had to. She really did. She knelt in front of the cage, grabbed him by the hip muscles, yanked him flush with the bars and licked him from stem to stern. He hissed, his cock growing longer. She began to lick that thick, bobbing erection in earnest. She was rough lapping him, but his flinch was accompanied by guttural groans of pleasure.

Drawing him into her mouth, she sucked. A growl tore from his throat. Encouragement to bob her head along his length. His hand fisted in her hair. She hummed her approval against his flesh. He actually cried out at that, brief, throttled, pained—but good pain, because his hand clenched tighter in her hair. She began to swirl her tongue as she stroked over him, making sure to tickle the sensitive spot just below the eye.

"Enough." He grabbed her face with both hands and urged her to her feet. "I want to fill you."

Fill me. She groaned but managed to come to her feet and dance a couple steps away. "How are you going to do that?" She turned her back to him, glanced coyly over her shoulder, and waggled her butt at him.

He wasn't having any of that. With a snarl he reached through the bars.

She continued to wiggle enticingly—until he seized her hips. He had a longer reach than she thought.

Yanking her naked buttocks against the bars, he tilted her to expose her sex, and plowed into her.

She felt every inch of that thick cock sink in. Gasped, long and loud.

He started thrusting, a hard, steady rhythm. A clang of metal accompanied each thwack of flesh. His hot thrusts, the bang of cold bars against her bottom, was a symphony of sensation. Her flesh sang with rising urgency.

"More." She closed her eyes and drank in the sensations. "Faster."

He slotted his arm though the bars and belted her hips, holding her in place for a pummeling. As he drove himself deeper and deeper into her wet, yielding sheath, he reached with the other hand to rub her groove, burnishing her clit until it was hard and ready to burst.

She arched into the cage, head and shoulders banging metal, a duet with his hip bones as his cock drove in and out with increasing insistence. He stroked her clit faster. She pressed back against him so hard the iron dented her flesh.

His breath billowed against her shoulder. His teeth opened over her flesh, his human's, but the action was his wolf. His incisors were sharp on her skin, and his growls dominated over groans. His human was in control, but not by much.

She didn't care. She wanted him, all of him, wild and free. "*Do it.*" She howled too, her animal calling to his.

He snarled. His teeth closed gently on the edge of her trapezius. Holding her with his arm and strangely gentle bite, he took one last long thrust. She was so wet he slid in to the hilt.

She screamed. He roared. They came together in a tumult of heat and wet and cries of pleasure.

She shuddered an eternity. Then she went limp in his arm. His strength held her upright, his breath rasping in her ear.

"That was..." He swallowed. "Sophia, I think I'm—"

"Noah?" Mason's voice came from the stairwell door.

Noah swore. "Just a minute, Mason." His bellow held an alpha's command.

Sophia tore herself from Noah's grasp. She snatched up her clothes and tried to put them on. Her muscles didn't work quite right and the spandex tank wouldn't go past her shoulders.

With a sympathetic *tsk,* Noah waved her over. Cautiously, she came. Taking the tank from her he winched it into a loop, lassoed her head then slid the material down her ribs like a sleeve. He took special care to settle her breasts in the cups, gently adjusting them.

Her heart beat a little harder. The big bad alpha was tender and caring and just as wonderful helping her dress as undress. She knew some human guys who could take lessons.

And here he was, stuck in a cage. "I have to go. Be careful, okay?"

"Always." His eyes were a burnished gold. "Stay safe with Mason."

"Of course. I'll be back in the morning to get you out."

He looked around the cell. "I'll be here. Or King will be."

Chapter Nineteen

Sophia left the jail with Mason. Now that, thanks to both Noah's massage and their sex, her tension was entirely gone, she realized how exhausted she was. She walked the blocks stumbling asleep on her feet, and the moment she got to her aunt's, she checked that the wards were up, locked the door, then fell into bed to snatch a few hours of rest.

Some bastard set the alarm for four thirty. It took her a moment to recall she was the bastard, needing to get to the jail before the sun rose. She showered, her mind on securing Noah's release before he went doggie.

Thoughts of Noah and the jail turned to memories of what they'd done at the jail. While the water ran like warm silk over her flesh, she remembered his hands doing the same, and more.

Swearing, she cranked the shower to cold, cleaned herself in a flurry of soap, rinsed quick, and leaped out.

She'd just managed to dry her overheated skin when her cell phone rang with the Techie Titan theme. *Gabriel?* She answered, "Who are you and what have you done with my nerd king brother? It's four-oh-crap in the morning."

"I'm still up from last night. I went dungeon crawling with some guildies. Look, I felt a surge of *death* magic...or I thought I did, but then it disappeared. I tried you but you turned your phone off again."

"I didn't turn it off." She'd slept through it, potentially worse from the brotherly scolding point of view. To distract him, she quickly added, "What did you do then?"

"I called cousin Daniel. He's all upset that you're, and I quote," Gabriel sucked in a big breath, "'She's the Blue from the prophecy but she's not taking it seriously enough especially considering since there's an evil wizard is involved, and it's all happening now!!' And I did not imagine the double bangs. Sophia, *what* in the poached eggs and hell is going on?"

"Well..." She glanced at the clock. She'd have to give him the insta-quick version. As she checked her luggage for clean clothes, she gave him a run-down, mumbling the stuff he'd yell at. Would Noah like the sexy skirt and tank top? Yes, but it was too obvious. She talked on autopilot, explaining her suspicions that Rodolphe might be the Hungry Ghost, that there was a group undermining the new alpha, and about the leadership challenge. Maybe skirt, heels, and blouse, but open the blouse an extra button? She categorically denied the death magic but was so distracted trying to decide between heels or flats that she said, "It's only good luck the alpha found his mate in time for the challenge—"

Fortunately, she stopped herself from babbling who Noah's new mate was.

Unfortunately, her brother was no dummy.

"Sophia Blue, you've mated a *shifter*? Something so forbidden you'll never again have to open your necklaces to get them on? How did you—?"

"Oops, you're breaking up. Gotta go."

Between the shower, her brother, and her clothing indecision, dawn was lightening the windows now. Panting in her race to get to Noah, she threw on her default clothes, the Full Banker of navy pants suit, ivory blouse, inch-heeled pumps, and pearls, and rushed downstairs.

A note from Mason was taped to the front door. He'd had to go on ahead.

Swearing, she ran the two and a half blocks to the jail. She got there just as the sun's disk cleared the horizon.

Mason sat on a bench outside the combination jail/courthouse. "Noah's already gone." He rose as she approached. "We didn't get to talk last night. I heard I missed all the excitement."

She bent hands to knees and panted. "Not all of it. Just the most embarrassing parts. How'd he get out?"

"The good news is, Jayden pulled some strings and Noah was released. The bad news is, Attila, Bonnie, and Clyde were released too."

"Who?" She straightened.

"The three idiot ex-lieutenants."

"No. Who's Jayden?"

Mason raised an eyebrow. "Black hair, black eyes, all attitude? Owns a really sweet bike I'd give my left nut to buy?"

"Oh, Jayden." Nameless Guy now had a name. "Is he a friend?" She reconsidered. "Or at least on our side?"

"Dunno. As much as he's ever on anybody's side, I guess."

"Is he pack?"

"No, though he runs with us sometimes. To me, he doesn't even smell like a wolf, but Noah has apparently had a few business dealings with him and says he's trustworthy enough. Frankly, the pack needs his money. Anyway, there's more."

"Bad news or good news?" But in her gut, she knew.

"Worse news. Ivan and Killer returned to demand Noah's head, reissuing the Alpha Challenge for tonight."

It hit her like a punch in the gut. She collapsed onto the bench next to Mason. "I was hoping they'd give up."

"Me too. In fact, strangely enough, they had." He sat next to her. "While Noah was still locked up, Jayden 'talked' with them. That boy has some seriously strange juju going on. But in this case it worked to our advantage. He convinced all five to crouch to Noah's dominance—it's a pack thing," he added to answer her puzzled look. "Basically they acknowledged Noah as alpha, kind of like swearing fealty. But by this morning, their attitude had changed one-eighty."

"Like someone else talked to them?"

"Threatened, more like."

"Wait. All five had given in?" She frowned as the implications hit her. "Then whoever's undermining Noah, it isn't the anti-alphas. Maybe not even part of the pack at all. Crap. I'd been rooting for Killer. Now we're in the exact same position we were in yesterday. Hunt and fight."

"And uh—" he blushed, "—the other thing.

Big strong Mason, blushing. She wondered what the last F stood for. "Does Noah have to accept the challenge?"

"This bogus? Not usually. Usually his lieutenants would rise up against the demanding assholes. But in this case, the pack members who *would* support Noah are off earning a living, or have vulnerable pups, or are too old or young to stand up to Ivan et al."

"So Noah's stuck."

"Probably. He went with Bonnie and Clyde to try one last time to reason with them, but I'm not holding out a lot of hope. That's where he is, by the way, or was until the sun rose. He said he'd meet us at your aunt's store."

"Got it." She started to stand, then paused at a thought and sank back onto the bench. "So if he has to go through with this challenge, how does he win?"

"Again, normally the hunt part would be simple. By the time alphas are old enough to lead, they're usually mated, so the challenged alpha and his mate lead the pack on a hunt where the alpha pair makes a kill and shares it with the pack."

A *kill?* She stifled a squeamish shudder. "And in this case?"

"On the plus side, Ivan and his buddies don't know Noah's mated."

"Can't they see his eyes have changed?"

"Gold isn't a common mated color. And some shifters change eye color like mood rings. They probably think Noah's just furious over the challenge. They'll see that as a good thing. That he's distracted, and worried how he'll miraculously find his mate by tonight, maybe jumping the first female who accepts him—"

The low, rough noise startled both of them—until she realized who it was. Her. She was growling. She cut it off with hot cheeks.

Mason politely pretended not to notice, talking on as if nothing had happened. "—when he's not distracted at all, since we know Noah has a true mate, don't we?"

Now didn't seem to be the time to bring up the fact that she probably wasn't his true mate either. "You said that's the good news. What's the bad?"

His eyebrows rose. “You don’t shift. Noah told me everything, Princess Sophia.”

Braid her broomstick. “The hunt has to be led by two wolves? Can’t I, I don’t know, dress up in tweeds, carry a rifle, and laugh about hunting wabbits?”

He shook his head. “The whole point of the challenge is to prove the alpha pair can lead the pack into a fertile future. Feeding and protecting the pack is important but ‘fertile’ applies to the viability of their offspring. They should be able to produce pups who can shift easily, which means a proper mate. Which is the last F in HUFF, by the way. Hunt, Fight, and, um, Fornicate.”

The way he said it made it clear the wolves generally used the shorter word. Her cheeks went from hot to on fire. That certainly explained why Noah had kneed Mason in the balls when he’d tried to tell her about that final F. “Okay, so the mate has to shift and hunt with her alpha. I might be able to learn to shift. Noah can try teaching me, starting at sunset—”

“Sorry, no.” Mason was already shaking his head. “You have to understand, wolves love custom. The more convoluted, the better. Traditionally the Challenge Hunt starts when the moon rises, but the full custom is ‘moonrise or sunset, whichever comes last’. Last night, moonrise was after midnight, which was why there was time for Noah to talk to the five. But due to the vagaries of the heavenly calendar, the moon won’t set until one thirty this afternoon, and *it doesn’t rise at all*.”

“The hunt starts at sunset,” she whispered.

“Exactly.” Mason’s grimace tightened to a full-fledged scowl. “Since the hex locks Noah in his Canidae form until then, he doesn’t have a mouth to teach you.”

"Then we'll have to find someone else." She snapped her fingers. "*I can shift*."

Mason startled. "You can?"

"Not yet, but I just remembered someone who said that. C'mon." She rose and started off. "What I don't understand is, why would someone outside the pack challenge Noah? Undermine him like this?"

"Greed?" Mason walked with her. "In return for protecting the pack, the alpha gets a cut of all pack earnings. Power and prestige play into it too."

"Yes, but if it's another wolf, aren't there easier ways to become alpha? Why the whole Challenge Hunt shtick? Doesn't that seem unnecessarily provocative to you?"

"As in provoking? Maybe. But what's he trying to provoke? Noah's protective instincts are already fired up. I don't know what else there'd be."

She didn't know either, but she had a vague, and terrifying, suspicion.

As they passed First Street, he said, "Where are we going?"

"Jayden's. When I said to him 'I know you're a shifter,' he replied 'I can shift'."

Mason's eyes widened. "Implying he wasn't born a shifter."

"Exactly. If Noah trusts him, I'll trust him too—for now. The hard part will be getting Jayden to teach me. He's not the kind of guy who seems naturally helpful. It'd be easier if I had leverage. Say, a big shotgun. Or a cannon. Or a battleship."

And then she remembered she had access to the one thing that made Jayden geek. The man who fixed his motorcycles.

She smiled.

"Whoa," Mason said. "Do I want to know what you're thinking? No, I do not. That smile bodes ill for someone. Not me, I hope."

"Not you. Here we are." She stepped onto the concrete pad in front of the pet store. Though the time was ungodly-thirty in the morning, the door was open, as if they were expected. She went in.

"Don't you ever sleep?" she asked the swirling darkness inside.

It resolved into the black-haired, black-eyed, very masculine form of the pet groomer she now knew as Jayden. He put his apron on, and she waited for the sexiness-amnesia to hit.

Sure enough, the instant the bib settled, she forgot to think of him as anything but a pet groomer. But she remembered the memory of it. "An enchanted apron?"

Jayden cocked a half smile. "Not the apron."

Which of course answered exactly nothing. "So what are you? A vampire? A godling? The rear half of a centaur?"

He threw back his head and laughed, a full belly laugh. "You're a proper match for Noah, aren't you, princess? We'd better get started. We don't have much time, and you have a long way to go." He started toward the glassed-in area of the grooming salon.

"Wait. What are we doing?"

He shot her a grin over his shoulder, absolutely appealing in spite of the apron. "What you came to learn, of course. Shifting."

She nearly clapped her hands. "You'll teach me? Without cajoling or threatening? Who are you and what have you done with Jayden?"

He laughed. "I assure you, I don't do everything for gain."

"Not buying it. Why? Because you owe Noah's pack a favor? Because Mason is the only one who can fix your bike? Some hidden gotcha?"

"None of those, Your Royal Highness. I'll teach you because it amuses me." With that he disappeared into the salon.

Mason whistled. "That can't be good."

She shrugged. "Doesn't matter. There's no one else in a five-hundred-mile radius who can teach a witch to shift."

"Good point. Look, it sounds like this'll take a while. I'm going to find Noah to give him an update, okay? Don't leave until I get back. He'll have my nuts for Waldorf salad if I leave you unprotected."

"You left me this morning."

"I'm now walking with a limp."

She suppressed a smile.

After Mason left, Sophia followed Jayden to the grooming area. "So what's first?" She came into the small room and shut the glass door behind her.

"Pin this to your underclothes. Make sure some part of it touches your skin." He handed her a small, white-enameled brooch shaped like a wolf. "You'll be shifting in no time."

"And then?"

"Nothing. It's a fully contained spell. All you have to do is activate it, so you won't even be breaking any more of your death seals."

She gaped at him. "How do you know about the seals?"

"Please. A witch who doesn't do magic? Unless you did a complete Evacuate or the evil Phere Burgot himself sucked your magic out, there's no way to keep it from expressing *other* than death seals."

"But...but you said we had a long way to go. I thought this would take all day."

"I said that to get rid of Mason. You and I need to talk without wolfie ears, princess."

"What? Why?" This was why she didn't trust the lying, secretive, conniving buzzard.

"I know that," he said.

"I beg your pardon?" She stared at him. "Did you just read my—"

"Oh please. Your expression shouted that you don't trust me. Besides, you're a smart woman, or you are now. Of course you don't trust me. You shouldn't trust me, or anybody."

"I trust Noah."

"Who originally didn't tell you about the hex that turns him into a puffball doggie." He scanned the store behind her.

"I understand why," she said. "It makes him vulnerable. But you—"

"Princess, I'd love to bicker all day," he said in a voice she'd use for backed-up drains. "But there's something else Noah isn't telling you. Something big. If you don't get it out of him before you try to lift the hex, wear a shit-proof mask for when it blows up in your face."

"There's a pleasant image. If this secret is so important, why don't you tell me?"

He jerked one shoulder, grimacing. "Not mine to tell. But do yourself and him a big favor. Bribe him, wheedle, coerce him—whatever you have to do, get it out of him." He raised one brow. "Me? I'd use sex."

"Why...you...I'd..."

"Yes dear, I know. Away you go, now. You have less than twenty-four hours to figure out how to break the hex—and more importantly, how to break Noah." He used two hands to shoo her, crowding her out of the grooming booth through the store. "Oh, and somewhere in there you may want to experiment with shifting. Walking as a wolf isn't as easy as I make it look."

"Wait!" She dug in her heels at the exit and held up the brooch. "How do I activate this?"

"Same way you get to Carnegie Hall. Practice." He grinned as he shut and locked the door behind her.

* * *

"Killer," sneered Rodolphe, the wizard known as X. "I hope you have a better tribute this time." He stepped into the trailer of the insipid he-wolf.

"Yes, master." The wolfman pointed at a fur-bitten female lying like a sack of potatoes on an even lumpier couch. Then he held up the stiletto. "And though it nearly cost us our lives, the blade has been blooded as you instructed. Twice." As he handed the stiletto over, he added in a mutter, "A better weapon than that siphon."

"Killer, you're an idiot." With a flick, Rodolphe activated the deadly blade—and plunged it into the sacrifice. The drugged-up creature barely mewled. "You don't understand how marvelous an invention this siphon is. Let me tell you a story."

With the other hand he slapped the siphon against the bitch's temple and activated it. "Once upon a time, witches held their rightful place as rulers of the earth. Then ignorant mundanes painted them as power-hungry monsters in fairy tales, and used the tales to incite a rebellion. The slaughter of witches in fairy tales paralleled witch hunts in real life."

The female barely gave a sigh as her head collapsed. Rodolphe moved the siphon to her breastbone. "Instead of rising up in retaliation, witches, led by goody-goodies Jean-Dion d'Avignon and Nostradamus, created the Witches' Council."

Rodolphe funneled the wolf's magic into both himself and the blade. Killer's eyes were glued to the female, wide in what, for any other being, would be horror. Killer, horrified. As if. "Then a truly great wizard—call him X—arose. He developed the siphon."

The siphoned magic curdled the blood on the blade, creating the magical poison. "The instrument let X snare magic that was cast by namby-pambies who didn't deserve it, and siphon it for his own use."

Rodolphe twisted the knife to get out the last drops of suffering. The siphon sucked them down greedily. "The short-sighted Council, rather than laud X, tried to lock him up. Asses."

He pulled out the knife and wiped it on the dying female. "So X worked long and hard to refine the instrument to, not only suck magic as it was cast, but to seize it directly from beings of magic."

Killer roused from his horrified freeze. "Fuckin' shifters, you mean."

"Yes, Killer. Shifters. But it still wasn't enough." The last of the power flowed into the siphon. "X developed an instrument which latched onto cast spells, then sent suckers which *swam up the spell-stream* to the mage, to suck magic *directly* from mages. He could take their power for his own!" Rodolphe chortled. "Now, most mages aren't more than a magical mouthful. Shifters are more substantial. But when X heard of a royal dual child, he knew he at last had the perfect power source."

"What's a fuckin' dual?"

"Killer, you ignorant ass." Rodolphe switched off the siphon and slid it into his inner pocket. "A dual is the product of a forbidden mating between a shifter and a witch. A child made of power who also possesses power. The perfect food."

Sheer revulsion twisted Killer's face.

Rodolphe slapped him. "You dare judge?"

Killer glared sullenly. "No, master."

"There's always a price to be paid for great advances. The trick is to make it come from someone else's wallet. Now, where was I? Oh yes. But the dual escaped and hid from X among the wolfpacks. Fortunately, X had attached an etheric eye to the child's familiar. Or as mundanes would say now, he 'bugged' the boy's raven. Then X developed a brilliant plan to flush the dual from hiding."

Rodolphe smiled, snapping on a rubber glove. Killer thought Rodolphe was helping him. If only he knew what a pawn he was.

"X allied himself with a brilliant former member of the Witches' Council who'd propitiously stripped all the private information he could before absconding...including the magical community census." Rodolphe carefully rubbed a deadly nightshade compound onto the blade. It sizzled as the death magic absorbed it. The venom was complete, so deadly not even an alpha wolf could survive it.

"A fuckin' census, master? How's that helpful."

"You barking idiot," Rodolphe spat. "That census had the location of *every pack on the continent*. All X had to do was develop minions in each pack and command them to give developing alphas a nudge just a little early."

"A nudge to challenge the old alpha?" Killer's eyes widened. "Like we did with Blackwood?"

So the wolfman wasn't entirely lacking in brains.

"An underdeveloped alpha, fighting a mature alpha might win or lose. But the dual, challenged before he was ready—well. He'd use his wizard's magic, you see? Then all X has to do is wait for the familiar to feel the surge of his master's magic. X trails the raven to the dual and *voila*! X has him."

"So you've found the fuckin' dual, master?"

"Not yet." Rodolphe sputtered it. "But the crow's on the move. It's only a matter of time." He pointed the poisoned knife at Killer and punctuated each word with a stab.

Killer blanched quite satisfactorily.

"And when the crow finds the dual—" Rodolphe retracted the blade with an angry flick and tossed it at Killer, who barely caught it, "—I'll be there to claim my reward."

Chapter Twenty

In the shelter of the pet store's entrance, Sophia unbuttoned her blouse, pinned the enameled brooch to her bra strap, and buttoned back up. Then she headed for the bookstore, where she hoped Mr. Kibbles would help her learn how to use the thing.

True, Mr. Kibbles was a cat, and she'd be a wolf. True again, she'd never seen Mr. Kibbles as anything but a cat. As children, she and her brother Gabriel had tried to make the cat change, taunting him unmercifully and hiding his food dish. She felt bad about it now, but they'd just been kids. Besides, Mr. Kibbles's reaction was to wash a forepaw or smooth his already perfect coat and generally indicate that frankly, children, he couldn't give a damn. He may have been a familiar, but as a haughty cat, he was darn near typecast.

Sophia knew he could help her best, though, because he changed forms, not as a shifter did with magic shifting muscle and bone and cloth, but as a spirit did, smoke to smoke, the only creature she knew who did. Well, aside from Jayden, who'd been as helpful as grease on a climbing rope.

"Yip, yip!"

The noise brought her attention to a small bit of fluff marching toward her up the sidewalk, glaring. She knew what that glare meant. *You didn't wait for Mason.*

"Sorry. We both thought I'd take longer at Jayden's. How'd things go at Bonnie and Clyde's?"

The dog looked away with a disgusted *grrr*.

"That's too bad. But I have good news. I can shift. Or I *will* be able to. I just have to practice."

She started again for the Uncommon. Noah marched alongside her, from his stiff gait only partially mollified.

At the store, she unlocked the door, then turned to him. "I'll need Mr. Kibbles to help me. Since you two don't get along..." She quirked a half smile, a sorry-but-could-you-stay-out expression.

Noah huffed the doggie version of a sigh. He yipped, *If I have to.* As Sophia opened the door, he started walking the perimeter of the building.

She went inside, strangely reassured. Sure, the wards were up, but no one would attack her unannounced while the little dog with the big heart was keeping guard.

In the kitchen, Mr. Kibbles was intent on his post-breakfast grooming.

She got rid of the newspapers she'd laid down for King then dropped into a half Lotus opposite the cat and studied him closely. He stood and gracefully stretched, his muscles sliding easily under his gleaming fur. He was all that was animal. She wanted to move like him, lithe, fast. To be like him, her senses sharp and living totally in the *now*.

She closed her eyes and focused inward. Slowly she opened her third eye. It was easier now that she'd unlocked part of her magic. When she was ready she looked at Mr. Kibbles.

He was so brilliant on the etheric she was nearly blinded. Squinting reduced the flare of light to a nimbus of pure gold. Whoa. She'd never looked at him this way before. That nimbus signaled a being of immense power and wisdom.

How do I use this? she asked the cat, mentally tapping the brooch attached to her bra strap.

Puny human. The haloed cat looked down his nose.

No need to diss me.

His glowing emerald eyes widened. *I'm not dissing you. Humans live inside their skins. Muffled. The field of self is meant to be larger; life is larger. Grow beyond your limitations, Sophia.*

Oh. She pushed her boundaries as he continued.

Greater speed and strength and sharper senses are yours when your self is outside your skin...yeow!

The cat was a windmill of scrabbling limbs, disappearing so fast there was a black hole in the nimbus where he'd been.

Wondering what had spooked him, she closed her mental eye and opened her physical.

She saw no difference. She still sat on the floor, although she now noticed the specks of dirt between the aged tiles, small motes of dust bouncing along in the eddy of air currents...

Wait. She wasn't *sitting* on the floor. Her eyes were simply the same height as when she was sitting.

She was standing, on four furred, pawed, legs.

Ooh. Pretty fur too. Not your typical gray wolf, she was pure white.

Probably because of the white enamel brooch, but she admired herself for a moment. Her limbs were slender but strong, her loins sleekly muscled. Her tail was bushy and her coat shone with health.

Hey, this isn't nearly the problem I thought it would be. She smiled, felt her mouth open, and her tongue loll. Ah yes, a wolfie grin. Deserved. This was going to be easy.

She strode for the door...using her two hind legs like a human. Her front legs stayed where they were. Back and front tangled, and she fell. Her muzzle hit tile, teeth cracking together. Since her spirit self was an inch outside her skin, she scraped off a few layers of *Sophia*.

"Ow!" she said only it came out "Yip!" It reminded her of poor King. Poor Noah, rather.

Mr. Kibbles snickered.

Know-it-all familiar. *You try changing from a simple left-right to coordinating four paws and a tail in two minutes flat.* She cautiously got her paws under her and tried again.

It took her hours just to learn to walk. Going human, she took off her shoes. Shifting back to wolf, she thought about walking on her toes, and that helped. Eventually Mr. Kibbles stopped snickering so she moved on, trying a trot. Her trailing front leg hit her surging rear, and she tripped and went down.

Mr. Kibbles started snickering again.

She lay on her side and growled at him. He jumped to a higher perch...and continued snickering. Stupid familiar.

She rested her head on the ground for just a moment. Mr. Kibbles's water dish was in her line of sight. Tired, hot, and thirsty, that water dish looked good. She rolled slowly to her feet and went wearily to the bowl to lap cool bliss.

Her long tongue darted out, slapped water, and splashed it all over. She tried again. As much liquid hit the floor and splashed onto her muzzle as went in her mouth.

She whimpered. She was a failure as a wolf. She could barely walk and to make matters worse, was a slob.

She tried to cry, but even that didn't work. Her nictitans—third eyelids she didn't even know wolves had—closed instead, and she only ended up with well-lubricated eyes.

As the noon siren blew, Mason limped in. "I am not leaving you this time, no matter what you say."

She contracted to human. "Didn't Noah tell you he's guarding me?"

"Noah's taking a break. I'm your guard for the lunch hour." His brown eyes darted around the kitchen and his belly rumbled.

"Want lunch?"

He gave her a sheepish grin. "That'd be good."

She fixed them tuna sandwiches. The task reoriented her. Five hours left, and self-pity wouldn't help Noah. She'd learn how to do this if it killed her.

Hope it doesn't come to that. "When's sunset?"

"Eight fifty." Mason bit off half the tuna sandwich. "Will you be ready?"

Will I? "Yes." She bit off nearly as much of her own sandwich with a determined chomp. She barely chewed before swallowing. She hadn't done anything this physical since mock-dueling her brother in college. She washed the sandwich down with milk. "I can walk and even trot if I concentrate. Cornering is still a problem, though."

Mason snorted. "Woods' paths are nothing *but* curves." He chomped the last of his sandwich, brushed off his hands, and stood. "Better get back to practicing then. Sounds like you'll need it."

"Thanks for the vote of confidence."

"You want false reassurance, go to an iota. Beta's job is to give you a swift kick in the butt."

"How about a swift job of the dishes?" She pointed.

"Love to, but you'll need the space for practice." He grinned and left.

By the time dusk rolled around she was exhausted, actually a good thing. Too tired to care which leg went where, things naturally fell into place.

Mr. Kibbles, with a strange rumble—a purr?—coming from his throat, head-butted her flank, the animal equivalent of a knuckle bump, and trotted out.

She was also hungry again but didn't eat. Hungry was good, right? It'd add fire and focus to the hunt. She might even be able to catch something small and furry...kill it...eat it...okay, maybe she'd go out for a cheeseburger after instead.

As the sky darkened, Sophia, tired but somewhat more confident, climbed back into her skin. Scant minutes after sunset, Noah strode into the kitchen.

For a moment all she could see were his golden eyes, the hard planes of his face, and the black hair curling around his ears. He was more handsome to her than ever.

He seized her by her upper arms and gazed deep into her eyes. His were filled with concern for her. "You don't have to do this."

"What happens if I don't? Can you meet this Challenge Hunt solo?"

His jaw clenched. "I won't lie to you. It'd be a... problem."

The growl underscoring "problem" clued her in that it would be a problem the way brain spasm migraines were "uncomfortable". "Noah, I've been practicing. I'll do fine. Well, as long as I don't have to kill...to eat...yeah."

He blew air. "Let me see you change."

That part at least was easy. She mentally touched the white enamel wolf and pushed outside her skin. Lolling at Noah, she sat on her wolf butt.

What hit the floor was not just her furred hips but something big and oval and puffy.

Her rump shot up, her feet scrabbling to get under her. She raised her tail and sniffed...damn, was she in heat?

She blinked up at Noah, and she must have looked shocked even for a wolf.

He looked...wistful. He stroked her head, gently. "You're as beautiful a wolf as you are a human, Sophia."

He thought she was *beautiful.* She needed to kiss him. She retracted into her skin, turning human under his hand. He stepped back as she extended vertically. He must have wanted her with equal need because when she was fully human but still slightly unfocused, he cupped her nape and pulled her in for a gentle but thorough kiss.

Her lips were starting to buzz and her heart to hammer when he stepped back. "If we're going to do this, it has to be now. Mason, Jayden!"

Two wolves trotted into the kitchen. One was dark gray with tan markings and Mason's big chocolate eyes. The other was black with black eyes.

The black wolf took a big sniff of the estrogen-filled kitchen and grinned at her.

She grinned back, all teeth. "Fuck you, Jayden."

The wolf only grinned wider.

"You two." Noah's tone was straight-up alpha. He pointed at both wolves, though his eye was on the black. "You will guard Sophia and keep her safe. If she has even a broken toenail at the end of this, I will hurt you badly."

The Jayden wolf yipped.

"If I'm dead after the hunt, then I'll come back and haunt you."

"Dead?" She blinked at him, a tingle of fear ripping down her middle. "What do you mean, dead? It's a hunt, not a fight. You can't die. How could you die?"

Noah's golden gaze was steady on her. "Sophia. Sweetheart. In the woods, there's no safety net."

"But surely with the whole pack there...?"

He took her face in his hands. "Most of the able adults are off earning a living. Some are at home with young pups. Aside from the four of us and Ivan's group, it'll be a few dozen females afraid for their young, some elderly, and a handful of teenagers."

"Then can't we hunt...I don't know, squirrels and rabbits? Smaller things that can't hurt us?"

"The purpose of a Challenge Hunt is to prove I—we—can feed the pack." He met her gaze steadily. "So the bigger the better. A deer if we can."

"Deer?" She swallowed hard. "With those big pokey things on their heads?"

He smiled. "It's okay. Antlers don't harden until fall. I'll aim for the nose or the rump to avoid the worst of the pokes." His smile disappeared. "Sophia, if we're doing this—if you're doing this with me—we have to go now."

Put that way, she had no choice. She put on her shoes and they went.

Noah drove a big SUV, Sophia sitting beside him. If her heart hadn't been pounding like a tympani, it would have been almost nice. As he drove, she put her phone on vibrate. She didn't want any distractions.

At the repair shop, Sophia shifted. Almost immediately her gaze found Noah's.

His expression was pensive. He sighed, unusual in such a self-contained, still man. "You really are quite beautiful, Sophia."

Her heart swelled.

Then he closed his eyes and...just rearranged. His black hair ran down his body like rapidly laying overlapping roof shingles. His limbs flowed like cream, forward and down. His face extended, ears sliding up.

In scant seconds, a huge black wolf stood in his place.

She'd seen his wolf before, but that was when her head was cracking open and he was under siege. Now she looked her fill.

He was sleek and muscled, his haunches roped and his chest deep. His withers would've come to human's collarbones, and he must have been his full six three from head to hip. Since the average natural wolf stood two to three feet tall and was no longer than five feet—and the average shifter only a little larger than that—he towered over them all.

His fur was solid black except for a few dark gray markings on his face and one wolf-shaped blaze on his chest. The gold of his eyes glowed even brighter from within his black mask.

Every hormone in her body exploded. The scent of her estrus was so strong she stopped breathing. Her wolf would have been perfectly happy to jump him right there. Thank goodness for the human in her who knew that, besides having places to go, they had witnesses—and that those witnesses were fully capable of laughing their fool heads off.

Sure enough, when Noah's first act was to come nuzzle and lick her, behind them was the explosive rasp of a wolfy cough.

Noah shot Jayden a glare. Jayden lolled. Even Mason whuffled, like a muffled laugh. It completely broke the mood.

Noah gave Mason a barked command. Mason managed to stop whuffling long enough to press his snout against a wolf-high spot on the wall, activating an almost invisible door. Noah led the way out. The door closed behind them.

They walked single-file, Noah trotting in the lead with his tail held high, Mason in the cleanup position. A trail cut through the field abutting the back of the store, winding its way through tall grass toward a smattering of stunted trees and thistles and shrubs at the edge of the forest.

Following the path, they entered the woods. Gradually the trees got taller, the trail narrower. Soon it became little more than a few broken twigs to the naked eye.

But to the nose...Sophia put her head down and snuffled. Scent blazed, shouting that this was an often-used way for the pack. She was traveling through the most amazing odors. Wildflowers and grass, but she also caught the powdery scent of moths and the bitter tang of bugs, and whiffs of stuff she hadn't even known had scents. In her constant nose-turning she tripped a couple times, until Jayden sniggered. Then she snapped her jaw shut and paid attention to where she was going.

But when they passed a well-marked oak, she nearly turned inside out, caught by the sheer complexity of smell. Stale bitterness was overlaid with a fresh, virile scent she identified as Noah's. Instinctively she knew this was a signpost for the pack's sacred territory, marked by their alpha. Other animals came here only at their own risk.

Awaiting them in the clearing was the pack—or what was left of it.

Noah had said there'd be the traitorous five plus cowed women, youth, and elderly. But Sophia had processed that information with her human brain, not her wolf.

The reek coming off the anti-alphas was abnormally strong. The others smelled tragically less than they should have.

Arcane Animal Husbandry said it was the scent-producing glands on their tails, less in the females and elderly because their tails were tucked. Their bodies and ears slumped even more than the submissiveness of followers would call for.

This was subservience from abasement and fear.

Her wolf flared with fury. The hope of future generations and the elders who should have been revered were scared and cowed, while those anti-alpha idiots, with strength and not much else, were preening and prancing like alphas.

She growled low in her throat.

The low-ranking wolves heard, abuse probably having attuned them to every nuance. Their heads came up, their eyes wide on her, a combination of wolf and human surprise.

One of the idiots finally saw her. Big, dark gray, with mean little eyes and markings like a skull on his chest. Ah yes, Ivan. He said, ***Who is she?***

Well, he hadn't really *said* it. But his meaning was clear enough through a combination of posture, ear-flagging, teeth-baring, growling, and sort of mental *push* on a group wavelength.

Noah snarled. When all attention was on him, he urged Sophia forward with his muzzle to stand before the pack. Then he used the gland on the top side of his tail to release pheromones onto her. Arcane Animal Husbandry told her this was standard animal behavior, an alpha identifying that which was his. He'd have done it to every member of his pack when he'd become alpha.

Experiencing it, it seemed less like "behavior" and more like high ritual.

Mason trotted in front of her, tail waving like a royal standard. ***Hail our queen.*** He turned to her and bowed over one bent foreleg.

Clyde! A smaller maize-colored wolf danced on delicate paws. ***You said I'd be queen.***

Bonnie was smaller as a wolf than Sophia had expected. She felt statuesque, almost regal in comparison. She stood taller, her tail unfurling and waving slightly.

Bonnie's ears went straight up and she bared her teeth at Sophia. Sophia didn't know exactly what that meant, but she did know Bonnie wasn't happy. Lolz. Sophia's tail only waved harder.

A cold nose poked Sophia's rear. She tucked tail and whipped around to confront Ivan. What the fuck, she tried to say, but all that came out was a low growl. Or maybe that was Noah.

Ivan's back stiffened in surprise. ***She's fertile.***

She's our queen, Mason said. Jayden, in a low undertone, added, ***Dumbshit.*** Mason continued, ***Of course she's fertile.***

I'm not fertile. I'm not your queen. Again nothing came out but a low burr from Sophia's throat, this one closer to a whimper than a growl.

Bonnie caught it. She looked down her nose at Sophia, the long muzzle making her disdain even more effective than a human. ***Is our queen dumb?***

Clyde made a hiccupping growl. A snicker, not as human as Jayden's, but insulting all the same. Ivan joined in, and Killer, then Marlowe following his brother's lead. Sophia realized belatedly that Attila was nowhere to be seen or smelled.

Enough! Noah braced large on his four paws, his raised coat making him even bigger, and gave them all a golden glare. ***Let's get this done.***

Let us, oh great king? Ivan's words were servile but his tone was just short of rude. ***A true Challenge Hunt belongs to the king and queen alone.***

Noah's eyes narrowed to slits, his lips peeled back to expose gleaming fangs; his low dangerous growl could have flayed the bark off trees. Sophia didn't need words to get that. He wasn't happy at all.

Jayden nudged her flank. ***He's going to tell them all to stuff it.*** Somehow he'd found a wavelength apart from the common band, his words clearer than the general mental push. ***They need him as alpha. Do something. Stop him.***

How? The word was as lost in her brain as all the others. She raised her eyebrows and popped her eyes instead. Hopefully the "What do I do, since I can't speak?" was clear enough.

Meanwhile Noah was barking, ***This is bullshit. I'm not risking* my mate *because you've got a hard-on for* me. *I'm abdicat—***

"All right, listen up, wolfies!" Sophia shifted to human so fast her hair burned. "Too much arguing, not enough hunting. Let's get going." She stalked away, shedding her humanity as she went.

She strode through a stunned silence. Hesitantly, several of the pack made almost reverent bows.

Stars and moon. Apparently quick shifting was a strength indicator to weres.

Then Bonnie yipped. ***Our queen is blind to the customs as well as dumb. We must howl first, for the good fortune of the hunt.***

Sophia bristled and turned to give Bonnie a good glare. If she made that *dumb* comment one more time she was so getting a rolled-up newspaper whacked across the nose.

Noah growled, ears up and fangs exposed. Sophia readied herself for another quick shift but he only said, ***Fine. If we're going to do this, let's do it.***

His voice raised in a strong howl. One by one, the others entered until it was a chorus. It was beyond eerie.

It went on long enough to get on Sophia's nerves. She waited, voiceless, feeling left out, feeling truly dumb.

But then she thought, hey, they were the ones howling before setting off on a hunt. Didn't that warn the prey? That was dumber than a sack of hammers.

Enough already. Sophia got off her haunches and set out. The others could follow or not.

Chapter Twenty-One

The howls died. Sophia smelled wolves trailing her but she refused to look, knowing her authority was already shaky.

Then she caught Bonnie's peeved push. ***How the hell does our queen know where she's going when she's not a real wolf?***

Sophia got a surge of pleasure. Yeah, maybe she wasn't a real wolf or even a hunter, but she was human with a brain and she knew where she was going. She knew where the deer hung out from past summers shining them—a kids-up-north thing.

She headed toward the Big Field.

Or at least where she thought the Big Field was. Some of the landmarks had changed over the years, and others looked different from a few feet lower down. Her strides became tentative.

Each snicker from Ivan goaded her. Each "poor dumb queen" from Bonnie rankled. Sophia started trotting, then running.

When they hit the clearing, Noah caught up to Sophia and ran beside her.

Joy sang through her, the deep, intrinsic pleasure of being alive and of running with her mate and her pack. She lengthened her stride, outdistancing even Noah.

She saw the gray stag first, warily emerging from the far copse. Instinct ripped through her, surging with unholy glee. She rode atop it, veering toward the tall, muscular animal. He bolted, but too late. She gained steadily. She was a yard behind the stag when he whirled.

She got a faceful of antlers. Not hardened yet, but the starlight lancing through trees glinted dangerously off twelve very sharp points. She clamped on the brakes, skidding stiff-legged in the turf.

Sophia, no! With a powerful leap, Noah surged over her head. She sucked in a breath. Would he land on the creature's deadly rack?

At the last minute he tucked his paws into his body, clearing the stag's crown with inches to spare, and landed on its withers. He spun, opened powerful jaws, and clamped onto its spine. A crunch later, the huge stag fell to its knees. Sophia froze. With a gasp, the stag went onto its side. Its last breath went out of it in a rattle.

She told herself that at least it had been quick and painless for the stag.

The rest of the pack caught up. In the general excitement, Killer edged into the woods' shadows behind Noah, where a dark human shape had appeared. The missing Attila?

Something went from human hand to wolf mouth.

The rest of the pack crowded around Noah and the stag, congratulating him, blocking her view of both Noah and Killer.

She nudged aside wolves until she could see.

Killer stood beside Noah, stray starlight glinting off metal clenched in the anti-alpha's teeth.

A blade.

Electric shock made her cry, *Noah!* But *still* nothing came out. She sprang desperately toward him—just as Killer jabbed his muzzle into Noah's flank.

Her mate's ears jerked back. He skipped away with a yip.

Sophia landed beside Killer. She snapped at him and snarled. Killer danced back.

Her mate's soft *whuffle* recalled her to him. Noah's stiff legs and pulled-back ears said something was very wrong. Immediately she went to him and sniffed his flank, where Killer had jabbed. She got a noseful of hot copper. She whined as blood welled up through his thick black fur and trickled down his coat.

How did this happen? Mason demanded.

Killer said, ***The stag's antlers must have stabbed him.*** If he'd held a knife in his mouth, he'd tossed it away, and Attila had grabbed it up. She didn't smell it or see it now.

Not antlers, Sophia tried to say, still stupidly mute, shook her head in a vigorous no. Noah had cleared the buck's crown like a bird.

No one paid attention.

Shift, Noah, Jayden said. ***That should heal it.***

Noah shifted. It was fast, but Sophia knew how instantly he'd done it before. Worse, he stifled a gasp and pressed a hand to his shirt-covered side. Intense pain crossed his face, suppressed so quickly, she almost thought she'd imagined it.

She slid nearer. He lifted his hand barely an inch and stared at it. Blood smeared his palm and darkened his shirt underneath. Only he and Sophia saw it.

Quickly he shifted back. ***The Hunt is successful. My mate and I will eat. Then the rest of you will taste in the order we give.*** Tail lifted like nothing was wrong, he trotted to the stag's belly.

Wait, what? *They'd* eat? As in, him and *her*? She started giving him as many no, not, never, uh-uh signals as she could short of waving her paws like a berserker puppet.

Jayden nosed her. He said on that private band, ***Just pretend.***

Oh. Yeah. She could do that. Panic subsided. She raised her own tail and strutted to Noah's side...where he'd opened the stag's belly with a powerful chomp. Under her fur, her face turned green.

She managed to pretend to sample *pâté de foie stag* for about two seconds before she stepped back.

Bonnie immediately took her place.

Sophia growled, low and angry. Wolf pecking order might normally give Bonnie first dibs, but some of those trembling females had less meat on them than fur on a hanger. Noah had said *they'd* choose the order, not nature, so Sophia growled louder.

Bonnie pretended not to hear.

That just pissed Sophia off.

So when Noah herded one of the elderly wolves toward the stag to take his place, Sophia found the thinnest female and nosed her in too, next to Bonnie.

Bonnie turned on the poor wolf, snarling and nipping to force her out. The wolf whimpered.

Righteous anger blazed through Sophia. She turned human, grabbed Bonnie by the hips and pulled her away.

Bonnie yowled. She jerked her hips away from Sophia and muscled back in on the deer.

Sophia grabbed Bonnie's tail with both hands and yanked.

Claws scrabbling, Bonnie came away from the carcass. With a bark she twisted and tried to bite Sophia.

Enough is enough. Sophia whacked her across the snout.

Bonnie turned human. It took her a while, muscle creaking and bones cracking. But when she stood facing Sophia, murder was in her eyes. "You're pretty happy for a woman who's just killed her mate."

"What are you talking about? The Hunt was successful."

"Sure." Bonnie smirked. "Noah won *this* challenge. Better if he'd lost. That would have only meant his exile. Now he'll be fighting Ivan—to his death."

*   *   *

With the pack busily feeding, Noah, Mason, Jayden, and Sophia returned to the garage.

The moment Noah was inside and out of sight of the pack, he sagged, a hand to his flank.

"What's wrong?" Sophia was immediately at his side, fussing like he was hers to fuss over.

"Nothing," he said wearily.

She yanked open his shirt to reveal his ribs. Dried brown blood streaked his sleek skin. She grabbed one of Mason's hand wipes and cleaned it off. Noah bore it stoically but now she could see the blackened skin, angry red lines radiating from the wound. It had to hurt like hell. "Not nothing."

Noah peered at his side. “Damn it. You’re right. Not nothing.” His voice was soft. “This looks like the wound that killed my mother.”

Sophia’s heart iced. “What did that fuck Killer do to you, that you’re not healing?”

“Let me see.” Jayden moved her gently aside, surprising in a man with his strength and shocking in a man with his annoyance factor. He examined Noah’s flank with a bunch of grave *hmms* and *tsks*. Even in those few moments, Noah’s pupils dilated severely and his mouth worked like it was dry. “Like your mother’s but deeper.”

She didn’t like any of it. “Magic?”

“Yes.” Jayden’s black eyes snapped. “Which is why shifting hasn’t healed it.”

“Killer’s no wizard. How’d he manage it?”

“I’d guess a knife treated with magical poison,” Jayden said. “Enhanced nightshade, from the looks of it.”

“That’s not deadly to shifters,” Sophia said.

“It is if it’s mixed with the target’s blood.”

She chilled. “This was planned? How lethal is it?”

“In an iota wolf, within minutes.” Jayden reached into his pocket. “An alpha takes longer to die, but not much. Hours. Unless we stop it, now.” He pulled out a flat silver disk.

“Hours?” Noah’s shock was clear. “My mother took days.”

“There are significant differences,” Jayden said. “That was regular magic, and a glancing blow. This is enhanced. Stabbed deep.”

“How do you know—?”

“What the hell do you think you’re using?” Sophia grabbed for the disk. “It’s silver.”

Jayden snatched it away. “It’s this or nothing. Noah?”

Noah removed his hand. Even in those few moments the poison had spread. Angry red stitched across his ribs like forks of toxic lightning. "Do what you have to. Stop this."

"Wait." Sophia jabbed her finger at the disk. "Not before I know what that thing does."

"It's an asp's compress, princess," Jayden said. "It'll suck the poison back to the point of entry and imprison it there. Once the poison is centralized, we can eventually extract it with a spell."

"How'd you happen to have it along?" Mason asked suspiciously.

"Please. When the anti-alphas lost at Bonnie and Clyde's, I knew they'd try something underhanded. I also have a disk for plague, bullets, and catastrophic hemorrhoids." He gave Mason a glare. "I mean hemorrhages. Now if you're all done proving how skeptical you are on your alpha's behalf...?"

Mason nodded reluctantly, and Jayden slapped the disk against Noah's skin.

Noah sucked in a pained breath.

"Hold still." Jayden counted three then lifted the disk away. It made a *thwuck* like a suction cup coming off, revealing a small circular red patch.

"That made it worse." Sophia snatched the disk from Jayden. It tingled in her fingers.

"It only looks it." Jayden was unrepentant. "The poison was drawn to the surface and confined. See?"

"I'm okay." Noah's words were a little gaspy. "I think I'm feeling better."

"Lucky Jayden." She put a little wolf in it. "I won't kill him immediately."

Noah gave her a small smile. Then he said to Jayden, "Now heal me."

"I hand you a minor miracle, and you want *more*?" Jayden grimaced. "Shifters. Look. Magical poison stabbed deep into a hexed werewolf is tricky enough. Add in your other little issue, and if I try to remove the poison the wrong way it'll irritate the hex—or any other magic on you—and make things worse."

Sophia's ears pricked. *Or any other magic on you.* Was that the secret Jayden had hinted at?

Mason growled. "You said that once the poison was centralized, you could extract it."

Jayden was already shaking his head. "I said we could *eventually* extract it. First we have to remove the hex. Then we'll see."

Sophia didn't like any of this. She examined the disk. Small runes were inscribed around its edge. Introductory arcane languages told her the symbols had to do with healing, but silver wasn't made for a werewolf.

So why had it worked?

"Then remove the damned hex," Noah said to Jayden. There was more than a little wolf in his growl.

Jayden gave an exaggerated sigh. "Any removal spell will remove the containment on the poison as well. Released poison, scant hours to live, remember?"

"Damn you." Mason crowded Jayden, almost chest-butting. "Sounds like convenient excuses."

"It's magic, not me." Jayden threw his hands in the air. "Ask her if you don't believe me."

Mason's head swiveled.

Sophia nodded reluctantly. "Single spells are easy. But layer two or more, and complexity zings off the scale."

"He's telling the truth?" Mason's jaw gaped.

"I don't know. But it's possible that, in trying to remove the hex, he'd release the poison." She liked this less and less. Five shitheads she knew and one she didn't—with powerful magic—were threatening her *mate*. And now a man who was supposed to be a friend was using silver on him?

She cracked her third eye to peek at the disk. The metal glowed with diamond-blue purity on the etheric, like a small white-hot star in her palm. It was a magic healing token all right.

For witches and wizards, not shifters.

She exploded "Why the hell did you use this? It's for witche—"

"I had to do *something* or he'd die." Jayden whirled to face her, fists on hips. "What would you have done?"

"I'd have brought disks for shifters, dumbass."

"*Enough.*" Noah's white-knuckled hand clamped to his side. "I don't care why, or even *what* at this point. Come morning, unless we find a way to reverse the hex, I'm facing Ivan as fifteen pounds of dog. Against a hundred pounds of wolf, I'm dead."

Silence. Sophia swallowed hard.

Then Jayden said, "This is more than a talisman can handle."

"I need this hex gone. Do whatever it takes."

Whatever it takes. Sophia stiffened. This was more than a few gewgaws could fix. Noah needed a real witch.

She'd have to do it. Which meant she'd have to break her second funeral seal. *Hands*.

Even at the thought, pain seared her palms and her fingers seized up. The disk slipped from them into her jacket pocket. She breathed through the pain. For Noah's life? She'd risk it. What the hell. It hadn't killed her last time, it might not this time either. Maybe next time, but that was then.

She opened her mouth to say she'd do it. That she'd use her magic. Mason spoke first.

"How?" he asked. "How do we get rid of the hex?"

"Carefully," Jayden said.

"No," Noah said. "We're out of time. Use brute force and deal with the fallout as best we can. You need to do it."

"Yes." She started to say. *Yes, I'll do it.*

But the instant she thought the words, a thousand razor blades of pain spun through her hands, up her arms, and sliced into her larynx.

Nothing more came out.

A voice dropped into the silence. "All right, I'll do it. But you know it will cost you."

The voice was Jayden's.

Chapter Twenty-Two

"Of course it costs, with you." Noah's face was grim. "What do you want?"

Eye my newt. Sophia mentally smacked herself. In hindsight it was obvious, though all of his previous magic could have been explained by his artifacts—the apron, the brooch, and the disk. But if he could remove a multilayer spell?

Jayden was a wizard.

Sophia seethed inside. Since Rodolphe, she didn't trust *any* witch or wizard except her brother. Not her aunt, not even herself. A wizard who charged favors for magic? Bottom of the trust pile.

"How did you know I could?" Jayden asked.

"I didn't," Noah said. "I just suspected. But my mother worked—" he grimaced, "—for one of your kind and the signs were there. Now stop delaying and do what you need to do."

She said, "Noah, don't. I'll do i-i-*hhh.*" Pain constricted her words, hands searing as if each of her fingers were lit like a firecracker.

"I don't want much." Jayden shrugged. "Name your firstborn after me."

"That's it?" Noah raised one brow. "All right, but only if my mate agrees to it."

"Done." Jayden plucked a thick wedge of blue chalk from the air, squatted, and began to draw on the garage's concrete floor.

"I do *not* like this," Mason growled.

"Hush now," Jayden said in a distracted murmur. "I have to get this right."

"Noah, don't," Sophia said again. "He's got his own agenda—"

"Princess, with all due respect, shut it." Jayden swept out a circle. "This is hard enough."

He closed the circle and her lips snapped shut. The spell was begun. Any interference now would only hurt Noah.

Jayden sketched a second circle, inscribing it inside the first, touching at their tops. A container circle, the kind that held magic on the inside rather than kept it out.

She was grudgingly impressed. He was doing serious magic, faster than even her most accomplished professors. She wondered why she'd never heard of him. The magical community was exceedingly small. Wizards powerful enough to reverse another witch's complex hex? Minuscule.

She knew them all. At least, all the lawful ones.

Could Jayden be...? Sophia's heart started pounding, like a drum rattling her ribcage. She'd seen photos of the Council's most wanted, but disguise spells, good enough to fool a witch, were not impossible. Especially fooling a witch who wasn't doing magic.

Vanishing the chalk, Jayden stood. “Okay, you can talk again.” He pointed to Noah and then the center of the circles. “Stand there.”

“Noah, wait.” Fear and need and love collided in her throat. She forced her words past the pain. “I-I’ll do it.”

Noah frowned at her.

A strange glint entered Jayden’s eye.

She ignored him to concentrate on Noah. “Don’t let him do magic on you. I don’t trust him. I’ll do it.”

“Sophia.” Noah cupped her chin, raising her face, and kissed her lips gently. “I saw what that cost you at Bonnie and Clyde’s. I don’t want you going through that again, especially when there are alternatives. Jayden knows what he’s doing, and once he’s given his word, he’s trustworthy.”

“Names have power.” She searched Noah’s golden eyes. “How do you know what he’ll do with our...” Her cheeks heated. “With *your* firstborn once it’s named the way he wants?”

Noah kissed her again. “He wouldn’t dare harm any child of mine, yours, or ours.” With a final kiss he released her and strode into the center of the circle.

He faced the intersection point as if he knew what it was. Maybe from growing up in that wizard’s home, he did. Jayden faced him across the point. Only a few inches separated them. Sophia was struck by how alike they were, wizard and shifter. Equally tall, lithely muscled, rangy builds, their black locks carelessly tousled, and handsome, chiseled faces. Even their skin tone was the same bronze.

“Ready?” Jayden said.

Noah smiled grimly. “No. But go ahead.”

Jayden joined his hands and swept both arms back toward his hip, like he was going to pop a volleyball.

"Wait," Sophia said. "The hex rebounded on a magic mirror with carved demons, then hit my picture. Are you compensating for that?"

Locked mid-gesture, Jayden gave a sarcastic eye roll. "I wasn't born yesterday, kid. I'm doing a reveal first." He released his joined fists at Noah. "Show!"

Magic shot into the circle. The air ignited with a whoosh of violet smoke that rose in a cylinder from chalk to ceiling. Violet haze washed back through the joined point to envelop Jayden. Sophia relaxed a bit, seeing that. Jayden had joined himself with Noah's confinement circle, so that whatever he flung at Noah would rebound on him. More dangerous for the witch, but it made for more efficient spell-casting. For the first time Jayden's magic was evident, glowing strong and clear. He must have been masking it, and the reveal stripped the mask away.

The magical poison also showed, a bilious sea urchin, spiny fingers waving, anchored to Noah's flank.

But there was no visible sign of the hex. The reveal didn't show the one thing they needed. "Damn it, Jayden! What's going on?"

"I don't know." The wizard's black eyes were narrowed, his clenched teeth bared. "This is like nothing I've ever seen. And that's saying a lot."

A buzz bit Sophia's ears. Not the normal hum of reveal magic, but the angry drone of a thousand riled hornets.

The smoke around Noah went red. He folded over suddenly, as if he'd been hit. His head kicked back. His face was drawn in severe pain, his skin dead white.

"You're hurting him," she shouted over the buzz. She barely kept herself from yanking Noah out of the circles, which would result in far more catastrophic pain. It took clutching her pearls so hard they nearly cracked.

"The poison is trying to latch onto my magic." Sweat trickled down Jayden's forehead. His hands, extended toward Noah, were stiff and tense, tendons white. "Trying to break out."

"Heavens above." Sophia dropped her pearls to clutch her hands. They were cold.

"What does that mean?" Mason's voice was dark with concern.

She swallowed an iceberg of fear to answer. "Using Jayden's power, the poison could break confinement, take over Noah's body then jump the gap to take over Jayden too."

"Hell."

"Yes." She held her arm out to Jayden. It shook slightly. "Use my power to resist."

"What about your death seals?" he yelled over the drone.

"A little Share Power won't break them." She hoped. But even if it did, she needed to do this, for Noah.

Jayden didn't wait for another invitation. He latched onto her wrist, his other hand still extended, quaking, toward Noah.

She chanted up a small Share. She'd already released a third of her power and her magic stirred deep in her core, her very cells, responding to Jayden's need, rising to her wrist to meet him.

He drew.

Her Sight showed her power pulsing from their joined hands into his aura. He converted the power into a pulse of magic aimed at the poison.

Spiny fingers shot up, trying to grab it. But Jayden's augmented magic sheared through the bilious poison's fingers like shurikens through vines.

The red haze faded to a pulsing violet.

"Did it work?" Mason shouted.

"Maybe," Jayden said. "I'm going to try to unravel the hex."

"How?" Sophia said. "You can't even see it."

"Like this." He snatched a purple wand from the air. Flicked it at Noah. "Unwind!" He spun the wand as if he would wrap the hex around it like cotton candy.

Sophia didn't see anything gathering on the wand. "It's not working."

And worse yet, as Jayden used up his magic, the poison surged. New fingerlets grew and latched onto his dimming power.

Jayden dropped the wand and switched to fighting the poison. "More power," he gasped at her. "Faster. *Now*."

For Noah. She snarled, "*Share all.*"

It wasn't complete—two thirds of her power was still sealed so she couldn't do a true Evacuate, and time would replenish it. But the released third burst from her, and from the battle Jayden fought, he'd need every drop.

He'd been gentle before. Now he sucked power out of her, not waiting until it rose to her wrist but yanking it directly from her cells. It hurt like hell.

She clenched her jaw and let him pull. Tears stung her eyes and her breathing collapsed into panting. Still he pulled, a thousand barbs tearing through her, shredding her flesh from the inside.

The poison's buzzing ebbed. Was her hearing failing...? Her physical eyes sprang open, tears trickling down her cheeks, but she ignored them to stare at the containment column.

The violet mist was thinning. Noah, his color returning to normal, slowly straightened.

The poison shrank to a dot...and disappeared from sight.

Sophia felt like the Hungry Ghost's straw, drawn and wrung out. When Jayden released her arm, she staggered.

Noah sprang toward her.

Jayden flung a hoarse, "Stop!"

Noah ignored him, knocking straight through the wall of magic. The purple smoke collapsed.

Jayden sagged with a grunt. "Damn it, I hadn't closed the connection yet."

Noah grabbed Sophia in his strong arms and held her tightly, like he'd never let go. "Love, are you all right?"

She felt like a burst, empty piñata, like a desiccated husk. But his arms, his warmth, eased the pain. She gave a weak nod.

His hand, caressing her hair, seemed still worried. "Jayden. The hex?"

"I don't know." Jayden drew a bushel of air in through flared nostrils, then let it out slowly. He looked wiped. "I did see enough to identify a layered weave before the poison tried to take over, and that only because Sophia aided." He paused. "That's some mate you have there." His tone was honestly admiring.

Her cheeks heated.

"I know," Noah said. "Did you neutralize the hex?"

"Maybe. I don't know." He sounded vexed.

Mason said, "But the poison disappeared. That means the hex is gone."

"Normally I'd agree. But I'm not sure. The hex, the poison, not to mention Noah's innate magic...this whole setup is strange." Jayden materialized a handkerchief and passed it over his brow.

Sophia peeked up from Noah's arms. "How?"

An annoyed grimace flashed across his face. "I don't know. That's what's strange about it."

Mason said, "If you're not sure the poison's gone, shouldn't you try again to remove it?"

Jayden was already shaking his head. "It nearly kicked our asses. I'll try again, but only after I know the hex is neutralized or Sophia has regenerated power. Better yet, both."

Mason's upper lip peeled up, like a wolf. "Noah may have to fight as a dog?"

Jayden didn't answer, his eyes bleak.

"If I do, so be it," Noah said. "What do we do now?"

Jayden's lids slid shut. "We wait for the sun."

Noah took Sophia's hand and led her behind one of the sets of shelves. Quietly he said, "This may be the last night of my life. I know you think our joining is because of the hex, that we're not truly mated. But for tonight—Sophia, I need you." His eyes, hot on her, underlined his request.

What could she say? He was brave and wise and kind and tomorrow he might die, fighting for his pack and her.

But the clincher was—she loved him. It might have been the hex, but her heart didn't seem to think so. And frankly, neither did her head.

She kissed him. "Yes, of course."

He took her to a small side office, closed the window blinds, came to her, and gently removed her coat. As he unbuttoned her blouse, he kissed her forehead, temple, cheek and nose. "I love your nose." He kissed it again. "If I lose tomorrow, I die a happy man."

"While I'm glad you like my snout of a nose, don't say that. If the hex isn't gone in the morning, I'll break my hands' seal and take care of it myself. Speaking of which..." Jayden had told her it was essential to get Noah's big secret out of him. "Now that you know my worst, maybe you can tell me yours—"

"Later." Noah put a long forefinger to her lips, silencing her.

Momentarily. "But—"

"Shh." He replaced finger with mouth, and kissed her.

He didn't say it, but both love and sorrow drove that kiss. His lips tenderly plied hers, the mate coaxing a response rather than the alpha demanding it.

She loved sweet and gentle but if this was the last time they'd be together, she wanted more.

She slid her hand along his fly and squeezed. He surged and groaned in response. Continuing to stroke denim, she curled a hand around his nape and backed with him to the couch. She sat, urging him down next to her.

When he hesitated, she tore off her blouse.

He collapsed onto the couch as if the sight of her lace-clad breasts took the strength from his body. But he quickly found it again. He pressed into her and kissed her, hands finding her breasts and cupping them. As their thighs seamed together, his kisses deepened, staccato thrusts of tongue interspersed with long swirls of hot lips.

His shifter's stubble rasped against her skin. It charged her with increased frenzy. She palmed his honed cheeks and levered her tongue toward his tonsils.

He chuckled and thumbed her nipples through her bra. "Not so fast," he murmured between kisses.

"Not so slow." She growled it. Somehow she'd acquired a wolf along the way, a wolf who drove her to grab hot heaven with her mate.

When he continued to simply kiss her and gently test the heft of her breasts, she took things out of his hands.

She reached behind her, unhooked her bra, tore it off, and threw it away.

Or rather she put things *into* his hands, because her taut breasts poured into his palms, filling them perfectly, her nipples tight and begging for his thumbs.

He made a sound that was half groan, half howl. His head dropped to the crook of her neck. His forehead was damp. "Sophia, you're so lovely. My wolf wants all of you, *now*. But my human wants to cherish you forever. I'm trying to give you time to adjust, to get ready—"

"*My* wolf says fuck that." She leaned into his hands, shimmying her nipples against the whorled skin of his palms—and landed a cupped hand on his groin.

He was erect under his jeans, practically bursting behind the zipper.

"You're ready. I'm ready. Let's get dirty." She stood and stripped off pants and panties and toed off her shoes. His eyes roved over her with gratifying hunger. The bulge in his jeans jacked up another size.

She climbed onto his lap, facing him, in her trouser socks and pearls. Not insanely sexy, but she was too desperate for him to care. "Kiss me." She grabbed his face and locked lips.

He wrapped arms around her naked back and returned her kiss with glorious abandon.

Her wolf howled her pleasure. Her human rolled her hips, rasping her dewing vulva against his heavy denim ridge. The friction sang up her nerves, urging her faster. She rippled against him, her heart thudding to keep up with her racing breath.

He broke off the kiss. "Wait," he panted. "I wanted to say—"

"No more talk." She silenced him the most effective way she could–she plastered her lips to his and thrust her tongue into his dark mouth. Then, to compound his interest and keep him taking care of business, she yanked, pushed, and unzipped until she'd fumbled open his jeans.

His erection sprang full and tall from the opening. She rose on her knees over him, took him in her hand and guided herself to perfection–

He grabbed her and flipped her onto her back on the couch. Spread her thighs and opened a hot, wet kiss on her pussy.

She shrieked. His fingers pressed into her flesh and his tongue slapped her clit. She howled.

"You want hard and hot? You're going to get so hard and hot you're going to spontaneously combust." He shifted, sucking lightly on her clit while grinding his stubbled jaw into her swollen labia. She thrashed under his mouth.

He thrust a finger inside her. His gold eyes flew up to hers. "Damn me, Sophia. You're already burning hot."

"Me? What about you?" She ground herself against his finger. "More."

He drove a second finger into her. He fell on her clit again with his slapping tongue and sucking mouth and masculine hunger.

She gloried in it, grabbing him by the ears and pulling and grinding harder. Her pearls rose and fell with her rapidly undulating chest, jewelry that, for the first time, wasn't staid and conservative but provocative and sexy with her nipples hard as nuts beyond them.

His fingers rode in and out of her pussy and he changed to straight sucking until her clit was hard and aching and she thought he'd draw her entire body out through it.

"Noah...stop sucking and fuck me now. *Please.*" She wailed it and somehow halfway through it changed to an eerie howl.

"You're so aroused. So very beautiful." His eyes were bright gold between her thighs. "Come for me first, my beautiful mate."

"No, I want—argh!"

He latched onto her pussy and sucked for all he was worth.

It was too much. She exploded in a sweet nova of bright stars. Too bright. She squeezed her eyes shut and thrashed against him as he tongue-whipped her clit to extend the orgasm.

Her wolf gloried in it. Her human was temporarily blitzed. She lay pliant as he shucked his pants. His erection had engorged to monstrous. He knelt between her wet, yielding thighs and fitted himself to her. The head of his cock pressed and spread her.

She was suddenly aware of the size of him versus the size of her, a second after it was too late.

He drove himself into her slick sex. To the hilt.

She gasped down to her toenails. He filled her and more. "You're...big, face to face. Wait."

He let out an intense groan. "Do you want me to stop?"

He was stretching her to her limits and beyond. She wriggled against him, caught like a butterfly. "Hell, no."

He smiled and backed off slightly. She gasped at the raw hollow ache in her pelvis. He surged forward again, filling her. And again. And yet again.

A wild need seized her. Her wolf driving her, she grabbed his hips and ground herself against him as if she could rattle his very bones.

His sexy grin exposed sharp, gleaming teeth. He began banging into her.

She yowled and met him thrust for thrust. His wolf was driving him too, joining them in a savage rhythm. Together they built higher and higher until she was lifted into the blue heavens themselves. She grasped his shoulders, fingers digging into muscles so taut they were iron. "*Mine.*"

His gaze blazed into hers. "*Mine,*" he agreed, and thrust to the very core of her being.

Power flooded her. She came, soaring like a bird. He came with her. They clasped each other and flew together through intense shuddering, shock and aftershock.

As their panting began to slow, he raised himself to hold her face in one hand. His gaze was tender. "I wanted to go slower. To show you reverence and honor."

"Showing how much I turn you on is good too." She yawned. Sobered. "That can't have been our last time. It's too soon. I just found you."

"Sweetheart. It won't be." He put his palm between her breasts. Took her hand and placed it over his heart.

It was an acknowledgment, and a pact. *True mates.*

If they survived the Witches' Council.

If he survived the fight.

Chapter Twenty-Three

They dressed and retreated to the main office. Sophia sat on a couch. Noah sat holding hands with her—he refused to let her go.

She said, "So Jayden mentioned there was something about you that I should know—"

"Yes, I..." His attention snapped toward the door. "Company's coming. I'll tell you later."

Mason and Jayden joined them, leaning against the walls, both of them staring out the office door with its clear view of the store's east window. Neither spoke but a muscle worked in Jayden's black-stubbled jaw.

The sex, Noah's warm body, and the temporary lull in terror made Sophia relax. She let down her guard—and the aftermath of tension and exertion crashed down on her, until she could barely keep her eyes open. She broke the silence to wake herself. "Where does the Challenge Fight take place?"

Mason said, "The field in back."

"In broad daylight? Aren't you afraid you'll be seen?"

"The field's shielded."

"What if the shield fails?"

"It can't. It's anchored to four talismans buried in the soil. They were just recharged, good for a couple years."

"Oh." If the shield failed, the talismans would act like a backup battery, in essence keeping the shield spell refreshed.

They were silent again. She slumped against Noah. She was painfully exhausted and he was so warm...

She stiffened. "What about Noah's poison? If it's not gone, will it interfere with the fight?"

Jayden answered. "Some. It'll slow him and make his movements stiff. But if the hex is gone, I'll be able to leach the poison."

"And if not?"

Noah said, "I'll have bigger problems than a little stiffness. Don't worry, Sophia." He rubbed her shoulder. "I've faced bigger opponents before."

"Over a hundred pounds bigger?"

He didn't answer.

They were silent again. She finally dropped off, dozing in Noah's arms. Her dreams were troubled. She was being chased by a horde of tiny wolves with mustaches. They'd just gotten their needle-sharp claws into her when she startled awake.

Noah was napping with his head canted back at an angle that wouldn't have been comfortable for a contortionist. She eased him down onto the couch, lay next to him, and pillowed her head on his chest. They both slept better then.

Mason woke them as the windows brightened with predawn. Sophia sat up and yawned. Jayden was leaning against the wall, seemingly nonchalant, but his black eyes were sharp on Noah. Next to Jayden, Mason watched Noah outright, not trying to hide his anxiety.

"Don't worry." Noah sat up and stretched as the first rays sparkled on the glass. "I feel fine. Better than fine. I feel exactly like my old self—" His form blurred and the tiny rat dog King popped into being standing on the couch cushions next to her. "*Yip*." He snapped it off as if it were a four-letter word.

"Yap, yap!" someone agreed.

That wasn't Noah.

Sophia swiveled to where Mason and Jayden stood by the window, bright sun streaming enthusiastically through the glass...only Mason stood there.

"Yap!"

Her eyes adjusted—down. Next to Mason quivered a very angry, black-haired miniature poodle.

She stifled a totally inappropriate laugh.

"Shit," Mason said. "What happened?"

He took the words right out of her mouth. "Jayden's spell not only failed—I think because Noah broke the spell before Jayden disconnected, some of Noah's hex rebounded on Jayden."

"Hell." Mason drove fingers through his hair, paced, then spun and flung a hand at the furiously yapping poodle. "Now how will he reverse the hex?"

"He won't." She pumped iron into her spine and stood. "I will."

Noah leaped in front of her, his little shaggy brows lowered like thunderclouds, his angry yip slicing through Jayden's barking. She could almost hear him saying, *Not for me you won't. You're not putting yourself in danger for me*.

"Noah." Kneeling, she took his cute doggie face between her hands. "Either I do this or you fight Ivan as an undersized dog. Your pack is at stake. So unless there are other alternatives—"

"Yip!" He jerked out of her hands to turn to Mason and growl.

Mason winced. "Uh, sorry, Noah. No."

"You can understand him?" she asked. "What is he saying?"

"I don't understand the words, but I know what he's saying." Mason's face reddened. "He wants me to challenge Ivan."

"And you won't? Just because you don't want to be alpha? Or are you too scared? I can't believe it. You'd let Noah stake his life against—"

"Sophia, no, that's not it. I *can't* fight Ivan. I'm, uh, his bond-brother."

Noah sat abruptly on his little hindquarters. He stared at his big lieutenant with surprise and consternation.

"It happened when I first came, okay? I went through a joining ceremony that involved very little sleep and a whole lot of alcohol. Next thing I knew Ivan and I were slapping cut palms together and I was pack—and his blood brother."

The black poodle started huffing, either the doggie version of a belly laugh, or he was hurking a hairball.

Noah yipped at the poodle. Sophia looked to Mason for translation.

"He said, 'You're no help.' Um, with a few more colorful terms added."

"Noah, please." Aunt Linda was missing, Gabriel was hundreds of miles away. Jayden had no magic, and Mason was handcuffed by the ties of kinship. It was devastatingly clear.

It was up to her. "I'll remove the hex."

All three males started yapping at her.

"Because yelling works so well." With a glance heavenward, she decided the issue by simply striding to the garage.

Mason followed automatically. Being queen had some perks. The poodle and rat dog came more reluctantly, yipping and yapping at each other the whole way.

"Where's your chalk?" she said. When Mason wordlessly handed her a chunk, she started refreshing Jayden's circles.

Mason stood next to her, watching closely. "How do you know it won't do the same thing to you that it did to Jayden?"

"I'm warding against it." She scribed a six-point star around the outer circle. Her movements were smooth, easy. Like riding a bike or swimming, it came right back.

"Won't the poison try to leap the gap?"

"Yes. I'll need your help to stop it." She finished the star, stepped out of her banker pumps and took off her socks, then traced her bare feet with chalk, muttering the words of a spell. Even the dogs stopped arguing to watch what she was doing.

"What is that?" Mason asked.

"I've rigged a sort of cutoff switch. If you see that I'm losing control, push me out of these." She pointed at the blue ringing her feet. "My power will automatically cut."

Jayden poodle trotted over to sniff the chalk markings. He nodded and his tail wagged.

"Glad you approve."

Mason squatted to touch the tracings around her feet. "How does it work?"

"It's advanced element theory," she said. "A witch's power comes from within, but visualization of that power is usually attached to an element, either earth, wind, fire or..."

His eyes glazed over. Poor Mason.

She took pity. "I'm pulling earth power. Break my ground, and it breaks the line of power."

"Oh." His gaze cleared and he stood. "Got it."

"Noah? I'll need you inside the circles."

The terrier yipped doubtfully. Even without words she knew where his concerns lay.

"Don't worry about me. The hex will be contained by the star and Mason will break in if your poison tries to take me over. And the pain..." She didn't like lying to him, but the pack needed him. And if he lost the fight when she could have made the difference, she wouldn't want to live with herself, anyway. "The pain will pass. C'mon Noah, let me do this for the pack. Or if not the pack, let me do this for us. For our future."

That finally did it. His jaw firmed. With a determined step he entered the inner circle, showing a profound level of trust in her, in the power and control of a witch he'd met only a few days before.

She blinked scratchy eyes.

Jayden barked. He seemed to be trying to tell her something. He poked her with his nose and barked again. It must be important.

She knelt, touched the white wolf brooch mentally and pushed her awareness outside her skin, accessing her wolf without shifting. She caught *layered*, then *backlash* and *rapid* and something like *tied at the tail*. Warning her against the rapid backlash of the poison? "I'll work as fast as I can. Step back."

She stood and closed her eyes, preparing to break her second seal.

To her surprise a third of her power, the power she'd given to Jayden, formed a lake at her feet, lapping at the shore of herself, waiting for her.

The lovemaking with Noah had apparently restored her more than she realized.

"Are you okay?" Mason said. "Your body snapped straight. Should I pull you out?"

"I'm okay. Starting the reveal." She mentally reimaged the water into sweet soil beneath her feet. Pictured herself as a tree, her roots extending deep into the life-giving earth. Drawing power smoothly into herself, she flung her spell into the circles' joined point.

Like Jayden's earlier reveal, a column of power shimmered up from the concrete under Noah's paws to the ceiling of the repair shop, rich brown because she was drawing earth magic. The power began to throb rhythmically. Her body throbbed in time with it.

But when she opened her witch's eye, nothing beyond a tiny pulsing point of red, the remains of the poison, showed.

Where was the hex?

"What's going on?" Mason said.

"Earth magic didn't reveal it. I'll have to try a multi-element spell. Don't worry—I'm still grounded with earth." She stirred up a little water magic and splashed the hex.

The power swirling around Noah brightened with blue streaks—but the hex didn't show.

She conjured up her wand, sparked red fire, and pumped it through the circles' joined point. The swirling smoke shimmered brighter.

"*Reveal.*" She blew the word into the containment on a puff of air. With the fourth element, the smoke suddenly glittered brilliantly, as if lit from within.

A tangle of magic was revealed glowing around the dog, a mummy's windings of vivid purples, yellows, reds, and blues.

She'd anticipated a complex, radically altered bur hex, so it took her a moment to realize what she was seeing.

"Your eyes are wide," Mason said. "Should I pull you out?"

"No. It's just that...it's a simple wrapping hex." Not hard to undo at all. Snip the magic anywhere, it unraveled. She wondered why Jayden hadn't managed it. He seemed like a competent enough mage.

Deep in Noah's flank, the poison flared.

No time to figure it out. She relaxed her grip on the multi-element reveal spell and pulled magical metal shears from the ground.

A wave of her hand sent the shears into the circle. They opened to snip the hex, like a steel Pac Man.

Chomp.

But instead of cutting through, the shears *cracked.* Another chomp, they shattered. Bits of metal fell to the concrete, wavered, and disappeared.

She stared, shocked.

"Sophia!" Mason. "What's happening?"

"The wrapping hex broke the shears. But no way a wrapping hex could have that much power...shit."

The poison surged toward her like an ocean wave.

Automatically she threw a wall of water-magic up with her left hand. The poison hit with acid splashes, spurting over the water wall and spraying the edge of the containing circle. She lifted more power from the earth and poured it into both water wall and circle, until it was almost gone.

"Sophia...?"

"*Not yet.*" She needed more power. That meant breaking her penultimate dome.

She touched the metal inlays on her wand. "I sing silver, I sing gold." As she chanted she stabbed the wand down, accessing the last of her earth magic. Mentally, she transformed the magic into a diamond drill.

Across from her, poison oozed along the chalk tracings, leaking along the line of connection. Pain bled into her soles. She clenched her teeth against it.

She pushed the pain aside to raise her mental drill. Putting the diamond tip against the glass dome that sealed her power, she revved the drill.

With a whirr, it bit in. The funeral barrier cracked.

Her hands began to burn. More pain bled into her feet. She kept drilling. More cracks began to open. Her legs throbbed from the leaking poison. Her hands were on fire.

She clenched her wand so tight her fingers ached. *For Noah*. She stopped drilling, forced all available power into the wand, and used the thing like a sledgehammer.

"I sing silver and gold. *Explode!*" She bashed the wand/hammer into her funeral seal.

The dome burst in a shower of glass. The lock didn't so much shatter as rupture.

Power screamed along her veins, blasting into her hands. She shrieked.

Mason said, "Damn it, Sophia. What do I do?"

"*Wait!*" Her palms swelled, her fingers puffed until her skin felt like cooked sausage casings about to explode.

She panted through the pain, tears sheeting down her cheeks. Clumsily fisting the freed magic, she fashioned a knife, and flung it against the hex wrappings.

Feedback sliced her with agony, but the knife flew fast and true. It hit the hex windings.

The knife shattered into dust.

"Sophia? Now?"

N-no. She didn't know if she spoke out loud or not.

She rapidly chewed her options. Direct power, no good. She waved a new blade edgewise across the windings. The knife *shooped* off like a skate on ice—skittering a half inch *above* the hex.

The poison surged, bulging its containment like a can of botulism about to burst. Dribbles of the nasty stuff ran in rivulets along the chalk. Pain eroded her concentration.

She could either fight the pain or cast one last spell.

Mason said, "If you don't answer me, I'm pulling you out."

She cast magic.

Panting, she let the death sacrifice burn her as she swept up a new knife with her wand. One last chance. Couldn't cut it. Compact it?

Her hands were too swollen and burnt to work a spell. The pain had dulled to a dark ache, not good news, like warming before freezing to death.

"*Shrink.*" With the last of her concentration, she flung her spell at the hex.

It hit and rebounded straight at her.

Mason yanked her back. She stumbled out of her foot tracings, the spell zapping so close to her ear she heard it whine past.

All magic abruptly cut off. The containment circle dropped. Her wall against the poison dissipated. That meant something, but she couldn't remember what. She was exhausted, barely alive, the funeral magic eating her from the inside. She slid to the floor, only Mason's strength keeping her from collapsing in a heap. Her muscles throbbed as if she'd been beaten. Her eyes wouldn't work.

A small tongue licked her fingers.

Yippy yippy. From somewhere far away a tiny bark tinkled.

The tongue worked up her knuckles, drawing the pain from her twisted joints. Calming the swelling. Her thoughts swirled, erratic, but she realized the healing tongue had to be Noah's.

Yippy yippity yip. Behind her. Either a third dog or a mosquito. That annoying? She was betting on the mosquito.

Panting, she twisted her head on the ground.

The piccolo barks came from the tiny pink mouth of a black toy poodle. Mad as a hornet, albeit a curly-haired, cutie-pie hornet.

Well, sure. That annoying? Had to be Jayden.

Tied at the tail... Jayden must have meant he was tied to Noah, a straight magical connection from the first unhexing attempt. Her shrink spell had rebounded into *him*. Jayden had gone from a miniature to a toy.

Yippy yip yip!

He was really mad about something. Something she'd forgotten...?

Noah's tongue started licking her other hand. He worked the swelling and pain out of her fingers. Healing her, as miraculously as after she'd broken her first funeral seal.

Suddenly Noah gave a pained bark and fell to the floor.

She struggled to sit up. The remaining death magic juddered through her, leaching her strength, and she only managed to roll up to one elbow. But beside her, Noah lay gasping. She parted the fur over his wound.

Red, angry lines radiated as big as a DVD.

Fear bled into her numb exhaustion. This was what Jayden had been trying to tell her. During her attempts to the cut hex, the poison had broken its containment. Probably made worse when Noah licked her hands, healing the worst of the broken death seal by taking it into himself.

Her wand, clamped in her wounded fingers, jerked down, pointing at her pocket. She rolled to her back. Her hand dove in...and came out with Jayden's healing disk. Thank goodness. She wouldn't have to do serious magic. She was alive, and Noah's healing had taken the worst edge off the death magic, but the seal shards still cut her nerves.

Managing to sit up, she pressed the disk to the ugly black lightning on Noah's flank. She blew gently on the disk, activating it with the lightest touch of air magic. She felt the *thwuck* when the thing started sucking the poison to a point. Her gasp of pain was a duet with Noah's soft whine.

She stopped blowing, but the disk didn't stop sucking. She tried a small flick of magic to remove it. Her hands burned. The disk still didn't stop.

She had no choice but to pull the thing off physically. The disk came off with a ripping sound and left a raw, naked circle. Noah was silent, but she felt his whole body tense and knew what it cost him.

But it had worked. The angry radiating lines had shrunk to the size of a half dollar.

Drawing up her knees, she slumped against them, exhausted and almost numb with pain. Wordlessly, Mason squatted to pick up the panting terrier. He carried him out of the garage. She pushed herself to weary feet, snagged her shoes, and limped behind. The toy poodle trotted in her wake.

Mason laid Noah carefully on the couch in the exact spot where her mate had held her, where they'd slept together in a more profound sharing of trust than even their sex.

Noah's golden eyes were open and calm. He'd stopped panting and seemed better. She sat next to him, resting her elbows on her knees.

Her magic hadn't worked.

She was a hereditary witch princess, a *magna cum laude* graduate of Nostradamus University. Her magic *never* failed.

Yet now, when she needed it most, despite suffering excruciating pain to use it, it had failed.

She had failed.

She buried her face in her hands. The skin on her right hand was cracked and bleeding. Blood leaked onto her cheeks, joining the trickle of shame seeping from her eyes.

Noah gave a soft bark. He tried to lick her ugly fingers.

She made a small noise of dismay and snatched her hand away from him. "That's how you got hurt before."

He rubbed up against her. Warmth and healing worked into her skin and bones.

Three little yips and the rest of her death pain drained away.

Amazement flooded her breast. "What was that?" She lifted her head and touched her wolf. "What did you say?"

Beyond them, Mason paced the office anxiously. "That's it then. We're done for." Even Jayden looked beaten.

Noah nuzzled her. His tail wagged. *I have confidence in you.*

Not the three words he'd used before, but he was counting on her. No time to go to pieces.

She sighed, released the wolf, and took several deep breaths. Time to pull out all the stops. Hard to do when she was only one step from the grave, but there was no choice. She was almost certain to fail.

But she needed to try.

Still, because she was almost certain to fail, she needed a backup plan. She found her phone and tried Aunt Linda's number. It went immediately to voicemail. She left a terse, "Emergency. Call me." She turned to the black poodle. "Jayden. Find Aunt Linda. Whether she can undo the hex or not, we need her. Bring her here. Mason. When does the fight take place?"

"When the sun clears the tall grass. This time of year, about 7:16."

She checked her phone for the time. Six thirty. They had forty-six minutes. She set one alarm for six forty-five and another for seven. "Jayden, try to make it within the hour, okay?"

He nodded and trotted off.

She could have attempted a search spell, but Aunt Linda was backup. She needed to save what magic she had for the main push.

She stood and started pacing. "Okay, thinking out loud, here. I tried magically cutting the hex wrappings, but that didn't work—plus the shears bounced a good half inch above the hex. My shrink spell too." She stopped. "Something invisible covers the hex." If she could remove the "something invisible", she could cut the hex wrappings. Hope stirred in her breast.

"Something?" Mason asked. "Like what?"

"Well..." She kicked into pacing again. "A repel or reverse wouldn't have broken the shears. But a hide, armor, or shield spell would..." Her brain whirled. A "hide" that wouldn't appear to a reveal spell? She'd need a special spell or amulet to see it, then. Both books and amulets were at her aunt's store. "Stars and moon. I have to go." She headed for the door.

"You know how to fix this, my queen?"

That spun her back. Mason's face glowed with an unnatural confidence in her, almost to the point of fanaticism.

When she was a page looking at Rodolphe, she'd worn exactly that expression. It made her feel all kinds of slimy.

"Mason, it's only an idea, and a long shot at that. You need to prepare Noah to fight the challenge as he is."

Mason's face fell so abruptly she had to add, "But it's an idea. There's still hope."

Chapter Twenty-Four

Sophia borrowed Noah's SUV and lumbered out of the drive. Six thirty-five. She had a little more than half an hour before the Challenge Fight. At the rate the small tank got up to speed, she wondered if it would've been faster to walk. Too late for that now. Turning the big vehicle onto the street was no better—it felt like she was driving a pirouetting elephant.

On the way to the bookstore, she phoned Gabriel.

He answered immediately. "What the hell is going on? I felt your magic flare from two states over. Definitely you this time. I left like a zillion voicemails. Only death magic causes that kind of pain—"

"Chew me out later, Gabriel. I'm alive, but if I'm going to stay that way, I need your help."

He huffed. "What?"

She was fiercely glad this wizard was her brother. When it came down to it, he'd give her what she needed, no questions asked.

She parked the SUV rather haphazardly across the street from the store and slammed out. "Bur hexes. Are they over or under?"

A short tapping of keys was followed by, "It depends. Shifters are over; wizards are under."

She swore. But it'd only confirmed what she'd begun to suspect. The other thing Jayden had been trying to tell her. *Layered.*

Every spell had a purpose and a strength. But each spell also had a natural layer, overlay or underlay. For a single spell it didn't mean anything.

Put two or more spells together and significance got cooking.

An itch spell was overlay. Hit with it, a person scratched like crazy. Unless the person had an underlay of armor. Then the itch spell hovered harmlessly on top.

Auntie's hex, hitting a pureblood shifter, *should* have been on top, easily cut by Sophia's neutralizations.

Which meant Noah was *at least part wizard*. Also duh-huhed why the wizard healing disk had worked on him. She jammed the key into the store lock.

Somewhere in his lineage, a mage had done the dirty deed with a shifter. Noah was a forbidden dual.

"Sophia?" Gabriel's voice sounded in her ear. "Talk to me. Why are you asking about layers? Noah's a wizard?"

Okay, not no questions asked. Should've expected that. Her brother's sharp mind was constantly working, prying and poking at facts like a sewing machine needle. Eventually he'd stitch things together. She didn't have time for it now.

"He's a shifter." She threw open the bookstore door and went inside, exquisitely aware that she wasn't answering the question.

"Then why are you asking about wizards?"

Her phone beeped. Six forty-five already? *Damn it.* "Duals are taboo." She ran to her aunt's talisman cabinet and threw it open. With two-thirds of her magic freed, the talismans' enthusiastic shouts were even louder.

"Taboo doesn't mean impossible," Gabriel said reasonably. "Not if you've got a boy witch and a girl shifter—or vice versa."

She and Noah had proved several times now that he was correct. But she still fought the idea. "It's *wrong*."

"I see." A beat. "But you love him?"

Her throat closed up on emotions so big they had no name. The one fact she couldn't fight. She managed, "Yes."

"Then it's not wrong. What have you tried, unhex-wise?"

And that was that. Sophia's heart swelled and she blinked back tears. Her brother would stand by her and Noah. "It's complicated by a magical poison." As she dug through the talismans trying to find one that would remove a stubborn hide or complex armor spell, she told him about the stabbing and her tries at removing the hex. In the background was fast typing. "Gabriel, what are you doing?"

"I made a spell database that's like a medical symptoms search. I've been looking for a chance to give it a workout."

"You and your databases." She gave a watery laugh. "Thanks." She meant more than just the hex.

"You'd do the same for me. Hmm. Invisible, repelling magic, but not physical attacks?" More clacking of keys. "It's a simple hide spell, Sophia. It would mask any witch magic Noah did, and also the hex." A pause. "Correction, my familiar says it would mask his witch magic except from his familiar."

"No, a reveal removes a simple hide. Mine didn't, and neither did Jayden's. And I know Jayden's worked because it removed his own hide."

"Jayden?"

"Never mind. It would take too long to explain. Check your database again. It can't be a *simple* hide..." She smacked her forehead. "Gabriel, your dearest sister is a couple cackles short of a full witch today. There is one very easy way a simple hide won't reveal." Mason had just been talking about it. The Challenge Fight field had a hide spell—fueled and renewed by talismans.

"Snap, crackle, and damn. The hide is being constantly refreshed."

"Yes. Noah must be wearing something magical that supports it."

"A ring? Earring? What does he always wear?"

"I don't know...wait. Yes, I do. His wolf pendant. Unless Jayden had seen Noah shirtless, he wouldn't know about it."

"Shirtless?"

Flames hit her cheeks. "Look, does your database tell you what breaks a hide-covered hex?"

"Just use the Laws of Precedence. Break the top spell first. The hide. But the hide won't break as long as the pendant renews it. Ergo, he has to take the pendant off."

"Right." Could a dog remove a pendant that had shifted in with him? Arcane Animals hadn't taught her that.

Well, she'd worry how Noah would remove his pendant while she drove back. Because if the hide wasn't a particularly stubborn or complex, she could break it easily once Noah removed his pendant. Turned out she hadn't needed to come here, after all. Chafing at the wasted time, she closed the cabinet. "I have to go. Thanks for everything."

About to sign off, she stopped. "Gabriel. I love you."

A sharp inhale let her know he understood. *She might not survive the day.* But he only said, "I love you too, Sophia. Be careful."

She put her phone away and started for the front door.

A melodious voice said, "Wait."

She spun. A handsome older man, his thick auburn hair frosted at the temples, stood with his powerful frame filling the doorway between the kitchen and the store.

Strangely, she wasn't scared. Somehow the man was familiar. Reassuring.

He raised a small cardboard box, like fancy bath salts, and approached her. "You'll need this."

"What is it?"

"Loose blue chalk. Your aunt uses it to mark patterns."

Sophia's phone beeped again. Fifteen minutes. And she still had to navigate the barge masquerading as a vehicle back upstream, worse because she'd parked it facing east and it would take a small country to do a U-turn.

"Well. I don't know what I'll need it for, but thanks." She held out her hands and the stranger tossed her the box.

"You're welcome." He winked one green eye.

As she trotted out, she realized that green iris surrounded a pupil that was oddly elongated. A cat's eye.

Good grief. That was Mr. Kibbles.

She managed to get the monster truck turned around by circling the block, only crunching two Minis on the way. Not really, but it was a near thing. She screeched to a halt outside the store and ran inside.

No Jayden. She ran to the garage. No Mason, no Noah. She sprinted out the people door.

The pack already circled in the field. It goosed her heart rate.

Shifters, both wolf and human, concentrated on the center. Wolf Ivan, standing amid the tall grass, howled his challenge. A heavyweight to wolf Noah's super-heavy, but the rat dog would be outclassed like a sack of flour.

She couldn't see Noah. Hopefully she'd gotten here before him—

"Start!" Mason called.

That kicked her heart into race.

Ivan leaped forward. Tall grass waved from the other direction, like a tiny nuclear submarine was displacing the tillers.

Noah, plowing through the grass, too short to be visible but running with the heart of an alpha.

Ivan the Wolf didn't make the connection. He stopped abruptly and howled again, triumphantly, and definitely premature.

Noah leaped into view and sank needle-sharp teeth into Ivan's underbelly.

Ivan yowled. He reared back on his hind legs and spun, flicking Noah off like water. The poor little dog tumbled into the grass. Ivan bounded to the other side of the ring where he fell to his hips to lick his belly, whimpering.

Sophia shouldered her way through to the front of the circle. Noah staggered to his feet, barely visible even close up.

The wound on his flank had opened again, oozing blood. His fur was matted with it and caked with grass and dirt. He shuddered on his little legs. He tried to take a step but was as stiff as a marionette.

Damn that poison. If they survived this she was turning Killer into a snake, making him into a pair of boots, and using the boots to kick all the anti-alphas' asses. "Noah! Your mother's medallion."

Bonnie booed. "No coaching!"

Sophia gave her a hairy eyeball, the facial equivalent of the finger.

Noah yipped. When she turned her attention to him, his trembling eased and his ears perked forward. She touched her white wolf. He said, *I knew you'd come.*

"I only left to figure out the spells. When your mother gave you the medallion, did she do anything special?"

"Shut up and fight," Clyde yelled.

Ivan stopped licking. With a growl he shook himself, rolled to his feet and started for Noah.

My mother kissed it. Noah turned to face Ivan.

Activated with love. The most powerful magic of all.

But there had to be a word or words. "What did she say?"

Too late. Ivan bounded the diameter of the circle toward Noah. Hunched down, hiding in the grass, Noah didn't answer. She held her breath. If Ivan fell for the same trick again, Noah might actually win this fight.

Ivan screeched to a halt, toenails digging into dirt, mere inches outside Noah's kill zone. Life was just a bowl of fuckberries.

Outside Noah's kill zone but not outside Ivan's. The wolf snapped up Noah's sturdy little dog body in huge deadly jaws.

Sophia gasped. Noah, as a wolf, had cracked the spine of a stag. What could Ivan do to a small dog?

"Stop!" Her heart hammering, she tried to burst into the ring. Hands grabbed her, held her back.

Ice exploded in her stomach as Noah squirmed and Ivan chomped—just as Noah wriggled loose. He fell out of Ivan's slobbery mouth, little legs scrambling. She breathed in relief. Too soon.

Noah was no cat. He hit the ground hard and lay gasping on his side for what seemed an eternity.

Ivan pounced. Sophia struggled harder against the hands. Everyone in the pack seemed determined to keep her from helping her mate. Maybe they knew something she didn't.

Noah managed at the last minute to suck in a breath, tuck his legs, and roll away, but he was slow and stiff. Damned poison.

Ivan spun on his paws, toenails scuffing up divots, and quickly shifted direction. He pounced again.

Noah rolled the other way. While Ivan scrabbled to change direction again, Noah creaked to his feet. He skittered to the side, but his limbs were awkward, and his whole body shouted his pain.

Ivan scrambled to come around. Even injured, Noah had more maneuverability, but Ivan had the greater reach. The wolf leaped again. Noah didn't change directions so much as prance stiffly sideways, barely evading Ivan.

Sophia shook off the well-meaning hands by backing out. Once loose she ran around the circle, following Noah, her fingers pressed to her wolf so hard her skin dented. "Noah, it's vital. What did your mother say?"

Ivan reared and spun on his hind legs, practically turning inside out before charging again. Noah shot one directed mental push at her before spinning to face Ivan.

Hide.

Ivan opened his jaws, fangs big as Noah's face, and chomped him.

She screamed.

Noah wasn't there. He'd dived between Ivan's legs. Ivan followed him, trying to bite him, and threw himself into a somersault.

Sophia forced herself to breathe. Now she could break the top spell. All she had to do was get Noah to remove his medallion.

Which would reveal his wizard magic.

It hit her then, the question of why Noah's mother had walled off his magic in the first place. That took a death sacrifice. What was so vital that she'd died to prevent anyone from knowing Noah was a wizard?

The answer stunned her with its simplicity. Its horror.

Rodolphe's siphon. It pulled magic from shifters—just like the siphon invented by the evil wizard Phere Burgot. Worse, Burgot had created a second siphon, spell or talisman, no one was sure—but it sucked a witch's power directly from her body.

Centuries had passed and Burgot was dead by now. But maybe another such evil wizard had risen.

Noah, a strong dual, having both innate magic and power?

He'd be an evil wizard's wet dream come true.

Things rearranged in her mind. Noah's original alpha fight, thrust on an immature alpha. This alpha challenge.

All to force him to reveal his magic?

No, impossible. Magic wasn't detectible in a person, only on a thing or in a spell—and even that only while the spell was active. Even after Noah used his power, nobody could trace him by it...

Except his familiar.

Noah's revealed power would call his familiar to him. If the evil mage followed the familiar... Damn it, she *couldn't* remove the hide spell.

"Go, Ivan!" Bonnie shouted.

Ivan ran after Noah with jaws snapping.

Noah dodged, slower. He was tiring. Then one dodge was too late.

Ivan slapped Noah with a paw like a hockey stick. The small dog flew into the circle of pack, bounced and hit the ground. He staggered drunkenly to his feet. His wound had opened completely, blood spilling in pulses.

Sophia's heart shot into her throat, pounding frantically. Her mouth went dry. It didn't matter who was after Noah or even why—if she didn't remove the hex, Ivan was going to kill him *now*.

She ran around the circle. "Noah, take off the medallion. *Hurry*." She had to believe his Canidae could shed a necklace his human wore.

He growled, started wriggling. A moment later, the pendant popped out of nowhere.

In her head, a single bell sounded, the deep, resonant gong of prophecy fulfilled.

HEART begins to beat.

Awe flooded her. She trembled—then clamped down on it. Job to do. She snapped open her third eye.

And saw...nothing. No spell shimmered into sight over the hex. She'd expected, once the hide spell wasn't continuously fueled, that it would become visible on the etheric. Whoever had crafted the spell was powerful and subtle. Even her third eye was blind.

She grabbed her wand out of her pocket, wound up, and hit Noah with a reveal. "*Revoke Hide*."

She'd pulled power without regard. The final funeral seal reverberated with the spell. Waves of pain and nausea juddered through her, bending her double.

A halo sparked around the dog and showed...nothing.

Her temples were pounding. Great galloping ghosts, who the hell could cast a spell that wouldn't reveal? Not even Gabriel could do that.

She was officially screwed. Without a way to see the hide spell she couldn't break it. She couldn't even weaken it.

Ivan pounced. Noah twisted but didn't get away fast enough. Ivan bounded after and caught Noah's rump with a swat, sending him stumbling.

Noah was definitely tiring now. Eventually he'd make another mistake, and then a fatal mistake.

Seeing the invisible was impossible, so what? She had to do it anyway, and she had to do it *now*.

A beam of sun hit her in the eye, dancing with dust.

An omen...no, a *clue*. Light beams were invisible, but dust revealed them. The hide spell might not be invisible if the loose blue chalk Mr. Kibbles had given her was magic.

She jammed her wand between her teeth and fumbled out the small box. Inside, a baggie with a twist tie confronted her. She untwisted, her fingers starting to sweat because it was entirely possible she was twisting the wrong way and actually making it more impossible to get at.

The wire fell apart. The baggie gaped. With a relieved huff she scooped out a handful of blue powder, sparkling in her Witch's Sight. Magic chalk.

Ivan pinned Noah to the ground with one paw. Noah kept twisting, barely avoiding Ivan's snapping jaws.

Heart hammering, Sophia threw the handful over the struggling pair.

"Hey," Bonnie said. Sophia ignored her.

Fuzzy strands sparked blue around the dog. Added benefit, Ivan sneezed, his paw coming up.

Noah wriggled out, panting and wheezing—his bright red blood smeared along the crushed grass.

No time for subtlety. Nothing held back. What the hell. She should have died four years ago.

Time to go out with a bang.

"I sing silver, I sing gold." She grabbed her wand out of her teeth and threw it at Noah. "Hide—*revoked*."

She smashed her last dome.

Chapter Twenty-Five

Sophia hit the funeral seal with the hammer of her will so hard the dome exploded. Her full power blared free. It sang forth exuberantly, streaming after the wand toward Noah.

The magic she'd used to confine it—the death sacrifice—flew back into her. The kick was so hard it folded her in two. All the air expelled from her lungs in a shocked gasp.

But that wasn't where she felt the brunt of it. Head, hands—heart.

The death magic exploded directly into her heart.

Her chest crushed with dark pain. *Heart attack.* She had maybe a second of consciousness to grab back her released power and use it to try to save herself.

A second Ivan would use to kill Noah.

A flight attendant once told her why, in an airplane, if the cabin suddenly depressurized, people were instructed to put on their own air mask before helping others. "Don an air mask, help another, save two lives. Help another who can't help you, and you've only saved one."

But in a plane, she'd have a few moments before oxygen deprivation killed. She had a second or two at the most, and so did Noah.

Her or him.

She chose him.

Her magic blasted into the flying wand just as it struck the hide spell. The wand sliced cleanly through.

Frayed ends of spell popped up as she keeled over. She lay on crushed grass, gasping, unable to breathe. Black tunneled her vision. She was heading into unconsciousness.

But as she lay there a strange thing happened. A magic wind rose, catching the frayed hide spell and unwinding it. The wrappings fell away. The hex underneath started to unravel. Strip after strip came loose.

Golden light lanced out from underneath.

Like a beached fish, she gasped on the crushed grass, wondering what was keeping her alive but even more awed by what she was seeing with the last of her etheric sight. Golden light was heavy-duty power, not simple shifter magic or even the power wielded by most witches.

As strip after strip of hex unwound, more light bled through, brighter and brighter. Green hissed as Noah's poison just burned away.

Her forehead broke out in beads of sweat. It looked like the mother of all primal magics was about to break free.

The hex tore. A blinding sheet of white light burst forth on the etheric. Colors danced in afterimage on her third eye, shards of blue and green and yellow.

With it burst a torrent of memory.

A small boy, dark-haired, stood in a warm kitchen. He had a cookie. He turned toward Sophia.

It was Noah.

He smiled. "This is great!"

A tall woman in slacks and a ruffled white apron appeared next to him. Her tawny hair descended in thick waves to the band at her waist. Her eyes were the same shape as Noah's, her nose the same elegant length. Their hair and mouths were different but even with the distance of memory Sophia could see this was a shifter, and his mother.

Noah's mother raised her head suddenly, her nostrils flared. "Simon."

A robed man appeared behind them. Sophia's last breath hitched.

It was a wizard prince.

His hair was black like Noah's. His mouth...that was Noah's sensual mouth.

"I hear," the wizard said. He had Noah's deadly stillness. "Take the boy out front..." His brows compressed and his eyes faded as if he was staring far into the distance. Then they snapped back to Noah's mother. "No. They're coming that way. Go out the back. Take the boy away, Hayley. Quickly."

It was memory, colored with a child's limited understanding. Witches had a technique to join memories with later adult perception, something like television captioning. With the last of her conscious will, Sophia synched up Noah's for him.

"Mother/Hayley/shifter," floated under the tawny-haired woman. "Hard man/Simon/wizard," was under the man.

Noises came from outside. "Bad men," the caption read. Then... "Wizards. Hunting."

Hunting...oh God. They were hunting Noah.

Simon pushed Hayley to go, then ran the other way as Noah's mother hustled Noah outside.

"Meeting the bad wizards," read the caption.

It erased.

Slowly came, "Holding them off. Fighting." The revised caption was dusted with surprise.

The memory played on. Wizards burst around the side of the house in a whirlwind of magic. Hayley grabbed Noah to her. The tightness of her grasp, the shaking of her body, told Sophia the woman knew they were dead.

Suddenly Simon appeared, wedging himself bodily between the attacking wizards and his family.

"Jumped," read the caption, but Sophia knew that wasn't right. Without training, Noah wouldn't know his father had transported, a horrendous power suck and rarely done. Yet Simon had used it to get there in time, to get between the wizards and Hayley and Noah. By the way Simon staggered, Sophia knew it took almost everything he had.

Not only very powerful, he must have loved them very much.

Sparks filled the air around the wizards, the roiling fury of a mage-battle with heavy magic. Shadows shifted and foreboding filled Sophia. Even though this was a memory, she mentally urged Hayley to go faster.

A cawing cut the air. Flying through the cloud of battle magic was a black bird.

"Raven!" Noah struggled in his mother's grasp.

Sophia thought at first it was Simon's familiar. But no, a cat bounded out of the house and attacked one of Simon's enemies.

Then a fourth enemy wizard followed the raven into the clearing. Unlike the dark-robed mages, he was clad in a shimmering pale robe with a thick white collar. The wizard didn't join the battle but stood apart from the rest, his collar undulating around his neck...not a collar. It was a ferret familiar.

The pale-robed wizard pointed. The raven cawed—and flew where the finger pointed, back-beating its wings as if appalled, but at the same time irresistibly compelled.

The bird had been magically bound by the enemy wizard.

Simon's face froze in an expression of despair so profound Sophia understood the truth.

The raven was in the power of the enemy wizard, and was the boy's familiar.

Noah's familiar.

"Raven!" Noah saw the bird and struggled free from his mother's arms to run toward it. "Beloved pet/Friend," was the subtitle. Even now, Noah didn't know.

"No!" Simon's arm shot out. The boy ran into a wall of air.

Simon swept his wand to point at the raven. A burst of magic pushed the bird up into the air, farther, farther, until it was a black speck in the sky. After Simon's own bodily transport, Sophia knew it was a suicidal use of power. He wouldn't have enough left to keep his family safe and his own life intact and still fight the remaining wizards and their familiars.

There'd be no happy ending here.

Simon's familiar joined him, fighting back to back. The remaining black-robed mages circled them, wands pointed. The ivory ferret and his master watched with unholy glee.

Noah's mother caught Noah, wrapped arms around him, and ran. Simon slashed at the enemy mages with wand and hand, covering their escape.

But as they ran, a ruby red beam of magic shot straight from Simon's heart. It bathed Noah and his mother as they ran toward the woods.

He'd unleashed his life magic to protect them.

Simon died.

The last black-robed man pointed his wand at the still-standing corpse and hit it with a blast of fire. The corpse fell.

Slowly, the adult Noah's mind captioned the frozen scene.

"Hard man/Simon/wizard," it started. Then it erased, replaced it with one word.

"Father."

Her heart contracted.

A couple coughs and it started beating smoothly.

Sophia opened her physical eyes. She was alive.

A wizard prince's life magic, sent straight from the heart, had kept Noah safe. In turn Noah, wizard prince and alpha wolf, had given it freely to his mate. To her. It had burned away her death magic and kept her alive.

The ring of pack was blinking, blinded by Noah's mage light ripping free, so brilliant even shifters could see. She gathered hands and legs under her.

Ivan stumbled around, snapping air.

A dark, horrible growl turned all their heads.

A huge black wolf, bigger and badder than anything, stood where only moments before the rat dog had been. His eyes were a brilliant gold, his body armored in a golden aura of magic.

Noah, finally made whole.

He stood there, their king, while their sight cleared. One by one they saw him. Awe filled their faces.

Hesitantly, one by one, they knelt.

Ivan was the last to see the haloed black wolf. In shock he whimpered and pressed his body close to the ground. He scuttled forward nearly on his belly and pawed entreatingly at Noah's foreleg.

Noah snarled. Ivan cringed and groveled. Noah barked. Ivan rolled onto his back, baring his belly and throat to Noah's huge tearing teeth.

Sophia couldn't watch; she couldn't look away.

Noah snuffled Ivan's throat...then nodded. He shifted, fluid and perfect, into a man.

Mason stepped into the ring. "This Challenge is over. The loser's penalty is death, but the winner may have mercy. What is your will for the challenger, my king?"

"Ivan." Even Noah's voice was golden, more resonant. "For your part in this, you are exiled from this pack for the rest of your natural life. You four." He pointed at Bonnie, Clyde, Killer, and Attila. "Wait for me in the store. Marlowe, with them. We'll discuss your roles in this later."

As they slunk away, the rest of the pack slowly came to their feet. Howls rose from the circle, even the humans eerily wolf-like. Noah nodded once.

He nodded a second time to Mason. Mason came to his side.

Then Noah nodded to Sophia.

The ring of pack turned outward, toward her, and again knelt.

Noah opened his arms wide.

She should have hesitated. Thought it over. Wolves took their ceremony seriously, and her actions would have grave consequences. But she was too glad to have him whole.

She ran to him. He enfolded her in his arms and she clung to him in her relief that he'd survived. That she'd survived.

A sharp caw cut through her relief. Overhead. It was an echo of Noah's childhood memory.

A black bird. A raven.

This was not memory.

* * *

That morning at sunrise, the raven landed despondently on a tree branch. He'd searched for days, starting at the first touch of dawn and not stopping until the last echoes of sunlight died from the sky.

This was the fifth morning since feeling his master's power flare. The pressure on his skull was unbearable. His brain was nearly exploding out his ears.

This was the day he'd go insane.

Regret tightened his chest. He thought he'd have longer.

He looked at the ground, so far below. Calling to him. Cool, damp with dew. He'd go insane, then die. No one would know.

Or care.

No. He had to believe, somewhere, his master would care. His master would feel it.

He sucked in a hard breath. He couldn't die. He was a familiar, damn it. Reservoir of magical wisdom. His master needed him.

He would not give up. Pain nearly killing him, he hefted himself from the branch and flapped awkwardly into the rising sun. He flapped without direction for what seemed like an eternity. Gradually the sun rose. His pain rose with it. Determination waned.

His wings were so heavy. So very heavy. He sank toward the ground. He'd rest, only a moment. Only a moment and he'd be on his way...so very heavy.

Golden power slashed through the morning. His master's magic flared bright in his eyes, startling a caw from him.

A wave of pure white light rushed toward him, over him. *Heart's magic*. It wasn't for him, so didn't cure him, but the sheer joy lifted his agony somewhat.

His master was nearby.

The raven gathered himself. It took every bit of strength and will he possessed, but he floundered east, his wings beating erratically.

His shoulders itched with the sensation of being followed. But there was no bitter taste, and the tympani pounding in his head drummed away caution. Pain nearly blinding him, the hope of meeting his master spurring him, he flew on.

The woods opened to a field. And there he was—tall, dark-haired, the grass waving like a green halo around him. Raven's master.

The wizard's arms were wrapped around a woman. She was crying, hugging him like she'd never let go. The raven sensed magic in her too, not so surprisingly, because magic called to magic. But his master's magical scent entwined with the witch's—as if they were mated shifters rather than witch and wizard.

If the raven hadn't been half crazy with pain, he would have paused.

Need made him spiral down.

As the raven landed, the change came. First his intermediate form, his body enlarging, arms emerging, wings shifting to his back. Feathers spreading, becoming short silky body hair everywhere except his huge black wings. He stood at the edge of the field, looking in amazement at his hands. His fingers were long, strong, bronzed.

One thing broke clear through the pain. He had *thumbs*. Oh, fucking *finally*.

His master caught sight of him. A strange look came over the wizard's face. His master's witch caught his master's expression, then looked toward him too.

"An angel," she said. He could hear her despite the length of the field, as if his ears were attuned to her voice as well as his master's.

"Not an angel." His master's brow was furrowed in puzzlement. "Someone...connected to me. R-Raven? No wait. Your name... I name you Bram."

Bram. The familiar's body convulsed again as his wings receded and disappeared. This time the healing magic was for him. His headache ebbed to a dull throb as the pressure on his brain eased and the damage began to heal.

He glanced down at himself. Black jeans topped solid, well-made boots. A plain tan T-shirt lay under a leather jacket. He was now a normal man in jeans and jacket, stylish without being fussy. He approved.

Bram went to greet his master, a fully functioning familiar at last. Automatically he said the words he'd been rehearsing since that first flare of magic a week ago.

"Master. Good to meet you. I will fetch you a wand, when you're ready... Oh, and an evil wizard was following me. He wants to kill you."

* * *

Feelings hit Noah, fast, hard, unsettling.

Love for Raven.

Hate for his father, for killing Raven...who wasn't dead.

Understanding that Raven wasn't his pet—wasn't even a raven at all. This was Bram, his familiar. Proof positive that Noah was the hard man's son. *His father's son.*

Disbelief. Love. Anger. And finally a trembling acceptance of the truth. He clutched Sophia, his only anchor in the maelstrom of revelations.

He was a wizard.

Sophia held him through the swirl of emotions. She hugged him and for a moment he believed everything would be all right.

Slow, sarcastic clapping broke that hope.

Noah whirled.

Sauntering toward them was a man, his aristocratic nose and noble brow almost a caricature of grandeur. His long flowing golden robe trailed through the grass, topped by a necklace that would have looked good on Henry VIII. Perched on his shoulder was a big brown bird, its wings slightly extended in the classic eagle pose. Pretense—it was a buzzard.

The last time Noah had seen this wizard, he'd worn a hoodie and jeans.

Rodolphe.

Chapter Twenty-Six

Sophia had thought it was finally over. Naturally that was when the overdressed asshole showed up. "Hello, Rodolphe. Why the hell are you still here?"

He laughed. "Stupid little witch. My dear, I'm behind everything. You didn't know? Ah, well, I'm not surprised. You always were a bit slow."

"What do you mean, behind everything?"

He laughed, mellifluous but with an artificial, practiced edge. "The break-in and theft at the bookstore that got you here? My doing. I was here for another, shall we say, project, and imagine my delight when I discovered Linda Blue was your aunt. After you were here, I started slow. I wanted you humiliated before I killed you. When you went to interrogate Marlowe, I rousted Killer from his whore and drove him to the trailer to accost you, to harass and manhandle you and maybe even break a few bones. Although he failed to get the job done." Rodolphe sniffed. "Killer and Attila's attack at the bookstore was also me, and their attacking you and your alpha at the wolf couple's house. Too bad your shifter friends showed up at the same time, or you'd have been comfortably dead."

She rolled her eyes. The ass was monologuing. Well, he always did love hearing himself talk—then what he said filtered through and made her blink. *You and your alpha,* not her dual. If Rodolphe was the wizard following Noah's raven, how could he not know? Brain chewing furiously on the implications, she only said, "You want me dead? But why?"

His lip raised in a snarl. "You ignorant slut. You thought you could send the human police after *me* and not pay the price? Of course I want you dead. Piddling-in-your-shoes scared and totally humiliated first, then very, very dead."

Noah stepped between them. "You'll have to go through me."

"So be it." Rodolphe bowed mockingly, then swept out a theatrical hand, palm up.

He had good fingers for it, long and artistic, but Sophia was no longer buying based on image alone.

The buzzard materialized a jewel-encrusted wand in its beak and dropped it into Rodolphe's waiting hand.

"A battle? You're kidding, right?" Sophia edged out from Noah's shadow. "I'm a multi-element witch. You're just a water wizard. You'll run out of power long before I do."

"Not anymore." Rodolphe flicked imagined dust off one sleeve with the tip of the wand. "I can get more magic."

"You mean more power."

He slashed the wand in frustration. Bits of glitter flew off. "What the fuck are you talking about?"

"Magic isn't the problem. There's an abundance of possibility. It's the power to use it that's the issue. I have more power." And far better control of her temper.

"Semantics." He eyed her with distaste. "You university-trained witches are such pains. Fine. I can get all the *power* I want."

It wasn't the university that set her apart, but she only said, "How?"

"Ah. I'm glad you asked." With his free hand, he reached into the breast of the robe, and slid out a long rod.

It was maybe ten or twelve inches, and a rosy pink. Talk about phallic substitutes. She wondered if it vibrated too.

Rodolphe dealt her a smug smile. "This sucks magic—pardon me, Miss Valedictorian, *power*—from shifters. Life energy. I have as much as I want to drain." He thumbed the rod and it started glowing. "Let me show you how this works." He pointed the rod at Noah. "On *him*."

"The hell you will." She leaped in front of her mate. Immediately the rod started beeping.

"Get out of the way. You're fucking up the readings." Rodolphe jabbed his wand at her. "I said, get out of the way. Or I'll hurt you."

Growling, Noah pushed her behind him. "Don't you dare threaten her."

The rod, now pointing at Noah, kept beeping. Rodolphe glanced down, then frowned. "Damn foreign crap." He shook the rod.

Noah stalked, wolf-silent, toward him.

Rodolphe's gaze rose. He went sheet white and snapped the rod up again.

Noah halted, palms up, his posture easy, ready.

Rodolphe said, "Screwed readings don't matter. I can drain any shifter, even an alpha."

Synapses fired in her brain. Again he'd said alpha, not dual. And "misreading" his instrument.

Rodolphe didn't know Noah was a wizard.

She sucked in a breath. Rodolphe *wasn't* the evil witch who'd tagged the raven Bram. But then who...?

"Are you so sure you can drain me?" Noah deliberately took another step toward Rodolphe. "Before I can reach you?" Another. "Before I *tear you to shreds*?"

"Y-yes." Sweat broke out on Rodolphe's forehead, glinting in the light of the sun. His hand, holding the rod, shook slightly. He glanced at his quaking hand and paled. "I could, but I won't. Because I don't want you." He tucked the rod away, then jabbed his jewel-encrusted wand at Noah. "I want her. Stand aside."

Noah stood his ground, arms crossed. "You'll have to get past me."

Sophia's heart filled with pride even as she clenched her fists to keep from smacking him upside the head. Her mate was no coward, but that bravery could get him killed.

Rodolphe's eyes narrowed. "You'd oppose a wizard of the Council? You, a mere shifter? You're insane."

"Not insane," Noah said. "In love."

Her jaw dropped. The hex talking? Except the hex was broken.

Noah had said the words. He truly was in love with her.

Her heart soared. Noah and her and true love, the kind with a future. Loving together, living together, making a home together...having children...puppies...what the hell would they have?

"Isn't that cute." Scorn dripped in Rodolphe's well-heeled voice. "I'm in luuurve." He started circling his wand, a tighter and tighter spiral aimed at Noah. When it pointed directly at him he'd release the spell. "That'll make it even more fun to kill you."

Didn't matter at this moment whether Noah's love was true or a trick of magic. Sophia had to stop Rodolphe.

"Wait." She stepped to the side, out of Noah's cover—and incidentally closer to her own wand where it lay in the grass after piercing Noah's spells. "It's me you want. Fight me."

Rodolphe's arm hesitated, putting a hold on the spell. Then he grinned.

Noah, with a short growl, stalked back between them. Sophia used the moment to snatch up her wand.

Rodolphe slid sideways to see her. "Are you challenging me to a duel, little witch? You know I'll win, even without draining fur-face there."

"You?" She matched him, again sliding out from behind Noah. "Puh-leeze. I could beat you with my learner's wand. A baby is stronger than you."

"Puh-leeze," Rodolphe mocked, still grinning, damn him. "You're an academic. All theory, no bite."

"Oh?" She motioned behind her back to Mason, to gather the pack and get them out of there, out of harm's way. Magical duels could get messy. "Let's find out."

Rodolphe was right—she'd never fought a duel for real. And right again, Beginning Magical Warfare (known familiarly as Spell Slinging 101) was her only official experience with the subject.

But she wasn't all theory, no bite. Her brother had tutored her.

Breathe, Sophia.

* * *

"Breathe deep to immerse yourself in the now."

Gabriel's slouchy college sweater vest, canvas slacks, and deck shoes were totally at odds with his six-five frame and shoulders that filled doorways. "Magic is a distance technique."

"Right." Sophia snapped her wand at him. Gouts of flame shot out, engulfing him.

When she released the flames, not a hair on him was scorched. But more, his vest was clean.

Mock duels were like paintball. Hits scored blobs of color. She hadn't even touched him.

He hit her with a powershot that knocked her off her feet. She went flying onto her butt.

She blinked up at him. "Why didn't my fire score?"

Gabriel shrugged. "I shielded."

Her whole body, on the other hand, looked like a bottle of ketchup had exploded on her. "Stars and comets." She scrambled to her feet. "What did I do wrong?"

"First off, you should have breathed. Then shielded."

Or she could be sneaky. She whispered, "Kat!"

Her familiar, in her favorite form of a tall, buxom redhead, her painted-on black catsuit dripping armament, drew two knives lightning fast and *shooped* them at Gabriel.

A foot from him they clanked like they'd hit a steel wall, and dropped.

"Shield, remember?" Gabriel said. "Guns and knives are good, but they need to be bespelled to get through."

"Fine." Sophia flicked her wand at Gabriel's familiar, a panther in his animal form. The panther was fast and agile but she used bullet magic, tight bursts of power, almost impossible to avoid.

The magic splattered like raindrops an inch away from his skin.

"Aw, come on! Familiars can't cast shield."

One dark brow rose. "They *can* wear amulets."

Which of course was when the panther leaped onto her, too fast to avoid, and the match was over.

"Your magic is better," she grumped. The panther was sniggering, a very annoying, self-congratulatory sound.

Gabriel helped her up. "It's not about magic, sis. It's about breathing. And preparation. Oh, and refusing to lose."

*   *   *

Sophia stood in the field, facing Rodolphe, and breathed as she readied her wand. Refusing to lose, hell yeah.

Noah stalked between Rodolphe and her *again*.

With a throttled noise of exasperation, she grabbed his shirt and tried to tug him out of the way. Like pulling on a cliff. She gave up and bonked her forehead on his back. Asshole alpha. Though potentially powerful as the son of a wizard prince, he had no training.

Rodolphe laughed. "Hide, Sophia. You never had the stomach to do the hard jobs. You hid behind rules and regulations then, and you're hiding behind a wolf now. You haven't changed. Oh wait, you have. You're out of practice and even weaker. I'll beat you easily."

Her fingers clenched her wand. Was he right? As a university student she'd been an overconfident, dogma-ridden witch, easily tricked. She'd gotten past that, but had she merely become a self-righteous mundane, hiding behind her bankerly pumps and pearls?

Not. Happening.

She tore off her conservative suit coat and dropped it to the grass. Kicking off her heels, she pushed up the sleeves of her white blouse. Too bad Kat was in the Bahamas. But in a way, this was better. Now she'd prove to everyone, including herself, that she wasn't hiding behind anything or anyone. That she had the guts to do the job.

Fighting was about breathing—and refusing to lose.

Free of her mundane carapace, she breathed better than ever. She moved out from behind Noah, her hand relaxed on her wand. Refusing to lose to this loser.

She was vaguely surprised when Noah didn't stalk between them, but whirled toward her, eyebrows raised.

"Wait," he said.

"Noah, stand aside. This won't be over until he's neutralized." Her eyes did not leave her enemy.

"Will it be over even then? Think. He doesn't know about my past." Noah pointed at the raven familiar, still standing there, staring obsessively at his hands. "If Rodolphe wasn't following Bram, who was?"

She'd thought of that, but one thing at a time.

Problem was, shit didn't come in gentle showers. It came in storms. Behind Bram, an ivory-robed man had appeared.

"Bravo. The father's son is worthy."

Chapter Twenty-Seven

The man looked ordinary, like an accountant—except for a very dangerous glint in his winter-pale eyes. He walked around the still-absorbed raven familiar, his calf-length robe far more utilitarian in the long grass than Rodolphe's. Quite plain for a wizard, except for his fur collar. *That fur collar...* When he raised his wand, it was without the ornate swoops and tells Rodolphe loved.

Without another word, he shot a bolt of magic straight at her and Noah.

Sophia hadn't done magic in years. Unsure of herself, she swept up a side-shield that would deflect rather than confront. The bolt of magic skittered off.

The unknown mage motioned to his neck, then to Sophia's right. His furry collar uncurled itself, jumped down and ran like a humping millipede to where the man had pointed.

A ferret familiar.

Memory flashed. The ivory robe, collar detaching... This was the evil wizard chasing Noah. The man who'd tagged the boy's raven familiar—the bastard who'd murdered Noah's family just to suck out Noah's power for himself.

He was *so* going down.

She slashed up her wand. Shouted "Sword", and skewered him with a blazing blade of flying magic.

He smiled.

That ripsaw smile sent a blood-curdling chill shuddering through her, the likes of which she hoped *never* to feel again.

He'd *wanted* her to strike at him.

The air stuck in her throat. Too late she remembered that, if this mage had gotten his hands on Burgot's shifter siphon, he could have also worked out how to siphon a witch's active magic, too.

Or worse, use her cast spell like a bomb's fuse to steal her inner power.

She couldn't call her spell back. She could only watch with sick horror as, one hand splayed on the breast of his robe as if he was idly posing for a picture, he swirled his wand with the other. He spun a vortex before him like the maw of a small tornado. The magic blade shot into it—and disappeared.

His vortex had eaten her magic.

Okay, that wasn't so bad. She pulled a deep breath through her nostrils and used the rush of oxygen to try to figure out what to do next...and then he flicked his wand.

Flecks of power, glittering a malignant red, emerged from the vortex and traced back along the line of her thrown spell. Like lighting the smoke trail of a snuffed candle lit the candle, those flecks were *tracing back to her*.

Okay, that was bad. She battled not to inhale, but even so, some of the bits found her nostrils and went up her nose.

Dozens of tiny barbed hooks sank into her brain.

Blood entered the ivory wizard's smile. He flicked the wand again.

A swarm of flecks released, headed for her. The first were only seeker hooks, meant to tether the supply line.

He was going to eat all her magic. To suck the power from the very core of her being.

Heart pumping in panic, she blew the air from her nose. "*Out.*" Not even a spell, she threw up a hasty mental image of the exploratory hooks blowing out with the air. Red flecks floated out before her face.

With a slash of will she sealed off all her power, walling it off behind a mundane facade that was half hope, half desperation.

Pinching her nostrils with a thumb and forefinger, she stopped breathing.

A cloud of hook magic pummeled her in the face like a swarm of buzzing, angry hornets.

She stood oh-so-still, steeling herself against the ping-ping-ping.

The cloud hesitated. Shuddering, it gathered and returned to its maker.

Her chest exploded in a desperate inhale. She trembled with horror at what had nearly happened. Sucking power, *life*. She'd read about it, studying Burgot. But she'd never dreamed a mage could actually be that evil. With that vortex he could take her power and not only leave her unable to defend herself and Noah, he could use it *against* Noah.

How could she fight that?

To buy herself time, she flashed the tip of her wand down, kindled a flame with a word, and burned a quick protective circle around Noah and herself.

The ivory wizard's smile quirked into an "Oh well". He motioned Rodolphe to Sophia's left. He flicked a finger at Rodolphe's buzzard and pointed behind her.

She didn't like his complacency at all. He was too confident, too relaxed. He'd done this before, many, many times... She was hit by a horrid suspicion. Maybe he'd come across Burgot's siphons and dressed up like him. But maybe, just maybe, this was the evil wizard himself.

The bane of the Witches' Council. It had taken the great Jean-Dion d'Avignon to defeat him before, and legend said that even the famous founder of the Council had only done it by tapping wild magic. Burgot was assumed to have died in exile.

Sophia began to wonder if rumors of his death were overly optimistic.

Rodolphe gave the ivory wizard a black glare. He never liked being ordered around. But he moved into position, and she and Noah were surrounded.

Four trained antagonists circled her, an untried wizard, and a familiar who'd just grown his big boy legs and stood gazing at his hands like they were the eighth wonder of the universe. Hell, even she wasn't much better; the mock-duels in college had been regulated non-fatal.

Okay. Start small and hope for the best.

And if that didn't work, cheat.

"Hey, ivory robe. Who the hell are you?" She pushed power into her protective circle. A shield rose from the ground, a cylinder of earth magic twinkling gold in the hot sun. Not much, but the best she could do on such short notice.

The wizard smirked. "You'd like to know, wouldn't you?"

She grinned back, all teeth. The great thing about evil was, the pool of henchmen was shallow. And peed in. Rodolphe was smarting from being ordered around, and she could use that. “Hey Rodolphe. Is that your boss?”

“No.” Rodolphe’s sneer said, *Me, have a boss? Please.*

“Stop,” the ivory-robed wizard said.

“He is my colleague.”

“Say nothing!”

Rodolphe’s operatic baritone rolled right over the ivory mage’s thin voice. “Of course you’re too stupid to recognize him. My colleague is—”

“—shut—”

“—Phere Burgot the Great.”

“—up.”

Damn it. Why did she have to be right? Burgot was still alive after all these centuries, probably from stealing wizard and shifter magic, siphoning it, eating it...it jolted her like a cut power line.

The real Hungry Ghost. She wasn’t swimming in the evil pool, she was splashing in a shark-infested, satanic septic tank.

She trembled.

“Steady,” Noah murmured. He aligned himself to her spine, to fight back to back.

His heat, his strength, ate through her shock. She managed, “You need a wand.”

“I’ll shift.”

“Magic is a distance technique.” She knew he’d understand the implication. As his wolf’s jaws took out one foe, the other three would be killing him with magic. “Powerful as your wolf is, you can only be in one place at a time. Unless you have a gun or throwing knives—and even those have to be bespelled to get through a magic shield—you won't reach them all before they mow you down."

"Magic shield, hmm? The familiars?"

That reassured her like nothing else could have. He understood to the point of working through the implications.

She said, "They have amulets."

"Ah."

Rodolphe started blasting with his wand at the earth outside her shield. He was a water mage so she didn't like that at all.

"Bram!" She shouted to get the familiar's attention. "Your master needs a wand—*hell.*"

Rodolphe whipped out a spray of water. It hit the churned ground and rebounded, carrying a load of dirt. Somehow he'd learned to mix elements since she'd seen him last. Burgot's doing, no doubt. And maybe that power sucker.

Mud magic splashed her shield. The shield glittered angrily as it burned the mud off. "Bram! A *wand.*"

"What?" The familiar looked up from his hands. His eyes glowed emerald green. Intelligence sharpened in them. "Where?"

"My aunt's store. Mason!"

"Here!" Mason's deep voice boomed from the garage, barely heard over Rodolphe's next explosion of mud. Her protective column hissed violently.

"Show Bram to the Uncommon—"

"Done." Mason morphed into his wolf and took off.

Bram leaped, melded into the raven, and flew after Noah's big lieutenant. Burgot shot a bolt after Bram, but the raven dodged easily, as if he'd anticipated it.

"Noah." She tossed her words over her shoulder. "I know you haven't done magic, but you have to try now."

"But magic killed my mother. Orphaned me. I can't...I won't...ah, fuck."

"Explode!" Burgot snapped his wand at them, unleashing a thunderball of power so big it hit her protective cylinder like a battering ram. The ground-deep shudder threw her to the earth.

She landed with her butt outside the circle.

Noah leaped over her, landing in front. He stood between her and Burgot, outside the circle, quivering with rage. "You want me, Burgot. Leave her alone."

Burgot only laughed. "What I want is your dual magic. I want you alive but docile, easy to drain—completely broken. Her death would do that nicely." He shrugged. "Besides, Rodolphe wants her dead for some reason."

He cocked his blood-red wand over his shoulder, preparatory to annihilating them both. "So dead she'll be."

* * *

Noah recognized the deadly glint of intent in Burgot's pale eyes. The ivory wizard was primed for what even Noah recognized as a killing stroke.

He was shocked by how strongly he needed to do one thing—protect Sophia. His wolf came forward with a snarl.

But even as his body automatically started to change, he held it off. His wolf was supernaturally fast, but Sophia was right—fast didn't equal instantaneous. Burgot and Rodolphe were on opposite sides of the field. No matter how quickly he dealt with one, the other would be free to kill her. Not to mention the two familiars, potentially as dangerous.

Hell. The only way to come out of this alive was with magic.

For years he'd hated and blamed his wizard father for the death of his mother. She'd made Noah promise never to use his magic. How could he ignore all that? How could he become a wizard, the very thing he'd railed against, vowed never to be? It felt like the last step to damnation.

How had it come to this? He was his mother's son. When had he slid so wholly over to the dark side? When he'd first seen Sophia, and was attracted to a witch? When he'd mated her?

Or when he'd realized his father had actually fought to save his mother and himself? When Noah had finally, after decades of pain, forgiven him for leaving them?

Didn't matter. Protecting Sophia meant acknowledging...using...*embracing* his wizard's nature.

That decided him. He'd do whatever it took, for her.

He sought the sparkles, the magic, that he'd suppressed for most of his life, tapped only briefly to deal with the treachery of the old alpha.

He couldn't find them.

His body iced. Had his magic somehow unraveled with the hide spell?

Count the steps, son. Down, down... Noah relaxed and went to the cool, unemotional place where the hard man—his father—had taught him to go.

And there it was. The tail of power twitched, just barely, in the center of his being, his navel. Relief welled in him. He touched his navel, reaching for his magic to fight.

What came forth was not a child's prickle of magic but a wizard prince's mature power. The torrent gushed like a river. He filled his hands with it, pure magic, overflowing his palms, streaming like a blast of windswept golden ribbons.

His deliberations in the cool place had taken fractions of a second. Burgot was just now snapping the blood-red wand forward.

Noah stood there, magic overflowing, and realized he had no idea what to do.

The shaft of killing magic, powerful as a cannon shot, barreled straight toward them, jarring Noah into a spontaneous response. His arm was already coming up when he figured out what was happening.

No magical training, but he knew how to fight. Block hard with soft. He threw his arm out, releasing his ribbons in a soft, fanning arc.

Burgot's hard shot hit the ribboned power like a cannonball caught by a streamer of woven silk. Noah's magic redirected Burgot's like a sling. It flew harmlessly to one side.

Squawk! Not quite harmlessly. It cannoned straight into Rodolphe's buzzard. The bird blasted into a puff of feathers.

A grim smile flashed in Noah's mind. Now it was two against three.

The golden-robed Rodolphe was bombarding Sophia with mud magic, but her blocks were precise and economical as she scrambled to her feet. He wondered why she didn't just return Rodolphe's blasts in kind, when she threw a fist of magic from her own wand, tossing Rodolphe onto his ass. She flung over her shoulder, "Noah! Don't use your magic directly against Burgot. He can suck power from spells and worse, use them to hook directly into your power—*yow!*"

Her high-pitched shriek was filled with pain and anger. He spun. She stood there, wand down, hand clutching her shoulder. Blood dripped from under her fingers. She slowly uncovered her shoulder. A burn charred the cloth and had ripped ugly and raw across her velvety skin.

Rodolphe was smirking. *Smirking*. Noah's rage rose from deep inside his heart.

He called up his magic...as Rodolphe pointed the pink rod at Noah. "Bye-bye, wolf."

Burgot shouted, "Wait!"

The beam lanced out. Noah felt the thing hit him, try to latch onto his very cells.

But he'd already called up his father's heritage, and his mage power grabbed the beam instead. Inch by inch, the cord of magic connecting him to Rodolphe turned from red to blue. Noah thought the wizard magic was pushing the sucker's magic back.

Until the blue reached Rodolphe. The siphon itself changed colors, from pink to blue—and power washed the other way.

Rodolphe's power flooded Noah. It hit him so hard it shoved him back. Squinting, he fought against it, planting his feet and leaning into it like fighting a hurricane.

Suddenly, it stopped. Noah opened his eyes.

Rodolphe's deflated husk dropped with a whisper to the grass.

Noah was horrified, but his training was already spinning him toward Sophia. He pressed his palm to her wound. His power rose again, more than even before. He didn't know how to use the magic but let his heart guide him, intuitively healing her as he'd heal himself.

Burgot sped toward Rodolphe's remains, gesturing at his familiar as he ran.

Out of the corner of his eye, Noah saw the ivory ferret boil up into a slender human male with a white brush of hair and a camouflage weapons vest shingled with knives. He slid two out and threw them in a single motion—straight at Sophia.

Noah whipped up a shield but Sophia was already blasting the ferret man with her free hand. Her magic actually lifted the small man off his feet and plowed him into the grass ten feet behind him.

Noah felt a rush of pride. She was stellar. A witch, yes, but *his* witch.

Burgot rummaged around in Rodolphe's remains and came up with the siphon, now pink again. He gave a satisfied, "Ah."

Noah didn't know what the wizard could do with the siphon, but he didn't like the supremely confident smirk sitting on the other man's lips.

At that moment he spotted a black dot in the air, heading his way. Raven. Burgot was rising to his feet. Noah focused on the other man. It would be a race to see who'd be ready first.

Grinning, Burgot pointed both wand and siphon at Noah just as Raven flapped over the field. Without looking, Noah held his hand up.

Caw! Raven dropped a short stick. Noah swept it out of the air, continuing the arc to curve up another soft shield as Burgot threw a blast at them. The shield caught Burgot's blast and threw it into the tree line. Noah shouted through the explosion of magic and branches, "Fight with us, Bram."

The raven plummeted, not so much landing next to them as turning inside out at the last moment. His human form was equally tall with Noah's.

As he landed Burgot threw another blast at them. The ferret familiar was just getting to his feet so Noah angled his shield block with a smile toward the ferret man. The familiar saw the blast rocketing toward him, eyes widening, and scrambled to dive out of its way.

Without words, Noah and Bram formed up back to back at the rim of the burned circle, Sophia sandwiched between.

She wasn't having any of that. She squirmed out from between their taller bodies and stood with her shoulders abutting their biceps, the three of them back to back to back.

Noah's heart smiled. His mate could take care of herself.

But the protective male inside him shouldered their triangle around until he, not Sophia, was the one facing Burgot. The ivory wizard bared yellowed teeth at him in a blood-curdling grin.

Gripping his new wand, Noah grinned back, letting his Canidae nature show a little fang. Burgot's smile faltered.

Noah was already raising his free hand to take advantage of the enemy's lapse. He whipped up a bolt of hard magic.

"*No,*" Sophia gasped. "He'll steal your magic. Close off your power, stop breathing—"

"Trust me." He threw the bolt of magic at Burgot.

Burgot only saw the poor dumb shifter playing into his hands. He touched the siphon to a pocket in his robe then swirled up a spell with it like a cyclone on its side. Its maw gaped where Noah's spell would have hit, if it had gone straight.

But Noah hadn't forgotten what Burgot could do. He'd thrown the ivory wizard a curve ball. Noah's spell careened harmlessly past, just out of reach.

Noah smiled. He'd faked Burgot into revealing his spell-sucking magic. This was why Mason never played poker with him. Noah was honest and trustworthy to his friends, but he could bluff the hell out of anyone, especially his enemies.

He slashed the wand, tagging his mother's black wolf pendent in the long grass.

This is for you, Mother.

With a flick of the wrist, he flung the pendent straight into Burgot's power vortex.

Sophia grabbed his forearm. "Not the medallion... damn."

The vortex vacuumed the solid pendent straight into Burgot's solar plexus. It skewered him through.

Burgot bent over, gasping.

The ferret man froze. Suddenly he collapsed into his animal form and ran away, tall grass waving. Bram changed to raven and took to the air, his caws sounding suspiciously like taunts.

"Stop! Pax." Gasping, Burgot raised both hands, uncurling slowly. Blood stained the front of his ivory robe. "Good fight." He attempted to smile. "Let's talk."

Noah's eyes narrowed. "Let's not."

"You were awesome." Sophia put a hand on Noah's biceps. "Come on. Let's get your mother's medallion."

"It was actually my father's. Given out of love." Noah glanced down at her as they started toward Burgot. With her hair mussed and her cheeks pink from the fight, she was even more beautiful to him. He had to bite down on his tongue to keep himself from sweeping her into his arms right then and there.

Her rosy color drained. "Oh hell."

Noah's head snapped up. Burgot was running away, Noah's medallion hanging by its thong from his clenched fingers. Sophia threw a bolt of power at Burgot's feet, but he blocked it with a hurried spell—just as a roar came from the street.

Burgot's ferret, now a man wearing ivory leather, spun a motorcycle to a stop at the edge of the repair shop's cobbled parking lot.

"Stop him!" Sophia ran after Burgot.

The wizard saw her and blasted earth up behind him, a tsunami shield of dirt and grass. Leaping after her, Noah grabbed her arm then yanked her back just before the heavy clods would have smashed into her.

Through the dirt veil Noah could see Burgot mount behind the familiar. They took off in a tight-throated roar.

Chapter Twenty-Eight

Sophia's heart pounded in her ears, fear and adrenaline pushing her to a diamond-hard focus. "We have to catch them." She reached for her white wolf.

Noah's hand on her wrist stopped her. "Even as wolves, we can't run as fast as a motorcycle. We need wheels. Mason!"

Mason rolled up the bay door as they ran for the garage. He disappeared into the shop.

"Which motorcycle?" she panted as she dashed through the door. She headed automatically for the store, but Noah stopped. Anxiety tugged her toward the connecting door, but her mate must have paused for a reason. She quivered in place.

"The only one with a prayer of catching that bike is the Ducati." He grimaced at the disassembled motorcycle. "Too bad we can't use it. I tried to fix it but—"

"Hell with that." She pointed her wand at the pile of engine parts. "Fix!"

Metal pieces flew, clanging together just as Mason ran back in with two helmets. He tossed one to Noah.

"Fix?" Noah stared at her, catching the helmet without looking. "Not *overhaulus machinus*, or *repairum cyclum* or something properly esoteric? *Fix*?"

"It worked." She dashed to the bike and put a hand on the throttle as she threw one leg over the seat. "I'll drive."

"Who'll fight Burgot? I'll drive." He nudged her back on the seat and settled in front of her.

"Can you even operate a motorcycle?"

He glared at her over his broad shoulder. Clamping the clutch, he flipped the key to on. Mason tossed her the second helmet. She was still fastening it as Noah roared out of the garage.

Burgot and his ferret were long gone, but above them, Bram cawed.

"What's he saying?" she asked Noah.

"I can't understand him...wait. Yes I can." There was wonder in his tone. "He's saying Burgot is headed for the highway."

"Got it." She cast a map spell and swept a hologram at Noah's eye level, a glowing orange line highlighting their shortest path to US 10. "That way."

Noah poured on the throttle, and it was all Sophia could do to hang on. He zipped along so fast Bram quickly fell behind.

They caught Burgot and his ferret hitting the freeway. The moment the wizard saw them, he started casting spells.

Sophia prepared to block.

But he didn't cast his magic at *them*. No, he tossed deadly spells *everywhere* else, at their bike, at the road in front of their bike—and worse, at random innocent traffic.

Sophia found out how much worse after the ferret zipped a quick pass around an old family station wagon, cutting it close, so close the car had to brake. Noah zoomed after. As she and Noah passed the station wagon, Sophia saw two car seats in back, a baby and toddler strapped in.

With a cackle, Burgot let loose a screaming rocket at the family wagon.

How could he even...? Horrified, she swung a shield in front of the car barely in time, got the angle wrong, and sent the rocket into the roadside grass. Turf burst into flame. Two degrees more and she'd have incinerated a farm.

She had to get off defense and onto offense. Reaching into her memory for her brother's training, she almost heard him say, *"Change up the rhythm of the attacks."* Right. She crammed in a quick blast of power to Burgot's front wheel.

With a flash of wand, the evil wizard intercepted her power before it struck, and bounced it into a car on the other side of the road. The car wobbled with the hit and started to skid before Sophia pulled it straight with a suction spell.

Inside, she bristled. Twice now, Burgot had used her own damned magic against her.

How could they stop him? Noah was busy keeping them on the road, and if Sophia had to use all her talent to protect the innocents, the few offensive opportunities she had wouldn't make any difference. If she could have created a big oil slick or something he couldn't divert...but no, she could just picture the pileup that would cause.

Maybe Rodolphe was right. Maybe she was hampered by her limits. Her conscience.

As if he'd heard her thoughts, Burgot glanced back and grinned savagely—and shot an arrow of fire magic into a barn.

The roof exploded in flames, magical tongues dancing from board to board. It would only be a moment before the fire found its way inside and hay would send the thing out of control.

Waving one hand, she filled the air over the roof with water vapor. Slashing the other, she cut a seed spell into the vapor. She had to let go of Noah to do it, but otherwise she wouldn't be able to do this fast enough.

Dark clouds boiled up and let loose with a downpour. *Wind—!*

A ramming spell smashed into her. Untethered, she started to topple from the bike. All she could see was the road below, zipping by so fast it was a blur. Her heart leaped into her throat. Hitting pavement would hurt.

Burgot had capitalized on her weakest moment. He was a seasoned battle mage, she wasn't, and several layers of her skin would pay for it.

Something jerked her back onto the bike. Noah's hand, fisted in her blouse. He yanked her back up and released her.

Her heart slid back down into her chest. That had been close.

She had to break the stalemate, but how? No oil slicks, Burgot intercepted offensive magic aimed at the bike, and the Hungry Ghost could suck any magic she threw directly at him...

The Hungry Ghost. That ravenous hunger made him scary, like greed, of the seven deadly sins. But like greed, it was also a bad thing. A potential weakness, if she could just figure out how.

The Ghost was never satisfied. Power, magic, he'd always want more.

Even when it was bad *for him.*

A plan birthed in her mind. If she threw power at him, he wouldn't shield. In fact, he'd latch onto it, suck it down, and ask for more.

Having felt her heart leap into her throat had inspired her. If she offer Burgot her magic to siphon, then waited until he was drawing as fast as he could with that straw of his throat... She'd used Share Power to share a thread of magic with Jayden, but that was nothing compared to the deluge of a complete Evacuate.

Like going from sipping water from a hose to having the thing shoved down his throat and cranked to full. His straw throat? He'd choke. Maybe burn him out.

Maybe—or maybe not.

Objections started to crowd out her idea. There was no certainty her Evacuate would short him out.

And she'd become irrevocably, forever mundane.

Give up her magic, forever. Damn it all to hell, she'd just gotten it back. Anguish clogged her throat. She nearly wept.

But if we continue like this, disaster will strike sooner or later.

Oh, and news flash. If the Hungry Ghost gets away with the Heart medallion, it'll be the end of the world as we know it.

She nearly wept—but she breathed instead. Fighting was about breathing. And preparation.

And refusing to lose.

She opened her third eye, reached deep, and targeted the motorcycle ahead of her.

"Blast!" She flung the spell at Burgot.

"Sophia, no!" Noah tried to intercept her magic. The motorcycle wobbled. He grabbed the handlebars to steady it, and her spell shot past them.

"Trust me," she whispered. His shoulders tensed, hopefully remembering when he'd said the same thing to her. But he didn't try to block her anymore.

Ahead, Burgot had spun up both a bloody grin and his wand. Touching his robe's breast first with the wand, he then spun the stick into the air. His vortex whirled into being just as her spell hit. The whirlpool sucked up her blast spell. She'd expected that, but not the hot rush of fear she felt when the seeking hooks flooded out.

She watched the deadly hooks coming and swallowed hard. *Refuse to lose. Breathe.*

They hit her. She flinched, but managed to breathe them in. She breathed again and let the hooks grab her. Sink in.

It felt like breathing razor blades. Her nose and lungs screamed. Then the hooks swam around her body—and embedded in her brain.

Her head exploded, worse than breaking her head seal. The rest of the cloud came, buzzing. She sucked them in too—and felt like a thousand hornets stung her from the inside. Her bloodstream lit with fire. The hooks sank into every corner of her body, every cell.

Jayden's drawing on her power had hurt. This was as excruciating as if her very cells were being hollowed.

Lightning sliced through her brain...and a light went out inside her head.

Trembling, she turned her third eye on herself. Her magic was a fierce ball of rainbow lights surrounding her like a globe. Red fire and yellow earth and green sea and blue sky—and a black pie-shaped wedge like a slice had been removed.

Part of her magic was dead.

She sobbed. And still Burgot drew, his hooks sinking deeper, drinking faster.

Noah reached back for her. "*Sophia.*"

"No." She swallowed and gripped his shirt in one hand, hanging on for dear life. "Let me...let me do this."

He jerked a glance back at her. Whatever he saw made him slow the motorcycle.

"No!" She tried to communicate her need through her clutching fingers. "Must...finish."

He glanced back again.

His golden eyes shimmered with unshed tears.

He knew. He knew what she was doing, and what it was costing her. And maybe even guessed why she had to do it.

Or maybe he just trusted her. Her heart hiccupped.

Just as another wedge went black. In conjunction, her arms went numb. Another link to her magic, dead. She closed her third eye, not being able to watch. But she felt the progress when her feet went numb then her legs.

Burgot was drawing as hard as he could through that little sniveling straw. Time to finish this.

Fury enveloped her. "You want my power? Choke on it. *Evacuate!*" With a roar she rammed every last bit of her power into the hooks.

They exploded as the energy hit them, pop-pop-pop. But her power was already roaring toward him like an ocean wave, huge and unstoppable.

The wall of power slammed into Burgot with such force that he lifted from the pillion seat and sailed into the air. He cartwheeled over the head of his familiar on the speeding bike, hitting the pavement with a wet smack. His limp body tumbled a few feet onto the hard shoulder as the ferret went roaring past.

Noah clamped on the handbrake and practically stood on the footbrake. Sophia slammed into his back. She couldn't feel it. Her body was numb. She tried to open her third eye. Either it didn't work...or her entire etheric world was now black.

The Ducati stopped inches from Burgot's still form. Noah kicked the stand and got off.

Sophia's chest felt empty. Her cells felt hollow. Her muscles wouldn't hold her. She tried to get off, wobbled—and crumpled onto the pavement.

Noah turned in time to catch her. His gaze flew over her face, her limp limbs. "Oh no, no." He eased her gently to the pavement as cars zipped past them, the wind buffeting them. She waited for his arms' healing to take effect. She felt his warmth and support...and emptiness.

Her body was dark. Her magic, her power—the thing that had defined her—was gone.

Ahead, the ferret man hit the brakes. She hardly cared.

Refuse to lose. "Noah." She flicked her eyes toward the familiar. "You can't let the ferret rescue Burgot or worse, take your mother's medallion."

Noah swung a hand toward the familiar. Without looking, he blasted the cycle. The ferret went ass over teakettle and face-planted on pavement.

She managed a grim smile. "Let's get your mother's wolf." She tried to rise. Noah had to help her. It took everything she had to get her dizziness under control. The sense of emptiness didn't leave her. She would have cried, but her eyes were too dry from the wind. She settled for fumbling off her helmet. With Noah's shoulder under her arm, his arm wrapped around her waist, she managed to get to Burgot.

The evil wizard's chest...rose. And fell. And rose again. She wasn't sure if she was glad or not.

To Noah, she said, "You'll have to..." She made a circular motion and pointed at his wrists and ankles.

"Right." Noah repeated the gesture, and magical zip ties wrapped the evil wizard.

By now Sophia felt as if she could stand on her own. Not that she felt less numb, but she was getting used to it. She lifted her arm from Noah's shoulder, tottered a moment, then nodded as she found her balance. "You should go restrain the ferret. I'll find your mother's medallion."

"Right."

She came across the pink rod first, the shifter siphon, in an inner breast pocket. A blue rod lay beside it.

She pulled both rods out and laid them on the pavement. She knew from Rodolphe that the pink siphoned shifter magic from their cells. Burgot had used it plus that tornado spell to try for Noah's dual magic. Why did he need a blue one...? Oh. The other probably sucked up cast magic. Maybe the blue rod plus the tornado was what had sucked her magic out.

If she hadn't felt numb, she would have wept.

Burgot woke as Sophia searched him for the medallion. *Heart beats for a wolf and a Blue...* This was the Heart piece. The fury in the evil wizard's eyes as she pulled it from an inner pocket was enough to tell her he knew exactly what it was.

As she pulled it out, for an instant, it dangled in front of his face.

He snapped his teeth at it as if he'd eat it—as if he were the Hungry Ghost in fact.

She yanked it away and clasped it to her breast. They locked gazes. Burgot slowly licked his lips.

She swallowed bile and turned away.

Noah returned and plucked up the pink siphon. It dangled from two fingertips as he glared at it, disgust clear on his face. "What do we do with this?"

"Both rods are dangerous. Only a truly wise creature can know what to do. If Kat were here, I'd ask her. As she isn't...well, without knowing who to trust, we need to keep them away from any mages for now. The medallion, too."

"Why my medallion?"

"It's a long story." She glanced at Burgot, who scowled at her. He seemed to know the medallion was significant, but in case he didn't know about the prophecy, she'd rather not fill him in. "I'll tell you later. My cousin Daniel has avoided the Council for months despite being mated to a wolf. Let's give them to him."

"A wizard prince mated to a shifter...?" Noah's disgust at the pink rod cleared to surprise. "Is the wolf named Zoe?"

"Yes."

"She's family. Yes, that's a sound plan. Speaking of wisdom creatures..."

Bram appeared in the sky over them, descending quickly. He transformed midair and touched down on one foot in human form.

"Take these to Zoe Light." Noah gave the siphons and medallion and instructions to Bram, who leaped into the air, transformed easily to Raven, and flew away with them.

Then Sophia called the Council police to come collect Burgot and his familiar—just before she passed out.

* * *

She regained consciousness to the soothing smell of chamomile tea, patchouli incense, and Aunt Linda's perfume.

"Are you sure she shouldn't be in a hospital?" Noah's deep tones thrummed with concern.

"I'm sure." That was Jayden's voice, unpeppered with sarcasm for a change. "Your little witch is very lucky. If she'd been with anyone but you, she'd have been a husk."

"I don't understand." That was Bram. "She's a witch—or she *was* a witch. But she's also a shifter? And my master is both a wolf and a wizard? That's forbidden. I don't understand how any of this happened."

"Some things, young one, are not meant to be understood." A soothing purr underlay the deep, melodious voice—Mr. Kibbles. "Just accepted and cherished."

"Shh." Aunt Linda's voice sounded nearby. "She's waking up." Footsteps shuffled closer.

Sophia's eyes fluttered open. The first thing she saw was Noah's face, relief instantly lighting his golden eyes. Auntie stood beaming beside him. Behind them were Mason, Jayden, Bram, and Mr. Kibbles. Everyone except for Noah and Aunt Linda had a cup of tea in their hands.

"Are you feeling better after your little nap?" Aunt Linda said.

Sophia blinked. She lay on a couch in the reading area of the Uncommon Night Owl Bookstore. She did feel a little better. Less empty...or maybe just more used to it now. The thought depressed her.

"Oh my, what's that grumpy face for? A nice cup of tea will cheer you up. Noah, be a dear and help Sophia sit while I get it?"

"What happened?" She tried to sit up. Noah helped her, easing pillows behind her back.

"Here, dear." Aunt Linda offered her a cup and saucer. "I've started some incense burning, that patchouli Gabriel got me for Christmas. Do you like it?"

Sophia stared at the tea without taking it. So normal. As if Aunt Linda hadn't disappeared...as if Sophia's magic hadn't disappeared too. "Where have you been?" Her gaze rose to her aunt's. "Didn't you know I was worried about you? How long does it take to find the reversal for a simple hex?" Which turned out not to be so simple, but that was beside the point.

"Here, dear," Linda repeated.

"Better take the tea," Mr. Kibbles said. "She won't explain anything until you've had some."

"And cookies," Auntie said. "The Misses Jamies sent over a batch."

"Oh, well, *cookies*." Giving in to the inevitable—Linda was a textile witch, but when she wanted to, she could be as irresistible as the most basic elements—Sophia took her tea. Noah snatched a couple cookies, dropped one on her saucer, sat, and snugged her feet in his lap while he munched the other cookie. Everyone else sat in chairs and on couches arranged in a sort of semicircle around her couch.

She took a perfunctory nibble of cookie. The sweet morsel stung her taste buds awake. Suddenly ravenous, she gobbled the cookie, then two more, and drank down the entire cup of tea. After which she felt stronger, almost herself.

Aunt Linda smirked. "Auntie knows best, dear."

"Yes, Aunt Linda." Now that the time for questions had come, Sophia found herself at a loss for words. *Am I really mated?* tangled with *Is my magic gone?* The answers might be too much for her to handle.

Noah laid a supportive, warm hand on her thigh.

It helped her to start. Still, she started small. "So Auntie. What's with the mirror?" She pointed. "Why do you have a malifier in your shop?"

Aunt Linda was gazing at Noah's hand with a beaming smile. She transferred her beam to Sophia. "Oh, that old thing? I found it at an estate sale. I couldn't let it fall into the wrong hands. Besides, I was taking a woodcarving class at the Y and needed a project."

Of course she did. "It's not a malifier?"

"Not anymore. It's a helping mirror."

"Then why did you leave? Didn't you know we needed you to unravel the hex?"

She tutted. "Dear Sophia. After I figured things out, my help was the last thing you needed."

"But the hex—"

"Didn't hurt Noah." She put down her tea and dimpled at Sophia. "In fact, it helped him."

"It turned him into a poofy dog!"

"Exactly." Aunt Linda actually smirked.

"During the day, when the raven was searching for him." Mr. Kibbles gave the first sane answer. "The animal form kept Noah's familiar from finding him—and the evil wizard, too."

"Also, it was the form most likely to bring him love," Auntie said.

Jayden choked.

"Oh, come on." Sophia snared another cookie. She had a feeling she was going to need the sugar. "You couldn't have known all that."

"But I did," Aunt Linda said. "I met Prince Simon and his mate Hayley years ago. Noah has his hair and her nose. He was obviously their missing boy."

"Of course we'd suspected when we first got to know Mason," Mr. Kibbles said. "He'd left his original pack to find a mate, but ended up here to help his cousin Zoe. He told us what had happened to Noah's mother and we put two and two together."

Auntie nodded. "Which is why I sent Noah a note suggesting he come here. To find out for sure if Mason's Blackwood cousin was the missing wizard prince."

"You did send that note." There was satisfaction in Noah's tone. "But my parents weren't mates. She worked for him."

"Such a tragic story," Mr. Kibbles said. "Simon fell in love with a shifter, and she with him. The Witches' Council would have executed one or both of them, so the couple pretended she simply worked for him."

"It's so fucked up." Jayden snorted. "Two adults can't be together, just because a bunch of asswipes on the Council decided their offspring might be too powerful to be controlled? Idiots."

Sophia felt her jaw go slack. Never mind the Council usually being revered—they were some of the most powerful witches on the planet. Jayden was talking about them like they were whiny kids. "What kind of wizard are you?" She searched his black eyes.

Something very old and very powerful looked back at her. She shivered.

Then he grinned. "Sorry. No spoilers."

Her cheeks burned. To cover her confusion she said quickly, "You mean shifter/witch matings aren't dangerous?"

"Of course they're dangerous. Duals are powerful, and power can be used for evil—or good." Jayden's grin widened. "Or even just for fun."

Mr. Kibbles shook his head. "The Council is very serious about the injunction. More so than if the problem were simply out-of-control duals."

"More than a problem with mad demi-gods, huh," Sophia said. "And the insanity thing?"

"Oh please," Jayden said. "The Council probably just drove those duals nuts with their badgering. Duals aren't statistically any more likely to go insane than any powerful magical being."

"How do you know—?"

"Back to my story," Aunt Linda said. "Improbably, Noah won the alpha fight against Scauth. Even sitting here blocks away, knitting, I felt him use his magic—which meant his familiar could feel it too, and find him."

"I tried to use it again," Noah said. "When fighting Ivan. I couldn't access it."

"Yes, dear," Linda said. "That was the hex. That's why we left the hex in place."

"You knew Raven was tagged?" Noah asked. "That he was looking for me? How, when nobody but Burgot saw what happened that day?"

"Hayley told the gist to Mason's mother before she passed," Mr. Kibbles said. "She told Mason, and he told us."

"You never told me," Noah ripped out.

The big beta wolf held up one hand. "I don't remember any of this."

"Don't blame him," Mr. Kibbles said soothingly. "The combination of Linda and a cup of chamomile tea can be very persuasive."

"I suppressed his memory of it before you even came, dear," Linda said to Noah.

"You *what?*" Mason's chocolate eyes narrowed and burned almost red.

"I couldn't have you blurting out the truth within the hearing of the old alpha's nasty lieutenants." She smiled placidly at him.

His gaze stayed narrow a dangerous moment longer before he sat back and sipped tea. "Good call."

They all digested that in silence a moment.

"So we knew Noah's familiar was tagged," Mr. Kibbles said. "Since the bird could lead the evil wizard Burgot straight to the dual he was seeking—"

"That's Noah," Jayden put in unnecessarily. Sophia glanced heavenward, a facial *what you gonna do?*

"The hex was perfect, forcing him into his animal during the day, exactly when the diurnal raven would be looking," Mr. Kibbles finished.

"And then I realized, here was Prince Simon's boy, all grown up." Auntie clasped her hands in delight. "A prince, an alpha, and unmated to boot. And here was my little niece, a princess and unmarried and—"

Sophia cleared her throat, pointedly.

Auntie's apple cheeks flushed, but her blue eyes twinkled. "I knew if I just got out of the way, all the mating details would work out."

Sophia's cheeks were on fire. Noah took her hand and smiled at her.

In his eyes, she felt beautiful. Her embarrassment faded. She smiled back, his power washing through her in a very tingly, pleasant way. "Why do you think we're mates?"

Auntie gave a pointed glance at the mirror in the back of the store. "Nobody else look." She waggled fingers at the mirror. "Reveal."

Traces of lovemaking still resonated, twinkling pink and blue and gold like fairy dust. Sophia blushed.

Auntie was beaming bright as a spotlight. "See? You didn't need me to break my hex."

"But I didn't break the hex." Sophia frowned. The events in the field seemed a lifetime ago. "I removed the hide spell, and the hex just unraveled."

"Yes, of course," Auntie said. "It was a helping hex. It wouldn't have been helpful to continue at that point, so it didn't."

Linda Logic. Why argue? Sophia took another cookie, biting into it thoughtfully. "Oh! I forgot in the rush of events, but what about the woman, the mundane who walked in on the hex taking affect? We need to do something about her before the Council finds out—"

"Your aunt already took care of her." Jayden's tone was solemn and the ancient look was back.

Sophia chilled. "Took care...? How?"

"I caught up with her and told her we were working on a magic trick for the charity talent show. Emphasized it was all mirrors." Auntie smiled impishly. "Why, what did you think he meant?"

Sophia laughed, saluted Aunt Linda with the quarter-moon cookie then popped the rest in her mouth and enjoyed.

Noah said, "One point bothers me. If the hex was supposed to help, why did I shift back naked every night?"

Noah, *naked*. Sophia's mouth dropped open at the image. She remembered she'd been chewing cookie and shut her jaw with a snap.

Auntie beamed. "Having you *au naturel* certainly sped things along sexually—"

"My wand," Sophia blurted—before she realized that was just as bad. "I mean, I had a question about it. When I first came, my wands were out, crossed on top of the cabinet."

"Crossed...in an X? Like a film rating?" If possible Auntie beamed brighter. "Maybe they also were trying to speed things along."

Sophia stared at Aunt Linda. How did she turn everything into *that* topic?

Mr. Kibbles said, "That was a portent, showing that your past and present would cross. Also it symbolized the unknown adversaries you'd face."

"Speaking of adversaries," Noah said. "Burgot was after me, but Rodolphe was after Sophia. How did they both end up here in Matinsfield?"

Sophia slapped a palm to her forehead. "That stupid magical census."

Noah frowned at her.

"You used your magic to survive the alpha fight, right? If Burgot wanted to goose young potential alphas into fighting, he had to know where the packs were. He'd need a list of the wolf shifter packs, and Rodolphe had stolen exactly that list before he was exiled. Damn it, I wish I'd never been a Council page."

Aunt Linda shook her head. "It's not your fault evil people misused your work."

Noah raised Sophia's hand to his mouth and kissed it. She squeezed his hand in return. His eyes on her were molten gold, and his mouth curved in a smile so edible she leaned up. Noah leaned down.

The *ka-shick* of a camera shutter froze them. "Don't mind me," Jayden said, tucking away his phone.

Noah glowered at the pet groomer.

Mr. Kibbles shook his head. "All that tragedy because Burgot wanted to add the power of a royal dual to his."

"Nobody should have control of that much power," Noah ripped out. "It's evil."

Sophia nodded. "That's why I stopped using mine."

"You're both idiots." Jayden snorted. "Noah, you couldn't be alpha if you didn't have power and control over your pack, right? And aren't they better with your leadership? That's definitely not evil."

"But what about me?" Sophia thought back to Rodolphe taking advantage of her naive arrogance. "Even though I meant it for good, my magic was used to do great harm."

"Please." Jayden made a rude noise. "You made a mistake. I think you went a little overboard with your *mea culpa*. A simple restitution to the transplant patient and a few hours of public service would have made you older, wiser, and still a potent force for good."

"You're only human, Sophia," Mr. Kibbles said. "You can only do your best."

"And anyway, it isn't the power that's bad," Auntie said placidly. "That's part of you, like your head and hands and heart. What's bad or good is how you use them."

Sophia startled at Linda's choice of words. She drew a deep breath and opened her mouth to ask one of her two vital questions. *Am I no longer a witch?*

"Speaking of head, hands, and heart," Jayden said with a pointed look at Noah. "Now might be a good time."

"Good time for what?" Sophia said.

"Sophia, sweetheart." Noah took her hands. "Wolf shifters do everything important, from challenges to joining rites, in front of the pack. And since these people are your pack...well." He went down on one knee in front of her. "You're the mate of my heart, the woman who complements me. Will you marry me?"

Her heart shouted *yes!* But she said, "Noah, I want to. But it started with the hex, and it's only been a few days..."

"You've been avoiding it for years," Auntie said in an undertone.

"Might as well say yes." Jayden grinned. "Your aunt will wear you down until you do."

Still Sophia hesitated. "But Noah is a wizard prince. I'm not...I may no longer be his match." She held her breath.

No one said anything. The significant looks they gave each other made her want to cry.

It was Jayden who broke the silence. "You're asking if you're still a witch princess. Wrong question. If you were *only* a witch princess, you'd be dead right now. That was some stunt you pulled, overloading Burgot. Anyone less powerful couldn't have done it at all. But somewhere along the way, you acquired a wolf, Sophia, and she saved you. Her own healing ability, and more, her tie to Noah's healing, kept you alive."

"But no more than that?" Her voice emerged in a broken whisper.

"You'll always be our queen," Mason said softly.

Her heart burst with contradictory feelings. Joy that she did truly have an inner wolf, at being Noah's mate and still having a place in his life, at being so accepted by his—*their*—pack.

But she also felt immense sorrow at losing that which, at one time, was the best, the most cherished part of her.

A single tear threaded down her cheek.

“For shit’s sake,” Jayden said. “Let me give you the rest. Your wolf kept you from dying. She healed you this far. She’ll probably heal you the rest of the way.”

“The *rest* of the way...?” Hope geysered through Sophia’s veins. “You mean I’ll still be a witch?”

“It’ll take time,” he cautioned. “And you can’t go around doing crap like that every day. A loud noise makes you temporarily deaf, but sustained loud noise makes the hearing loss permanent. So take it easy with the spells. But I don’t see why you can’t make a full recovery.”

“Well, then. My answer is—” She thrust her cup at her aunt and reached for Noah, arms wrapping around him like she’d never let go. “Yes. Yes, yes, oh yes!”

Epilogue

Burgot and his ferret were tried in front of the Witches' Council. Both were found guilty on multiple counts of magical murder. The ferret was sentenced to life imprisonment.

Burgot was also found guilty of high treason against witch kind, and thrown into magical solitary confinement, a place known as the Pit, from which there was no escape.

Sophia and Noah discovered Rodolphe was behind the murders in Killer's trailer. Sophia had vowed to make whoever was responsible pay, and she felt as if she hadn't done enough justice for those poor murder victims—until Noah reminded her that Rodolphe's draining at the hands of his own weapon was true poetic justice.

Noah reluctantly left his wolf medallion with Sophia's cousin Daniel Light for safekeeping. Burgot was imprisoned, but there were other mages just as hungry for power. If any others heard of the Key to Magic, they'd have to fight this battle all over again.

Then all that was left was figuring out how to keep their relationship secret from the Council—the biggest battle of all.

*　*　*

A few days later, Sophia snuggled with Noah on the couch in his bachelor apartment, ninety percent of the place taken up by an entertainment center in the living room, a beer fridge in the kitchen, and king-size bed in the bedroom.

"What are we going to do?" She sighed and nestled her head against his shoulder. "The Council won't let us be together and I don't think I can even pretend to cook and clean for you."

"I could be *your* domestic." He kissed her forehead lightly.

"Please. You, domestic?" She turned up her face for more kisses. "You're the epitome of wild."

"Mmm." His mouth found hers and showed her just how wild he could be, a little bit of teeth, a little bit of tongue, and a whole lotta heat. After her lips were buzzing, he said, "Do we have to tell them anything? Maybe without your full powers they won't care."

"I still have the genes, even though they're not expressing at the moment. Any children would still be powerful."

"Mmm." He continued nibbling down her neck, sending shivers of need through her.

"Although it *has* been five years since the last census. They won't do another for five more." She lifted her chin to give him better access. "But I think they'll catch on then, when we're both listed living at the same address along with one or two wolflets."

He jerked straight. "You want kids?"

"Well...yes." Her heart plunged into cold water. "Don't you?"

"Yes. Oh, Sophia, *yes*." He seized her mouth in a kiss that devoured her, so hot her hair felt ready to burst into flames. Relief coursed through her, followed by desire so strong and sweet she wanted to drag him into the bedroom and get a start on making those wolflets immediately.

He pulled back. His nostrils flared and he growled. She shivered at the sound, pure beast. *Her* beast.

He lifted her in his powerful arms and carried her to the bedroom. Laying her down, he stripped her of her clothes.

Then he got rid of his. She got to watch. His belly appeared first as he stripped off his T-shirt, ridged abs quickly pummeling in and out with his excited breath. Then his chest, the heavy muscles lifting as the shirt went over his head then collapsing to a perfect W bracketed by powerful arms. His collarbones winged under a throat so strong she wanted to lick it like an ice cream cone.

Until he unbelted, unsnapped, and unzipped, and she wanted to do the same thing to what was revealed. A couple flips of his feet removed his shoes, a quick push sent everything to the floor, and she was confronted by his naked desire for her, cock jutting proudly from his hips.

Stars, he was gorgeous. Powerful body, gold eyes bright as newly minted coins, full of desire for her...she wanted all that, wanted *him*, but she wanted *more*.

She held out her arms. "Noah. I love you."

"That's not the hex talking, is it?" He came into her embrace and kissed her, hot and fierce.

"You know it isn't." She backed off, her eyes searching his. "But I know you might not feel the same—"

"Fuck, Sophia, I loved you the moment I saw your picture. Every second I spent with you, every facet of your personality that was revealed only made me love you more. *I love you*. And I want to show you how much."

She knew by college that guys showed their love through sex. Sex like hers and Noah's? She'd show him back.

The first time was hot and fast. They came together in an explosion of tongues, hands and pumping hips. When they lay sweaty and breathless, then...well, then the beast proved he could play.

"I have a surprise for you," she said.

"I do too." He held up a plastic ring, thickened with a fingertip-size barrel at the top. Intrigued, she waited.

He stroked himself to fullness, then slipped the ring around the root of his erection. He pointed to his cock, taking her attention off the ring. "This is yours. You get to do with it whatever you want."

"Mine?" She licked her lips. "*Whatever?*"

It nodded eagerly. He smiled.

She bent and petted it with her tongue. He sucked in a breath. She tickled the tip. He groaned.

"Anything, hmm?" She pushed his cock down against his belly, straddled his hips, and carefully eased herself forward, sliding him flat under her. She was wet with excitement and her pussy slid along his length like going down a slide. He groaned louder. So she did it again. And again, pumping along him over and over.

As she pumped, she wrapped her arms around his neck and kissed him like they were mating mouths. Each thrust of her tongue caused a corresponding jump of his cock under her, nudging the swollen softness of her sex.

She stilled when he cupped her breasts, one in each hand, and gently thumbed her nipples erect. He half-sat and kissed her, his tongue tangling with hers. Laying back and bringing her down flush with him, he started rolling his hips under her, his cock sliding along her slit, mimicking the tangle of their tongues. Each roll tugged at her until she was squirming and her belly went taut with longing.

Finally she couldn't stand it any more. Sitting up, she raised herself, dripping, from his hips to settle the head of his erection at the entrance of her body. Then she slid slowly down.

He groaned the whole way, a long moan forced through gritted teeth, expelling air when the final inch of her spread to take him. She wriggled, her pelvis achingly full.

He reached for the ring between them and squeezed the thickened part. It started vibrating, directly against her clit.

She squealed. Her hips popped up at the surge of sensation and she nearly came off.

He grabbed her waist, held her on, and thrust up. He began thrusting hard, beating against her in an ever-quickening tempo.

She moaned, leaned forward to wrap her arms around his neck, and hung on for the ride. He began to pause at the height of each thrust to grind against her. It pressed the tiny vibrator into her soft, wet flesh. Her breath sped up with each grinding buzz.

She couldn't keep still. Her mouth fell open and her teeth caught the tender lobe of his ear. She nibbled gently as he rose and fell under her. His breath was harsh on her shoulder, dampening her skin. She pressed closer, rubbing her nipples into his chest, then flattening her breasts against him. His abs scrubbed her belly. His shoulders under her arms dewed. The mated smell, rising with the heat of his skin, was strong.

She began to churn against him in her own rhythm, slightly out of sync with his. They pistoned again and again and then out of the blue a thrust would come together, so hard their skin smacked and her eyes popped open and her clit hit the buzzer and sang.

She soared higher, sensations like sweet alarms ringing her nipples, pussy, and everything in between. He synced his thrusts with her and they drove into each other like fighters, doubling the impact. She gasped with each smack. Her nipples were tight nubs and his cock had swollen fatter. About to come, she straightened on his hips.

He changed rhythm, harder, slower. Deeper. She released him to hang onto his wrists. Each thrust of his powerful hips raised her in the air. She flew for a split second each time he recovered for another thrust. He bounced her on his hips until she was nearly crazy with need and love.

Wrapping arms around her back, he thrust one last time, so powerfully it felt as if he were touching her soul. Joy ripped through her. She began to come, strong contractions that released powerful waves of color and light and happiness.

One thing would make her joy complete.

She slid a hand between them, razzed a bit of magic, and broke the ring open.

And then he shouted and they were coming together, hard spasms of ecstasy that shot and burst like fireworks. It was almost frightening how hard they came. They clutched each other in sweaty arms and gasped and cried out as orgasm ripped them bare.

It ebbed only slowly. She came to with her head resting in the damp crook of his neck, his cheek against her crown. His arms relaxed, holding her loosely as her heart slowed. He said, "Your magic...?"

"Surprise." She raised her eyes and, arms still wrapped around his neck, gazed into his softly glowing gold eyes. "Just a bit, but it's a start. That was amazing."

He said, "That's how much I love you. And if you let me, I'll show you how much every day for the rest of our lives."

She released a depressed sigh. "If the Council lets us."

"Hey." He took her chin in his fingertips and raised her face to his. Searched her eyes. "We have five years. Maybe we can give our house two addresses. We'll figure it out. And in the meantime..." Inside her, his cock started to fatten.

Her eyes widened. "There are apparently advantages to mating an alpha wolf."

"There certainly are." He began to bounce her again.

"Say." She closed her eyes and enjoyed. "You never did tell me. How many babies do shifters have at a time?"

"In the wild? The average is five."

She shrieked, every muscle shouting *stop*. "That's *average*?"

"Relax." He chuckled. "It's different mating with a human. My mother only had me."

"Oh. Good."

* * *

And so they were married discreetly in the little church next to the bookstore.

Jayden swept in as Sophia finished dressing to give her a mischievous grin. He said, "Sticking it to the Witches'

Council. I'm proud of you, kid." When he swept out, she saw the pink bow, the one briefly worn by King, nestled in among the baby's breath and roses of her bouquet. She smiled.

Mason was the best man and her aunt the maid of honor. Her brother Gabriel gave her away. Mr. Kibbles was the wedding planner and the Misses Jamies sat in the back row and passed out programs and tissues.

Her familiar Kat, who'd felt her use of magic all the way in the Bahamas, made it back for the wedding. She spent the whole ceremony staring at Bram...who was still gazing at his hands. Wouldn't have worked anyway. She was a cat and he was a bird. Or maybe that was really why she was staring at him.

Their wolf pack filled both sides of the church. With Ivan gone, the women were starting to come out of their shells. With Noah guiding local businesses, the workers were starting to return to Matinsfield. Killer, for his part in the murder of wolves, was sent to jail. Bonnie and Clyde and Killer's little brother Marlowe were already mellowing, and Noah allowed Attila to stay on the condition he take anger management classes. Several new jobs opened up in town, which brought back even more of the pack workers.

As Sophia waited in the vestibule, Aunt Linda gave her the "talk". Not the one about the wedding night, thank goodness. But about head, hands, and heart. Apparently the reason she'd lived through releasing her death magic wasn't just her wolf's connection to Noah, but also the wizard prince's love for her. He'd not only soothed her and getting her through the worst of the pain like a birthing coach, but he brought some serious countermagic to bear. The combination of shifter magic being drenched and deep-seated in life plus Noah's own power far overshadowed her death magic. It was further aided by his father's life magic, which had also come from the heart. Noah's love protected her.

Magic was all about potentials, and thank goodness for that.

At the reception, she sat side by side with her new husband at the head table, watching their guests chat, delighting in the joy of wolf pups and witch kids racing around together.

"Who would have thought it?" She leaned into Noah's strength and briefly rested her head in the crook of his neck. "A witch who rejected magic ending up with, not only all her magic, but also with shifter magic—and mated to an alpha who is also a wizard prince."

"Which I desperately didn't want to be." He kissed the top of her head then leaned back to smile at her. "But somehow both of us, in throwing away our powers, found an even better power."

She lifted her head and smiled into his eyes. "What's that?"

His golden eyes held forever. "The power of love."

Dear Reader,

Thanks for reading! My greatest joy as an author comes from you joining me here in my book world. I hope you've found entertainment and pleasure in these pages for a time, and that you'll come back to join me soon. ♥

~Mary

Want to hear about new releases? Sign up for my newsletter!
http://www.maryhughesbooks.com/Newsletter.html

A Request

If you enjoyed this book, I'd really appreciate it if you'd take a moment to review it online. You can help prospective readers find new books to love by writing a few sentences about what you enjoyed.

Thanks for taking the time to do a review!

Curious to find out what happens next with the prophecy? Continue reading for the first chapter from *Mind Mates, Pull of the Moon Book 4*.

Pretty little shifter, wizard prince—their taboo love could burn the barriers between worlds.

Mind Mates

Pull of the Moon Book 4

Shifter Emma Singer has more problems than she can shake her pretty wolf tail at. Her father has been executed, and her mother and brother plan to sell her to a pack alpha for his harem. Even the wicked little crush she has on her boss is doomed—why would six-and-a-half feet of hot, handsome, royal wizard want a boring, good-girl, iota shifter like her? Not to mention her only power is going berserker—that's a real relation-shipwreck!

Gabriel Light is a wizard prince who turned his back on his exceptional powers after he was accused of causing his parents' death. Now he pours his intellect into his tech business, and hides his naughty, forbidden lust for his pretty shifter clerk. But when his sister is imprisoned, and Emma is kidnapped, it's time for this alpha geek-wizard to decloak with all laser cannons blazing. Only one problem—with Emma at his side, how can he stay focused, with his inner wolf howling to have her?

Emma's father left behind a journal. When Gabriel and Emma accidentally release its hidden magic, they learn that together, they hold a key to power beyond imagining—if they can stay alive long enough to use it. But when Emma unleashes her berserker wolf on their enemies, can Gabriel draw her back from the brink before she destroys everyone in her path?

Warning: Contains a hot wizard prince panting to bring out a good-girl shifter's naughty side. Accidental voyeurism, deliberate orgasms, a jealous rival wizard, and fun with prophecy

Enjoy the following chapter from *Mind Mates*:

Swaying atop the three-story ladder, Emma Singer swallowed hard and forced herself to climb higher.

Her fingers curled tighter around the rungs as she neared the metal braces of the Choice Buy's exposed-structure ceiling. An Employee Appreciation Day banner drooped from her clenched hand.

"Damn. This good-girl shtick is getting old."

Wolf shifters, even iotas, weren't afraid of heights, but her stomach slid toward her legs the higher she got, maybe knowing something she didn't.

She glanced down and immediately wished she hadn't.

From the hushed, rarefied heights, her fellow Techie Titans looked like ants gathered around the home-theater setup, where their boss was installing a game. The huge flat-panel was reduced to postage-stamp size by her height.

Strangely, her six-foot-five boss looked just as imposing as usual.

"Hurry up, Emma." Brant the Blundering, the gangly teen who'd pulled down the streamer in the first place, called from the base of the ladder. He was built like a puppy who hadn't grown into his paws—and was as coordinated too.

Swallowing her vertigo, she stretched to refasten the crepe paper to a joist.

"More to the right." Brant waved an arm to demonstrate, hand like an oven mitt on a broomstick.

He hit the ladder and knocked it sideways.

Emma tottered, arms pinwheeling. The streamer fluttered away, waving mockingly in crepe paper's version of the finger.

No good deed goes unpunished flashed through her thoughts as she toppled off. The ladder rocked a few times before righting itself with a *kerchunk*.

It seemed an eternity for Emma to fall the three stories. Below, Brant's wide eyes followed her descent. She had time to wonder if there was a twelve-stepper for acute volunteeritis.

Well. This is gonna hurt.

"Emma!" In the nick of time her boss, Dr. Gabriel Light, swooped in, doing his usual hero thing.

He caught her.

She landed in his strong arms (no problem). They were tight around her (no problem). His scent, masculine and heady, filled her sudden sucked breath (still no problem, or not much of one).

Automatically she clung to his broad shoulders, hard muscles under her fingers, her inner wolf wagging its tail (starting to be a problem). Her fingers threaded into his silky hair (definitely trekking into problem territory). Her lips, a whisper from his chiseled jaw, his delectable earlobe, opened, her tongue aching to swipe a taste.

Red-alert problem.

"Emma, you're safe. Trust me." Behind his plain glasses, his lids lifted to her. His irises were a startling, star-shot blue-green, like the moon sparkling off a warm sea, making her want to dive in and do the breaststroke.

For all that he dressed like a junior college professor, the man was teeth-achingly beautiful.

She tried to swallow, but her tongue had swollen to fill her mouth and nothing happened. She tried again, managing to pant and gulp at the same time, swallowed wrong, and started coughing uncontrollably.

Dr. Light set her on her feet—by sliding her down his sleek, muscular, cotton-and-male-smelling chest, oh *yum*—and rubbed her between her shoulders to ease her.

His big, warm palm did ease her cough, but the breadth of his hand filled the entire area between her shoulder blades and made the rest of her clench with aching desire. Gabriel Light wasn't simply lead Techie Titan—he was their nerd king, and he was built like royalty.

The little iota wolf in Emma yipped happily.

But she, her human self, wasn't so pleased. Despite her interest in him, he'd never shown anything more than kindly concern. The last thing she wanted was to be a poor lovesick fool.

But he smelled so *good*.

"Are you all right?" Dr. Light, one arm clasped around her, slid a long, large finger under her chin. Tilting her head up, he gazed deep into her eyes. His own were sympathetic.

She stopped breathing at the oceans of tenderness in that gaze—fraternal tenderness, but so damned gorgeous.

Plus side, no breath meant her hacking cough stopped, long enough for her to wheeze with what air remained in her lungs, "I'm fine."

One corner of his mouth tipped up in a gentle semi-smile. "You always say that. 'I'm fine.' Whether you are or not. You're not a trainee anymore, Emma. It's okay not to be fine. You won't get fired. It's okay to admit you need help."

An iota wolf, admit to being vulnerable? Hell no, it wasn't okay. Her breath surged back in a rush. She was bottom of the pack, and worse, built like a kitten, tiny and cute to the point that she had to buy her clothes in the kids' section at WallyWorld and one of her nicknames was Piglet. She could never *ever* be caught out as needy and vulnerable, surrounded by apex predators all day.

She wasn't sure whether she meant her shifter pack or the six-foot-five walking sex bomb who was her boss.

Human boss, she reminded herself. Who didn't seem to have a *clue* she was interested in him.

"I'm *fine,*" she repeated through clenched teeth.

"Are you?" His gaze shifted to her mouth, and she stopped breathing again. "That's bad for your teeth, you know. Relax."

He eased the chiding words with a slide of his finger along her jaw, the rough whorls of the pad caressing her flesh. His touch raised tremors in her that shimmered down her throat, waking nipples and belly and wolf.

Oh, to grab him, hook a leg behind his, and take him down to the floor—with her underneath.

She was strong and tricky and might have tried it in private, except he moved like he'd studied martial arts and knew what to do. A warrior's grace hinted at an extremely muscular body lurking beneath his sweater vests and slouchy pants. She'd probably only embarrass herself.

Her wolf didn't seem to care. It was panting and lifting its tail, and her human wasn't far behind.

So naturally, when her eyes were big pools of do-me and she was spurting pheromones like a department store perfumery, her alpha wolf Bruiser prowled into the store.

* * *

Bzz-bzzt. A buzz like an angry hornet stung wizard prince Gabriel Light's ears the moment the predator slunk into the store.

Cap'n Crunch me. Gabriel had magically alarmed the door for just such an event, but why now, when he'd finally gotten a semi-innocent excuse to wrap his arms around this warm bundle of soft, sweet-smelling heaven?

Emma. It felt like he'd been dying to hold her forever. Now, with her in his arms, was the first time in months he could breathe.

But that buzzing alarm told him the approaching beast was male, a wolf shifter, and, from that level of sting, Emma's alpha. The beast was not going to appreciate seeing her in another man's arms.

She started trembling, no doubt in response to the alpha's rampant fight-club stench, a musk even Gabriel could smell. He tried to ease her tension with a joke.

"Hey, Emma. How many tickles does it take to make an octopus laugh?"

She skewered him with a disbelieving stare, icing his flesh. He'd blundered, she didn't understand he was trying to comfort her, *nobody gets my skewed sense of humor...* Then she gulped and said, "Eight? Like, um, eight legs?"

Immediately his world brightened. "Nope. Ten tickles. Get it? Tentacles?"

She managed a tiny laugh, tinkling bells to his ears, and her body relaxed slightly under his arms. "That was *such* a dad joke."

He loved that she, of all the people he knew, actually laughed at his jokes. He smiled into her eyes like a besotted fool.

Of course, that was when the he-wolf prowled into view.

Gabriel wondered how far he could get with the wolf by protesting his intentions were honorable. Probably not far. The creature was only barely in human form.

The wolfman was medium height but had a face like a dented shovel and a body like a trash compactor, his muscles-on-muscles popping in a stringy T-shirt that barely qualified past no-shirt-no-shoes-no-service.

Worse, with the hair sprouting everywhere, nose elongating like a snout, and lengthening canines, this alpha was dangerously pissed.

Hard to reason with a pissed-off wolf. They tended to bite first then ask questions...never.

Yet instead of releasing Emma, Gabriel's hand dropped from her clenched jaw to open protectively on her back.

"The fuck?" the wolfman snarled.

Something inside Gabriel snarled right back.

He throttled it. Whether his own masculine instincts or maybe he'd developed a wolf to complement Emma's, *down boy*. Diplomacy first. "This isn't what it seems—"

"I know." The he-wolf tapped his snout. "Good thing too, or you'd already have my fist in your face. Let her go. *Now*."

Briefly Gabriel clenched his eyes. The wolf didn't smell it, but Gabriel really reeked of desire. He'd magicked up a way to hide the odor because of the Witches' Council.

Witches tangling bed sheets with wolves was a huge taboo—punishable by anything up to and including the headsman's axe. He'd have risked the ultra-close shave, but the Council Enforcers usually hit the female with the worst of the punishment.

He couldn't stand the idea of one hair on Emma's head being harmed.

Trying to deescalate the situation, Gabriel loosened his arms around her. But he couldn't quite let her go. "Sorry, sir." He forced a smile and managed a creditable professionalese. "Store's closed. Private party."

"In the middle of the fuckin' day?"

"Yes, sir. A special recognition celebration." He had a small one every month, but this month they'd had record sales, so he closed the store early, locked the doors, and put on a real shindig. He wondered momentarily how the he-wolf had gotten in. Maybe with the caterers. "You'll have to leave."

"Not without her."

"Sir, what part of private eludes you?"

The wolf held up one ham hand and slowly curled his fingers. "What part of my fist eludes *you?* If I'm leaving, so is my cousin."

Probably not by DNA. "Cousin" was a common cover story for pack members living together, caring for each other, *getting naked together...* Gabriel's arms tightened around the pretty little shifter. The he-wolf growled in response. Gabriel would have to let go of her.

Soon.

At least the creature didn't know Gabriel was a witch. No one would, unless he was working active magic. If the wolfman *had* known, he would've attacked immediately. The Witches' Council's taboo meant most wolves had no use for witches, and some actively hated them.

Let her go.

Problem was, if he stepped away now the alpha would see Gabriel's intentions were no longer perfectly honorable.

Slouchy pants only covered so many inches of rock-hard hey-how-ya-doin'?

The wolf stalked nearer.

Let her go.

Not yet.

Hell and cornflakes, Gabriel had been constantly aroused, ever since Emma started working at his store two months ago. Her pretty face, pert body, and sparkling personality called to everything in him.

What nailed it was that she actually got his weird sense of humor.

The he-wolf prowled the edge of Gabriel's kill zone. Getting steamed.

Gabriel really needed to let Emma go.

But none of it seemed to matter squat, not Witches' Council headsman nor the hairy promise of death, not when his dreams had become reality at last, and he had her soft, curvy body in his arms.

"Dr. Light, it's okay." Emma's sweet voice snared his attention. "I know this, um, man."

She gazed up into his face so adoringly he fell into her big brown eyes, momentarily blotting the alpha shifter from his awareness.

Which was when the wolfman grabbed Emma's delicate arm in one hairy ham hand and yanked her out of Gabriel's embrace.

Yanked her so hard she stumbled.

Fury seized Gabriel. He grabbed the wolf's slab of a shoulder and shoved him back, popping Emma loose. Stalking after, Gabriel tore off his glasses to glare down at the he-wolf. Bad idea to challenge an alpha, but *this beast dared touch Emma.*

The wolfman's ears lengthened and definite fangs flashed. "What the fuck do you think you're doing?"

Gabriel ripped out, "*Nobody* manhandles a woman, or *any* being, in my...in our store." His jaw clenched against his slip of the tongue. At pains to blend in, he didn't advertise the fact that he owned this Choice Buy. Hell, head Techie Titan was bad enough. He'd taken great care to stay under both mundane and magical radars, to the point of wearing glasses he didn't need. Huffing a calming breath, he put said glasses back in place.

"That is my cousin, and I'm head of the family." The he-wolf's eyes narrowed, spitting fire. "You interferin' in family business?"

While the wolfman spoke, his hairy hand dipped behind his back—where a concealed gun or knife would be.

Damn it. Gabriel played the wimpy nerd to humans and potion geek to witches to avoid exactly this.

Mentally, he called up a shield spell. Violence was about to erupt.

"Enough!" Emma wedged her tiny self between them, shoulders back, chin up, and chest puffed like an irate cat's fur. "Bruiser—I mean Bruce. Leave Dr. Light alone."

Gabriel found himself a little surprised and a lot impressed. She was standing up to a wolf twice her size and her alpha to boot.

This was a totally new side to her. In the couple months she'd worked here, she'd only ever been diffident. Eager to please.

Always saying "I'm fine". He found himself even more intrigued with the pretty little wolf. And more anxious to defend her. He started to cut in.

She slashed him a glance, a clear "back off" in her eyes.

He hesitated. If this was a wolf thing, his interfering could harm her pack standing.

Fine, he'd back off—for now. He stepped to the side, a hand cocked near his waist. Not for a gun, but ready to plunge under the sweater vest for the row of charged magical talismans that studded his belt.

"I don't like your attitude, missy. We're going." Bruiser grabbed Emma and hauled her toward the door.

She dug in her heels. "*No.*"

The wolfman slapped her face, so hard it left a red mark on her creamy cheek.

Gabriel forgot all his talismans, took one step, and planted a fist in the wolfman's snout. *Bam.*

Bruiser rocked back on his heels. His hand sprang open, releasing Emma.

Shocked gasps from the employees gave way to a quiet cheer or two.

Mentally, Gabriel facepalmed. He was a crunchy-even-in-milk *idiot.* Yeah, that punch felt satisfying, but it as good as announced that he'd had a raging hard-on for sweet, soft Emma for two months. A freeze potion or calm amulet would've worked more subtly.

Bruiser straightened, rubbing his snout. "Why you...you *fucker...*"

Gabriel shifted his weight to the balls of his feet. This could get ugly.

"You heard Dr. Light." Another male dressed in Choice Buy blue, equally tall with Gabriel, glided up to stand beside him. "Private party."

Male, not man, his black hair and low, growling bass hinting at his panther heritage. This was Gabriel's familiar, Pan, in his human form. If Gabriel had become a powerful battle mage, it was mainly due to Pan's wisdom and teaching.

Which meant the panther was going to kick his butt later for being so obvious. But in private.

Casually, almost negligently, Pan slid a foot forward into a fighting stance. He pointed toward the exit. "Leave."

One by one, the store employees cinched up behind Pan and Gabriel. Gabriel didn't need to see their expressions to know they were glaring buckets at the wolfman, because the bully paled and fell back a step.

Blustering, "This isn't over," the he-wolf spun and marched out.

Pan rolled his golden eyes.

Gabriel jerked his chin at the wolfman, and Pan, reading him flawlessly, followed.

"Thank you, Dr. Light." Emma appeared in front of Gabriel, her eyes shining up at him. "I could've probably handled him, but your solution was much more elegant."

"It was nothing." His cheeks heated. Elegant? He'd been fury-driven stupid and clumsy.

But at her words, something male inside him puffed its chest and yodeled.

She took a step closer, placing fingertips on his sweater vest. "You're being modest."

The chest-beater started fantasizing, picturing her throwing herself into his arms—and bed—in thanks. His cock rose in anticipation.

Before the fool penis and chest-beater could take over, his phone rang.

Two scoops of damn it.

He'd shunted the store phones to the answering service. Only a few people had his direct line. His thoughts arrowed to his pregnant sister, Sophia. "I need to take this. Excuse me?"

Emma stepped back with a nod and a sigh. His cock sighed and stepped back too.

He tapped the headset he always wore in the store. Most witches had trouble using advanced technology—their connection with the basic quantum uncertainty that was magic interfered with anything electrical—but he'd developed spells to prevent such interference.

After his parents died in a magically triggered plane crash, he'd made it his life's work.

In case it wasn't his sister, he spieled off, "Choice Buy, Techie Titan Gabriel Light speaking. How may I help you?"

"Gabriel, it's Sophia." His sister's voice was low and stressed, almost breathless.

His own breath hitched. "What's wrong? Is it the babies?"

Sophia had married alpha wolf shifter Noah Blackwood in semi-secrecy last month, the forbidden witch/shifter coupling in defiance of the Witches' Council taboo.

At first Gabriel was happy for his sister. Noah was a fine male and loved Sophia to pieces. Then Gabriel's familiar Pan had done a bit of research into the Council laws. Gabriel had already known intermagical cavorting was a felony. Life in prison for a witch caught doing the horizontal tango with a shifter.

But a witch princess having children with an alpha wolf? Death sentence.

Sophia said, "The babies are fine."

He breathed in relief.

"But I'm not. Gabriel, a Council Enforcer is about to jail me, and you're my one phone call. I'm accused of *Coeuntia cum Lupo*."

Mating with a wolf. Gabriel's worst fears had been realized.

About Mary Hughes

Mary Hughes (written Hug-he's but possibly pronounced throat warbler mangrove) writes smart and sassy stories of action and love.

She's a bona fide computer geek and performing flutist. (And piccolo, but we don't talk about that.) When this USA Today Bestselling Author isn't busy finding the missing </> tag or blowing her lungs out, she's on the couch reading or binging on The Flash, Elementary, NCIS, or Wynonna Earp...and petting the cats that inevitably end up on her lap.

Mary's online and would love to hear from you!
Newsletter http://www.maryhughesbooks.com/Newsletter.html
Facebook http://www.facebook.com/MaryHughesAuthor
Twitter http://www.twitter.com/MaryHughesBooks
Instagram https://www.instagram.com/maryhughesbooks
BookBub https://www.bookbub.com/authors/mary-hughes
Goodreads
http://www.goodreads.com/author/show/279140.Mary_Hughes
Website http://www.maryhughesbooks.com/
Blog http://maryhughesbooks.blogspot.com/

www.ingramcontent.com/pod-product-compliance
Lightning Source LLC
Chambersburg PA
CBHW030333310726
48979CB00001B/8

* 9 7 8 1 9 4 0 9 5 8 2 6 2 *